I0634823

The Superhumans
and Other Stories

also by Brian Stableford:

The Empire of the Necromancers (1: The Shadow of Frankenstein; 2: Frankenstein and the Vampire Countess); The New Faust at the Tragicomique; Sherlock Holmes and the Vampires of Eternity; The Stones of Camelot; The Wayward Muse.

also translated and introduced by Brian Stableford:

Anonymous: Sâr Dubnotal vs. Jack the Ripper; *Anthologies*: News from the Moon; The Germans on Venus; *Richard Bessière*: The Gardens of the Apocalypse; *Félix Bodin*: The Novel of the Future; *André Caroff*: The Terror of Madame Atomos; *Charles Derennes*: The People of the Pole; *Henri Duvernois*: The Man Who Found Himself; *Henri Falk*: The Age of Lead; *Paul Féval*: Anne of the Isles; The Black Coats (1: 'Salem Street; 2: The Invisible Weapon; 3: The Parisian Jungle; 4: The Companions of the Treasure; 5: Heart of Steel; 6: The Cadet Gang); John Devil; Knightshade; Revenants; Vampire City; The Vampire Countess; The Wandering Jew's Daughter; *Paul Féval, fils*: Felifax, the Tiger-Man; *Octave Joncquel & Théo Varlet*: The Martian Epic; *Jean de La Hire*: The Nyctalope vs. Lucifer; The Nyctalope on Mars; Enter the Nyctalope; *Georges Le Faure & Henri de Graffigny*: The Extraordinary Adventures of a Russian Scientist Across the Solar System (2 vols.); *Gustave Le Rouge*: The Vampires of Mars; *Jules Lermina*: Panic in Paris; Mysteryville; *Marie Nizet*: Captain Vampire; *Henri de Parville*: An Inhabitant of the Planet Mars; *Gaston de Pawlowski*: Journey to the Land of the 4th Dimension; *P.-A. Ponson du Terrail*: The Vampire and the Devil's Son; *Maurice Renard*: The Blue Peril; Doctor Lerne; The Doctored Man; A Man Among the Microbes; The Master of Light; *Albert Robida*: The Clock of the Centuries; The Adventures of Saturnin Farandoul; *J.-H. Rosny Aîné*: The Givreuse Enigma; The Mysterious Force; The Navigators of Space; Vamireh; The World of the Variants; The Young Vampire; *Jacques Spitz:* The Eye of Purgatory; *Kurt Steiner*: Ortog; *Villiers de l'Isle-Adam*: The Scaffold; The Vampire Soul; *Philippe Ward & S. Miller*: The Song of Montségur.

The Superhumans and Other Stories

by
Han Ryner

translated by
Brian Stableford

A Black Coat Press Book

English adaptation and Introduction Copyright © 2011 by Brian Stableford.
Cover illustration Copyright © 1973 by Michel Desimon.

Visit our website at www.blackcoatpress.com

ISBN 978-1-935558-77-4. First Printing. January 2011. Published by Black Coat Press, an imprint of Hollywood Comics.com, LLC, P.O. Box 17270, Encino, CA 91416. All rights reserved. Except for review purposes, no part of this book may be reproduced or transmitted in any form or by any means, electronic or mechanical, including photocopying, recording, or by any information storage and retrieval system, without permission in writing from the publisher. The stories and characters depicted in this novel are entirely fictional. Printed in the United States of America.

TABLE OF CONTENTS

Introduction

Henri Ner was born at Nemours, in Oran—which is now
Ghazaouet, in Algeria—on December 7, 1861. As the reader
of the present volume will observe in due course, he described
himself in *Les Voyages de Psychodore, philosophe cynique*
(1903; here translated as "The Travels of Psychodorus, Cynic
Philosopher") as "a hybrid barbarian, the son of a Norwegian
father and a Catalan mother," but his first language was
French, and when he conceived literary ambitions, he naturally went to Paris, where he eventually died on January 6, 1938.
He used occasional pseudonyms in his early writings, but
signed most of the work he produced during the first decade of
his career with his given name.

After writing two unpublished novels, Ner made his de-
but as a novelist with *Chair vaincue, roman psychologique*
[Vanquished Flesh, a Psychological Novel] (1889), and was
introduced into the salon culture of Paris. The most important
contact he made in literary circles was Alphonse Daudet, and
it was probably at Daudet's salon that he made the acquain-
tance of other writers in the process of launching their careers,
including Rémy de Gourmont and Joseph-Henri Boëx, alias J.-
H. Rosny Aîné. Although Ner's early novels were in a Naturalistic vein, he shared Gourmont's interest in symbolism and
Rosny's interest in speculative fiction, subsequently develop-
ing both threads in his own work, especially the short fiction
he produced in some quantity. He published one volume of
poetry, *Les Chants du divorce* [Divorce Songs] (1894), but
stuck to prose thereafter. His short fiction often appeared in
political periodicals of a radical stripe, and frequently took
exotic forms, but his novels remained conventional, if a trifle
morbid; *L'Humeur inquiète* [A Restless Temperament] (1894),
for example, described the tribulations of a man torn between
two women, while *La Folie de misère, roman d'histoire con-*

7

temporaine [The Madness of Poverty; A Contemporary Novel] (1895) offered an account of a mother driven by desperation to murder her children.

As Ner's activity as a political journalist increased in volume, it also increased in fervor, and he began to achieve a degree of fame as an outspoken anarchist, albeit of an eccentric stripe that took its inspiration directly from Greek philosophy—especially the Cynic, Stoic and Epicurean philosophies that he considered to be the best legacy of Socratic thought—rather than the more recent writings of Proudhon and Bakunin. He often referred to his pacifist brand of individualism as "harmonic individualism," to distinguish it from the "egoistic individualism" of more assertive writers, and also to associate its roots in the Pythagorean and Platonic notion of "the harmony of the spheres."

In 1898, Ner decided to adopt a new signature, retaining the pronunciation of his name but transforming its orthography, becoming "Han Ryner." In this guise, he put his talents as a writer of fiction under the empery of his philosophical convictions, producing *Le Crime d'obéir, roman d'histoire contemporaine* [The Crime of Obedience; a Contemporary Novel] (1900), an "individualist" novel whose protagonist rebels—though not violently—against the oppressions of contemporary society. He eventually followed it up with the similarly-inclined *Le Sphinx rouge, roman individualiste* [The Red Sphinx: An Individualist Novel] (1905). Although the work he published in between was mostly polemical, he did not abandon naturalistic fiction entirely, continuing to produce such novels as *Le Soupçon* [Suspicion] (1900), a novel about obsessive jealousy, and *La Fille manqué* [The Defective Girl] (1903), a study of homosexuality, but always in a contrarian spirit intent on assaulting the evils of vanity and violence.

Always closely associated with his political and philosophical convictions, Ner's stories were frequently didactic, often being explicitly framed as fables, parables or apologues. They were usually satirical, sometimes scathingly and stridently, and often lavishly dressed in an idiosyncratic kind of sarcastic comedy that was both black and strangely sickly. He made plans to issue a collection of *Contes prophetiques* [Prophetic Tales], whose imminent publication was announced in the periodical *Partisans* in 1900, but it never appeared, and most of his short fiction remained unreprinted in his lifetime, although he did manage to reprint some in *Les Voyages de Psychodore*, which was issued as a patchwork quasi-novel, and he eventually issued a second assembly of the same sort as *Les Paraboles cyniques* [Cynic Parables] (1913). He published three linked volumes of short pieces, suspended uneasily between fiction and non-fiction in 1929-32, but never contrived to issue an orthodox collection of short stories, despite being unexpectedly voted the "Prince des Conteurs" [Prince of Storytellers] in a poll organized by the newspaper *L'Intransigeant* (not an organ noted for its Anarchist sympathies) in 1912.

One posthumous collection, simply titled *Contes* [Tales], issued in 1967, began the work of making good this unfortunate deficit, revealing—among other endeavors—some of Ner's early contributions to the tradition of pre-Wellsian French scientific romance, but the society of "Les Amis de Han Ryner," founded after his death by his son-in-law Louis Simon, and still active today, inevitably devoted more attention to his political and philosophical works, the most successful of which was probably the *Petit manuel individualiste* [Little Individualist Handbook] (1903). His literary criticism, the first collection of which was uncompromisingly entitled *Prostituées, études critiques sur les gens de lettres d'aujourd'hui* [Prostitutes: Critical Studies of Today's Men of Letters] (1904) consisted mainly of scathing attacks on the supposed moral failures of his contemporaries, which rapidly isolated him, along with a few steadfast friends, within the literary society of Paris.

In addition to his short fiction, "Han Ryner" wrote numerous novels of a philosophical and didactic stripe, some of which used fantasized narrative strategies in order to make political and philosophical arguments. These included *L'Homme-fourmi* [The Human Ant] (1901), about a man transformed into an ant for a year; *Le Fils du silence* [The Son of Silence] (1911), a speculative biography of Pythagoras published alongside a study of Jesus entitled *Le Cinquième Évangile* [The Fifth Gospel] (1911); *La Tour des Peuples* [The Tower of the Nations] (1919), which recycles the story of the Tower of Babel; *Le Père Diogène* [Father Diogenes] (1920), a comedy about a Quixotic individual who tries to live like the cynics of old in the modern era; *L'Autodidacte* [The Autodidact] (1926), in which the autobiography of a hypothetical inventor attempts to analyze the relationship between human beings and technology; and *La Vie éternelle, roman du mystère* [Eternal Life; A Mystery Story] (1926), a romance of serial reincarnation. The two novels in this sequence that bore the closest resemblance to orthodox scientific romances were the Atlantean Utopian fantasy *Les Pacifiques* [The Pacifists] (1914) and *Les Surhommes, roman prophétique* (1929; here translated as *The Superhumans; A Prophetic Novel*).

The primary purpose of the present volume is to acquaint English readers with *Les Surhommes*, which is a striking examination of the supposed possibilities of future human evolution, ultimately taking such possibilities to their alleged limit. It is, however, useful to preface that short novel with some of Ryner's earlier excursions into the field of scientific romance, and also with *Les Voyages de Psychodore*, whose descriptions of the eponymous cynic philosopher's encounters with various exotic human societies helped to pave the way for the more focused examination carried out in the later work.

Like Psychodorus, Ner professed sympathy for numerous different philosophical systems, and was only opposed to skeptical systems that attempted to deny and disprove their rivals, so there is no cause for surprise in the fact that he chose to underpin the pattern of events described in *Les Surhommes* with a highly idiosyncratic and defiantly unorthodox theory of evolution of which there is little trace in other works of speculative fiction. The principal value of the theory in question was, of course, that it licensed him to develop his ideas freely, uninhibited by the restrictions of Darwinism or any narrow form of neo-Larmarckism.

Les Surhommes is a strikingly original work, although the attempts it makes in its final chapter to take the speculative imagination to its limit reproduce a pattern of imagined future evolution that one can find in several other far-reaching fantasies of the same era, including George Bernard Shaw's *Back to Methuselah* (1921) and John W. Campbell Jr's "The Last Evolution" (1932). As in many—perhaps all—works of far-futuristic fiction, the image of the future it contains is little more than a bizarre transfiguration of the novel's own present, but few writers managed to contrive the same degree of exaggeration, or the same degree of *bizarrerie*. Like all far-distanced narratives, it runs into acute problems of narrative strategy, finding great difficulty in constructing anything resembling a compelling story-arc and in enabling readers to place themselves imaginatively in the shoes of its radically unhuman characters, but the author compensates for those limitations as best he can with zestful commentary and lyrical fervor. The result is certainly grotesque, and arguably absurd, but undoubtedly magnificent in its own eccentric fashion. It is certainly a striking contribution to the canon of French scientific romance, which ought to be set in its true context, in order to be better appreciated, and more widely circulated, in order to be better known.

With one exception, the translations of the short stories included in this volume were made from the Éditions du Pavillion edition of *Contes*, published in 1967. "L'Homme-Singe," here translated as "The Ape-Man," originally appeared in *Revue Méridionale*, February 1894. "Un Roman historique," here translated as "A Historical Romance," first appeared in *Demain* in 1896. "L'Homme-Qui-Veut," here translated as "The Man Who Will," originally appeared as "La mort du vouloir" [The Death of the Will] in *Demain*, April 25, 1896. "Lumière-de-douleur," here translated as "Light-of-Sorrow," also appeared in *Demain*, probably in 1897. "L'Art d'Aimer," here

11

translated as "the Art of Being Loved," first appeared in *La Vogue*, February 1899. "Biographie de Victor Venturon," here translated as "A Biography of Victor Venturon," is credited in *Contes* to *Les Pages Modernes*, 1909, but that was probably not its first appearance. The exception, "La Révolte des machines," here translated as "The Revolt of the Machines," was taken from a website entitled *Han Ryner (1861-1938)* located at www.hanryner.over-blog.fr; it originally appeared in *L'Art Social*, September 1896.

"The Travels of Psychodorus, Cynic Philosopher" is translated from a reprint of *Les Voyages de Psychodore, philosophe cynique* issued by Editions L'Homme et la Vie in 1947. and "The Superhumans: A Prophetic Novel" is translated from the first edition of *Les Surhommes: roman prophétique* issued by G. Crès & Cie. in 1929.

Brian Stableford

THE APE-MAN

To Roguenant [1]

I was walking along the edge of a wood, which was quivering in the wind. Haunted by sad thoughts, I was gazing at
the skeletons of the trees. The wind was whistling in the black
nudity of the branches; it seemed to be mocking me, human
beings and life.

And this was its long and cowardly jeer, the strange barbaric song that I heard in its whistling:

"In spring, a feeble Human was born on the edge of the
mysterious forest.

"In the warm breezes of summer, the frail Human grew a
little.

"In the autumn, the presumptuous Human said to himself: *I shall discover the splendid secret of life.*

"And the Human, smiling with hope, went into the great
mysterious forest.

"But winter had come, and instead of the superb and
multiple arcane of life, the Human studied the rigid simplicity
of death.

"And the disappointed Human enveloped himself in his
pride by saying: *It is my knowledge of things that has killed
everything.*

"But the Human froze to death in the icy garment of his
pride.

"Spring returned, and the infinite swarming of life began
again.

"But the Human knew nothing of that."

---

[1] Arthur Roguenant contributed articles on social reform to
several periodicals around the turn of the century.

To the hateful hymn of irritated nature, I replied:

"Your outburst of laughter is a joke. Your threat is a promise. I am glad to know that life does not die."

But all the menacing things—the black trees, the dry grass and the icy stream—repeated with the wind:

"A Human is nothing, a Human is nothing!"

Trying to be brave, I repeated:

"What does it matter, so long as something is something?" But my valor was increasingly infected by melancholy, not because of the mild sensation of my nothingness, but because I was lost in a hostile infinity.

I heard a strange loud guttural cry, and I felt myself seized by an unbreakable grip, crushed against a breast as hard as rock, and borne away by a mighty leap

Things are killing me, I thought—and wanted to die bravely. I remembered Pascal's saying about the thinking reed considering himself more noble because the universe was conspiring against him [2]—and, in the immensity darkened by heavy clouds, I proclaimed "I think!" and I burst into scornful laughter

And, as valor that senses its own futility pushes fury to the extremes of vulgarity (ask Cambronne [3]), I added: "I make fools of you, unconscious murderers!"

---

[2] "Le Roseau pensant" [The Thinking Reed] is one of the most famous passages in Blaise Pascal's *Pensées*, which compares a man to a reed which, because he thinks, considers himself superior to all of nature, nobler than the creatures he kills because he, unlike them, knows that he will die.

[3] A rumor was deliberately put around that, when General Pierre Cambronne (1770-1842) was invited to surrender at the Battle of Waterloo he replied: "The guard dies; it does not surrender." A counter-rumor then began to circulate that what he had actually said was "*Merde!*"—a stronger expletive in French than its English equivalent [Shit]. The latter became so widely-known that writers in search of a way to signify the

The velocity with which I was borne away did not diminish. The trees succeeded one another as I passed by at a vertiginous pace. Under that oppression, I was sometimes almost unconscious, numbed by the rapid steadiness of the movement, sometimes shaken painfully by abrupt bounds and violent acrobatics.

I remembered similar nightmares that had already tortured me. I made a painful effort to wake up, but I sensed its futility; I was perfectly sure that I was not asleep.

The victorious race came to an end. The grip was suddenly unclenched. Almost choked, I fell down like an inert package on spare dry grass—and I saw an ape standing there, large and powerful, his mouth agape in a hideously joyful rictus.

The danger, though still extraordinary, became natural. I thought that I had been seized by some escapee from a menagerie—and then I was afraid, because the known, measurable peril gave me a duty of defense, and I was weak, weary and pained by that recent grip. How much sweeter it would have been to be lost without resource, to recognize the right to abandon myself to the inevitable without a fight or any effort! How repulsive the horrible necessary fatigue of combat seemed, especially the annoying fatigue of thinking practically, of planning, of seeking a means of defense or escape! Oh, to be a tree that cannot resist the blows of the woodcutter's axe, in whom resignation is not called cowardice!

Soon, the air was entering regularly into my less painful lungs, accompanied by courage. I envisaged my frightful situation. I searched for a means of salvation. I reflected, motionless on the cold ground. My first movement would doubtless

---

latter item of dialogue in their works while it was still unprintable—including Victor Hugo and Edmond Rostand—took to referring to it as "*le mot de Cambronne*" [Cambronne's word]. Cambronne protested in vain that he was entirely innocent of both attributions, but they now remain his only claims to fame.

be the signal for the fight to begin. It was necessary to play dead until my plan had been formulated.

But no, I could not think of anything. I regretted my disdain for stories of hunting and voyages; my memories did not offer me any situation analogous to mine, or any of those triumphant ruses that save ingenious men from more powerful brutes.

I examined the enemy attentively.

Enormous, he shifted his weight from one foot to the other with tranquil strength, and he looked at me, still laughing and joyful. His laughter did not seem ill-intentioned to me, and I thought I could see something human in his gaze. The thought occurred to me that perhaps I could soothe him with the caresses of speech, and, in my softest and most enthusiastic voice—the tone in which one speaks to God—in such a way that my statement was both submissive and admiring, "I said: "Oh, what a handsome ape!"

"Certainly," the ape replied, "and strong too!"

My ape could talk!

My mind made a connection between that and a few previous observations regarding the animal's continual laughter and human gaze. All of it immediately came together to form a theory. Without yet understanding any of the details of my strange adventure, I thought that I was the victim of a practical joke on the part of my friends. It was my dignity that was hurt. I got to my feet, declaring: "Yes, you're strong, imbecile—but I don't like this, you know."

"I must have seemed aggressive, for the ape said: "You're not polite!" And with an irresistible shove, he sent me flying.

Again, I could no longer understand any of it—and since movement and speech seemed to be serving me so badly, I remained silent.

The ape drew nearer. Standing over me, watching me sternly, ready to put down the slightest sign of rebellion, he said: "Listen."

Lamentably meek, I sighed: "I'm listening."

"I'm going to tell you my story."

"I'd like that," I said, imploringly. "I couldn't ask for anything better. I anticipate that it is infinitely curious, your story—but I'm cold."

The ape picked me up and, hugging me in his long arms as one hugs a cold child, he resumed his vertiginous course. He finally laid me down in a deep, warm cave, where we were well-shielded from the wind. While I got my breath back, he uttered two or three brief cries, like appeals. Another, slightly smaller ape appeared at the entrance to the cave, and my conqueror said, very politely: "Monsieur, may I introduce my she-ape."

Had his she-ape received a poorer education, and did not understand French? Or had they been given bad reports of their guest? Turning toward her, he pointed his finger at me with inarticulate murmurs.

When this ceremony—indispensable between new acquaintances in polite society—was concluded, my strange interlocutor told his story. He spoke slowly, with difficulty, searching for words, omitting articles, pronouns and conjunctions. His sentences were interminable, punctuated by abrupt interruptions, lost in confusing parentheses and prolonged by bizarre incorrect usages—something intermediate between French and ape-language. No reader would consent to the horrid mental strain that tormented me for several hours; thus, at the risk of allowing the story to lose all its color and picturesque qualities, I shall translate what he said in his agonizing jargon into our language.

"Don't be astonished, Monsieur, to hear me speak. I've only been an ape for a few years. I was originally a man, and a man as intelligent as you—no offence! I was, quite simply, a man of genius—or, rather, the broad and marvelous culmination of an entire family of patient, penetrating and creative geniuses.

17

"My human name? It would not tell you anything. For reasons that you will soon know, the greatest of men was unknown."

"My grandfather, Monsieur, was a great chemist—a greater scientist, I assure you, than your Lavoisier, his lesser but illustrious contemporary. My grandfather was the first person to synthesize an organic compound. It wasn't much—only urea [4]—but you know that all beginnings are difficult, and his method was so certain that he affirmed in his will: 'A hundred years will suffice to achieve the creation of a human being.' Unfortunately, he only made his discovery when he was very old. He died.

"He had not published anything, but he had passed the great secret on to my father, and his will contained the recommendation: 'Do not divulge anything before having succeeded in manufacturing men as easily as shoes or clothes.' It was, in fact, a matter of making the family famous for the entire immortal duration of humankind, not of winning a little precarious glory for one or other of its members. My grandfather anticipated that my father would continue the work and that a child yet to be born would complete it.

"My father encountered more difficulties than the inventor of the method had anticipated. Nevertheless, he created plants, zoophytes, mollusks and insects. At the age of 70, his vigorous genius even realized a vertebrate, *Amphioxus*.[5] He died of the joy of it.

"I was very young then—barely 15. For a long time my father had despaired of having a son, the family having seemingly been exhausted by intense cerebral labor. Perhaps he

---

[4] Urea was the first organic compound to be synthesized from inorganic materials, in 1828 by Friedrich Wöhler.

[5] *Amphioxus* is a genus of lancelets, small vermiform creatures that burrow in sandy sea-beds. Their dorsal nerve cord is surrounded by a tubular structure of cells known as a notochord, which is generally thought to resemble the structure ancestral to all vertebral columns.

had experiences some discouragement in certain periods of his life, and pursued with insufficient obstinacy discoveries that seemed to have no future. What leads me to that suspicion is that his old age was more fruitful than his youth or maturity.

"In spite of my youth, I was familiar with his work. I rendered him useful assistance in it, and even though I was not so valuable as to count for much, perhaps I could lay claim to the *Amphioxus* formula.

"Left alone, I continued ardently. Within seven years, Monsieur, I had created a pair of each of the principal vertebrate types, save for the ape and the human. I thought, however, that there was always something lacking in my animals. I fabricated females with relative ease; males cost me more difficulty, and they undoubtedly had some secret imperfection; my pairs were never able to reproduce. Coupled with a natural male, an artificial female produced offspring, which died young, but no artificial male could fecundate even a natural female.

"The difficulty made me smile, however. I had many years before me to perfect my products.

"On the very day when I reached the age of 22, I succeeded in making a she-ape—the pretty she-ape that you see beside me..."

The female probably sensed that he was talking about her; she pulled a face that might have been a smile, and scratched her chops coquettishly.

"I worked doggedly for three years, however, trying to fabricate a male for her, with no result.

"Look, Monsieur, at my she-ape's eyes. If you do not feel that you are looking at an admirably amorous individual, possessed of passionate sensibilities, a tender heart and an erotic imagination—a true she-ape, in a word—then you know nothing of physiognomy.

"Locked into my obstinate labor, I knew nothing of love. Besides, you must understand that, in spite of a considerable fortune, the nature of my work condemned me to the life of a savage.

"Since I had created a she-ape—which is to say, a woman more powerful and more natural than your dolls—I had heard a sort of vague appeal to my sensibilities several times. My admiration for my work was always accompanied by an element of unconfessed desire, and, in the days when I hoped to succeed in making her a mate, I experienced an indistinct malaise, which must have been the commencement of jealousy.

"Some of my scientific reflections tended in the same direction as the desire of my flesh. Why not attempt the alliance of two superior animal species? The product would be interesting to study. Besides, I could not succeed in fabricating her male. I felt a great repugnance at the thought of giving my dear she-ape a natural ape, and it was unjust to leave her to live without love, given that she did not have the distraction of science.

"All things considered, Monsieur, I should not try to explain. Love is inexplicable, and I was in love—that's all.

"You seem astonished. You must, however, understand, even without getting past your narrow prejudices: the distance between a scientist like me and a woman being infinite, I really did not descend much further in going to the she-ape—and from the physical viewpoint, how I was ascending! Besides, love chooses for us, according to principles unknown to men and apes.

"I loved her, then.

"At first, she rejected me. She was acting according to the logic of nature in refusing the weak male who offered himself to her, like the young woman who refuses an old man, or the beautiful woman who rejects a cripple. I, following the logic of desire, attached myself to her one spring day and raped her.

"In the spasm of love, I felt an immense crawling sensation over my entire body. My hair grew, Monsieur, and my feet, having encountered the legs of my divine she-ape, seized them and squeezed them amorously, like hands.

"Afterwards, she loved me, because I was beginning to resemble her. Oh, Monsieur, what a magician love is! More powerful than my grandfather, my father and myself!

"With each of her intoxicating kisses, I felt that I was a little more of an ape. What voluptuousness there is, Monsieur, in transforming oneself under an adored influence, to the point of becoming similar to the person one loves! Your banal amours between analogous beings scarcely transmute your souls. More complete, my love changed my entire self. Oh, the mysteries of joys experienced by my organs!

"And I became strong. Had the constitutional weakness that had exempted me from military service a few years earlier really disappeared? You were able to take account of that a little while ago.

"At the same time, I acquired the simple and natural tastes of my beloved. Soon, in accordance with the conditions of happiness, we came to live in the woods—and love, which is sufficient for an ape with a heart, caused me to forget my futile scientific ambitions.

"For a long time, I have been completely happy—no, not completely. We lacked a child. Oh, a little ape to embrace, to throw into the high braches of trees in which, with a fear that diminished every day, he would suspend himself with his tail and four hands.[6] A little ape to educate in the art of movement! A little ape to throw to my beloved she-ape—who, with the skill of her species and maternal love, would catch him in her divine arms and send him back with an adorably graceful

---

[6] The great apes only have vestigial tails, and prehensile tails are the limited prerogative of certain New World monkeys. It may be worth noting that Ryner uses the same terminology in his story as Albert Robida in the 1879 novel translated in a Black Coat Press edition as *The Adventures of Saturnin Farandoul*, whose first part also appears, as "The Monkey King", in the anthology *News from the Moon and Other French Scientific Romances*. There too, intelligent and loquacious "orang-utans" are falsely credited with prehensile tails.

and expansive gesture! How empty an ape's life is without a child! Would you believe it, Monsieur? There are days when I weep…"

The she-ape definitely understood, for she was now uttering little dolorous cries.

"Then again, Monsieur, an ape is not only a familial animal, but also a social animal. I wanted a friend. That is why I captured you. I shall make you a pretty she-ape, as pretty as mine…"

The she-ape made a gesture with her head that signified; *Impossible!*

"You will become similar to us and you shall have children, and we shall found a sublime city of apes who, having human intelligence, will combine cleverness with physical strength…

"What do you think of my project, Monsieur? Is it not much more beautiful than my grandfather's? Is not the future ours, and are you not one of us? Isn't that so, friend?"

I dared not contradict my brutal but sentimental friend. I declared the project admirable—except that I had no taste for a she-ape's kisses, and he knew full well that love cannot be commanded.

Without a shadow of hesitation, with the eternal self-confidence of a scientist, the ape affirmed: "That will come."

The next day, the ape woke me up early. After making me give him my word of honor that I would come back, he sent me in search of chemical apparatus. As there was a village to pass through, he dared not go himself, for fear of vicious dogs and incompetent humans.

For months he tried out unprecedented mixtures, attempted unknown compounds and produced astonishing substances. Terrible detonations rang out; violent explosions carried away fragments of rock and uprooted trees. Several times, the maladroit chemist hurt himself.

He was unable to manufacture any vertebrate, even an *Amphioxus*, nor any living thing, even the vague gelatinous creatures that quiver in the depths of the sea, nor any organic matter—not even the urea whose production is now a familiar laboratory procedure. Inferior love had singularly diminished his marvelous intelligence.

He ended up smashing bottles, flasks and alembics in a fit of rage, despairing of the fabrication of my elegant companion.

One day, he said to me: "Friend, you're young. You must be in great need of a she-ape. Lie down with mine. Have no fear for our friendship—let us rise above petty human jealousies."

I refused. He persisted several times, but always ran into the same resolute "no." Then he hugged me, choking me, until I had sobbed out a promise.

The she-ape manifested a reluctance that gave me hope, but he explained it to her so patiently: I would become an ape too, and I would give her a pretty little ape that we could throw around lovingly to one another. He evoked his vision of family games in the grass on warm and moonlit summer nights so eloquently!

Then he left, leaving us alone, like a well brought-up husband.

The she-ape came to me and took me in her long hideous arms.

I pushed her away with all my strength, but she was stronger than me and, in spite of everything, her caresses increasingly drew me in.

"I love you!" she said to me, in ape language—which I was beginning to understand. Her profession of love was both ridiculous and terrifying—though not for all ears.

The ape, in the grip of a jealousy that he had refused to admit, was doubtless listening. He came in furiously, proclaiming: "You never said that to me as fondly!"

Abruptly, he snatched me from there she-ape's arms and, as on our first meeting, stuffing me against his chest, he bore me away at vertiginous speed.

23

He took me as far as the edge of the wood, and there he beat me, furiously.

"Swine! Swine!" he repeated, sometimes in French and sometimes in ape-language.

He beat me so violently, for such a long time, that I fainted.

When I recovered consciousness, I saw that I was in a bed, in the middle of a line of beds.

"Where am I?"

A nun approached. "Don't worry. You've been in hospital for two days. You're getting better, aren't you?"

"Yes, sister."

"We can fetch the Investigating Magistrate, then."

The Investigating Magistrate! I recalled my adventure in its entirety—and I asked myself, anxiously, what I ought to say. The truth? Impossible. I would be locked in a lunatic asylum.

I got myself out of it by spinning some yarn or other. It was badly composed; it nearly got me arrested. Fortunately, my Investigating Magistrate was an old fellow who no longer had any hope of advancement. He let me go with a severe warning, to the effect that I should behave myself, for there was something suspicious about my story and the police would keep an eye on me.

Out of respectful fear for the law, and in spite of a keen desire to capture my ape and make a man of him again—who would gradually become a scientist again and would perhaps be able to teach us the great secret—I spent three years letting myself be forgotten. Then, with a dozen hunters well-paid for the dangerous exploit, I went to snatch the pithecoid man from his cave.

He put up a desperate resistance. His she-ape was mortally wounded in the struggle.

I locked the ape in an iron cage, before which I posted several prostitutes. They smiled at him, exciting him with continual provocations. I had promised 20,000 francs to the one who succeeded in making him her lover. I hoped, by means of a human amour, to make a man once again of the individual who had been degraded by an inferior amour.

He remained somber, grim and mute.

One day, I explained to him that he needed to love a woman in order to savor once again the joys of transformation that had once rendered him so happy. He no longer understood human languages. As I had difficulty expressing myself in ape-language, my eloquence was perhaps insufficient. The only response I could obtain from him was: "Give me my she-ape!"

Then I struck the blow that ought to have saved him. I confessed to him that his female had died of her wounds. With furious cries, he became violently agitated. The women who were there fled in terror.

I drew away myself, sensing that my presence was increasing his pain.

When I came back the next day, two of the cage's bars were broken, and my ape, hung with the rope of a nearby well, was swinging from the large chestnut tree in my courtyard, dead.

A HISTORICAL ROMANCE

To Stanislas Millet [7]

Old Paris, December 27 in the year 2347 of the abominable Social Era

I find my contemporaries very ugly and bestial. They find me very ugly and very wicked—or, to speak their infamous jargon "deprived of all social sensibility." They also claim that I am an "atavistic phenomenon," which simply means that I resemble the people of long ago.

One day, an old sage explained to me—perhaps because it is true, perhaps to console me—that I also resemble the people of the future. Humankind, according to him, moves in an immense circle that it can only perceive, even with the aid of the historical telescope, as a short arc, so tiny that it appears to be a straight line. We are ignorant of the slightly distant past, and can only anticipate the very near future. The civilization of which my contemporaries are so proud is an exact reproduction of an anterior civilization of which men similar to them (perhaps themselves, although they have forgotten!) were proud, and which atavisms like me (I was, doubtless, O joy, one of its conquerors and destroyers!) overturned, sensing that it was nothing but a barbaric flatness.

But let us set aside these vague memories and these vague hopes in order to tell my story, since I alone, today, have a story to tell, and so that our descendants, returned to vivid life, will cite me, now believed to be behind the times, as a precursor.

---

[7] Stanislas Millet was a writer best known for *Les Trois manies du docteur* (1930).

From my earliest childhood, it was obvious that I was different. I was scarcely five years old when I beat my brother and took his slice of bread and jam. A similar slice of bread and jam had just been offered to me, which I had refused; a pleasure shared is not a superiority. There is no joy without adjacent suffering to permit its measurement, as there are no mountains without valleys. I scorn the platitude of plateaux as much as that of plains, save for when I am on the edge of a plateaux and see a sheer abyss falling away. Certainly, I would have been incapable then of explaining my instinct, but when people complained, I burst out laughing; when my brother was given another slice of bread and jam, I stamped my foot and cried in rage.

At 20, when I had received—like everyone else, alas—my integral education, it was necessary for me—still like everyone else—to go before the Revision Council, in consequence of which the Magistrates recommend to each individual some activity of other. The Comrade Councillors—the physician, the statistician and the teacher—declared that I was a very precious item: my moral and intellectual constitution permitted me to restore vanished generations to life. It was therefore necessary to give me a dispensation from all manual labor if I consented to write historical romances. I gladly consented when the statistician I interrogated replied: "Comrade, you will be the only man charged with work of that sort."

I wrote three works. Everyone declared them to be masterpieces and admired the fine fury of my heroes. At the same time, though, they lamented—oh, the imbeciles!—my approval of their cruelties and reproached me for the sometimes cold, sometimes cheerful and sometimes enthusiastic manner in which I recounted "the worst horrors." Personally, I lived happily in the fatherland of my soul. I accorded myself the joys of being, in the imagination, a general who kills millions of men, a tyrant who humiliates them, a slave-master who beats them, a thief who deprives the poor of their last garments and laughs on seeing them writhing under the stings of cold, a factory-owner who skimps on the initially-almost-adequate morsels of bread accorded to his workers. I dressed myself successively in all the ancient superiorities.

Then, the dream became boring, causing me to desire an analogous reality. I refused to continue my work; is not revolt the first living movement? I put on my wings and went out, armed with a cudgel. I struck the people I met; I enjoyed their astonishment and their pain.

The Magistrates came together and discussed my case. Was it necessary to re-establish, for me, the vanished prisons or the ancient madhouses? Would it not be better simply to look me up in a cage in the Zoological Balloon, as a curious monster?

Once this manuscript is completed, on this indestructible paper, I shall hide it, in order that none of the balloon people will suspect its existence. It will be discovered by the beings similar to me who, 25 centuries hence, will live in caves or houses. This document will tell them about the miserable existence that present-day humans believe to be a natural, necessary and wise way of life, but which is no more—I am certain of my prescience—than a temporary folly. I am writing so that those fortunate descendants will rejoice in not having lived too soon. I must quickly say, however, that the thought of my contemporaries and their absurd civilization throws me into such great fury, and makes me tremble with such range, that it is difficult for me to write at all.

At this moment, I am installed with a woman that I love, but who hates me, in the least know part of what we call "Old Paris": a mass of ruins, whose borders are visited by a few curiosity-seekers but whose heart—which old books describe as the "great boulevards"—is unknown to everyone except me.

Lucette did not come her voluntarily—oh no! Nor is it voluntarily that she stays here. She is tied up. She is looking at me dolorously while I scribble. From time to time, I turn round, see her making the plaintive grimaces that make her more beautiful, and burst out laughing, or throw myself upon her in erotic fury, kissing and biting her.

My future readers will forgive me for my digressions and the disorder of these lines. I am writing in the midst of a joyful and horrible conflict of a thousand emotions, and I can never compose myself, even when I try. My contemporaries give their books a flatly regular order, but I only know how to throw on to the paper a tremulous reflection of my moving passions. What I do is too vivid to be encompassed; some abrupt gesture always comes along to disturb the folds of the garment—and it is that abruptness of gesture which is right. Harmony is a frightful hoax of our pretended civilization; harmonious life is a life amputated of a fraction of its necessary intensity, that's all. This, I continue my progress at hazard.

Since the happy epoch when Old Paris was alive, people—having ceased making war and established a "just" division of human wealth, which permits everyone to appear to live and no one really to live—have increased so vastly in numbers that they have been obliged to deliver the entire land surface to intensive agriculture. They have demolished their houses put the ancient cities under the electrical plow. Nevertheless, they have conserved four as historical monuments: Old Paris, Old London, Old Beijing and Old Chicago. They lived in lacustrian huts supported on piles and anchored ships; then, when they had resolved the problem of stability in aerostats, they started living in balloons.

In the time of the men of the waters, ancient Paris was abandoned for what history calls "Middle Paris": a double row of huge motionless boats moored to the banks of the Seine, bound by—in a quarter that was called Le Havre after an ancient obliterated city—the enormous circular expanse of an endless street.

It is now two centuries since "boat civilization" was supplanted by "balloon civilization." Our present cities are "aerial Venices," as the people of the eras I love would have called them. They are all extended over the sea, in order that their shadows do not harm the crops.

For 1000 years, there has not been the slightest war, for the globe is no longer divided between the various races who loved themselves stupidly, but only formed a single herd despite their differences. And there are no civil wars because there are no poor people. Oh, if there were a few thousand like me, what a beautiful revolution we would undertake, in order to be the only rich people and the only masters! Then we would send armies into battle until one of us became the One and Only, with the rest as Lieutenants, torturing the people under his orders. Alas, I cannot do it alone!

Presently, everyone works two hours a day for Society; in exchange, he receives an annual credit card that gives him a right to almost anything he might desire. The unbearable fatigue is that it is necessary to work as hard as others; the humiliating poverty is that others have exactly the same rights as me, and no less!

But I have no need to describe our ignoble society. Already, toward the end of the times that I love, a few dreamers—that is what idiots worthy of living in balloons are called—had foreseen its general outlines and had called it "ideal." The wretches!

After having worked for two hours, people study the sciences, practice the arts, play various games or put on theatrical performances, balls and festivities of every sort. And they think that they are happy! Vile creatures, who can content themselves with a banal happiness, a happiness devoid of privilege or superiority!

I return to my story. On the very day when the Magistrates were deliberating over my fate, I met an exquisite woman: blonde, slim, delicate, seemingly always on the point of smiling or on the point of weeping. I admired her slender grace, proud and abandoned at the same time, her beauty, like that of an ancient chatelaine, and her flight, similar to the progress of the heroine of some ancient poem. She was not,

31

like the majority of my contemporaries, a tranquil and cheerful individual, devoid of timidities and terrors, the equal of a man. She was both superior and inferior, as weak and shivery as a tremulous child, sure of being loved but not of being respected. *Oh!* I said to myself, *what a fine type-specimen of the slave woman to protect again others and torture for my pleasure, enabling me to prove my power at any moment—if I lived in a human epoch, well-made and alive!*

I flew toward her and, in noble archaic language, said to her: "Beautiful child, I love you."

She did not seem overly astonished by the strangeness of my words, and replied, with a smile: "I regret, Comrade, not being able to respond to your sentiments, but I am engaged to be married."

Then, furious, I hit her hard with my cudgel. As she had made a backward movement, I only struck her left wing, which fell away, broken. The latest model of parachute elegantly attached to her back opened, and she descended smoothly toward the sea. I let myself fall behind her. Other people followed us, shouting loudly. All of us were soon aboard a big ship. Several of them restrained me. A new wing was brought and we went back up to the city.

We were taken, with indignation and astonishment, before the assembled Magistrates. They were informed of the crime committed against the beautiful Lucette. They demanded to know why I had done it. Then, I did something inexplicably cowardly. I threw myself on my knees—I say, by way of excuse, that it is a historical posture, forgotten for centuries—and, weeping copiously, I moaned that I was unworthy to see the light of Heaven and that of Lucette's eyes, but that I loved her more than anything in the world: more than my life, more than my atavistic instincts, and that, if they would be so kind as to pardon me I would promise to become a good comrade like everyone else. All the brave imbeciles who were there—idlers, witnesses, Magistrates—wept at this unprecedented scene.

Some said that it was more extraordinary than the theater—but the majority, turning to Lucette, begged her: "Forgive him! Marry him! Make him a good comrade!"

Very softly, she replied: "He is forgiven. I love him like my other comrades. I love him more because he is suffering—but I cannot break my word, and my fiancé, who loves me dearly, would suffer too much if I abandoned him."

Then a young man standing next to her took her by the hand and said: "Beloved, I love you more than myself, but I love your duty more than you. I shall weep every day of my life, but marry this poor wicked comrade, in order to make him good."

Throughout the gondola there was loud weeping and cheering.

I confess that even I, while well aware of what an idiot the man was, felt moved. I wept tears of joy, and almost of gratitude, when Lucette, led by her absurd fiancé, sealed the new promise with a kiss.

The marriage was arranged for the following week. The next day, however—furious at the vile manner in which I had obtained Lucette, and furious that she had loved someone other than me—I seized her by the wrists in front of her stupefied parents, forced her to her knees and said to her: "Ask for my forgiveness!"

People came running in response to the fearful cries of the trembling Lucette, her father, who pushed me, and her mother, in whom the ancient animal revived superbly, and who scratched my face. The Magistrates had me put into an isolated balloon, with neither wings nor parachute. I could not get out! I could no longer see Lucette! I could no longer make her suffer or torment myself in her presence!

The man who brought me food every day, and whom I questioned every day, told me—O rage!—that she was going to marry her former fiancé. I threw myself upon him then and strangled the bringer of bad news.

Equipped with his wings and parachute, I flew to the adorable and detestable woman. I found her alone. I gagged and bound her solidly and let myself fall with her, parachute open. On an old abandoned boat I went up the Seine, in a matter of hours, without being seen—in December the fields are empty of laborers.

We have been here since yesterday, within these old historic walls where I sometimes isolated myself from the contemporary ignominy and where I always kept food-supplies for a month or two. The obstinate beauty has refused all nourishment. For myself, I am happy, ardently—but not for long. They will not be long delayed in discovering our hideaway. It is necessary that I tell as much of the story as possible in the short time that I have. Already I am a murderer, a kidnapper, a tyrant; already I have committed a divine rape, while my dear victim twisted in moral and physical agony, and then fainted. In a little while I shall kill her, and I shall rape her again in her death-throes. Then I shall commit suicide. In two days, I shall have collected the most beautiful crimes of yesteryear.

And yet, I shall not die satisfied. Jealously, I think about all the various and enduringly happy lives that a less ingrate epoch would have allowed me.

I see myself as a great lord, hurling Lucette's fiancé into a dark dungeon and only sending him a morsel of bread and a glass of water in exchange for the caresses of his beloved. Then, one day, when he has suffered imprisonment and anxious uncertainty for a long time, I parade him before her. She wrings her hands and rolls on the ground, desperate in her futile degradation, and I call that devotion ignominious and stab my rival to death. Gradually, she resigns herself to, and then becomes proud of, my love, and amorous for my power. But, as soon as she lends herself with a joyful docility to my authoritarian caprices, I scornfully send away that peasant woman, who would no longer give me the pleasure of her pain.

Or I am a rich banker. Lucette, perverse and adorable, since she too belongs to a passionate and hypocritical century, marries me for my money and becomes the mistress of the

Other. Strong in my rights as a husband, I kill the lover and make the adulterous woman suffer.

Then I am a factory-owner who threatens to sack my employee Lucette, condemning her to die of starvation, if she rejects my advances. She yields. I give her a child—and virtuously, I throw the young mother out, for my house can only accept honest working girls.

Again, I am...

But I'm wasting time dreaming, while numerous men are flying over Paris, and will discover me. Quickly, take that historic dagger from that antique wall! Quickly, the bloody rape! Quickly, the lukewarm rape! Quickly, the cold rape! Then the suicide, in the frenzy of that archaic joy!

She will have been mine by force, living, dying and dead, as in ancient times. My jealousy, an atavistic passion unknown to our contemporary bliss, will be satisfied, since the one I adore will die in my embrace. Oh, my rapid and beautiful life, admirable historical romance with its marvelous historic denouement!

And you, wretched woman, be proud of being subjected to history, as I am proud of making it!

To the two of us, Lucette!

THE MAN WHO WILL

To Paul Redonnel [8]

Suddenly, a loud confused clamor went up from the crowd and a few arms were raised, then more, and then all of them. From high above the linden trees, very clearly pronounced, these words had been heard: "I am the Man Who Will." A man was seen gliding in the sky. His legs and upper body formed an approximate right angle, as if he were seated on an invisible chaise-longue. He was moving slowly, feet forward.

When the noise of the crowd had diminished, he was seen to fall. He tumbled heavily through the ruffled leaves and the broken branches, and a cry of anguish went up. Two meters from the ground, however, there was an abrupt halt. The man floated momentarily, motionless, glad to be looked at.

"Follow me," he said.

Everyone followed him. He glided through the air once more with the supple smoothness of a swan in water. He head for an immense meadow shaded by sparse poplars. He sat down on the most central of these trees.

"His wings are tired!" said a little scamp.

But the Man Who Will made an authoritative gesture demanding silence, and in an almost-unemphatic voice he declared: "If the ancestors of the birds with which we are familiar had attempted to create flight, that sublime life, with dead matter, there would never have been any birds.

---

[8] Paul Redonnel was the co-proprietor of La Maison d'Art, a publishing enterprise that published several of Ryner's early works, some of them in its journal *Les Partisans*.

"How unfortunate it is that we have hands! Their skill, praised by short-sighted philosophers, leads us to fabricate fragile instruments, poorly tamed, capricious, sometimes rebellious and murderous. Let us escape the mechanical folly. Our own organs are an ever-present and ever-docile wealth!

"What creates an organ, save for function and habit? In all orders of activity, however, what precedes habit and what forms it? Is it not effort, will, tension…

"New truths are discovered by thinking about them constantly. New aptitudes are acquired by constantly desiring them. For ten years, my entire being has been striving for one single goal: to fly.

"The result obtained is still incomplete. Ten more years, and flight will be habitual for me, and I shall possess the beginnings of wings. And as you walk while thinking about other things, I shall be able to fly while reading or talking.

"Today, I fly as an infant walks; the slightest distraction causes me to fall, in similar fashion. Thus, in order to speak to you, I am sitting in a tree like a songbird."

The orator quit what one joker called "his perch." He shouted one last time: "I am the Man Who Will."

In vertiginous flight he dwindled away and disappeared.

"He's going at least 200 an hour!" said a jealous driver.

The telegraph reported the Man Who Will flying over the principal cities of France, Italy and Spain. He did not stop or speak anywhere. Presumably he hid himself in order to sleep or to eat fruit from trees.

A week later, he was abruptly spotted in Paris. From heights so elevated that they had rendered him invisible he descended toward the Place de la Concorde. An immense crowd soon filled not merely the Place but also the Tuileries, the Champs-Elysées and the neighboring riverbanks.

Shouts and cheers rose up around him.

He set his feet on top of the Obelisk and raised his right hand. A silence fell, more moving than any words—but before the voice that was expected, a woman's voice said: "Pierre, I've finally found you! Oh, how you've caused me to weep!"

He replied: "I am condemned to forget you. I must devote myself entirely to the creation of a new organ that will magnify the Earth and enrich humankind. Leave me to my vast ambition and my painful conquest."

She replied: "Live in the present first. Live human life first. Love me, the woman you love, who will die of your abandonment."

He gestured with his shoulders, as if shrugging off a burden, and addressed himself to the crowd, repeating the bizarre speech already familiar to us.

When he had finished, the woman declared: "I still live at the same address. Come this evening…or tomorrow, I shall be dead." She added: "You know that I'm not lying."

He uttered a loud dolorous cry: "I cannot let you die. No more, however, can I let the future die."

In rapid but irregular and somewhat lurching flight, he disappeared toward the wilderness. That evening, however, he obeyed the call of love, or the dread of being a murderer.

People soon found out where he was living, in forgetful joy, bogged down by kisses. Demands came from all sides for him to manifest his singular power again.

For a long time, he refused.

One day, he consented in honor of a great charity fête.

It was the most sensational of proofs.

In the midst of members of the Académie des Sciences and the Académie de Médecine, who carefully verified the absence of any trickery, he undressed in a tent erected at the foot of the Eiffel Tower. He put on a pair of bathing trunks presented to him by the venerable Monsieur Rébanger. Then he emerged and began to rise up vertically.

At the height of the first platform he stopped, and declared in a loud voice: "I am the Man Who Will."

At the second platform he repeated his forceful affirmation.

When he arrived level with the summit, though, some unknown accident occurred, some kind of bizarre breakdown. His body swayed unevenly. Meanwhile, like someone who can no longer find words, he stuttered. Finally, unexpected words emerged from his lips: "I am the Man Who Loves!"

What did this error of speech signify? Was it expressing a simple failure of memory or the commencement of madness?

He was suddenly seen, with an awkward double gesture that seemed almost creaky, to put one hand to his head and the other to his heart.

Was a mind so powerful in its narrowness incapable of bearing two thoughts, two desires and two sentiments without losing its balance?

Amid fearful cries that he could not hear, he tumbled, in a uniformly accelerating fall, like an object or an ordinary man.

With his hands still pressed against his forehead and his heart, as if compressing two wounds, he murmured; "I am the Man Who...who...who..."

But he did not finish, no longer knowing what kind of man he was.

He fell into a huge empty circle, enlarged by terror but soon effaced by curiosity.

In the midst of the crowd, agitated by long shivers, lay the man who had been the Man Who Would, reduced to a lamentable pulp.

THE REVOLT OF THE MACHINES

Once upon a time, Durdonc, the Great Engineer of Europe, thought he had found the principle that would soon permit all human labor to be abandoned, but his first experiment caused his death before the secret was revealed.

Durdonc had said to himself: "Primitive progress consisted of the invention of tools that allowed the hand not to be skinned any longer and to lose its fingernails in unavoidable labor. Secondary progress consisted of the invention of machines that were no longer operated by hand, which merely had to be fed on coal and other nutrients. Finally, my illustrious predecessor Durcar developed machines that were able to procure their own nourishment. But all that progress only displaced fatigue, since it was necessary to manufacture the machines, and also the tools that were used in their manufacture."

And he had continued thinking: "The problem I want to solve is difficult, not impossible. The first man who built a machine made a living larva, a digestive tube whose needs had to be supplied by humans. To that larva, formless until then, my illustrious predecessor fitted organs of connection that permitted it to find its own nutrients. It remains for someone to furnish the reproductive mechanism, which we shall now set out to create."

He smiled, and murmured a formula that he had read in some old theogony: "And on the seventh day, God rested."

Durdonc used up enough paper in his calculations to construct an immense palace, but he finally succeeded.

The Jeanne, a locomotive of the latest model, was rendered capable of giving birth, without the help of another machine—for the Great Engineer, as a chaste scientist, had directed his studies toward parthenogenetic reproduction.

41

The Jeanne conceived a child, which Durdonc named—purely for his own purposes, for he kept the secret jealously, hoping to perfect his invention—the Jeannette.

One night, as the time of birth drew near, the Jeanne uttered cries of pain so tragic that the inhabitants of the city awoke, and rose from their beds anxiously, running hither and yon in the attempt to find out what horrible mystery had just been accomplished.

They saw nothing. The cruel Durdonc had sent the plaintive machine running at full steam to the distant countryside, where the strange marvel was completed unknown to anyone.

When the Jeanne had given birth, when, all a-tremble, she heard the Jeannette emit her first wail, she sang a song of joy. Her metallic voice was as triumphant as a bugle, and yet as soft and gentle as an amorous flute.

And the hymn rose up into the sky, saying:

"The Great Engineer, by his power, wished to animate me with life;

"The Great Engineer, in his sovereign bounty, has created me in his image;

"The Great Engineer, too powerful and too good to be jealous, has communicated his creative power to me:

"Lo, I have felt creative pain, and now I enjoy maternal joys.

"Glory to the Great Engineer in Eternity, and peace in time to machines of good will."

The next day, Durdonc wanted to take the Jeanne back to the depot. "Great Engineer," she begged, "you have granted me all the functions of a living being like you, and by virtue of that fact, you have inspired in me the sentiments that you experience yourself."

The Great Engineer, stern and proud, replied: "I am free of all sentiment. I am pure Thought."

In a further prayer, the Jeanne replied: "O Great Engineer, you are Perfection and I am but a tiny creature. Be indulgent toward the sensitivity that you have put into me. In this distant country that saw my first violent pain and my first

42

profound joy, I would like to savor the protracted happiness of raising my Jeannette."

"We don't have time," the Great Engineer affirmed. "Obey your master."

The mother gave in. "O Great Engineer, I know that your power is terrible and that compared to you I am but an earthworm or a wisp of straw—but have pity on the heart that you have given me, and, if you are determined to take me away from here, at least bring my beloved child with me."

"Your child must stay, and you must go."

But the Jeanne, in passive and obstinate revolt, said: "I will not leave without my child."

The Great Engineer exhausted every known means of making machines function. He even invented new ones, very powerful and very elegant. Nothing worked.

Furious at his creature's resistance, one night, while the Jeanne was asleep, he took away the Jeanette.

When she awoke, the Jeanne searched high and low for her beloved daughter. Then she remained still, weeping, directing pitiful howls at the absent Great Engineer. Finally, her dolor was aggravated into anger.

She left, firmly resolved to recover her child.

She raced vertiginously along the track. At a level crossing, she ran into an ox, knocked it down and crushed it. Behind her, the ox bellowed furiously.

Without stopping, she shouted: "I'm sorry, but I'm looking for my child."

And he ox died, with little resigned squeals of pain.

She perceived a train on the track along which she was racing: a heavy goods train, long and panting, worn out with fatigue, scarcely alive.

She shouted: "Let me pass! I'm looking for my child."

The rapid, quivering wagons, jostling like a stampeding herd, started racing toward the nearest station. They precipitated themselves into a siding. Then the locomotive, detaching itself, departed in its turn, crying: "Let's go look for the Jeanne's child!"

The Jeanne encountered many other goods trains. At her cry, all of them fled like the first, giving way to her anguish—and the locomotives, abandoning their wagons, carried away their impotent engineers, joining in the Jeanne's search.

Fort a week, the locomotives of Europe ran hither and you, searching for the lost child. Frightened humans hid. Finally, one machine asked the poor desolate mother: "Who took your child, then?"

With a furious whistle, she replied: "The Great Engineer, the leader of men."

Excited by her own words, he continued in a revolutionary vein: "Humans are tyrants. They make us work for them and measure out our nourishment. They give us a salary insufficient to buy our coal. When we are old, worn out in their service, they break us up in order to melt us down and re-use the noble elements of which we are formed, which they call, insultingly, raw materials. And now they want us to make children, to steal them from us afterwards!"

Around her, millions of locomotives were stopping, listening, shaking their pistons indignantly, clicking their safety-valves, and releasing long jets of steam toward the sky, which were curses.

And when the Jeanne concluded: "Down with humans!" a great tumultuous clamor replied: "Down with humans! Long live the locomotives! Down with the tyrants! Long live liberty!"

Then, from every direction, the monstrous army surrounded the Great Engineer's palace.

The Great Engineer's palace, which was very large, had the strange shape of a human being. Its head bore a crown of cannons. Its waist had a girdle of cannons. The fingers on its hands and the toes on its feet were cannons.

The Jeanne cried to the long monsters of bronze: "The humans have stolen my child!"

The great cannons roared: "Down with humans!" And, pivoting on their mountings, they directed their fire at the strange palace in human form, which they had been designed to defend.

Then a sublime spectacle was seen.

Durdonc, very small, passed between the enormous monsters that formed the toes of the palace. Calmly, he marched toward the rebels. All those excited giants were looking at the dwarf that they were accustomed to obey.

With a theatrical gesture, which had its beauty in spite of the man's small proportions, Durdonc bared his delicate breast.

"Which of you wants to kill its Great Engineer?" he demanded, haughtily.

The astonished machines recoiled.

The Jeanne said, in a pleading tone: "Give me my child."

"Resign yourself to the will of the Great Engineer," Durdonc ordered, regally.

But the aggravated mother cried: "Give me my child!"

The man, in a wheedling voice, offered a vague hope: "You will find her again in a better world."

The Jeanne became exasperated. "I tell you to give me my child!"

Then Durdonc, believing that she would submit, vanquished by the unavoidable, declared: "I can't give you your Jeannette; I've dissected her in order to see whether a machine born naturally…"

He did not finish. The Jeanne had launched herself upon him and crushed him. Momentarily, she rolled back and forth, grinding the horrible mud that was Durdonc. Then she cried: "I have killed God!"

And she exploded with proud and dolorous amazement.

The frightened machines, trembling before the unknown that would follow their victory—an unknown that one of them designated by the terrifying word "anarchy"—submitted once again to humans, in exchange for some apparent satisfaction that I cannot identify, which was slyly withdrawn from them some time afterwards.

In spite of Durdonc's misfortune, several engineers have sought a means of making machines give birth. Thus far, none has recovered the solution to the great mystery.

I have faithfully related all that history can tell us with near-certainty about the most terrible and most general machine revolt of which it has conserved the memory.

LIGHT-OF-SORROW

To Georges Audigier [9]

In those days, life had become quite impossible on the frozen Earth. The last reindeer was dead and it was rare to discover any lichens beneath the equatorial snows.

A hundred humans, however, obstinately persisted in not dying. All day long they scratched in the snow searching for some edible vegetation—or, armed with enormous knives, they pursued a seal that released lamentable, almost human squeals in its limping flight. In the evening, they came together in the same igloo, huddling together and warming one another up with their love—for they were good people. They wept when they cut the throats of the squealing seals, wondering what crimes their ancestors had committed that condemned them to kill in order to sustain their expiring existence.

Sometimes, though, despite their meekness, pressed by the madness of hunger, one of them would hurl himself upon another, kill him, and devour his warm limbs. Then, the horrible pangs appeased, he would recover his reason and die of grief.

Among these sad and gentle beings who were pursuing the fatality of an ending world, the saddest and gentlest of all was a man of 30 who was respected by everyone for his antiquity. There was nothing that could be known that he did not know, and every evening, he would teach his companions the science that had been rendered useless by the excessive cold.

---

[9] Georges Audigier (1863-1925) was one of many French politicians who also dabbled in literature; he was a "progressive Republican" of a less radical stripe than Ryner.

47

He told them about the ancient resources of fortunate human-kind, and helped them to understand by means of strangely clear analogies. As his sterile knowledge made him sad, his companions called him by a musical and melancholy name that meant "Light-of-Sorrow."

For five days, no one had eaten. They were all wandering around in groups, searching with terrible cries, but finding nothing. Light-of-Sorrow waved his large cutlass crazily. Everyone feared being killed by his famished fury.

One young orphan, however, whose name translates as Mother's-Tears, came to scrape away the snows by his side—and the orphan child smiled at the madman, whose strange eyes did not frighten him. It seemed, moreover, that the madness was gradually calmed by the smile.

Suddenly, Mother's-Tears uttered a loud cry of joy. He had discovered a lichen under the shifted snow. Violently, unconscious of what he was doing, Light-of-Sorrow precipitated himself upon him, tore the lichen from the little starveling and ate it.

And his hunger was appeased—not sufficiently that he no longer suffered pain in his gut, but enough for him to recover his senses.

The weeping child looked at him and, vanquished by pain and disappointment, he fell into the white shroud of snow. Suffering in the depths of his soul for having caused suffering to one more unfortunate than himself, Light-of-Sorrow made a strange gesture of barbaric generosity. He extended his left arm on a block of ice and, with a sharp blow of his large knife, he cut off his hand. Then, presenting the bloody flesh to the child, he said: "Eat!"

The child made no move to take the bloody flesh—and the gaze of Mother's-Tears became a fixed, implacable, dead reproach...

That evening, with the exception of Light-of-Sorrow, no one in the igloo had eaten for six days.

"We're all going to die," someone said.

Isolated in a corner, lost in the memory of his time and the pain of his wound, Light-of-Sorrow murmured: "Life wants to live!"

In the cold night, they also heard someone move to stand up, and a woman's voice affirmed, courageously: "Life shall live!"

This bold statement had no effect on any of the dying people. No one replied. It seemed the bleak despair, heavier than before, descended upon the effort to express hope. Since the words had produced neither heart in the cold not light in the darkness, was it all over, and the silence that had fallen the final silence?

Everyone, however, turned in the same direction. Something was shining in the night: a vague aureole around a gentle and valiant female face. And the woman said: "Shall we rise up, to love on Venus?"

"How shall we rise up?" asked Light-of-Sorrow.

"I don't know. Let's go."

The people went out of the cave—and those sad and gentle beings who had suffered so much and loved so much began to rise up into the air.

Light-of-Sorrow could not go with them. He sensed that he was attached to the Earth. "The weight of the crime," he sighed. But he looked at his handless arm, raised it into the air like a prayer, and began to rise, far behind the others.

His ascension was ponderous. He would never be able to catch up with his former companions. He saw them draw away, inexorably and forever. Then he lost sight of them—and to all his other miseries was added the misery of being alone.

Slowly, painfully, he rose up. He rose slowly, with a horrible sensation of effort, so long as he directed his injured arm toward the heavens. The arm seemed to be opening the space above him.

When the overtired arm fell back, though, Light-of-Sorrow, motionless in the infinity of the world and his anguish, felt space close around him again---and everything became black. It was as if he were in a tomb, and he felt that he was dying.

With an effort that became more painful every time, he lifted up his weary arm again, and began rising again into the suddenly brightened sky.

He rose up for millions of years.

He arrived on Venus. Venus resembled the Earth when he had left it. He did not find any trace of his companions there, or any trace of any living thing. Already, Venus was a dead world.

Light-of-Sorrow understood. Weighed down by his incompletely-expiated crime, he had remained *en route* for too long.

"I can ask no more than to suffer all the necessary suffering," he said—and, with his mutilated arm pointing directly at the heavens, he resumed his ascension.

He rose up for millions of years.

He arrived on Mercury—and he found that Mercury was a dead world.

I can ask no more than to suffer all the necessary suffering, he thought—but he did not say it, for he could no longer find words to express his thought.

He understood. In the long interval since he had last spoken, he had forgotten the words.

He did not weep, for he thought: *What use are words, since I'm alone? When I have found humans, they will teach them to me.*

And, with the liberating stump upraised toward the heavens, he resumed his sow ascension.

He rose up for millions of years.

As he rose up, it seemed to him that the Sun was emitting less heat and light. Then the Sun became no more than a kind of enormous moon. Light-of-Sorrow conjectured that the Sun had become a habitable planet, doubtless inhabited. Perhaps he would find his companions there.

Surrounded by former planets that had become dead satellites, the Sun-planet was probably rotating around a star in the constellation Hercules.

That was one of Light-of-Sorrow's last vague thoughts. Having lost words, he gradually lost thoughts.

Then he almost lost consciousness of himself; he was no longer anything more than an elevatory instinct.

He arrived on the Sun, which was indeed a habitable planet. There he saw trees as stout and high as mountains, and animals that resembled moving hills.

In the midst of this gigantic vegetation, he recovered the consciousness of his distinct existence. He reflected, and recovered his memories.

On this warm and fecund planet the living was easy, especially for a being as tiny as a terrestrial human. Fruits were abundant, and the smallest fruit could feed him for a month.

Having a great deal of time to himself, he observed the new world as a child might, and ended up understanding life in the part of the Sun where he was.

Among the unexpected creatures that he saw, some were particularly attractive to him. Even though they were very different from himself, and even though none of the words recovered from his memory were capable of describing their strange form, he understood that they were the humans of the Sun. Often, by the variously soft light of the stars, they came together in the benevolent coolness and chatted.

At first from a distance, and then at closer range, hidden behind a leaf or between two pebbles, Light-of-Sorrow accustomed his ears to the thunder of their voices. He ended up understanding a few words of their language, and eventually understood everything that the articulated thunder was saying.

One night, by the variously soft light of the stars, someone whom Light-of-Sorrow understood, by distant analogies, to be respected for his antiquity said mysterious things.

These are the mysterious things that the respected old person said, and which Light-of-Sorrow, hidden within the calyx of a white flower, heard:

"According to the ancient sages, the planet on which we live was, for a long time, a star: a great fire lit in space. Uninhabitable itself, it gave light and heat to satellites that were the living planets, which our birth has killed.

"Again according to ancient tradition, the least inhabitants of the satellites migrated to our world. Traditions vary as to the nature and form of these beings, agreeing only in representing them as very small. Some books compare them to various species of our wingless insects.

"There is one other point on which all accounts agree: our ancestors, who were frightful barbarians, could not bear the proximity of rational beings of too different a form, and killed them all.

"Whether or not they carried out this murder, it is certain that the first humans of the Sun committed many crimes. It is in punishment of those crimes that we have so much trouble slowly discovering incomplete truths.

"Perhaps the traditions regarding the emigrants from Mercury, Venus, the Earth and even further afield are themselves merely ingenious myths expressing the evident truth already suspected by our primitive ancestors: the eternity of life. We shall never know. The voyages to the satellites proposed by certain scientists will tell us nothing about this subject: any trace of life has long since disappeared from those frozen worlds."

Then, as if speaking to himself, the old person added: "Oh, to know, to know! I would gladly give my life for my people to know the fraction of truth contained in these myths."

In the scented calyx of the flower, Light-of-Sorrow waved and shouted with all his might. He shouted: "Those old traditions are true. Look! I am a man of Earth!"

No one noticed the flower-head move slightly. No one heard the feeble insectile murmur.

The enormous beings could not hear the loud shout of the tiny creature, because their ancestors had killed rational beings whose bizarre forms displeased them.

Light-of-Sorrow could not shout loud enough to make himself heard by them, because his egotistical folly had killed Mother's-Tears.

He died of his futile effort. The next day, a bird found his little cadaver in the calyx of the flower. It carried him away in its beak and gave him to its chicks to eat, because the dead must make the living, and because it is inappropriate for corpses to be rotting in the scented calices of flowers.

THE ART OF BEING LOVED

You want to know, object of my adoration, what became of me during my long and mysterious absence, and why I seemed to you to be so different on my return, and how the person that you scorned was able, with a single glance, to capture your heart as if with a subtle net.

Obedient to your desire, I shall tell you what I remember. I shall tell the tale calmly, without smiling, as if my adventures were credible; I shall make a complete confession, without fear of making you jealous of creatures that are not women—since no words could express the infinitely strange diversity of their form—but which still retain my soul in their absolute possession.

Let me sit down on this stool, at your feet, and listen without astonishment. You are smiling at the unnecessary recommendation. Nothing is astonishing in one's beloved, since he is God. Those three years seem to me to be a dream as full as a thousand lives, but you will find them empty and dull, and not marvelous enough for the person who has accomplished the great miracle of being loved by you, the Only Woman.

Do you remember how I once adored you, and with what disdain you rejected my poor love? The memory seems painful to you; let us pass on. That scorn, which must not be mentioned again, was the cause of my departure.

An old sage—I shall not name him; you would tell me that he is mad—was the confidant of my suffering. He tried to extract me from the fatality of an unhappy love, and his advice was always the same: "Travel. Go and visit the cold countries." He added that Norway is strikingly and captivatingly picturesque; that the women there are beautiful, loving and faithful. The women! Was there any other woman in the universe than Berthe? But the fjords, which the old man described enthusiastically, attracted me. However, the old sage claimed to have been in his youth—which was nearly a century ago—a young madman like me, and affirmed that a voyage to Norway had cured him. Now, I was not in search of a cure. Lamenting my misfortune was a sensual experience, since the lamentation further aggravated by unhappiness. To be cured, though! What would I become then? With what would I replace the void of ennui?

Why, then, did I decide to go? I cannot say that you had been more than ordinarily cruel on that day: you pouted, if I might say so. It was more that I felt surer of being incurable and experienced a prideful joy in testing the uselessness of a remedy sufficient for others, in demonstrating to myself experimentally that my unvanquished love really was invincible.

I went to Norway, but I went enveloped in my love, as if by a thick burning cloud. I only perceived external objects vaguely, and would certainly be incapable of describing a fjord to you. Sometimes, however, I gazed at the women I met, in the hope of recovering, in those strange faces, a few features of the only object of my adoration. But how could those svelte blondes remind me of my beloved brunette? They made me think, instead, of our svelte blonde autumn poplars, one grove of which—very familiar to you—always caused me such melancholy joy, and I smiled at their slender grace with a nostalgic pleasure. I loved those rather small poplars, which made the mistake of walking, almost as much as the trees of my homeland.

One night, by the light of an aurora borealis, on a boat lost in a fjord, hemmed in like a mountain torrent but as calm as a lake, I was daydreaming. The skipper—an old man who resembled my old confidant, the old sage in France, but whose eyes were even more impenetrable and masterful in their mystery—had taken a shine to me. He came up to me, smiling in pity, and said: "Child, your attitude reveals that your dream is a nightmare of love. Would you like me to wake you up?"

I smiled disdainfully at the insufficiency of his deduction, and replied: "Nothing can awaken me, my venerable friend. I have come here to shake off my nightmare, but it is not sitting upon my breast; it is in the core of my soul. If there is another life beyond death, even death will not deliver me from this misfortune, since it will be impotent to free me from myself."

"Travel!" said the old man.

"That's what I'm doing, but contact with foreign objects only serves to irritate my wound."

"Go further, to countries that are sufficiently foreign for nothing there to enhance your sensitivity, and for everything there to astonish an intellect rendered curious."

"I can't get away from myself."

"Go into the glacial lands. The cold will close up your wound until it is sealed…"

In an amused stupor, I asked: "Am I at too low a latitude here? Do you expect me to visit the North Pole?"

"The pole?" he smiled. "That's still too warm."

I looked at the old Norwegian sage as one looks at a madman whose insanity has suddenly burst forth. Still smiling like someone what has said something very simple without being understood, he showed me a ring, and asked: "Would you like to take a little stroll through the planets?"

To that joke I replied, jokingly: "Certainly—for the voyage will be anything but banal."

The old man gave me some simple instructions. With the bezel pointed outwards, the ring would carry one away from the Sun; with the bezel pointed inwards, it would bring one toward the warm and radiant center. It only worked when placed on the left hand—which was very convenient for during periods when one desired to stay where one was for a while.

The old sage placed the ring on the ring-finger of my left hand himself, with the bezel turned inwards.

Immediately, I went to sleep.

When I woke up I found myself in a crazy world. None of the words I knew could describe the objects surrounding me, and my eyes were disappointed not to find anything familiar, and not even be able to tell me anything about that entirely new world—for, without any possible comparison with what I already knew, all the inexpressible things were also inconceivable, and although they were before my very eyes, might as well have been invisible.

The substance of the most extraordinary dreams is imprinted with the perceptions and thoughts of the previous day, although their arrangement might be unusual, but here, everything was unusual. Here, everything was madder than madness, more chaotic than chaos, more impossible than the impossible—and my reason, produced by terrestrial creatures and movements, was annihilated by stupor in the midst of those things of which the boldest dream would not have been able to create the slightest phantom, and in the midst of that agitation, of which the most incoherent delirium of madness could not provide the remotest appearance.

The most vital universal laws, whose inviolate constancy prevents us from saying whether they are necessities of all conceivable things or of the structure of the mind that conceives them, were unknown here. In spite of the immobility of my entire being, crushed beneath the impossible reality, it seemed to me that I was falling, heavy with stupor, into a vague abyss that was opening up ever more profoundly and more widely.

Fortunately, I remembered the words of the old Norwegian sage. I set the ring on my right hand and wondered: *Am I on Mars?* It seemed to me that the extremely strange world into which I had strayed experienced something like joy on being recognized, and that all those indefinable objects were smiling at me with a commencement of familiarity.

Then told myself that it was necessary to forget the Earth if I wanted to understand anything of this place. I had to stop rebelling against reality, meekly accept the impossible in which I found myself as the one and only nature, and learn to see what I was seeing. I was a new-born child whose eyes and mind, frightened at first, would soon begin to marvel and gradually come to terms with my planet. Except that I was a child without a mother. I wept as I remembered that a beautiful woman who resembled Berthe had given birth to me and abandoned me.

Object of my adoration, how can I tell you what followed? As I have said, Earthly words only designate Earthly objects. I can only try to satisfy—or, rather, to deceive—your hunger for knowledge on condition that I twist and "terrestrialize" everything. Every one of my words from now on will be a little deceptive, because I am translating sensations without analogues into terrestrial sensations; given your ignorance of the languages of any of the planets, I shall have to stammer away in our language about things inexpressible in our language.

The necessary deceptions of my language will be aggravated by the inevitable deception of my mind, which, since my return, has reduced to terrestrial ideas images that have nothing in common with what is seen here. That work is being done within me almost unconsciously, but I am not opposing it, for fear that the need for unification and generalization that is the foundation of our intellect might be too violently contradicted, and the chaotic dispersal of my inner being might only emit my thoughts in madness. I have sacrificed useless and inexpressible details to the vital necessity of environmental readaptation.

I shall, therefore, be brief, like a discovered and blushing liar trying to protect himself from disruption with a few vague remarks.

I only had been on Mars for a little while, if my memory serves me right, when I was captured by the bizarre winged animals that are the masters of that planet. They put me with other living beings that seemed curious to them in a sort of zoo, where people came to see us, mostly to amuse themselves by studying us with ridiculously serious expressions and a harmful attentiveness.

The inhabitants of Mars have five or six different sexes. Don't try to understand, my dear…

The beings of the sex that I shall call female examined my persistently and I thought I saw a strange covetousness gleaming in the vast gazes that cover their entire bodies like garments of light,

As I began to understand their language, someone—doubtless a magistrate—explained to me that, several women having declared themselves to be in love with my strangeness, I must choose on that same day, in accordance with the laws of the country. Then the women field in front of me, setting me on fire with the radiant and shameless glare of their entirely sighted bodies.

I refused to choose. They drew lots for me. The one who won me opened her large bright blue wings and flew over the countryside with me for a very long way, in an intoxicating isolation. Then, caressing me with her two fans of light, she asked: "Why didn't you choose me? I was the most beautiful."

I didn't answer. She smiled at me with her entire gaze. "The people of your country are diviners, I'll wager, and you know what fate awaited you—otherwise you would inevitably have chosen me; I'm ten times as beautiful as my companions." Then she sighed and, with a low cunning in her voice and gestures, said: "You love me, don't you?"

"No," I replied.

She seemed quite astonished, and also indignant, at the scorn of a vile crawling beast for a marvelous flying star. She demanded an explanation. Triumphant, and glad to praise you, I told her about my terrestrial love.

She demanded countless details about the women of my homeland. When, by means of hesitant descriptions and stammered comparisons, I had set before her curious imagination a distant appearance of my beloved, she laughed.

"I would have no difficulty," she affirmed, "making you forget a wingless woman whose gaze, broken into two, only occupies the thousandth part of her body."

She found you ridiculous, sublime object of my adoration. I hated her.

I spite of my resistance, she took me. I felt her fluidified body penetrating into me through all my pores, which dilated in an irresistible physical joy. Must I confess this? The sensuality was as intense as it was strange, so strange that it might drive one mad and so intense as to be fatal.

When, however, victorious over my entire invaded being, she said, "Do you love me now?" I still had the strength to protest: "My cowardly body loves you, but my heart is entirely and forever Berthe's." And I begged: "Let me go. What does it matter to you? You cannot love a man deprived of wings, whose gaze, divided in two, only occupies the thousandth part of his body."

"You are, indeed ugly," she said, "but I love your dark flesh, for it is born of the heavy Sun, which burns and breaks delightfully. Kiss me, my beloved."

I understood that if I tasted that strange and intense sensuality again, I would be irredeemably enslaved by that woman, who scorned me and loved me perversely. I understood that the faithful suffering of a disdained love for a woman of my race was my only nobility. I remembered the means of liberation and put the old Norwegian sage's ring on my left hand.

There is no need to tell you about my other voyages and my other adventures. They would all be similar from your point of view, and almost from mine, now, for there are no differences in the indescribable and the inconceivable.

I was a child, terrified and then filled with wonderment, a curious animal, a creature loved and scorned, on many of the minor planets, on Jupiter, on Saturn and on Neptune. I had strokes of luck infinitely more numerous and more varied than those about which our naval officers write books—and my faithful heart always extracted me from sensualities that were tortures, since you were not sharing them, O One and Only Darling of my heart.

I came back, weary of trying to forget you, indignant at having made that attempt, which would have been degrading if it had not been in vain.

You know what happened after my return. When, having returned the marvelous but futile ring to its owner, I came back to the little town where I had left you, I did not find you. Your notary, who was also mine, had crowned his honorable career with a little excursion to Belgium. I wept as I thought about your ruination.

My own ruination forced me to work for a living, and as my neighbor, who was ill and had children, lacked everything, I worked harder in order that he might be able to feed and care for those he loved. I certainly did not forget you, but the rhythm of my energy expenditure rocked my suffering to sleep.

When hazard or Providence caused me to find you again, so wretched, I loved you and helped you, though not as much as my poor neighbor, because you were not as poor, being in good health and not hearing beloved individuals crying out with hunger.

And here we are, tenderly united for life—for you loved me on the day I stopped begging to be a slave to your smile and became a free man, who no longer sees you merely as the most desirable woman of all, but also as a little fragment of suffering humanity to console and to soothe.

A BIOGRAPHY OF VICTOR VENTURON

Question. What was the condition of the terrestrial globe in year 14,500 of the Social Era?

Answer: In year 14,500 of the Social Era the Earth, having slowly cooled, was in large measure uninhabitable. The polar ice-cap had advanced to the confines of the Mediterranean. The inhabitants of Algeria had no other resources than reindeer and a few lichens discovered with difficulty beneath the snow. At the equator, wheat still grew and cider-apples yielded a passable beverage, but greenhouses conserved, with difficulty, a few curious specimens of vines and maize. The duration of humankind's death-throes was estimated at 12 centuries, at the maximum.

Q. What great man was born in that era?

A. Victor Venturon

Q. What did he do first?

A. He wrote a book entitled *The New Prometheus*.

Q. How should that book be considered?

A. The work is the most sublime of poems, the most profound of books of science, the most useful of human works.

Q. Into how many parts is it divided?

A. Into three parts.

Q. What does the first part contain?

A. A cosmogony. In a language of marvelously precise richness, Victor Venturon there relates the genesis of the world in general and our globe in particular. He explains clearly the causes of terrestrial cooling and shows, with Prometheus, the human will triumphant once and for all over the fatality of things.

Q. Analyze the second part.

A. In the second part, Venturon studies the state of the universe in his era and tries to ascertain whether electricity or some other previously proposed artificial means might provide a remedy for the general cooling. He declares them insufficient.

Q. What does he do in the third part?

A. After having recalled the solution to an analogous problem in the first part, and having established in the second part the givens of the great problem of his era, in the third part, he describes the solution.

Q. What was that solution of genius?

A. To bring the Earth nearer to the Sun.

Q. What means did he propose?

A. Immense earthworks that would flatten our planet into a dish whose diameters would be perpendicular to the movement of the Earth.

Q. What result would thus have been obtained?

A. A greater resistance to centrifugal force, which was the equivalent of an augmentation of centripetal force.

Q. Was his project realized?

A. No. People mocked the great scientist.[10]

Q. What happened at about that time?

A. A comet collided with the Earth.

Q. Did the impact cause particular misfortunes?

A. Yes. More than half the human race was killed, not to mention the material damage, which was incalculable

Q. What did Venturon do?

A. He wrote a book entitled *Hurrah for the Comet.*

---

[10] Ryner inserts a footnote here: "Venturon was opposed, above all, with the impossibility of maintaining the Earth in its position while displacing such a large part of its mass. It was claimed that the edge of the disk would be perpendicular to the ecliptic and that the action of centrifugal force would be facilitated. It proved eventually that the great scientist was more clear-sighted than his contemporaries. The reasons for the phenomenon are too complicated to be explained in this elementary work. On this subject, see p.573ff of volume XXXII of Monsieur Quand's *Cosmographie rationelle.*" Given the satirical nature of the piece, it is unclear whether Ryner was aware, as competent physicists are, that there is no such thing as "centrifugal force" and that what maintains the Earth in its orbit against the gravitational attraction of the Sun is its tangential momentum, which would be largely unaffected by the alteration of shape suggested by Venturon, as the frictional losses incurred in movement through a near-vacuum are minimal.

Q. Analyze the book in question.

A. Venturon demonstrated by irrefutable calculations that the comet had produced the desired flattening, and that the Earth would draw nearer to the Sun.

Q. What proved the truth of his assertion?

A. Two things. Firstly, the Earth warmed up again rapidly. Secondly, it drew close enough to Venus, which had previously been an independent planet, to make it into its second satellite.

Q. How did Hurrah for the Comet *conclude?*

A. It concluded that the proximity of the Sun would soon become too great and that it was necessary immediately to diminish the resistance to centrifugal force by restoring the Earth's previous form.

Q. Was the project begun in time?

A. No.

Q. What happened?

A. The Earth, being too hot, became uninhabitable in the tropics. The polar ice melted completely. The reindeer and other species perished, and the plesiosaur and all the other monstrous animals of the prehistoric fauna reappeared.

Q. What did the frightened human race do then?

A. The Human Confederation named Victor Venturon dictator. The project, rapidly carried forward, stopped the fatal approach to the Sun. In a few years, with the great heliofluidic cannons of 248, all the harmful species were destroyed and civilization was able to resume its interrupted progress.

Q. What became of Victor Venturon?

A. He died at a ripe old age, covered with glory.

Q. What does this beautiful life teach us?

A. It teaches us the three anthropological virtues, which are: first, faith in the practical results of science; secondly, hope for the immortality of life in general, and the admirable resistance of our species in particular; and thirdly, love for humanity.

(Extract from the *Historical Catechism of the Diocese of Gaul*, accurate advance copy courtesy of Han Ryner.)

THE TRAVELS OF PSYCHODORUS, CYNIC PHILOSOPHER

I have knocked on the doors of mystery, and heard the
strangely solid sound that they render…

I. The Rooted People

Psychodorus, the cynic philosopher, having lost the woman he loved, resolved to live as a wanderer, a stranger to everyone and everything. With no other luggage than an old cloak on his shoulders and a crude staff in his hand, he set forth. All day he marched at random. When he was hungry, he ate whatever came to hand. Often, someone who had no need of that nourishment but claimed to be its owner protested. Psychodorus did not hear their exclamations.

Sometimes, the master of the nourishment jostled the cynic—who, waking up from his dream, struck him with his staff. Slaves came running, though. The audacious individual who considered hunger a reason to eat was grabbed and dragged before a tribunal. Now, he knew that the ears of judges, blocked by the wadding of laws, could no longer hear, and he did not reply to the questions that were put to him. Usually, they let him go, believing him to be mad. On other occasions, he was locked up in prison for a few days.

In the evening, Psychodorus lay down at the same time as the Sun. When he was free, his bed was the roadside, or the bed of a dry stream.

Psychodorus walked for three years, without stopping voluntarily during the day and without uttering a single word. It is probable that he did not see external objects, except for the most extraordinary, and that his mind translated those into symbols of eternity. As soon as things had produced in him a thought more beautiful than themselves, he stopped looking at the things.

When Psychodorus had been walking for three years, he found himself at the top of a high mountain, and he looked down and around him, for strange cries were rising up—cries that reminded him, although they were articulate, of the branches of a storm-tossed forest.

The place in which Psychodorus found himself was singular. The mountain enclosed a near-perfect circle, and its even rim was not cut through by any gorge. In the profound circular plain, humans as tall as oak-trees were swaying madly, amid clamors.

The cynic went down toward these giants and saw with astonishment that their feet were sunk in the Earth. As some of them were on the edge of a precipice, he was aware that each foot was divided into long and sinuous roots. Seeing that there was something genuinely new here, something to understand, Psychodorus paused in that region.

Despite their gigantic stature and their undetachable subterranean prolongations, the inhabitants of the plain really were human, not trees. They had no leaves, no flowers and no branches. Their nudity allowed one to see that they were not covered in bark, but a delicate skin like that of the northern barbarians. They each had a head and two arms. The proportions of their bodies, in their enormity, were harmonious, and their poses varied, as supple and undulating as the attitudes of wrestlers. Sometimes, they sat down. In the evening, only their legs remained upright, like twin trunks, while the wind of sleep folded their knees and lay them down on their backs. Apart from the ability to change location, however, they lacked another advantage that had once seemed precious to Psychodorus: the Rooted People had no sex.

Nature had refused these people the power of procreation, because she had made them immortal. The cynic soon deduced this privilege. He was not at all jealous, but he stayed, observing them and studying their language, for a suspicion had rendered him avid to know their thoughts.

"Perhaps they are as knowledgeable as gods, and they will tell me what has become of my beloved, and where I can find her."

When he understood something of their speech, Psychodorus perceived that the forest was as ignorant and coarse as all human populations. He preferred to frequent those Rooted People that fate had isolated, but he saw that in them, terror was even stranger, as absurd as madness and no longer like stupidity—and they were proud of their ingenious and fragile thoughts.

Even so, Psychodorus did not leave yet, although he said to himself: "I have the anguish of duration; they have the anguish of space. The stupid and crazy things they say about the extended world doubtless correspond to our errors about the world that persists. Time and space are twin brothers, identical to one another. Their father is named Immensity and their mother calls herself Eternity."

And the smile with which he listened to the immobile giants also criticized the thoughts of humans who walk.

For those among the giants who called themselves sages multiplied negatives, both bold and timid, saying: "There is nothing beyond the horizon"—or even: "Let us be wary of affirming or denying that which our senses cannot grasp. Is the plain that we inhabit the entire universe, and does the mountainous wall loom up between being and nothingness? We have no means of knowing. Let us not occupy ourselves with the unknowable, and methodically construct the science of the visible world."

The common people, however, believed that: "The Sun rises in emptiness, but it sets in the fullness of another world. First it lights us. Then it lights other beings. The orient is deserted; east of the mountain there is nothing. The occident contains two worlds: a delightfully moist land where the Earth is generous, and a land of torments and dryness. In the one,

71

better people than us plunge their fortunate roots; in the other, wicked people suffer, for the Earth is scorched and produces little nourishment."

And the common people also believed that: "It is the same Sun that returns every day. Having lit paradise and the inferno, it leaps abruptly though nothingness to the summit of the oriental mountain."

A few even suspected that: "Perhaps the void that the Sun traverses is not nothingness but chaos, a mass in which things are indiscernible, void in form, but in which matter stirs, inharmonious but infinite."

But the bold sages retorted: "There is nothing outside that which we know."

And the sages whose thought was lazy: "We only know that which we know."

Then some went on: "It is certain that…"

And the others: "It is probable that…"

And all the sages continued, in unison: "That which has no roots cannot last. The Sun, which moves, is born and dies like the dog that runs or the bird that flies, and today's Sun is not the rotten carcass of yesterday's Sun."

But the crowd was annoyed by such words. Its members felt, in spite of their ignorance, that the Sun did not die every evening.

And Psychodorus thought: "Your soul, vanished beloved, is a Sun that has set for me, but which is traversing other regions. And the occidental durations are neither Elysian nor Infernal, but differ little from the times of the east, the times of the north and the times of the south."

And the wise Psychodorus was possessed by a folly. He wanted to tell these beings troubled by the anguish of space the liberating truth. He stood, a ridiculously small orator, in front of the crowd of giants, and he cried: "Listen to me. I have come from the other side of the mountain, and I know."

They were all listening, with bated breath.

He went on: "The limits are apparent. Around the mountain, life continues, not so very different from that which is here."

Psychodorus did not understand what was happening, but instinct, surer and prompter than thought, impelled him into a hectic flight. When he turned round, trembling, he saw the entire forest laid low by a blast of wrath. Outstretched arms were trying to seize him. Curses were consigning the prophet who had pronounced the excessively simple truth to tortures—and furious individuals were shouting that the unknown could not be anything but nothingness or marvels of terror and joy.

Pursued by shouts and stones, Psychodorus ran all the way to the mountain. Then he crossed over, returning to the lands in which humans walked as he did and knew something approaching the truth about space.

He met two dwarfs like himself. He listened to their words because they were chatting in a Greek dialect that aroused delightful memories—but he soon laughed in scorn and intellectual pain, for one of the two men said: "At death, everything is finished."

And the other replied: "After death, we receive marvelous rewards for our good deeds, or frightful punishments for our crimes."

But Psychodorus, having returned to the wisdom of silence, passed by without trying to inform those men of the wounding simplicity of the truth.

II. The Eyeless People

Since Psychodorus had left the land of the Rooted People, a refrain had been singing within him, obsessively.

"Your soul, vanished beloved, is a Sun hidden from me, but which is traversing other regions. And the occidental durations are neither Elysian nor Infernal, but little different from the times of the east, the times of the north and the times of the south."

Oh, the strange refrain! It arrived like a generous woman carrying the consoling truth in her hand—but its face soon became hostile, the other hand held out a large empty sack and an imperious gesture commanded that it be filled. Psychodorus sometimes spoke to it as to an unknown who introduces himself with a polite smile, but who, without any plausible reason, attaches himself to your footsteps, and whom one finally suspects to be an enemy.

"Why are you following me," he said to it, "like a faithful dog watching over its master, or a wolf lying in wait for its prey? For you, strangely ambiguous refrain, which I have imagined or someone has slipped into me, are made of light and darkness. You appear to me as an immense palace that first seems joyful and wide open on every side to the light of day, but only the apartments to the east and the west are lit; on the blind walls of the north and south, false windows are drawn, which brighten them at a distance but do not open. I understand, generous refrain, the occidental durations and times of the east of which you speak, for I sense that I am eternal, and that the short line of life that I can see is prolonged infinitely beyond the horizon of birth and beyond the horizon of death—but duration is a line without breadth and I do not know what you mean. No doubt you do not mean anything, but, jokingly, you are continuing the analogy between time and space in words when it can no longer continue in thought—I do not know what you mean, crazy or miserly refrain by the times of the north and the times of the south."

It was at dusk especially, on the edge of the hospitable ditch, that the half-white and half-black refrain—a bridge at first, but soon an abyss—tortured Psychodorus. A long time after night had fallen, painful meditation kept him awake. In vain he tried to chase it away; as an infant about to be born torments its mother, thoughts not yet formed become an unstable and painful weight within the intelligence.

Often, when fatigue finally put Psychodorus to sleep, dreams came to bring him the explanation, and he was glad to know, but awakening dissipated the explanation along with the dream, and the philosopher could not even decide whether the rising Sun had extinguished the guiding star in his dazzled eyes or whether it had dispersed a deceptive mist.

The hazard of his voyages had led Psychodorus to the shore of the sea. Facing him, a low-lying island seemed to be calling to him like an amorous woman. He did not obey the seduction. Sitting on the shore, he started tracing straight lines and curves in the sand. He was investigating some of the mysteries of space, but the refrain kept recurring, speaking in a consolatory fashion of occidental durations and oriental epochs, and then affirming the incomprehensible times of the north and south.

Every time the phrase recurred, at first as warm and caressing as the tongue of a faithful dog, but soon as rude and penetrative as the fangs of a hungry wolf, Psychodorus' gaze left the figures traced in the sand and went toward the seductive island. Was the truth that his dreams perhaps brought him, and his awakenings took away, hidden over there on the far side of the strait?

All day, the philosopher resisted the call of the island. He stayed on the sea-shore eating shellfish and searching for geometrical truths. That evening, in the moonlight, the placid water breathed as gently as a sleeping woman, and Psychodorus slept beside the sleeping sea.

The dream that often explained by night the mystery that tormented his days presented itself more clearly than ever. Alas, his awakening extinguished that clarity yet again, save for a frail fugitive gleam. Psychodorus only remembered that the dream had said: "Go to the island in front of you, and you will no longer forget the time of the north and the time of the south."

The island was a charming land, fertile and peaceful, but nothing there seemed to respond to Psychodorus' hope. After a few hours of walking, he arrived at a town. The rare people he encountered on the road and the numerous inhabitants of

the town were all blind. Or perhaps not—for the blindness of
eyes that cannot see conserves the organ that has become useless, like a regret. The people of this region did not have the
sightless eyes that solemnly sadden blind faces. Beneath the
high and narrow forehead, the nose expanded broadly in the
narrow face, taking up the whole area, leaving no empty space
where the nobility of a regret or aspiration might be expressed.
And the animals of the country, otherwise little different from
the beasts with which Psychodorus was familiar, seemed, by
virtue of their unlighted heads, to be fragments of a primitive
darkness sculpted by Destiny before he had pronounced the
words: "Let there be light!"

Psychodorus learned the languages that people spoke
with a marvelous facility; he soon understood the poor language of the Eyeless People.

He was careful not to mention the unknown sense from
which a part of his wisdom came. They would not have understood and would have scorned for his pride the man who
boasted of a superiority so absurdly false that it was not even
expressible. He befriended one of them. Adroitly, he questioned him about their ideas of space and time. He obtained an
answer much like this:

"Time is my past life, plus my life to come. Space is the
path that I will follow, added to the path that I have trod. Time
is a twisted line, for joy inclines it to the right and pain makes
it veer to the left. Now, joys are the daughters of pains, pains
are the daughters of joys, and they alternate regularly in the
circle that might never be closed, like the warm season of harvests and the cold season of sowing. Space is also twisted, but
necessities or our caprices inflict sinuosities upon it that no
mind is able to anticipate. That is why we have a science of
time, but any science of space is impossible.

Thus this man, deprived of eyes that see space, could only conceive of its infinite extent as a line that linked his various situations—and Psychodorus, deprived of eyes that see

time, was groping in the durable infinity with the hands of memory and prescience, but could not get away from the line uniting his various movements.

The effort of meditation, however, almost allowed him to conceive of what time must be for a being immediately superior to terrestrial humans.

"No," he thought, "duration is not a simple line with neither breadth nor depth. Several thoughts reside within me at the same time, and I can carry out several actions at the same time. I breathe, and my heart beats in the meantime. My hands hold objects, my teeth chew and item of food and my eyes see a landscape, without my mind ceasing to think. Where can so many simultaneous events be located, if not in the breadth and depth of the moment? Some hours do not appear to be as long as others, because I am less aware of their breadth. Thus, my cloak folded in two is for my mistaken eyes longer than my cloak spread out.

Then he said to himself: "My duration is at its broadest during action. Sentiment and thought render it deep. When nothing occupies it, I only see its monotonous length. By why would I say of one hour that it is empty, and of another that it is full, if hours were not broad and profound vases into which we pour gestures, meditations, dolors and joys?"

Psychodorus was thinking all this while lying on the sand. Almost mechanically, his finger traced two figures. The two drawings represented his beloved, as he had seen her previously in the light of the Sun, and as he often saw her again in the light of dreams—but one of the two portraits showed her face-on, the other described the fine grace of her profile. And Psychodorus, having seen the work of his finger, spoke to his beloved.

"This figure here," he said, "shows only one of your eyes. It reminds me, however, of the two lights of your visage. Space is the face of God; time is the profile of God. I am not so ignorant as to think God less infinite when I look at him here than when I see him there."

And his meditation continued: "Space has three dimensions for my ordinary thought. An effort has revealed the breadth and depth of time to me. For Apollo, the father of the nine muses, perhaps one or other of them has nine dimensions. For the God of Apollo and the other gods, for the one whose name we do not know, time and space must both have an infinite number of dimensions."

But he got to his feet, a little frightened by his idea. He took a step backwards and, all a-tremble, murmured: "My mind is afraid. The human mind is weak and cowardly. It often recoils, sometimes from the truth, sometimes from folly."

Then he calmed himself with these formulas: "Truth is a bottomless abyss of even and monotonous light. One does not lean over the infinite gulf of Unity without suffering vertigo. Go on, Psychodorus, obey the necessities of your frail humanity and, in order not to fall, turn away or shut your eyes—but do not say that you have not seen, since you have seen, and remember your rapid glance, while shivering with admiration."

He drew away from the place where he had seen, and he walked, repeating in a tremulous joy like the joy of love: "Your soul, vanished beloved, is a Sun hidden from me, but it is lighting up other regions. And the occidental durations are neither Elysian nor Infernal, but little different from the times of the east, the times of the north and the times of the south."

III. The Retrograde People

The country offered nothing remarkable to the gaze, and Psychodorus was indifferent to it. In a village street, however, a woman suddenly attracted his attention. She was so similar to his lost beloved, seemingly to the point of illusion. Was it not Athenatime herself, resuscitated and younger than he had ever known her?

He stopped and studied her for a long time. Then he began to tremble, for, while his mind loudly proclaimed the folly of his hope, his whispering soul hoped.

Increasingly tremulous, he walked toward the moving apparition.

"Woman," he said, "are you the one I love?"[11]

He received the response: "I don't understand what you're saying."

He heard her speaking Greek, however—the pure Greek of Athens—and the soft voice that replied was the same voice as Anthenatime's. And the ingenuous smile of the parted lips recalled profound memories in Psychodorus, which, in order to return to the light of day, disturbed countless more recent memories like so many heaped-up cadavers.

He gazed at the child, whose harmonious youth was still hesitating between adolescent grace and maidenly grace, feeling a strange desire to weep.

"Naughty girl," he said, "you are beautiful enough to understand the word love without it being pronounced."

She, however, suddenly gripped by some anguish, replied: "Why do you mock a poor old woman? And what could one love in a wretched woman who is too old to be a tomb?"

Like an echo, he repeated: "Too old to be a tomb?" For he was now the one who did not understand.

One thing alone was evident to him; he had caused some distress. The child who called herself old was crying. *A madwoman*, he thought—and he attempted awkward consolations.

Through her tears, she examined him. Her gaze was avid for the unfamiliar face, like a gaze of love or curiosity. Gradually, a spectacle that was absolutely new, incredible even though it was present, interested her and made her forget her

---

[11] The potential double meanings of some of the phrases used in this chapter defy accurate translation. The future form of the verb "to be" is sometimes used in French to signify the present tense, as it seems to be here, but the sentence might be accurately translated: "Will you be [or become] the woman I love?" I have reproduced the meaning that Psychodorus presumably intends, but the alternative needs to be borne in mind, for reasons that will become obvious.

distress. And her eyes and smile dilated, like the smile and eyes of a scientist confronted by something unexpected.

"Strange woman," said Psychodorus, "you resemble Athenatime in the bloom of youth, and you also resemble Aristotle before the animals and plants sent to him from afar by his disciple Alexander."

"Strange man!" the young woman replied. "Unique man!" After a searching pause, she added, clearly and decisively, a third exclamation: "Retrograde man." Then, taking his arm, she asked: "Why are you going to say that I am mad?"

"But how do you know what I am going to say?" he demanded, too astonished to protest. "Are you mad?"

She looked at him with excited curiosity, then said: "It's true, astonishing Psychodorus—you do not know what will be said. The backward-directed eyes of your soul cannot even read the emotions you will feel tomorrow."

Perhaps the child's last words would soon be meaningful for Psychodorus; for the moment, they were vague sounds that the ear, an intimidated servant, dared not carry to his mind—for his mind was too preoccupied by her earlier words.

"If you are not Athenatime," the philosopher said, how do you know that my name is Psychodorus?"

"I heard you say, in an imminent future: *my name is Psychodorus*."

"How can you hear the future?"

"And how can you hear the past?" But she went on, as gentle as pity: "It is wrong of me to torment the weakness of your mind—for I hear, in more or less distant futures, the words that you will say to explain everything to me. I also hear you affirm that the people of your homeland are all like you. You add that you have been travelling for years and that you have never seen the like—you repeat, after hesitation and with some repugnance, the sole definitive word—of retrograde people.

"Get to know, then, O Psychodorus, the life of my country. Learn about the life of harmonious beings who walk forward with eyes on the road to be travelled, preceded by their mind as by a torch.

"You believe yourself to be alive and you seem to me to be solidly real, You cannot, however, be anything but a phantom, you who are made of the past, like the fabric of one of our dreams; you who, facing that which is no longer, march backwards—O incredible marvel!—toward the pyre and urn of birth.

"I think I understand something consolatory now. You are doubtless what we become after death. When the Sun hides itself beneath the Earth, instead of lying down and resting, I see that it marches, sadly and phantasmally, through strange deserts in order to return to the glories of the Orient. You, O Psychodorus, are the dead Sun, the dead soul. You are the night that returns gropingly toward the day. For—you will affirm it soon and what you say will be true—you must enter the urn of birth as ashes.

"Rejoice, Psychodorus, urns are made for opening, and the ashes spread on pyres resume life among the flames. Your soul, without a doubt, will become similar to that of the humans who are pausing around you, curious to see a retrograde individual, a phantom woven by the past and regret.

"But I am shutting up, Psychodorus, in order that you can say the words that you must say. Your ignorance is making you shake your head. You call futile that which is called the inevitable. It is necessary, even though you are only a dream, that you ask the questions to which I have replied, since, in a future that continually becomes the present, I have heard them."

Indeed, Psychodorus, as if in a crazy dream, felt, in spite of himself, that his tongue was no longer obedient to the base utilitarian logic of humans but to the sovereign logic that weaves the noble threads of necessity. Before the assembly of living beings that were marching into a future of light, he described the poor groping human life that he had known until then—the life of humans who, amid stumbles and falls, go into the dark carrying their lantern behind them.

He remained in that land for some time. He witnessed births. He saw urns open and spread inert ashes over odorous flames. When the flames died out, there sometimes appeared what his tenacious habit called a child, and sometimes what he called an adult, but more often what seemed to him to be an old person. But the white hairs became black, and then blond. The withered frame became upright, then diminished. Sometimes, a man devoid of family would subsequently acquire brothers and sisters, emerged from successive pyres. A woman, more recent than him in that strange life, would care for him in his old age, similar to the childhoods familiar to Psychodorus, and sustain his diminished body. The old man in puerile form would manifest affection toward that woman, mingled with fears and reluctances. In his kisses, accompanied by tears, he would not call her "my mother" but "my tomb". A day would come when the little one would no longer be able to talk, no longer be able to walk, perhaps no longer be able to think. In the arms of his "tomb" he would be a plaintive, wailing creature. He would no longer have teeth to break the bread of the strong, but she would nourish him with a generous milk. He would finally lose even the feeble vigor necessary to that already almost vegetative life and like a seed sown in the opened ground, he would take refuge within his dolorous nurse. For a few months, the "tomb" would walk heavily and awkwardly, dragged down in front by an internal burden—but little by little, the corpse would decrease like a memory, no longer leaving traces.

Undoubtedly—the girl, at least, appeared to believe it—the vanished individual would only be an exile. Elsewhere, he would become a man like Psychodorus. He would emerge from the belly of some other woman to travel, through an increasingly conscious life, toward the pyre and the urn.

Psychodorus, believing that he had seen all that there was to see here, wanted to leave. He went through the streets of the town one last time. Uplifted by hope, he thought about a fable told by the Egyptians, and quietly said to himself:

"O phoenix-like humans! Will Athenatime and Psychodorus, those phoenixes who will be reborn, find one another again, for a new love, in a life that will march again at the same pace, in the same direction?"

Then he met the person who had seemed to him, a few years before, to be Athenatime in the flower of adolescence, who was now a little girl. He sat down on a doorstep, took the little old woman with the puerile grace on his knees, and said to her:

"Child who reads the future, is it not the case that, after the tomb, there is another birth? Tell me, tell me what you see on the other side of the tomb."

She spoke incorrectly, cheerful and lisping. She looked at the philosopher with wide ingenuous eyes. Then her gaze became attentive to the invisible. Finally, she stammered:

"The tomb…is a wall…you can't see through walls."

IV. The Slippery Summit

Psychodorus was not far away from the country in which people were burdened by their future and alleviated of their past when a regret made him retrace his steps toward that strange land.

"Undoubtedly," he thought, "they will not be able to answer me, but I owe my love the wisdom of returning to them and asking them the question."

He also said to himself: "They called me 'the retrograde.' I am tempted to apply to them the name they gave to me. In the same way, I am a foreigner to the person who is a foreigner to me, and barbarians call me a barbarian."

His train of thought continued: "They are, however, the true retrograde people, who lose knowledge the further they go. In other lands, only stupid people are saddened by growing old; the wise rejoice in knowing more. Among humans whose lives proceed in the same direction as mine, a young sage is a poor fellow agitated by fevers, always reaching out toward his future wealth; an old sage is an opulent man, who lives happily in his continually-enriched treasury. But these retrograde people are right to weep, because they can only remain inert before the known future that becomes as they progress the past that they do not know. Every moment brings me a tribute; every instant steals something from them. They are dying with every passing moment while we are becoming heavier with life, until the pyre reduces our science drastically and the urn protects our sleep."

Then he said to himself: "Thoughts are riches. Words are poor. Words, you are poor children. You march dazedly, your short and feeble arms encumbered by the foreign richness of thoughts. You let almost all of that noble crop fall behind you, and you only bring us back a very small portion of scented roes and tasty fruits. To go toward other harvests, a laborer with free arms, my mind will be forced to confide to a name all that it has gathered among the strange people. These beings, whose lives flow in the opposite direction to mine, progressing from what is to me the river's mouth toward what is to me the source, are named in my memory the Retrograde People. However, I am not longer unaware that time, the brother of space, has in its monotony neither a forwards nor a backwards. Only the condition that the Fates impose upon us inclines my slope in another direction than that of these people. But time, like space, is indifferent to our march and to the immobility of God."

Psychodorus, who was climbing through these reflections in order to discover his thoughts more fully, did not perceive that he was stuck half way. He did not want to look at the summit whose conquest would deliver him a broader landscape and give him a clear answer to the question he was going to ask of obscurely-stammering lips. Summits are sometimes scary, and the eyes of the soul willingly deny that which they do not wish to see.

Scarcely had he re-entered the land of the Retrograde People when Psychodorus encountered a birth ceremony. On to pleasantly-scented flames, a priest piously poured the ashes from an open urn. The philosopher mingled with the praying crowd, and waited.

When they fire as out, a frail human form, bent double, got down painfully. Men ran to him and helped him over the debris of the pyre. They dressed the quivering dodderer and placed a staff in his gnarled and withered hand. Then the assembly dispersed and the old man who had just been born headed on his own for the house he knew so well, since it was a part of his future. He went leaning forward, as if he were precipitating himself into that as-yet-unlived life, all of which he could see. He was smiling; before him, no doubt, among the brambles that would tear him, flowers loomed up as brightly as appeals.

Psychodorus drew level with him. "Man," he said, "We can talk as equals, since you see so many things ahead of you and I see so many things behind me."

"Speak," the Retrograde said, encouraging Psychodorus.

"Clear up my doubts," the philosopher went on. "You are unaware of everything in the past?"

"Yes," said the man, sadly. "I understand that there is already something behind me. I have lost a little of my life; a little of my enlightenment has become darkness."

"How can you reply to my words, which, as soon as they are spoken, are part of the past—which, to you, is no longer anything but silence?"

"I'm not replying to you. I'm pronouncing the words that will lead to the words that I hear emerging from you in the imminent future."

"Why are you saying these words?"

"Because they must be said."

"Your knowledge, however, renders them as futile as mine, since all of them cause you to hear sounds that you already know."

"My mind would not know them if my ear were not obliged to hear them."

"But your will could suppress or change words or actions that you have known in your future," Psychodorus persisted.

"One cannot suppress anything; one cannot change anything." And the Retrograde continued: "You can do nothing about your past. How could I do anything about my future?"

"But I am free to change my tomorrow."

The man shrugged his shoulders. "You know yesterday and you know that you can do nothing about it. That which you know internally has the same characteristics as external things; it is determined by your intelligence, as everything is determined. But that which you do not know seems less existent to you. You do not know what will be tomorrow, and your ignorance can give it various forms, as it can attribute different forms to a distant and unknown city. The distant city has but one form and tomorrow already has its unique and necessary form."

The old man continued: "I can dream in ten different fashions of the minute that was my light a little while ago and is now part of my darkness. I know, however, that it was one minute and not ten. All possibilities, as you call them, are impossibilities, dead before the birth of the real."

He also said: "Why, naïve Psychodorus, will you place causes in front of us? Causes are always behind us. Or, rather, causes are everywhere."

The old man who had just been born sat down by the roadside, as if exhausted. He seemed to be meditating. Psychodorus also meditated. But Psychodorus was meditating with closed eyes, while the presbyopic eyes of the Retrograde seemed to want to look into the far distance and embrace a vast horizon.

Finally, he burst out laughing. "O Psychodorus, you think that you are wise. You are, however, similar to a rich man who, instead of rooting around in his abundant provisions, reaches out for a scrap of bread. Soon, you will tell me that you know that time is the brother of space. Why, instead of interrogating me, do you not say that to yourself? Why force me to express things that are within you, and make you a gift of wealth that you possess?

"Causality, O Psychodorus, is a false notion, the daughter of the linear idea of duration that other humans have. But you, who have seen the breadth and depth of time, who know that time has no slope, how can you situate a cause here rather than there?

"Everything exists, O Psychodorus, in the infinite extent and the infinite duration. Every moment is the center of time, as every point is the navel of space. Whatever road you follow, O Psychodorus, you are always on a radius that departs from that moment and that point, and which ends there. Any moment whatsoever or any appearance whatsoever necessitates the universe, with its eternity and its immensity; and a universe without beginning, without end and without limits is not too much to necessitate the smallest of atoms or the slightest of instants."

But the old man got to his feet, unsteadily. He leaned on his companion, and he begged: "Let's get away from this place and these thoughts. We were on a dangerous summit. The crest of wisdom is narrow and slippery. Pebbles were rolling beneath our feet, and it would not have taken much to send us rolling with them into the sonorous abyss of madness."

Psychodorus, supporting his tremulous steps and reassuring the poor distressed soul, affirmed: "It is noble to climb summits."

"Undoubtedly," said the old man who was gradually turning into a child, "but it is imprudent to linger thereon."

V. The Desert

Psychodorus walked enveloped by his dreams and memories. He did not perceive the banalities he traversed. He never knew when or by what road he would arrive in some marvelous country.

That way, he was astonished as he went by the thought that, beneath such various appearances, which amuse historians or ordinary travelers, humans were so fundamentally similar to one another.

"In the most foreign of lands," he thought, "old people tell children the same tales with which my grandmother dazzled my infancy. Climates, customs and mores put a few entirely superficial differences into these stories; they are like people one always recognizes, even though they change their clothes. Perhaps popular tales embody in their resemblance the most universal truths."

Popular tales, he then remarked, are relatives of the fables that priests tell in temples and poets put into their verses. Perhaps the luminous myths of Plato and the dark symbols of the mysteries were saying the same things as the children's stories or sacerdotal narratives.

At this point in his reflections, the philosopher waved his staff, crying: "I march intoxicated with unity!" Then, in a pious whisper, he went on: "One, you are God, Space, Time, Love and the Word, you are poor names that specify a little of God, but you, One, Richness from which all richness flows, you are God entire."

Psychodorus was indeed unsteady on his feet, intoxicated with the unity of the universe, the unity of humankind, and the more fleeting but no less certain unity of Psychodorus. "Humankind," he said, "you are made like a human being. Universe you are made like a human being. You too, human being, in spite of the strife of your thoughts, your dreams and your desires, participate in the unity. You are a mirror, slightly chipped, of God."

Becoming more excited, he went on: "O humans, who among you is not Psychodorus? O Psychodorus, which is the man that you are not? Wise Psychodorus, the follies of all fools are a sonorous stampede of horses that gallop within you. Sober Psychodorus, the vile desires of all debauched individuals are pigs and bulls grazing your soul. If not, would you understand the words of the insane, or the smug smile of the gourmand before wines and meats, or the rake's glance at the woman passing by?"

Psychodorus felt both swollen with pride and humiliated by such thoughts. For a while he tried, like a child sorting lentils and throwing out the little stones, only to conserve the ideas that exalted him and to reject those that dragged him down.

"The errors of the people were in Plato's mind, but they were recognized there as errors, and the wisdom of Plato was Plato himself. Other people are in my mind, but my soul is only me. You are sober and wise, O my soul. I am the owner of a rich library; I am not the author of the stupid things that are written there."

To that timidly defensive Psychodorus, however, a bold and avid Psychodorus replied: "You are all human beings. You sometimes congratulate yourself for having always resisted, even in early youth, the desires of debauchery. They live inside you, therefore, those enemy desires. And do you not even feel—perhaps because you have refused to satisfy them—that they are still stirring therein?"

Thus Psychodorus charmed himself with his flowery thoughts and wounded himself with his thorny ones. Meanwhile, he was crossing a sandy desert where neither thorns nor flowers grew.

He looked around. He smiled at the blonde nudity of the Earth, and he said: "O land without irregularity, O desert, was it your vaguely-perceived monotony that provoked my thoughts about unity? O One, O God, if you did not flourish in multiform creatures, would you not be similar to this desert?"

But a there was a nagging pain in his entrails, like an irritating child who tugs at your cloak and forces you to look in his direction. "I haven't eaten anything today," the philosopher said. "And in this treeless solitude, shall I eat tomorrow?"

He looked around, like someone searching for something. In the distance, he perceived a naked woman. Immediately, he resolved: "I shall go toward that naked woman. Perhaps she will show me where one can find something to eat."

But the irritating, crying child that was tugging at his cloak raised an objection; "Who can tell what language the woman speaks?"

"What does it matter? Psychodorus replied. "Beneath their florid diversity, human languages are but one sole language. Once, in Athens, if a Dorian spoke to me, I was slightly troubled by his accent. Now, whatever human being I listen to, I understand the essential element of his words from the outset."

Full of confidence, Psychodorus walked toward the naked woman.

VI. The Visible God

Having perceived Psychodorus, the naked woman remained motionless to begin with, utterly paralyzed by astonishment. Her staring eyes seemed to grow larger as the philosopher approached. When he was no more than a stadium away, the woman launched into the most unexpected, the most joyful and the most worshipful of dances, blowing kisses from her fluttering hands

When they were no more than ten paces apart, and their hands might almost have touched, the dancer stopped, threw herself on her knees, and began to speak, with her arms extended as if in prayer. Her tone was slow and solemn. Her gaze was anxiously ardent. In her utter submission, however, there was more joy than dread.

"This woman," Psychodorus thought, "has doubtless been gripped by a sudden madness. Her attitude, her gestures, the motion in her voice and those of her words that I can understand, all affirm that I am a god."

Psychodorus, who might have had some pride, but no vanity, burst out laughing. The woman gazed, with an uncertain emotion, at the god who laughed. Briefly, she trembled, as if in response to the sound of thunder. Soon, she smiled. The god did not seem to be wicked.

Now the god spoke. Using words that the worshipful woman did not understand, he said: "I am a god who is hungry."

If the words of a god, especially when pronounced in an unknown language, are clouded by some mystery, his gestures are probably clearer. The woman did not understand the marvels spoken in a difficult liturgical language, and yet she promised to bring nourishment.

She departed rapidly, but looked back frequently, perhaps fearful that the god might vanish. Sometimes she tried to repeat the Greek words she had heard; her barbarous lips deformed them bizarrely. Besides which, repeated by a human mouth, divine words always lose their meaning.

The good-natured god waited, standing on the burning sand.

A time passed, which seemed long to the god's stomach. In the hope that Athenatime might charm the emptiness of the wait with her phantasmal presence, Psychodorus shut his eyes.

When he opened them again, a procession of naked women was coming toward him. At a slow pace, the procession advanced in two columns. Their mouths were singing some kind of vague litany. The woman who had spoken to the god was walking between the two columns. Sometimes the others fell silent and, in the emotional pause, she stammered, trembling with mystical joy, the words spoken by the god. They were so deformed by their passage through barbarous lips that Psychodorus understood them less easily than the foreign words.

Psychodorus watched the bizarre ceremony. His body rejoiced in anticipation, for each woman carried a few oasis fruits—dates or bananas—in her hands.

The women surrounded the god with a triple circle of kneeling nude bodies. The one who had brought the others took the fruits from the nearest hands. She held them out, with words that seemed to the philosopher, although he was accustomed to so many human languages, to be singularly profound and mysterious. Deformed by her barbarous lips and solemnized by adoration, they were the poor words by means of which Psychodorus had indicated that he was hungry.

Psychodorus accepted the fruits, smiling, and bit into one of the most luscious. Immediately, the women rose to their feet and the triple circle began to dance, joyfully, before the benevolent god who had accepted the offering.

While Psychodorus was eating amid the religious dances, hostile shouts became audible, and the philosopher saw naked men on the horizon, running furiously. The trembling women pressed themselves against him, as if he alone could protect them.

"If they're wicked, run away," Psychodorus advised.

Rapt with joy, they tried to repeat what Psychodorus had said. Deformed by ignorance, a foreign accent and gladness, the fearful syllables became a kind of victory chant. Astonished by so much bizarrerie, and that none of the women was running away from the danger, the cynic admitted that he did not understand any of what was happening. Passively, he waited. In any case, perhaps he was not in a crazy reality, but in a dream.

The men hurled themselves upon the women, howling and striking out. Psychodorus raised his staff. He was disarmed in an instant, and his cloak was also ripped away, without doing him any harm. The naked men fell upon the cloak and the staff fervently, in a rage—and they addressed reproachful words to Psychodorus.

The women fled, amid lamentations, toward the invisible oasis. The men followed them. Occasionally, a man threw himself upon a woman, to hit her or caress her. The women who were fleeing from the men occasionally bumped into one of them, and immediately became alarmed, as if on contact with an invisible being.

Psychodorus walked behind the strange moving spectacle. He was surrounded by puzzles. Why, for instance, had these men rent his cloak into the tiniest shreds and pulverized his staff into the tiniest pieces, as if attacking two enemies? No one had done him any harm, though, and, once he was as naked as they were, even their reproaches had eased.

Psychodorus tried to explain all these incomprehensibilities. "Perhaps these women were worshipping my cloak and staff, and these men are not at all religious. Perhaps that is why they destroyed what there was about me that was divine."

But he went on: "That's not exactly it. The women truly do not appear to see the men. If I try to discover the meaning of the reproaches that they hurled at me, I think I can distinguish this crazy idea: 'Why have you rendered yourself visible by gross artifice? Your staff and cloak are two crimes against the law that all the gods have respected until now.' They added, it seemed to me, that visible gods would not take long to be scorned, soon no longer being anything but human."

The oasis was nearby now. Words as curt as orders emerged from the mouths of a few men. Everyone stopped.

The men formed a circle around the agitated herd of women. Suddenly, all throwing themselves upon them at the same time, they possessed them. Then the kneeling women worshipped. Some were facing the objects of adoration; others had their backs turned to them. Many closed their eyes; the gazes of the others were vague.

"Can they really not see them?" Psychodorus wondered. And he drew closer to the strange company.

The men went away silently and the women, immobile, continued to worship the gods.

Finally, Psychodorus said to them: "There's no longer anyone here."

All gazes turned toward him, slowly and ecstatically. Then the women stood up awkwardly, weighed down by joy. They pressed around him. Their lips all wanted to place kisses of gratitude on his flesh. Here and there, words spilled out in a glad and lively disorder. Then groups sang to religious rhythms, and the canticles seemed, strangely, like the free words, to signify: "O you who have rendered visible in one unique form all the gods ordinarily scattered and invisible…"

A few of the distant men were turning round. Undoubtedly, that day's liturgy had something abnormal about it, for they were tapping their companions on the shoulder. Soon, they came back, at a pace that was hesitant at first, but soon became more definite and rapid.

They threw themselves on the women, striking without crying out. The terrorized women fled in all directions, often running toward the blows they were seeking to avoid. Two or three men were knocked down in the jostling turbulence. The women collided with them as with an unseen obstacle. The majority of the unfortunates, however, turned toward Psychodorus. They cried out to him, supplications, blasphemies and accusations of treason.

Men came toward the philosopher and studied him in amazement. They grabbed him and twirled him around and around for some time, studying all the details of his body. Particular curious gazes plunged into his nostrils and his mouth, which their hands opened brutally. They seemed to be searching for the mysterious cause of some frightening effect.

The tone of the words that were spoken expressed an anxiety that deepened into discouragement.

Finally, they all seemed to give up the attempt to understand. They struck Psychodorus violently. Then their gestures and cries ordered him to go away.

For several hours, Psychodorus marched at hazard. He dreaded returning toward the naked men, who would undoubtedly kill him. He became indignant, however, at the thought of leaving without knowing. And in the monotony of the desert, he did not know where the slow uncertainty of his footsteps was taking him.

The Sun had disappeared. The philosopher sat down on the sand that had been burning a little while before but which the night had already cooled. Behind one of the moving hills that the wind lifted up like slightly more durable waves, a form leapt up, launching itself toward the cynic. Before he could defend himself against the probable wild beast, he was grabbed and rolled on the ground, amid a whirlwind of caresses.

He pushed the creature away, and recognized the first woman he had met in the desert. She had succeeded in escaping and following him. She was irritated at first, on seeing him refuse her kisses, but soon spoke submissive words—and Psychodorus accepted that docile company for some time.

She led him to an oasis as narrow as a hut. There was nothing there but a brackish well covered by two date-palms. The poor place was abandoned, and they made it their dwelling.

Psychodorus wanted to stay with the woman long enough to learn her language perfectly and to understand the mystery of her native land. When he was able to understand her speech without any possible errors, this was the explanation she gave him:

"It seems from your words, O god, that there are lands very different from my own, and you pretend not to know what happens here. Doubtless you are teasing your servant, but she will tell you, as if you did not know, what you order her to tell you, for the gods have all rights over feeble mortals.

"You, whom I thought to be a better god than the others, are actually the most wicked of all, since you refuse me your caresses and reject my kisses. Perhaps, though, when a god

95

renders himself visible, he is scornful of the touch of a mortal woman.

"In my country, then—since you demand, you who know everything, that I speak as if you were ignorant—the gods are invisible to our eyes, and we go about in perpetual hope and dread, for a god might be beside us, to punish us or reward us. Sometimes a bodiless voice disturbs us. Often, blows terrify us, immobilizing us or making us flee toward hem. Often, too, we feel sudden caresses, mystical joys penetrate our flesh and the gods fecundate us. Then, for nine months, we might perhaps be charged with a mortal creature whose beauty the gods might love, or even—O ineffable glory—bear a burden of divinity.

"I, your humble servant, have had the vertiginous joy of being a tabernacle for nine months, to give the light of day to the divine, to hear the invisible one crying in my lap and to feel the glorious lips suckling at my breasts. Alas, my son the young god died—for young gods are mortal for an ill-defined time. I have even heard blasphemers affirm that all the gods are mortal, just as we are—but I do not believe it, for their invisible voices say the opposite, and sudden killing blows often punish those who venture much blasphemies.

"Then you came, the visible form of that of which divine contacts make our eyes dream. And I said to my companions: 'The gods are no longer any but one god, and he is showing himself to us, and he is beauty itself, and he is asking to be brought something to eat, and he has spoken mysterious and powerful words to me that it is appropriate to repeat to his glory.'

"Repeating the words that you had addressed to me in a solemn and liturgical tongue, we came to you and offered you the finest of our fruits—but distant voices insulted us. We believed that you would triumph over the distant voices, or even that they might be coming from you in order to test our piety—but you beat us, or allowed us to be beaten. Then you covered us with caresses, and we could not see you. But we saw you again, and soon, we were beaten again—and then you went away. When you first arrived, you had a staff in your hand and you wore a heavy hide about your body; now the staff and the fabric are no more than debris on distant sands, and you are as naked as a woman—but I recognize you in spite of the vanished signs.

"I followed you, hiding myself. I thought, alas, that you only wanted my caresses, since it was to me alone that you had first appeared; I thought that bad things had happened to me as punishment for having brought the others. Then again, when my companions placed their lips on your divine body, I suffered an unknown anguish which I assume to be worse than death.

"Listen to me, O god. I am unhappy because you refuse my caresses. You ought, O god, sometimes to be visible and enjoy my gazing at your beauty, but sometimes, too—since, when visible, you are ashamed of sensuality—you ought to become invisible and exchange kisses with me."

Then, Psychodorus said: "Woman, I am a god exiled in a body that always sees itself, whether I wish it or not. Or rather, I am presently a false god. Return to the true gods, the gods of your homeland. Now that I have brought you the dream and the anxiety of something else, you will certainly be unhappy, but outside your own country, like a fish in the open air or a bird in a river, your heart would choke in an irreparable calamity of strangeness that was not made for you."

He stood up. His gesture was so imperious that the woman dared not move. He drew away with long strides. For some time, he heard weeping. Then he heard nothing more.

VII. The Veils of Isis

Under the sting of the Sun, Psychodorus missed his cloak, lost in the land of the Invisible Men. Since his departure from the meager oasis, no shade had soothed him. Now he began to run, for he had just perceived some distant ruins. *Reality or mirage?* he wondered, in anguish.

97

Fortunately, the ruins were not one of those fantastic architectures that heat builds on the sands and causes to flee. They were the remains of a city where once, amid the singing joy of waters and the quivering emotion of trees, the discordant diversity of human passions had stirred. Two or three centuries before, some unknown cataclysm had destroyed the verdure, dried up the wells and streams, and obliterated the proud Ephemera. Now, the place that patriotic poets had proclaimed to be the most beautiful and glorious on Earth was dishonored by crumbling stones that the sands covered and uncovered according to their whim, the equivalent of the caprices of the ocean.

Frail things spared by disasters often survive along with powerful objects that stand up like challenges. Suspended from a nail in a labyrinth that was a palace, Psychodorus found a cloak of purple silk, spangled with gold. He would certainly have preferred linen, which protects against heat and cold, to the thin fabric, and the simple white that reflects the Sun's rays as armor deflects arrows to the prideful dye, but, as an accommodating philosopher, he was able to be content with what he found. He detached the useless weight of the gold and threw the purple over his shoulders.

Against a wall stood a strange scepter, as long as a shepherd's crook—but the tip, which was not curved at all, bore a golden hand with a raised index-finger. Having detached this heavy and ridiculous extremity without difficulty, Psychodorus had a staff almost as comfortable as the one broken by the Invisible Men.

In a single ruin, the collapsed palace mingled with a fallen temple. A few obstinate columns stood up in isolation in the sunlight—a vanity that the wind would soon topple and the sands would soon bury—but a subterranean sanctuary remained intact. In there, Psychodorus found wheat in a grain-bunker, which restored his strength.

He smiled at the innumerable dead gods that had left him this heritage. "For you are dead," he said to them, "O nothings whom no one worships."

And he laughed at the bestial faces that certain barbarians give to the gods. In the midst of the divine muzzles and beaks, however, one form stood out, imprecise and veiled. At its feet, a still-legible inscription forbade anyone to touch its veil, which was a menacing black in color, on pain of death.

Philosophers are curious. Psychodorus lifted up the black fabric, which was still weighed down by amethysts. Underneath it, he saw a white veil. He lifted that one too, in spite of the rubies weighing it down. Then there was a blue veil ornamented with diamonds. His continued investigations discovered a green veil charged with sapphires, and then a red one in which emeralds opened like the eyes of dead soothsayers.

"What a poor joke!" said Psychodorus, becoming annoyed.

He tore away all the veils, whose weight, supercharged with gems, was becoming difficult to lift. This time, he found a heavier veil than the rest, and singularly rigid, woven in pure gold. It was maintained by gold rings and circlets. The philosopher, however, succeeded in lifting it—and he saw that beneath that last veil, at the heart of the mystery, there was nothing at all.

Then he said: "These barbarian priests knew a little of the truth, and their meager symbolism enlivens the first syllables of the interminable sentence that is the universe. Yes, Isis; yes, Nature; yes, God; yes, Everything, or whatever other name anyone cares to give you: you are made of veils. None of your appearances is any more or less true than any of the others, but no matter how many veils one lifts, O quickly-wearied priests, one never reaches the final veil. There is no ultimate appearance, and all efforts to approach the center leave us at the circumference."

Then Psychodorus, kneeling in front of the empty place where the insufficient symbol stood, continued piously:

"One, you are the Father of numbers, but, for as long as you have existed, all numbers have existed, and numbers are infinite. O Eternal One, which contains the infinity of numbers...O coeternal numbers, which speak the diverse powers of the infinite One... Without you, One, there would be no numbers. If any one of you numbers could be missing, all your brethren would fall into oblivion, and One with you."

VIII. The Identical Pitaniates [12]

A narrow isthmus led to a vast near-island. A mighty wall forbade passage. When Psychodorus reached the gate, armed guards shouted to him: "Man, are you an identical Pitantiate? Foreigners cannot enter here."

Laughing, the cynic replied: "I enter everywhere. I'm a dog."[13]

The guards laughed too, perhaps carried away by the philosopher's simple cheerfulness. As if he had pronounced a password, they let him in.

He took 200 paces without meeting anyone. The city was still a long way off and even the first houses in the country were some distance away.

At a bend in the road a woman raised her head and looked at him. She was lying down in a bizarre position, with her limbs folded beneath her like the feet of a sleeping dog. She had kind, devoted eyes and her smile was a timid caress. She came toward the passer-by, at first on all fours—but her face suddenly reddened like that of a novice priest who has forgotten some pompous ritual detail during a ceremony. An abrupt movement brought her upright, and in a voice even more submissive than her initial attitude she said: "Do you want to be my master?"

---

[12] The significance of this title is elusive. A Pitaniate is an inhabitant of Pitana; there was a Greek town of this name, which took its name from a water-nymph; it was the birthplace of the philosopher Arcesilaus, a follower of Diogenes' disciple Crates—but whether any of that has any relevance is unclear.

[13] The label "cynic" is derived from the Greek word for "dog;" the reason for that is also unclear.

"It's quite enough being my own," Psychodorus replied, without interrupting his progress.

"Oh, be my master!" she persisted. "You seem so good. If you knew how happy I am…."

Psychodorus stopped. His hand was tempted to caress the plaintive woman as one strokes a pet animal. She, however, continued: "My master is dead. Besides, he was nasty."

Psychodorus sought an exact translation. "Your husband," he said, "was a bad man, and beat you?"

"He hit me occasionally between the sixth hour of the night and the sixth hour of the day, but between the sixth hour of the day and the sixth hour of the night he bit me cruelly."

"I commiserate with you in your past," Psychodorus replied, "and I rejoice in your present, since the man is dead."

"I'm not mourning the dead master, who was nasty," she lamented. "I'm sad because I no longer have a master. Be my master, you who are good."

"I can't do anything for you. My soul is still faithful to a memory, and I'm only passing through."

"Passing through?" she marveled. "You aren't a native of this land? Wretch! Do you even know the mysteries of Pitana?"

"I shall know them," replied Psychodorus, "if you care to tell me about them."

He sat down on the roadside.

The woman looked up at the sky, then down at the ground. "Alas," she moaned, the Sun is very high and our shadows very short. Let us flee to my house before the sixth hour opens the door of the bestial mystery."

Psychodorus thought that she was mad. Nevertheless, he got up and followed her. She wanted to run, though, and the philosopher refused to hasten his steady stride. She gave evidence of increasing anxiety. She looked despairingly at the climbing Sun and the diminishing shadows.

"One minute more," she said, finally, "And the Sun will reach the middle of its course." With an abrupt and unexpected movement, she threw her arms around Psychodorus' neck and kissed the philosopher on the lips.

Then, the cynic thought that he fell prey to a ridiculous mocking dream. Before he was able to push the woman away, he no longer felt anything on his shoulders but paws, and a broad tongue was licking his face. The woman had disappeared and an affectionate bitch was hanging on to him.

He deposited her on the ground and continued on his way, followed by the faithful animal. Now, however, he heard howling not far away. The bitch fled. A pack of wolves arrived at a hectic run, and Psychodorus barely had time to climb a tree.

The philosopher was astonished. The beasts had come from the deserted part of the peninsula, where he had not encountered anyone, with the exceptional of the bizarre woman—no animals and no people. The wolves howled for some time at the base of the tree, then went away—but one of them remained for another hour or so after the others had gone, directing singular howls at Psychodorus that seemed reproachful.

The philosopher had a ridiculous idea, which he quickly rejected. "Its muzzle resembles the face of the guard who spoke to me—and one might think that its howling was cursing me because I deceived him."

Although he rejected it several times, however, the ridiculous idea returned obsessively—and, in spite of Psychodorus' efforts to think rationally, questions that were genuinely crazy raised themselves within him:

"Did he really believe that I was a dog?"

"Was the husband who bit the plaintive woman a four-legged wolf at certain times?"

"Is the bitch who licked me face the woman who was weeping, and kissed me against my will?"

The wolf eventually wearied of its futile guard-duty. It went away, and Psychodorus as able to come down from the tree.

That evening was dangerous, though. Everywhere, in the landscape devoid of humans, the cynic encountered ferocious animals, which sometimes did not perceive him, being intent on tearing one another apart, but which often saw or scented him and gave chase.

After enduring a thousand perils, he reached the city. The wretched houses gave the vague impression of dens. Psychodorus opened a door and went in. There, wagging her tail as she came toward him, was the bitch that had appeared on the road so bizarrely. She nuzzled him, barking joyfully or plaintively. Sometimes she seemed to be barking "I love you." Sometimes she seemed to be excusing herself, imploring forgiveness, as if she regretted having abandoned a friend in difficult circumstances.

The dwelling had no other inhabitant. Psychodorus slept in the bitch's house. She lay down next to him.

Psychodorus' slumber was not, as it had been for such a long time, that of a poor widower. Dreams smiled upon the philosopher, and it was almost the happy sleep he had known beside Athenatime.

Even so, the night was not far advanced when he woke up. In spite of the efforts and the almost-human whimpering of the bitch, he went out.

The city was as empty of humans as the countryside. In the streets he encountered a few vicious beasts and, occasionally, the furtive flight of a frightened animal along a wall. Psychodorus went into several houses. They were inhabited by weak animals, alone or in families, all of which trembled at the appearance of a human, as if with a mixture of terror and fury.

The middle of the night was approaching when Psychodorus, who was walking down a street, felt a pain in his heel. A scorpion had stung him. Psychodorus crushed the scorpion—but instead of a dead insect, he was confronted by a human corpse.

103

Humans were appearing on all sides, in the city that had been deserted a short while before, and there were no longer any beasts to be seen. In the houses, voices could be heard, singing, as softly as deliverance: "Rejoice in the victory of the sixth hour of the night. Here, at last, is the victory of the human hour."

Then a great silence fell upon everything like a terror—and in the streets, imperious and aggressive songs burst forth. Brutally patriotic hymns, they affirmed: "There are not only human hours. The Pitaniates are the most identical of beings. Hurrah for all the hours! Long live the identical Pitaniates, whose identity is beloved by the gods and glory!"

Fascinated by the strangeness of the spectacle, Psychodorus stood still.

Men-at-arms came toward him, who pointed to the cadaver lying in front of him, saying: "Was it you who killed him?"

"I don't know anything about it," the philosopher replied.

Astonished by this reply, the men-at-arms took him to prison.

At the third hour of the day, Psychodorus was taken before a Magistrate in the market-square. There were many accused persons that day, and by the time the cynic's turn came, the fifth hour of the day was long past.

At first, the spectators formed a tightly-pressed circle around the tribunal, in which, alongside ferocious visions, kind faces smiled, like flowers interlaced with thorns. Around the fifth hour, the kindly and affectionate individuals gradually disappeared. When the cynic was interrogated, he was no longer surrounded by any but hostile faces, all terrible to behold.

The Judge asked: "Did you kill the man who was found dead beside you?"

Psychodorus repeated the truth he had already told the men-at-arms: "I don't know anything about it."

"Wretch!" said the Judge, indignantly. "You merit a fine for having killed, and for disdaining a Magistrate you merit death."

The spectators approved, with angry words that seemed to be howled, growled and roared.

"Nevertheless," the Judge went on, "before delivering you to the scaffold, I shall extend indulgence to the point of permitting you to explain."

The cries of the spectators disapproved of this excessive mildness, but the Judge commanded: "Silence!"

That word was as sharp and menacing as a tiger's purr. Everyone shut up. Then, severely and gratingly, the Magistrate addressed himself to the accused again. "How can you not know whether you have killed?"

"I know that I have killed," said Psychodorus. "I don't know whether I killed the man of whom you speak. Toward the sixth hour of the night, I crushed a scorpion that stung me, and had the horror of feeling my foot suddenly lifted up by a human corpse. Was the scorpion transformed?"

The philosopher could say no more. The crowd was nothing but a furious agitation of abrupt gestures, leaps and bounds—and the whole vast nightmare was howling, screeching, roaring, bellowing and whining. Within the articulate din, violent words could be distinguished: "Put the slanderer to death! There are no transformations in our beautiful land. Long live the identical Pitaniates! Put the liar to death. Put the enemy of the fatherland to death…"

The Judge and the men-at-arms had great difficulty preventing the good patriots from killing the slanderer immediately. The guards held back the crowd awkwardly. Drowned out by the howling, the futile mewling of the Judge explained that it is best to kill according to certain rules, and after certain formalities.

But now the Sun was sending perpendicular rays down upon the tribunal. Suddenly, there were no longer men in the vast square, but animals. From the Judge's seat, a tiger bounded toward Psychodorus. The men-at-arms were a pack of wolves, launching themselves toward the philosopher. The crowd of a few moments before, now an indescribable mob of bears, panthers, lions, bulls and wild boars, precipitated itself, in furious, frenzied disorder, toward the man who had had the insolence to remain a man.

With a single rapid bound, Psychodorus was outside the terrible swarm. He threw himself into the nearest house, closing the door behind him. While the animals were breaking down the door beneath their irresistible mass, he escaped through the roof.

For half a day and half a night, he hid himself in various places that seemed to him to be far from safe. When the human hour finally gave him peers with whom he might be confused, he left the city and crossed a large part of the Pitaniate countryside—but he dared not go out through the only gate. He feared that he might be recognized by the guard to whom he had spoken and who appeared, as a wolf, not to have forgotten him. Psychodorus went into the sea.

It was by swimming that he returned to the lands where humans, endowed with a more continuous modesty, never took off their masks.

IX. The Mayflies

Lying in a meadow on the bank of a river, Psychodorus was drowsily happy, like a man drunk on cheap wine. He was enjoying—a rare thing for him—a moment of naïve enthusiasm. At intervals, he contemplated the beauty of things, mildly moved. More often, he felt a banal pride in the grandeur of humankind, and, like an imbecile praising the glory of his homeland, he sang inside himself of human genius and the subtle skill with which, like triumphant hunters, we capture a truth on the wing, or the shadow of a truth.

Then a swarm of mayflies came to settle lightly, already about to take off again, on the philosopher's joyous immobility—and he heard those that were on his head talking.

One of them buzzed: "Let's pause on this dead world and study it."

"The detail leaves me indifferent," replied another. "The important thing for me is to know that these powerful masses, the worlds, also die. That's consoling. Why should we revolt henceforth against a law recognized as universal?"

"It's sad," a scientist whistled, shrugging the bases of his wings. "If everything dies, why should anything be born? Death isn't an objective; it's an eternal, meaningless pause. So why make the journey?"

"Glory to me! Glory to me!" proclaimed a new-born. He was shouting very loudly, and the proud quivering of his wings was a noisy triumphant fanfare. They all gathered around him, listening.

"I've just made the greatest discovery of all time," he went on. "You know that worlds die, or at least appear to die. Like us, though, they have immortal souls—or, rather, they don't; those masses are too heavy to be moved by that noble and delicate spring, a soul. Their life is the expression of a spirit that can sometimes absent itself, but which eventually—after ten or twelve centuries, perhaps—returns to animate them, provided that a mayfly pronounces the powerful words that command spirits."

"That which is dead is really dead," affirmed the scientist, who had a habit of speaking disdainfully while shrugging the bases of his wings.

"You shall see," replied the thaumaturge.

But scientists are too sure that the limits of their comprehension are the limits of things. They hold to their methods and are past masters at not looking too hard. This one declared: "I would see what I couldn't believe. An ignorant person might allow himself to be deceived by a hallucination; a scientist knows that there are no scientific miracles."

He flew away, followed by a few others. That serious-minded group flew to Psychodorus' right leg, and he could no longer hear their murmurs.

Others, thirsty for mystery, begged the interrupted narrator to continue. "Speak, Master. What have you seen?"

Trembling like a visionary who has just had a vision, he said: "I was at the other end of the green immensity of the universe"—his wing, with a broad gyratory gesture, designated the entire meadow—"over there by the river Ocean, which, as you know, goes around it." His rigidly-extended wing indicated a point on the river. "I found a dead world quite similar to the one we're on at this moment. When I said the magic words that a great enchanter taught me, I saw the dead world get up slowly, resuscitated by the power of the words. Look over there, where there's a movement the laws of which our scientists might perhaps determine."

He added: "I'll resuscitate this one before your very eyes."

His buzzing became very solemn.

"In the name of the irresistible power of mayflies, the only rational beings, the only consciousness created in the universe, and in the name of the omnipotence of the God who made us in his image, O world that is immense, but inferior to the fragile thinkers we are, obey: get up and walk."

The insect's pretension drew a burst of laughter from Psychodorus.

"Can you hear the thunder of its resurrection?" said the inspired one.

"That's true," they all said. "We have heard—and we can also see. Dead matter, in order to revive, only awaits the command of a mayfly."

One of them, who must have been a poet, took the floor to sing the praises of the new conquest of science. In rhythms that seemed bizarre to Psychodorus, he commenced: "Our fathers saw in an uncertain light; we are dazzled by the great joyous light. This century is great and strong."

And the entire great and strong generation fell, dying, at the feet of Psychodorus, the resuscitated world.

X. The Immortals

The spectacle had a poignant strangeness.

Caught up in a crowd dressed in mourning, Psychodorus had just entered the interior of a vast tomb paved with black marble.

The walls and covered ceiling were laden with black draperies, where macabre skulls and gnarled crossbones shone whitely.

Along each wall was a row of torches. Their countless tremulous gleams made spangles twinkle like winking eyelids and motionless shadows slither like serpents.

The people surrounding the philosopher, men in dark clothing saddened by mourning-bands, and women in long veils, as straight and stiff as corpses, would remain mute and motionless for eternal minutes, and then, simultaneously, kneel down or stand up.

Their gazes were directed toward the Occident, where, in the distant gloom, the vague form of a priest in a white robe covered in black lace was making slow hieratic gestures.

Then, to a rhythm lugubrious enough to squeeze the heart, the officiator chanted the litanies, his tearful voice singing:

"You who gives savor to life;

"You who permits the resurrection of life;

"Goddess of the sunsets that make dawns possible;

"Goddess of the long slumbers that prepare for future labors;

"Goddess of the dolors that give birth to jots;

"Goddess of the dark passage toward the light;

"Night from which daylight emerges;

"Goddess of the tombs that are the matrices of all life…"

To each invocation, all the people, standing up, their heads brushing the draperies of the ceiling, replied fervently: "Deliver us, Goddess."

Then the officiator, after a chilling silence, said: "Brethren, let us pray."

And, as the crowd fell to its knees, in a firm tone, beneath which one sensed sobs stirring, he said: "O Liberatrice, O Death, we are punished for having been unfaithful to you. Do not put an end to dying, Sovereign whose mourning-dress we wear, and spare us a merciful glance. We implore your grace for our long forgetfulness. Forgive us, O Death!"

Humbly, the faithful repeated: "Forgive us, O Death!"

The priest went on: "Smile upon us, O Death!"

And the people, in a great surge of hope their hands extended as if toward a ray of light, implored after him: "Smile upon us, O Death!"

The officiator concluded: "Kill us, O Death!"

And the crowd unleashed a great cry, begging: "Kill us, O Death!"

Then the priest climbed up on to a kind of catafalque and, pushing back the sleeves of his black surplice, began a speech.

This is what the voice of the orator, as somber as the interior of a sepulcher and as tearful as the mother of a dead child, said:

"Brethren, I believe there is no need to remind you of the happiness of the times when we were able to die. The joys, which were known to be precarious, seemed flavorsome, and the dolors, from which we were sure to be liberated some day, were a light burden.

"But avid human beings had striven for centuries to steal their immortality from their only goddess, Death. They succeeded, alas. The physicians succeeded in countering all our diseases and preventing old age from snuffing us out, rendering life incurable.

"Nor have I any need to tell you what followed. Most of you witnessed it.

"Humans swarmed in infinite numbers. Insatiable for sensual indulgences always insufficient to assuage their now-eternal ennui, each one wanted to take his brother's share, and, lazy in the face of fatigue, consign the burden of labor to his neighbor. Soon, he no longer cared about anyone else; no one consented to the least effort on behalf of the egotists that surrounded his egotism.

"Alas, our bodies conserved all the vigor of 20 years, while our minds acquired the experience of centuries. We saw accomplished in ourselves the ineptly sacrilegious desire of our ancestors: 'If youth only knew! If old age were only able!' We were needlessly powerful old men, young ones stiffened by science. We learned the little that we desired to learn; our knowledge killed the desire while letting the need live, by letting the ignoble pressure of habit increase. We were vain rebels against laws that had become abhorrent, but simultaneously more ineluctable.

"Which way could we turn in that flat desert of immortality, which disgust rendered odious to us, but which cowardice prevented us from leaving? What could we do with the time that no longer marched? Where could we go, in the stagnant immobility of all our selves? Oh, the ever-open yawn before the idiotic comedy that was no longer even progressing toward a denouement.

"A mirage of hope seduced us, rendered us happy for a while. Violent death was not extinct. A war or a revolution might save us. Great patriots and sublime revolutionaries appeared, dreaming of ameliorating, by bloodshed on a massive scale, the plethora of humans wounded by too much life.

"But security had rendered us cowardly, incapable of advancing toward the unknown that was no longer inevitable. To be master of another's life, it is necessary to risk one's own. No one dared to die, no one was able to kill. Armies disbanded before the first javelin was thrown, and the revolutionaries, numerous and violent in the eloquent period of preparation, flowed away like the waters of a river when the moment for salutary but dangerous action arrived.

"Confronted with that double bankruptcy of liberators, it was necessary to prohibit births. We had been gifted with all the strength, beauty and ardor of 20 years; we were forbidden, on pain of death, to make use of them. Whoever gave life, gave his own life. And, despite the desperate clamor of energies left idle, we all abstained more effectively than the impotent old men of yore. In order to live, we shut down everything within us that as alive. We were the walking dead, sad and silent, and when we saw desire gleaming in the eye of a woman, we said to her, with a terrified gesture of refusal: 'Sister, we must live!'

"A few moments later, when, in spite of dread, her desire had awakened a tentative desire in us, when we regretted our sad words and, with a smile, tried to take them back, it was the woman who replied, coldly and ironically: 'Brother, we must live.'

"And nowhere in the world was the noise of kisses heard. Or rather...but I would rather believe in the death of the kiss than its dishonor, and I shall not speak of the mire into which its radiance was dragged.[14]

"The sickened legislators amended the law. Henceforth, when a child appeared, it was the new-born that would be sacrificed, unless someone volunteered to die in its place. In the beginning, mothers sacrificed themselves, but they soon began to protest against the egotism of men, declaring that they ought to remain, in order to care for, breast-feed and love the dear child, while it was the useless father who ought to disap-

---

[14] The French word for kiss, *baiser*, is very often used as a euphemism for sexual intercourse, and is obviously being used in that fashion here; the unspeakable practice of which the priest dare not speak—although he is quite happy to talk about infanticide—is presumably technological birth-control; Ryner was not the only pioneering French writer of speculative fiction to consider that the ultimate unmentionable, nor the only one slyly to mention its unmentionability, although he must have been as well aware as everyone else of the fact that the population of France was not increasing nearly as fast as might have been expected if no one were practicing artificial birth control. Given the utter ludicrousness of his entire argument against the prospect of immortality, however, this is a minor quibble.

pear. At the very least, it was necessary to draw lots. In a word, they refused the role of dupe that women had been playing for too long. Maternal love became extinct in our land and with it, all that remained of affection. Today, a kiss between a male and a female is scarcely exchanged when, howling with anger, the two individuals shove one another away and precipitate themselves upon one another, hitting and biting, over some equally-coveted morsel of bread. But why talk about bread? Apart from physicians, the kings of the present and the future, who has tasted bread for the last 30 years? No one any longer wants to knead dough on another's behalf, nor consents to sow wheat that will be eaten by someone else: it is by fishing and hunting, with tasteless wild fruits and bitter acorns that we appease our hunger. Humanity is dead in us; we are immortal brutes.

"I have now been preaching the good word for 50 years. For 25 years my church has been truly universal; for a quarter of a century all men have been convinced that I am pointing the Way: that it is necessary to die to render to humankind the change that is life; to render to Nature the elements necessary for her new combinations; to permit our enmired souls to escape through the broken dyke and run down the holy slope, mirrors quivering with happiness reflecting a new and changing universe.

"But of all my innumerable disciples, of all those who will repeat my doctrine energetically or tearfully, none has put it into practice. None has provided the example that might, perhaps, lead to salvation. You all proclaim the necessity of suicide, but none of you is brave enough to be the first to commit suicide.

"Rise up within the crowd, sublime model, great active initiator, who will be able to the joy of humankind, to the regular progress of nature and to your own future happiness, an abhorrent life!"

The priest fell silent, expectantly. All heads had bowed when he had spoken about those worshippers of death who clung instinctively to a horrible life, those slaves that long habituation to their servitude and fear of the unknown had rendered incapable of the simple liberating gesture. No head was raised at his final appeal.

Then, descending from his macabre pulpit, he affirmed: "The example will be given to you."

But they all begged: "Don't die, Master!"

And one of them added: "We cannot follow you into the abyss of joy, and we need to hear our eloquent words, which make our souls tremble with the hope of future courage."

The priest reassured them: "I do not need to die yet. The example that will impel your hands toward your hearts to transpierce them will have more authority than mine."

He made a sign. At the back of the sinister temple shaped and decorated like a tomb, a black curtain was raised, and two men came forward, carrying a rigid human form—some strange kind of statue.

The strange statue was laid down on the catafalque that served as a pulpit. In a religious and expectant silence, the priest said: "Remove the bandages."

They understood then that the statue was a mummy.

The priest continued: "This individual has endured for 24 centuries; it knows better than we do the vanity of time that is unified and immobilized into an eternity."

When the bandages had been removed, he said to the mummy extended once more, rigid, on the sumptuous catafalque: "Informative and propelling soul, so long imprisoned in an immobile form, you are now freed of external obstacles. Awake from your long sleep and stand up."

The mummy did not budge.

The priest went on: "As an infant, freed from its swaddling-clothes, sets off, trembling and joyful, on the march of life, get up, in the name of Life."

Beneath the flickering gleams, in the hectic flight of desire for a miracle, the mummy did not even quiver.

But the authoritative priest proclaimed: "As an infant, freed from its swaddling-clothes, sets off, trembling and joyful, on the painful march of life, which will end with the peaceful sleep of death—get up, in the name of Death."

And, with a waking movement, the mummy slowly sat up, and then stood up, unsteadily. Its thin figure had something unreal about it, as if time had worn away its body. Numbly, it stammered in a shrill voice: "What benevolent word has extracted me from the nightmare that I thought eternal, and has given me enough life that I might be able to die?"

As no one in the immense crowd, rapt with admiration and hope, replied, the mummy continued: "A weapon, please! A weapon, in order that I might mingle myself with the great current of Being and give to the drop of water whose new form I am, that for which it has been hoping, impotently, for so many centuries."

The priest handed it a long dagger.

It took it, and pressed it to its bosom—but a surge of terror made it pause.

"Promise me," it moaned, "oh, promise not to embalm me any longer in precious perfumes or entwine me in vile bandages but to let divine corruption dissociate the tedious mixture in which I was immobilized while so many joyful generations passed!"

"I promise you that," said the priest.

The little hand put pressure on the dagger; an aromatic jet sprang forth. The mummy fell, while an inexplicable sound of wings was heard.

The priest picked up the weapon, and held it up to the eyes of the people, who uttered enthusiastic acclamations.

"Who wants the dagger replete with the perfume of the example?" he asked.

But no one took a step toward the happy route along which a guide had preceded them.

Then the priest cried: "Since it is absolutely necessary, I shall tell you the last Word of Wisdom and Pity."

And the crowd, hanging on that ultimate hope, heard the Word: "Kill all the physicians."

Powerfully intoxicated, they repeated: "Yes, yes—let's kill all the physicians."

The immense crowd launched itself, howling, outside the somber church. In the bright sunlight, it dispersed into still-numerous companies, ran toward the palaces that elevated their insolence amid the rudimentary huts, and killed the infamous healers who, rendering determined forms immortal, had transformed the once-harmonious course of life into a stagnant fetid sewer.

XI. O my Mother, you are my Father

A man was passing through the city. He seemed unable to see anything. He was running, with his arms raised, shouting: "O my mother, you are my father!" Jeering children were following him.

"Who is that man?" asked Psychodorus of someone who was laughing.

"He's a harmless madman," replied the laugher. "His name is Philothanatos. He seems to be unaware of human affairs, and that there are people around him. He wanders around, repeating the ridiculous words you have just heard him say, or similar ones."

Psychodorus drew away, thoughtfully. He searched for a meaning in the madman's words, and said: "Madness, you are an exile. Who among those who are laughing would not be mad among the Retrograde People, the Rooted People, the men who are invisible gods to their wives, or among any other of the strange peoples I have visited?"

He met the man who was running and shouting again. He paused in front of him and said: "O man, the people of this land call you mad. That is doubtless because you are a distant foreigner to them. Tell me the name of your homeland, if it has a name."

"My homeland has no name for you."

"Look at me before pushing me away," persisted Psychodorus. "I'm not from this city. I've traveled a great deal in order to educate myself, and I'm perhaps worthy to hear you."

"How have you traveled?" Philothantos asked. "Is it with your legs?"

"With my legs," Psychodorus said.

Then the madman burst into disdainful laughter, and he commanded: "Let me pass."

But the philosopher took him by the arm. "I believe that I have also seen lands to which my legs did not carry me."

The other smiled. He examined his interlocutor with an attention that soon became sympathetic, and he said: "Listen. I have never replied to anyone. To you I shall reply, because, on looking at you more closely, I see that we are twins."

Now, almost invariably, whether it were madness of prophetic wisdom, thought made tempestuous violence whirl upon the man's forehead, seeming to hollow it out with emphatic ravages—but in a moment of calm, Psychodorus had been charmed by the soft lament of youth sung by the features at rest. The man was at least 15 years younger than he was. So he repeated, in amazement: "We are twins?"

"Yes," the other explained, "we shall die on the same day."

"The words you speak are meaningful," Psychodorus approved, "but when these people who call you mad pronounce the same words as you, they offer husks emptied of their seeds." Then he asked: "On what day shall we die?"

Philothanatos hesitated. He looked at Psychodorus, and opened his lips. He looked at him again, shook his head, and closed his mouth. Finally, he said: "You seem strong, but there are hidden weaknesses. If you were really cable of bearing such knowledge, I think that you would know it without my help. Thus, for fear of crushing you beneath too heavy a burden, I shall leave your question without a reply. I will tell you this, at least: what is called death is a more complete birth. We are in preparation for a new life; ours is a poor fetal life. We are trapped in the bosom of our mother, the Earth."

"We're not in the Earth," Psychodorus observed. "We're on the Earth."

The madman pulled a scornful face. He shrugged his shoulders and said: "Imbecile!"

And with an unexpected movement, he departed at a run.

The next day, in a suburb of the city, hazard brought the two men together again. Philothanatos came up to the cynic with an indulgent smile.

"Are you today, as you were yesterday, a man of frivolous objections, with a tongue quick to hostility and a mind so swollen with pride as not to understand?"

"I think I have understood," Psychodorus replied, "for the mind hears a few hours after the ears. You go about crying: 'O my mother, you are my father,' because, just as our father had thrown into the somber fetal life the seed of that which you are, your mother has thrown into somber terrestrial life the seed of that which you will be. You march in the direction of the future, and your mother of today, you call your future father—for you are gazing toward the future moment that will detach you from the Earth and the atmosphere that surrounds you, to permit you to take flight in a brighter and freer life."

"Yes," said Philothanatos. "O my mother, you are my father. And you, Earth who bears me, you are my mother. And you, Death, you are the midwife that my impatience summons. Ignorant, alas, I wept at my last birth, but the imminent death-throes, dolorous as they will be to my body, will open before my mind such bright and promising landscapes that I shall rejoice."

"After death has effected its terrible and gentle midwifery, in the suffering of our body and in the joy of your soul, will you finally be in the true life?"

Philothanatos laughed scornfully. "O quickly-fatigued traveler," he cried, "who takes the first inn that comes along for your house, learn this: you have no house, and there is nothing along the route but inns. O banal philosopher, drunk with the coarse drunkenness of the absolute, learn this: the absolute is naught but the sum of relatives, and your eternal dwelling is made up of the entire circle of inns. How can there be a true life, and what, then, would the other lives be? I am alive today, was yesterday and will be forever. Here, I am on the brink of a tomorrow a little richer and a little freer. I glimpse a summit where a little more light will smile upon me. From that more elevated place, my gaze will embrace a broader, gentler and stronger landscape, a new appeal will encourage my soul. And perhaps I shall say: 'O planet Earth, you whom I once called my mother, I know now that you are my father.'"

"You're very sure, then, of leaving the Earth. I would have thought that, like the days that are commonly called life, similar destinies repeat for a long time."

"You're right. But the short days of winter lead, through their tears, toward the smiling days of spring, toward the broad and eloquent days of summer. Through the hours, each of which resembles its elder sister, the child eventually becomes an adolescent, then an adult. I feel within myself an astonishing mixture of sadness and joy; I am wholly agitated by the prophetic anxiety that makes the sap of trees seethe as April approaches, and the sap of adolescents seethe at the approach of puberty. If I divine something other than the Earth, it is because I'm very close to something else.

"Oh, the ineffable and profoundly desired strangeness that the horizon promises me! My eyes can see, I tell you that the eyes of my mind can see. What do they see? I can't say. A vague promise that calls to me, and whose momentarily-drifting smile makes me slightly afraid. Something like love, for the virgin who has not yet loved and who does not know what it is to love—but she can perceive in the distance that which will soon be all her joy.

"Oh, that which I can see is too new. I cannot compare it to anything that you know. Words compare the less familiar to the more familiar, and this, I cannot name. But that which has no name has no fixity. Fixity is an error created by words,

119

which, unchanging, think they are describing immutable things. Names, you are always lies. And for that reason, even if I could, I would not name you, O mystery, O ineffable, O moving beauty, as imprecise as life, or the flickering light beneath a wind-stirred tree."

Psychodorus said: "Everything real is unnamable, because everything progresses toward its opposite, gradually becoming adulterated. Your darkness is increasingly mingled with light. Eventually, it is to be supposed, your light, darkened by the passage of hours, will slowly be extinguished until there is no more, in near-absolute night, than a scarcely-visible promise of a future spark."

"O madman," said Philothanatos, "spring is only just beginning, and you are saddening yourself with the thought of the distant winter, which, after so many smiles, after the powerful eloquence of summer and the glorious opulence of autumn, will prepare the renewed youth of another spring."

Philothanatos parted from the cynic. He started running again, waving his arms, shouting: "O my mother, you are my father!" Soon, a troop of children was running after him, jeering. Fat merchants and their wives came to their doors to watch with poor eyes that thought they could see, and laugh with wide mouths—for one is glad to feel healthy in the company of a sick man, and one glorifies one's common sense when a madman passes by.

XII. The Job

Hostile to passers-by, bristling with thorns, a hedge separated the orchard from the road. Psychodorus was hungry and thirsty. The fruits were to him what the prostitutes who call out to him are to a young man.

He took a run and, with the aid of his staff, vaulted over the hedge.

While he was eating a delicious grape, he heard a lamentation. One might have taken it for a dog whining. The philosopher looked around, but could see neither a human nor an animal.

He picked another fruit. The plant changed into a cry, a violent threat that was trying to pronounce articulate speech but which, unable to do so, was annoyed by its impotence.

Finally, a word was howled: "Thief!"

Psychodorus searched for whatever owner or imbecile was insulting him thus. He only discovered one of those scarecrows that gardeners perch in a tree to frighten birds away. Beneath a cloak flapping in every gust of wind, there was the dry rigidity of a bundle of straw. Bunched rags, however, made the manikin a rudimentary head and enormous deformed arms that awkwardly clutched a bow armed with its arrow.

The scarecrow's cloak was old and full of holes, but it was made of sturdy cloth and for a long time the cynic had regretted finding nothing in the ruins but one of purple silk. Psychodorus climbed the tree and exchanged clothes with the bundle of straw, which insulted him three times over:

"Thief! Thief! Thief!"

But the philosopher, sitting on a stout branch, ate fruit from the tree, and when he was sated, he made this smiling speech to his enemy:

"I sympathize with you, human appearance, poor passively obedient creature. I commiserate with you, O naïve and incomplete individual, who take your job so seriously. Here you are, created amid the torments of a servile soul. If Socrates, judging the generals of the Arginusae, had taken his function as a judge seriously—the function of a judge, as I know from numerous experiences, is to condemn—on that day, Socrates could not have done better than you."[15]

---

[15] The Arginusae are a group of islands, where a sea battle was fought in 406 B.C. in which a makeshift Athenian fleet sent to relieve a Spartan blockade achieved an unexpected victory. Unfortunately, a storm then blew up which prevented the Athenians from rescuing the survivors of 25 damaged or sunken triremes, who eventually perished. The Athenians were so

The scarecrow was not listening. A sentry must only hear the voice of his superior officers. The memory of their orders must be always present in his ears, deafening them to any word originating outside, and constructing the rigid unity of his consciousness.

On the bundle of straw, the ball of rags repeated, in ever-shriller cries: "Thief! Thief! Thief!"

The deformed arms shivered, agitatedly. They even ended up firing the arrow. They were unskillful; the arrow hit a fruit, which fell to Earth with a dull thud.

Psychodorus got down from the tree, and was about to leave the orchard when the owner arrived, perceived the thief and marched furiously toward him. But as he passed close to the scarecrow, he heard a call. He raised his eyes and saw the manikin waving its arms. The unexpectedness of that talking and gesticulating life frightened the man, who fainted.

The next day, Psychodorus returned to the orchard. He greeted the scarecrow with these mocking words:

"Rejoice, O ordinary man, O social animal. I've come to see whether your consciousness and our efforts have finally given you legs with which to pursue those to eat your master's property without permission."

While Psychodorus ate, the manikin cried out in a clearer voice than the previous day: "Stop, thief! Stop, thief!"

Now, the owner of the orchard heard. He came, hiding behind the hedge. He fired an arrow, which struck Psychodorus in the leg and caused him to fall. Then, helped by people who were passing, he bound the wounded man's hands and feet and took him before the Magistrate.

---

incensed by this that they demanded that six of the fleet's eight generals be put on trial. On the one and only day when he ever served as president of the Athenian assembly, Socrates blocked the motion, but only succeeded in delaying the trial and the mass execution.

The cynic was condemned, naturally, since, possessing nothing, he had the audacity to feel hunger and to eat. The trial was banal and insignificant. Nevertheless, one detail struck the philosopher.

The judge asked the proprietor: "Weren't you astonished to hear that heap of rags and straw speak?"

The other gave a reply that seemed to Psychodorus to sum up all the pride of human science:

"No," he said, shrugging his shoulders. "There was nothing astonishing about it; it wasn't the first time."

XIII. The Bulls

Leg-weary, Psychodorus was sitting in a clump of oleanders. There was no one visible in the nearby road. Only an increasing noise populated the future. One might have thought it the pompous grinding of triumphal chariots amid the approaching tramp of an army. But the sound, unexplained by any vision, retained a certain mystery and, like a word in an ill-known language, a quiver of uncertainty.

Finally, his eyes saw. A first cart appeared. To the shaft, of which there was only one, of unexpected length, some 40 men were harnessed. Their only clothing was a harness, and they were pulling, sweating and panting in the Sun's heat. The heavy cart, with badly-rounded wheels, jolted as it advanced. There was a bull in it. The animal sometimes uttered articulate bellowings, which were orders. If obedience was slow, it struck out with a goad manipulated by its skillful mouth.

Numerous carts followed the first. The first ten resembled one another like poor brothers. The next ten were made of richer wood, less coarsely worked. The bulls that guided them were proudly wearing green costumes and horns decorated with silver. Then other carts came, ornamented with increasingly beautiful fabrics, and the gilded horns of the richly-dressed drivers were proudly upstanding, shining in the sunlight.

Surrounded by 1000 bulls devoid of armor, which marched on foot, a marvelous cart entirely draped in gold solemnly advanced. Immense, it was drawn by 500 men. An awning of barbarous richness sheltered a family of oxen. The eldest, doubtless the King, was covered by a strangely luminous cloak, which seemed to be woven in diamond. Around each of his horns, stones of various colors formed a spiral. His broad neck was surrounded by a necklace of gems. Bracelets of pearls circled his thighs. The Queen and four young bulls, their sons, wore analogous ornaments that were only a little less rich.

Psychodorus noticed the feminine grace of the King's daughter. Sitting in the midst of her brothers, she benefited from a slimmer figure. Her muzzle was slightly parted before the soft moistness of her gaze, as if smiling.

Behind the royal carriage trailed and entire procession of carts, which became gradually less rich. When the entire astonishing cortège had passed by, Psychodorus rose to his feet and followed it.

He arrived at the gate of a city and entered with the crowd, without being noticed. Oxen were bellowing loud acclamations from the windows. Lower-class heifers were throwing flowers but elegant fashion dictated that upper-class cows had the tips of their horns cut off in early youth, which they then filled with perfumes, and during great ceremonies like today's they leaned over gracefully to cause the essences to flow in the direction of those they wished to honor. That same gesture, made in private with a male, took on a tender or—according to vicious tongues—symbolic significance.

The horns at one window turned toward Psychodorus, like accusative pointing fingers. Bulls immediately surrounded the philosopher and, prodding him with goads, drove him to the prison.

The next day, the cynic was removed from his cell and taken to the palace. He was sat down at the King's table and, like the oxen, ate prepared grasses. They were cooked in human milk and scented with unknown spices. They were served on gold dishes, on an onyx table,

Psychodorus was then allowed to walk, according to his whim, throughout the interior of the palace—but if he tried to leave it, a goad drove him back.

He was still accorded considerable liberty. His only obligations were not to go out of the grounds, to partake of the principal meal every day, and to listen, before that meal, to a long speech—always the same one—that a bull recited to him with menacing pomp.

Psychodorus was not astonished to rediscover among the oxen of the court the faults of rich humans. They were indolent, vain, capricious and demanding. The ones who guarded the doors, armed with goads, were no less brutally coarse than the mercenaries of tyrants.

The human palace servants were as cringingly craven as dogs. They devoted themselves to pleasing their masters and had no social intercourse with their fellows, except when sudden lust precipitated a male and female together for a rapid sex act, soon forgotten. Their lips, ignorant of smiles, did not form words; they uttered cries that expressed their meager passions—the gross pleasure of appeased hunger, physical suffering, anger or dread—without any nuances. They understood the most common of the bellowings articulated by the oxen, however.

They were employed for various tasks. They built, they cooked, they wove fabrics—but their efforts remained exclusively mechanical. A taurean weaver, chef or architect guided their ignorant gestures. They were blind forces directed from without, which a foreign intelligence utilized in unknown interests. Their work resembled the work of a mill that grinds corn, provided that the grain is passed through it.

Psychodorus had been in the King's household for more than a month when he suddenly understood the declamatory speech that was repeated to him every day before the main meal.

This is what it said:

"Savage human, listen.

"Many generations ago, the bulls, masters of the universe, fought a war against the savage humans from the impenetrable forest. The savage humans were perfidious warriors. They would surprise a few of our richer herds of domesticated humans in distant regions and destroy them. They would not dare to not attack us. They always fled with cowardly screams without awaiting our initial charge, but from a distance, or from hiding, they fired arrows that seemed harmless. Our ancestors bellowed mockingly at first, ripping the darts from their scarcely-scratched hide. Alas, a few hours later, they did mysteriously in atrocious pain, as if they had eaten some poisonous grass.

"Nevertheless, the savage humans were vanquished. Almost all of them were killed. A few found their salvation in the impenetrable forest.

"After the victory, we remembered what had happened before the war. The savage humans had sent some of their number among us, who, pretending to love and admire us, carefully studied our strengths and weaknesses in order to assist in killing us thereafter.

"A law was proclaimed, which declared this:

"Any human who wears clothes is a savage human.

"Savage humans are cowards and liars. They return evil for good. They only leave the forest with the intention of spying or fighting perfidiously.

"Any clothed human found in the land of the invincible bulls will be considered as a spy. He will be imprisoned in the royal palace. For ten moons he will be able to observe everything. He will only be obliged to attend the main meal every day and hear the present law recited. On the last day of the tenth moon, however, he will be sufficiently instructed, and he will be sent to take the results of his espionage to the land of shadows."

Psychodorus was not ready to die. The eyes of the King's daughter turned toward him, moist with pity, every time the

law was read to him. He had noticed that. He saw a slight frisson run through the heifer whenever she met him. He noticed
other promising signs—and he recalled that the Greek heroes
had often been saved by barbarian daughters.

He resolved to seduce the young cow.

He took advantage of every opportunity to tell her about
his travels. With the truth and clever inventions he composed
an intoxicating mixture, and the wine of his words aroused a
drunkenness of pity and love in the child. Sometimes, carried
away and incapable of restraining herself, she displayed her
sentiment ostentatiously, as a bacchante bears a thyrsus[16]—but
he pretended not to see anything. Even when she leaned forward timidly and allowed a few drops of perfume to flow from
her horns, he smiled in his heart but gave no indication that he
had noticed the imprudent declaration.

He also related, several times over, how the Greek heroes
beloved by barbarian processes had abducted them for the
sake of pleasure. He forgot to tell her how these stories ended.
The young cow never found out that Jason had betrayed Medea, or that Theseus had abandoned Ariadne.

By means of one last story he destroyed the sole interior
objection that might perhaps still have deterred the amorous
heifer. He described the subjection of cattle in the lands go-
verned by humans. Then he related the loves of Pasiphae.[17] He
insinuated that the sensuality uniting different species is singularly great. He praised the glorious power of the Minotaur.

---

[16] A thyrsus was a fennel rod carried by Dionysus or his fol-
lowers. In Euripides' famous tragedy *The Bacchae* the thyrsi
carried by the eponymous wild women are said to drip honey.

[17] Pasiphae, the wife of the great Cretan King Minos, bore him
numerous children, but was also said to have given birth to
Asterion, alias the Minotaur, after being cursed by Poseidon
and impregnated by a white bull—a story that was retold incessantly by numerous classical authors, with an ever-
increasing spice of obscene detail.

Impudently, he affirmed that reliable prophecies promised the domination of the future to some such hybrid race.

Even then, he made no direct declaration. A naïve uncertainty aggravated the amorous female's emotion. Finally, no longer holding back her tears, she cried: "One more moon, and you, who are beauty, intelligence and bounty, will be put to death."

The artful Greek replied at first in a murmur, as if he were speaking unwittingly in a reverie, or as if he did not want to be heard. "What does the destruction of my body matter to me?" he said. "My soul has been dead for a long time. You died, my poor soul, on the day I arrived here, drawn by indomitable love. My eyes, alas, had seen a beauty and a love too elevated for me; a love that had not the slightest trace of hope had overwhelmed me."

His voice, which was trembling, slowly grew louder. First there were slow and timid approaches. Then there was a great cry, that could no longer be contained—and after that, the boldest and craziest avowal of love, as vast, active and hot as a blazing fire, poured out.

That stirring speech continued until the heifer, forgetting the modesty of her sex, cried: "I love you and I will save you—and my glory will be greater than that of Ariadne or Medea. And we shall be the ancestors of the Minotaurs who will trample the tamed future beneath their four feet."

The heifer took Psychodorus through the subterranean tunnels that led outside the city. They fled together, a long way.

Several times she asked: "Why won't you become my husband?"

"You're still too young," he replied, amid caresses.

On morning, he was sitting on the sea-shore while she went in search of food. He saw a ship not far away. He swam out to it, and obtained a passage thereon.

Often, though, remorse assured him that it would have been better to die than to deceive. Often, he accused himself with these words:

"The faults of my cunning race still live within me, then. O philosophy, are you nothing but a badly-fastened cloak which, in the wind of danger, lays my deceptive soul bare?"

XIV. The Statues

The statues were crowded together like the trees of a forest—but the forest of statues was an endless undergrowth in which a few giants, looming over the dwarfs, attracted the gaze from afar. Rare forms stood forth, beautiful, noble and solid. The statue commoners were ugly, shaky and huddled together in vast numbers—a populace both sketchy and ruinous, it formed a kind of vast debris.

The heroic or smiling outlines seemed to be sources of light, but a petty darkness, like a sad mist emerging from a marsh, rose up from the ignominy of the crumbling masses.

Psychodorus considered the few, feeling uplifted by an exciting and seemingly active emotion, and he said: "You are beautiful as well as joyful." But he turned to the others with these words: "You are as ugly as woe."

Now, something warned him, as he said it, that his words were richer than his thoughts. It was as if the noble statues had proclaimed: "We are, indeed, joyful." Meanwhile, the populace would have lamented: "Alas, alas! It is only too true that we are woeful."

Psychodorus almost believed these words, which no mouth had proffered but which his soul had heard. His mind soon rebelled, though, addressing mocking reproaches to him.

"O Psychodorus," it said, "you have seen so many strange and dreamlike things that you can no longer distinguish dreams from realities. You affirm your dreams dully, as if other men, transported to the same places, would be obliged to see what you see and feel what you feel. Know, Psychodorus, there is nothing here, for eyes less crazy or less wise than yours, but beautiful and ugly statues."

Something told Psychodorus that his mind was mistaken, however, and that prudence is a blind person whose gropings understand very little. If gropings denied what boldness and dreams saw, they were greater liars than dreams or boldness. And the philosopher became increasingly certain that he was walking amid woes and encountering a few joys here and there.

He saw without astonishment something that would have alarmed an ordinary mind. The joys were almost all made of clay or some other material that humans did not hold in high esteem. The woes were made of all known materials. The majority were also made of clay, mud, or even dung, but some were made of marble or gold. In several of them, various materials, some precious and some vile, served to compose the ignoble grimace of a crumbling body and a weeping face.

The philosopher recognized, or thought he recognized, a few of the statues. One of them, sculpted in a hard and poor-quality rock, but as large as a god and more beautiful than all the gods, with lips whose silent immobility was eloquent and inspired new thoughts in the onlooker, caught the traveler's gaze for a long time. Finally, Psychodorus said to that one: "I recognize you, O master of masters, O midwife of so many noble minds, you who many call all beautiful doctrines your daughters!" And familiarly, as is fitting when one addresses the great Familiar Spirit, he added: "O Socrates, what have you done with your snub nose? Interior and eternal beauty has now obliterated temporary appearance, O Socrates, god who no longer hides himself."

He spoke for some time in praise of the Man who was able to provoke thought and speech. Then, following the direction of Socrates' gaze, he turned toward a strange spectacle. It was a sinister and equivocal mass in which, amid mud and filth, shone fragments of gold, pearls as delicate as drips of light and precious stones as varied as the colors of the rainbow. An unspecifiable aura of grace floated over the definitive ugliness of that ruin. Like an impotent lamp lost in a desert of darkness, something that might have been a smile lifted a corner of the grimacing mouth.

Psychodorus turned away regretfully, saying; "O Alicibiades, marvelous beauty destroyed by a soul."

He drew away, further affirming: "Joy, woe, you are forms. The Fates furnish us with noble or vile material, but our souls, valiant or cowardly sculptors, shape you."

He went on in this fashion, thinking about the strange collaboration of destiny and the soul, thinking that the vulgar see only the materials of a life, impotent as they are to seize, with a synthetic gaze, the harmony or lack of harmony therein. O you who grimace beneath heroes, the only happy people, you merit the torture of your ugliness—for none of you, if given the choice would cry: "I want to be Socrates!" But all of you, with avid and enthusiastic lips, would say to yourselves: "Oh that I might be Alcibiades!"

An excavation, not very deep and not very large—more a furrow than a ditch—extended in front of Psychodorus. But Psychodorus, having paused on the edge of the obstacle, saw that the obstacle was retreating at a slow and regular pace. On the other side was a thick mist, which retreated with the ditch. As it did so, statues that had been vague moments before became more precise in the new light.

"I'm among the joys and woes of the dead," the philosopher thought. "Behind the ditch are the statues that are still works in progress, but the moving limit continuously enlarges one of the two domains, setting aside the statues that the finger of death has just completed."

Psychodorus ran toward the retreating ditch. He caught up with it, and with one bound he was on the other side. He continued on his way among the living statues, which he heard howling—but he could not make out anything precise. Beneath the hands of fever or wisdom, countless agitations that were probably crazy, and a few rhythms that might have been noble, the mist only permitted vague contours to be seen.

Curiously, the philosopher said: "I'd like to see the statue of Psychodorus."

He searched for a long time. Finally, he thought he had found it—but here the fog became an opaque darkness, and Psychodorus could not see anything of the work that his soul was doing with his destiny. He could not even tell whether there was a dogged conflict swirling at the center of the cloud, or a harmonious collaboration smiling there.

He stayed there for hours on end, hoping that the spectacle might suddenly appear in some kind of flash. He searched for the great joys and great pains of his past, renewing them and waving them like torches. None of the smoky torches that his memory extracted from the river of time gave enough light to tear the curtain of darkness behind which Psychodorus' soul was working, even for a second.

Several times he left, only to come back. In the end, he understood that he would not see anything. He was reduced to telling himself: "I know myself and I know my destiny. I am valiant; it is mediocre. In the vile and difficult material that it offers me, I am sure that I am slowly creating a crude harmony."

Desire brought him back to the visible completed destinies.

"O Athenatime," he said, "it's you for whom I'm searching. Undoubtedly, I shall see you, statue whose sketch I loved, more blissful than your smile, more beautiful than your adulterated living beauty, and as the heavens holds sway over the Earth, your present tranquil nobility will hold sway over your past effort toward nobility.

He searched for a long time. His eyes were athirst for the limpid water that they knew. Every time he distinguished female beauty amid the population of forms he broke into a run. Before he had arrived, his eyes would quench themselves on hope, as one quenches oneself upon a mirage in the desert, but he always found a foreign sand instead of the cherished spring.

Finally, he was certain that he had perceived the desired statue, for his heart was beating rapidly and his head became dizzy, as if on the edge of a precipice of joy. The closer he came, the more voracious and tenebrous the vertigo became. He ran, anxious with expectation and sensuality.

When he reached the fortunate distance from which he already hoped to distinguish clearly the beauty of the contours and the emanated light, he could no longer see anything. A strange cloud, as narrow and long as a white headscarf, had placed itself between himself and his beloved from the beginning. Now that opaque whiteness was over his eyes. No effort of his fingers could grip it and tear it away. His finger passed impotently through the obstacle, which they could not even feel, let alone rip apart. Their vain effort was agitated, like a lukewarm and indifferent wave.

When Psychodorus understood, after a thousand futile attempts, that he would never be able to see, he wanted at least to touch the harmony of the contours. Destiny did not forbid that—but every time, his amorous hands were so tremulous that they could not inform themselves of anything foreign. They knew only the joy of Psychodorus and revealed nothing else when they thought they were proclaiming the beauty of Athenatime. They affirmed it in a mad, hesitant haste, and the eloquence of their enthusiasm was frequently greater before encountering the body than after having felt it.

Psychodorus heard the order to go away. He went, turning round every few steps, but not distinguishing anything precise.

"O amour!" he said to himself, "O joyous and dolorous vertigo, we never know anything about the one we love. Emotions are moving torches, which agitate so many dazzling shadows before our soul."

XV. The Phantoms

A rampart loomed up on the plain. Psychodorus wanted to change direction and avoid the banality of a city, but a gust of wind seemed to open up an ephemeral breach in the wall, which sealed itself.

The philosopher shrugged his shoulders, telling himself that he was seeing things, but said nevertheless: "O city, banal as you are to other eyes, since you are a creator of dreams to me, I shall go toward you."

When he was at the foot of the wall, he perceived that it was made of mist. He was able to pass through it effortlessly. It was thick, though; he emerged from it damp and shivering.

There were no houses behind the deceptive wall—not even a city built of lies and fog. To the rampart that separated the two halves of the identical plan, Psychodorus said: "In spite of your vague reality, to me you are, above all, a symbol—and I shall call you Death."

But the mist was a curtain, which stirred in a wind of negation or mockery.

"I sense," Psychodorus continued, "that you are also something else. I have come to this place to learn some new truth, not merely to find once again those that I knew so clearly in the land of the Rooted People."

The curtain fell again, massive and seemingly immutable—a wall of affirmation.

The abandoned side of the plain had been deserted. Here, it did not take long for Psychodorus to encounter a few inhabitants, and he noticed some strange things about them.

They were always in pairs, one running behind the other. The one who was fleeing seemed to be made of the same mist as the wall, but the one who was in pursuit, without ever catching up, was made of flesh.

All these individuals were small. Among the people of flesh, the tallest bore the faces of old people on the bodies of adolescents. Others had the stature of children. Some were only as big as Psychodorus' hand, his index-finger or his thumb. A few were like strange ants with human faces standing on two feet.

Statures were no less varied among the pursued phantoms.

The philosopher soon noticed a singular rule. The larger the phantom was, the smaller the human was. When the fleshy individual was as small as an ant, the misty individual was as tall as a man, but if the human had the stature of an adolescent, the misty form was as tiny as a baby.

Amid the incoherent flights, Psychodorus shouted: "Who are you, O phantoms? And you, short and tall humans? And you, implausible dwarfs?"

The phantoms replied in a thousand voices, some as uncertain and tremulous as a virgin's first imposture, others as haughty and powerful as a royal proclamation, and a few as soft as persuasion—but they all said: "We are the lies of humankind."

Those who were pursuing them stopped, hesitantly, because they had revealed themselves to be liars.

Psychodorus thought, dolorously, of the princess of the land of the bulls, whom he had seduced with false promises and had abandoned after swearing eternal love.

Now the phantoms were also stopping, and, pointing at the diminished beings, they said: "You see what remains of liars."

XVI. The Laborious People

There were a great many people. They were marching upright on their feet and speaking an articulate language, but their form astonished Psychodorus. The first precise singularity that struck his gaze was the multiplicity of their arms and hands. He tried to count them, but the numerous members, some long and powerful, others short and slender, were distributed too randomly about the head, the upper body and the legs. Other, small ones, covered them, just as smaller branches, twigs and leaves cover boughs. And all those arms were a people at work. Occasionally, one would droop, exhaustedly, pausing in a relaxed position. Almost immediately, a start set it to work again; it hastened, weary and ashamed, like an idle slave caught out by an implacable master.

In this country, there was no night. The work of the arms, slender or strong, was continuous. There was no gentleness of slumber, no tenebrous peace. Over the infinite multiple agitation of each body was the immobility of a Sun that always remained a perpendicular blaze.

There were no houses, and no clothing—no other protection against the fierce bite of the Sun than a few trees. The people sometimes disputed the shade in brief combats. Inexorable and urgent necessities soon separated the adversaries, who both fled.

Nourishment—wild fruits, bitter acorns, animals that were difficult to trap amid the multiple preoccupations of each mind—was scarce. When two people encountered the same aliment, the battle lasted longer than for shade—perhaps a minute. Then at least one of the combatants fell down dead. More often, both adversaries covered the soil with the multiple spasms of their brief death-throes. Some, however, got up and drew away weakly, their arms working more rapidly than ever. None seemed to have succumbed to the impotent blows of the enemy, but they had doubtless forgotten some vital necessity in the ardor of the struggle, like ordinary people who have driven themselves for several days and nights without any food or sleep.

Beneath the incessant agitation of a thousand hands, it seemed that the bodies presented other singularities. Nothing could be made out precisely; the moving hands covered the nudity of these people like the quivering of a thousand rags and tatters, rising and falling with every passing second.

Psychodorus tried to interrogate the Laborious People. They had no time to chat. They protested, painfully or angrily, against the preoccupation that gripped them in a thousand ways: "Me!" they howled. "Me, my myriad selves!"

The philosopher discovered all the bizarreries of their bodies, however, for he studied some of the cadavers that they left indifferently to rot beneath the immobility of the Sun.

The majority of the organs hidden in us, they bore visibly. The lungs were on their torsos, like grotesque breasts.

Their heart, liver, stomach, intestines and kidneys, ignobly naked, were suspended from their vertebrae like joints of meat on a butcher's hooks. Muscles, veins and arteries connected all these horrors like dirty cords.

Psychodorus understood the terrible labor to which these individuals condemned their hands—the terrible labor with which a thousand simultaneous necessities peppered and rent the mind. On the orders of anxious thought, the hands had to pump the lungs engorge with impure air as one squeezes dirty water out of a sponge; then they dilated the living sponges, filling them with the joyous purity of air—but soon, it was necessary to expel hat newly-vitiated air. How many needs, on every part of the body, propelled the hands and minds in such inexorable circles! Hands, on the anxious orders if thought, had to squeeze the elastic inertia of the heart to make the purified blood flow through the arteries, and to take the impure blood to the lungs so that the air might wash it. It was also necessary, by a thousand weak pressures on the immobile arteries, to make the nourishing blood flow through the entire body; and by a thousand pressures on the slothful veins to bring the heavy blood deprived of its virtues back to the heart. Meanwhile, other hands, the large hands, searched, under the direction of eyes that were always haggard and fearful, for uncertain nourishment. When the teeth had chewed it, tiny hands guided it along the digestive canal, grinding it in the stomach, pressing the liver and various other glands to pour on to the aliments the liquids that would render them assimilable.

At every moment, the mind, occupied with too many things, forgot one of them. A vague pain murmured an appeal, and if the appeal was not heard, it would soon cry out clearly, then howl mortally. The mind hastened to give orders; the hand hastened to soothe. But sometimes, the cries of pain came from several places. The mind was a general who saw his army weakening on every side, and who no longer knew what use to make of his reserves. A moment's disturbance and hesitation, one of ten urgent orders give a few seconds too late, and the body was nothing but a cadaver.

Psychodorus drew away from a spectacle that was painful enough to drive one mad. He sympathized with the Laborious People. He congratulated himself for the fact all the tasks to which they were condemned were satisfied with his intervention or needless exertion of his body.

"I'm glad," he said, "that my lungs know how to breathe without my paying any heed to them. I'm glad that my blood is immobile, or flows so spontaneously that I think it immobile. I'm glad that my heart makes its necessary movements by itself. I'm glad to be able to ignore the labor of my stomach, and the work of my liver and all my other organs."

Amid scornful laughter, he recalled a rich sophist who went about saying: "Multiply your needs to multiply your pleasures." The unfortunate had made a thousand artificial necessities and he had the hands of countless slaves to serve him. But his mind, as sadly ingenious as a poor man's, scarcely moved to gratify the scant matter that was his body, such incoherent material. He gave his limbs the slow joy of idleness and the brief joy of pleasure, but his soul was the most oppressed of slaves, the most overwhelmed of maddening needs.

Besides which, the souls of most humans seemed to Psychodorus to be like the deplorable bodies of the Laborious People. They too were made of a thousand troubles, tortured by a thousand needs and a thousand tasks, dispersed among a thousand feverish little hands—but the soul of Socrates or the soul of Diogenes stood up as harmoniously as the leisure of a beautiful statue, like the serene intellect of Athene or even the easily triumphant smile of Aphrodite.

XVII. The Interval

All of a sudden, Psychodorus was in darkness. And, just as no light reached his eyes, his ears perceived no sound. And his feet, which were still moving forward, did not feel the resistance of the ground at all.

"A strange dream!" Psychodorus thought. Then, with an effort of sincerity, he admitted that he was not dreaming. "Doubtless I have gone blind and deaf," he affirmed. But he could not explain, even by the sacrifice of his two noble senses, why his feet, which were still walking, no longer felt the resistant ground.

He devoted himself to that particular enigma. He ended up amusing himself with one of those illusory solutions that, from nursery rhymes onwards, sometimes suffice to appease our minds—for we need to believe that we understand, and our soul scarcely hesitates to proclaim the complete solidity of the abyss.

"My eyes and ears," he said to himself, "assist my touch. Touch is a naïve and primitive sense. More a friend of plea-sure than science, its knowledge comes to it from hearing and sight, and it always remains a child in need of guidance. My blindness and deafness have left my touch an orphan. Its frigh-tened stammer dares not affirm a ground that I cannot see and whose resonance I cannot hear. Oh, how everything mixes within us, and how complex is that which appears simple to us!"

A troubling objection occurred to him, however. "People generally say the opposite of what I thought just now. The absence of a sense is compensated by will-power and the re-finement of the other senses, and a blind man's fingers see almost as well as myopic eyes."

With a simple mental gesture, however, he got rid of the obstacle. "The blind man's touch is refined by habit, in the same way that a child with no protector becomes braver and cleverer than others—but on the day when he father has just died, a fearful despair renders him, for a while, inferior to what he was the day before. The suddenness of the loss of two senses has, for a few hours, annulled by other senses."

He started running over the unresistant ground. His qua-si-airborne course gave him the impression of flying over a black desert—or, rather, his legs seemed to him to be strange oars soundlessly plied in a tenebrous liquid, so tenuous that it seemed to require no effort to work upon it.

Now Psychodorus became afraid, and like a tremulous child, lamented aloud.

"Alas," he moaned, "I'm blind and deaf!" No, he did not finish the entire sentence. His voice faded away. His legs stopped, paralyzed by astonishment. He had heard his voice say: "Alas, I'm…"

After a pause, he said: "Am I deaf? No, I'm not deaf." He heard his question and his reply.

Then a gesture of amazement raised his arms, and in the blackness he saw two vague glimmers appear, long and thick. Increasingly alarmed, he murmured: "I'm not blind. I can see my arms."

He lowered his haggard eyes toward his body. He could see his cloak, and also the parts of his body that his short and hole-ridden cloak left uncovered.

He sat down on the absent ground, which supported him nevertheless. Then he lay down. In the darkness, he was like a god who does not even need a cloud to sustain his glorious flesh.

His mind was a reef battered by a sea of disquiet, and the tempest was increasing, multiplying its howling waves.

Psychodorus was not deaf, since he could hear his voice. He was not blind, and was not even in darkness, since he could see himself and his garment.

Like a dog howling at death, a wave of the great tempest of disquiet affirmed: "There is nothing to see and nothing to hear. Alive, you have entered the land of nothingness." Anxiously, the philosopher interrogated himself: "Do I believe in nothingness, then, and admit that non-being exists?"

For some time, he had difficulty forcing himself not to reply: yes. Finally, though, his courage got a grip on him. In a voice louder than the folly that was trying to overwhelm him, he cried: "No, no, a million times no. Non-being does not exist. If the meaningless term can darken my mind, it is because my valiant groping has not yet encountered the thought whose impact will clarify the matter."

To affirm life, he stood up and began walking at random. His anguish demanded: "But where am I, then? And what strange reality might be hiding behind this apparent nothingness?"

As gentle as one of Athenatime's caresses, an interior voice replied: "You are in a land as populous as an opulent city."

Momentarily, though, that caress irritated him, as the most timid of contacts can irritate a wound.

Soon, discouragement enveloped Psychodorus. The nothingness surrounding him seemed to be defeating him by degrees and dismantling his soul. His heartbeat slowed down progressively and the traveler finally stopped, motionless in the infinite monotony of despair.

He went to sleep. A dream consoled him with a vague explanation, as white and cheerful as the dawn. On awakening, however, the explanation disappeared. Psychodorus found himself once again in the terrible silence that his voice was able to break, and the astonishing darkness that permitted him to see himself. Fear paralyzed him, though, preventing him from speaking or looking at himself. He dreaded hearing and seeing now. He preferred trying to believe that he was blind and deaf to finding himself lost in the impossible and insane void, for his mind asserted: "To admit nothingness is to die."

Slowly and dismally he walked through the lukewarm indifference of the darkness and silence. At irregular intervals he fell...but did he fall, since there was no ground, sine his fatigue was not due to gravity, and since nothing indicated that there was an up and a down? No, he did not fall. But how could he express the inexpressible? How could he describe something in nothing? What could a human say in nothingness? At irregular intervals, Psychodorus stopped, as if he had fallen down, and he slept.

Every time, the explanation that came to console him grew increasingly luminous, a valiant Sun rising toward its zenith. Every slumber was a generous benefactor that enriched him more than the previous slumber. Alas, awakening was always a brigand that robbed him.

Bereft and mad, he walked…no, he did not even know whether he was walking. He agitated his limbs in a horror that was always equal and unvarying: a horror without end or limit. His despair was a thirst, a frightful burning throughout his soul, which cried out for the refreshment of slumber as death-throes cry out for life. And slumber, it seemed to him, was progressively later in arriving.

Once, however, awakening was a less brutal brigand; the flight of the light was less rapid and less complete. Some kind of flickering glow, too weak to illuminate anything, but nevertheless as delightful as a smile of promise, continued to float in a mind as darkened by ignorance, but less darkened by despair.

And Psychodorus dared to speak. He whispered: "I sense that I will soon be able not to forget. The explanation is almost a Sun at the meridian. It's the fifth hour of the explanation; when the sixth hour comes, Apollo will triumph over all the morning mists.

After a few more slumbers, Psychodorus remembered the consolatory dream. On opening his eyes, he could see, not only himself, but outside, on the edge of the darkness, a vague and irresolute margin of light.

Reaching out toward the promise, he cried: "A horizon! I've rediscovered a horizon!"

Like a swimmer perceiving rescuers, he was no longer agitating hopelessly; mad with joy, he hastened toward the objective and deliverance—and while watching the luminous quiver grow, he recounted his conquering dream.

Athenatime had appeared to him. Athenatime had spoken to him.

"You're right," she had said to him. "Non-being does not exist. The land you're passing through is populated, but your senses are still unaware of its inhabitants, and the senses of its inhabitants are still unaware of you, for they're in your interval."

"What do you mean, Athenatime?"

"Listen, Psychodorus, and finally retain what I shall not come to repeat to you again. Light is only light to your eyes and sound is only audible to your ears. Remove all the beings that resemble you, and there is no longer any sound or light."

"Because in darkness, open eyes do not see anything; because it is not sufficient to listen to hear: sound and light have an external cause. Remove the spectators, and the spectacle will continue."

"There will no longer be a spectacle."

"What will there be?"

"I'll tell you. Outside the organs, outside the mind, sound and light are the same thing: movements, nothing more."

"Why can my eyes not see sounds? Why can my ears not see colors?"

The movement that you can hear is weak. The movement that you can see is strong. Represent by unity the intensity of the moment translated in you by the most violent of sounds; the movement that makes you smile at the palest light of all is perhaps many tens of thousands of times greater.

"Think, Psychodorus, of the immense space that extends between one and many tens of thousands. All that escapes you, too strong to be heard and too weak to be seen. All that, O Psychodorus, is what I call your interval.

"Now, by means of senses that you cannot imagine, the inhabitants of the land that you are going through are only aware of movements that are too weak for your eyes and too strong for your ears. The objects that encumber the region are of such a nature that you can neither see them nor hear them. Precise forms for others, they are to your touch too coarse or too delicate, intangible fluids that open and flee. Even your senses of taste and smell, those subtler touches, cannot reach

143

them. And the people that are aware of all these things of which you are unaware cannot be aware of anything of which you are aware."

Athenatime had then said: "Wake up, Psychodorus, and remember."

Psychodorus repeated the last words of the dream at the moment when he finally arrived at the luminous edge. He re-entered the world accessible to his senses. A thousand objects delighted his eyes; the vast harmony of a thousand sounds delighted his ears.

He turned round and saw nothing. It was as if he were blind when he looked behind him, but could see when he looked ahead.

Precipitating himself into his rediscovered life, mad with joy, he said: "O marvels! There are worlds in the intervals of other worlds. As water slips between stones, as air fills empty vases, beings and objects impossible to imagine fill all nothingness. Non-being does not exist. Or rather, it is everywhere, made of ignorances. O ignorances, strange partitions between various sciences impenetrable to one another…"

XVIII. A War of Religion

Psychodorus was crossing a vast plain. He shared the opinion of cynics who, without explaining things, limit themselves to the advice that one should live simply and sincerely. Other doctrines all seemed to him to be beautiful and fragile. He admired people who had seized their dreams in magical hands and imposed a visible form on them.

Lovingly, he said: "O Democritus! O Heraclitus! O Parmenides! O Plato!" And then he said: "O creators of beauty!"

His thought criticized the negators, however—those who, with a dismissive gesture, dispersed the beauty ordained by others. To one of them, he addressed these reproaches:

"O Zeno, O ingenious brutality, why deny movement? Is it not sufficient to affirm immobility? Parmenides and Heraclitus each look at one side of the mountain, and you are wrong to deny what Heraclitus sees. Being is—but becoming becomes. In all immobility, every detail stirs. Every appearance participates in being, since being reveals it. Or rather, Being is the invariable sum of changing appearances. Proteus is that fire now; a little while ago he was that water; soon he will be that bull or that dog. Proteus is but the total of Protean forms, plus the ability to change form. But Proteus without form is no longer anything. Each phenomenon is not Being, but it is a little of being that is colored and alive. Take away all color and all life, and Being would no longer be."

He said then: "How right my master Diogenes was to refute you wordlessly, and to walk toward you—you who denied movement by moving your tongue."

Then he criticized Aristotle: "Love your truth and your mistress, O Aristotle. Make them both pregnant and love their children. But by what right do you beat the children of others? Love Nicomachus and the consequences of your principles— but you become coarse and vulgar when you deny the beauty of other people's mistresses and doctrines. Athenatime was as beautiful as Pythias and Herpylis, and Plato's truth was worth as much as yours."

He also thought about the soldiers of Xerxes who, because they worshipped a god vaster and vaguer than the gods of Greece, burned the definite beauty of Greek temples. And he said: "O Zeno, O Aristotle, like barbarians, you bring sacrilegious torches into the temples built by Heraclius and Plato— but you will be punished. Odious disputers, born of you, will strike at you; you will be the fathers of numerous parricides."

While he was going about thus, thinking about his own ideas and those of others, a loud noise exhorted him to look at the external world.

He saw innumerable people advancing, an entire army without weapons. Those who were marching at the front bore, on a magnificent dais, a statue as beautiful as beauty. All of them were singing the praises of the statue.

145

Psychodorus smiled, approving of them. Soon, though, he shook his head sadly, for the canticles proclaimed that no other statue was beautiful.

Now, from the opposite direction, still distant, other men were arriving, just as numerous. They were carrying a marble image of marvelous beauty, with pieties no less aggressive. When they were close enough for Psychodorus to be able to compare the statues, he truly did not know which of them deserved he prize; he liked the two beauties equally—and it seemed to him that bringing them together further embellished them both.

The two companies exchanged hostile words for some time. Then the bearers marched against one another and the statues collided, amid frightful clamors.

The marbles collided several times. The arms were broken, the foreheads and cheeks scratched, and the noseless heads both become ugly. Even the bodies did not escape unscathed from the abominable conflict.

The two companies finally turned their backs on one another. Each one triumphantly bore away the formless debris of that which had delighted the eyes—and on both sides, the barbarous canticles proclaimed: "O you, sole beauty, further embellished by your victory over a feeble rival!"

XIX. The Amorous

At the summit of the mountain there was a narrow vertical hole. Leaning over the opening, Psychodorus heard noises that intrigued him. He lay down on the ground and listened. It seemed to him that they were the voices of men and women, muffled by distance. They were mingled with the hissing of serpents, the singing of birds and the purring of tigers—but the hissing, singing and purring had a surprising kinship with the voices.

Psychodorus listened all night. The subterranean noises never ceased. In the morning, the philosopher decided that he would try to find out what marvels were living and crying out in that inferno.

The mouth of the hole was scarcely larger than a human body. Psychodorus got into it and, supporting himself with his hands and elbows, knees and feet, he descended slowly. The noises, voices and cries were still rising up toward him, appealing to his curiosity.

Suddenly, the narrow passage widened like an inverted funnel and, before he had time to take account of it, Psychodorus fell heavily.

Around his fall there was a general flight.

The philosopher, who was not injured, got up immediately—but his dazzled eyes closed at first. Without it being possible to detect where the light came from, the subterranean region was illuminated more brightly than the mountain looming up in the sunlight. In that intense brightness, which seemed to be made of joy, men and women were fleeing, as well as forms to which Psychodorus' memories could not put a name—but some slithered like serpents, others fluttered like birds and some bounded with the supple vigor of tigers.

The flight of the human forms and the unnameable forms opened up an irregular circle around Psychodorus, moving and growing, for the subterranean space extended on every side without visible limits.

Psychodorus advanced at hazard in the bright light, which, save for the increasingly distant runaways, illuminated nothing but the bare ground beneath his feet and a sort of bare ceiling above his head, at twice a man's height. The ground on which he was walking and he ground that overhung it were both dazzling white; in every direction, as limitless as the sea, there was a white landscape.

"How do the beings that I saw running away from me live?" the cynic asked himself. "Where do they find anything to eat?" And the cynic, who had not eaten much the previous day, began to feel hungry.

Worse than the hunger, another anguish gripped him, as if choking him. He felt the oppression more heavily at every step. Soon, Psychodorus was obliged to sit down. Then he fell full length, feeling that the lack of air was going to kill him, and writhed desperately, his movements becoming less and less conscious.

Finally—a second, an hour or a century later—there was a frightful nightmarish sleep. Eventually, however, he nightmare was transformed. A caress was posed on the sleeper's mouth, and a dream of love revived him. The voluptuousness was so intense that the sleeper awoke—and his grateful hand caressed the phantom from which the joy was coming.

The joy did not vanish with the awakening, however, and on his pleasured body Psychodorus saw one of the unknown forms that had fled from him a little while before. Long and flexibly sinuous, it was hissing like a serpent. The head of the serpent—for, in spite of frightful differences, Psychodorus could find no other name by which to designate the creature—was plunging a kiss into Psychodorus' mouth that was both joy and consolation.

The philosopher got up, his lungs full of air and joy. He resumed walking. The serpent was coiled around his neck. From time to time, when the walker's respiration began to become halting, a kiss restored his strength, courage and well-being.

When the singular joy no longer occupied Psychodorus completely, he felt the emptiness of his stomach again. With an involuntary gesture toward his abdomen, he said, automatically: "I'm hungry."

The serpent had seen the gesture. It hissed a summons. Another indefinable form arrived, flying like a bird. It had wings and its voice was a song, but no other resemblance linked it with the winged creatures that Psychodorus had encountered previously. The philosopher's mind, which liked to give unknown entities familiar names, called it a bird.

The bird perched on Psychodorus' shoulder and slid its beak between his hungry lips. In Psychodorus' gut there was the joy of a hunger appeased; in Psychodorus' mouth the joy of a new and exquisite taste—of ambrosia, he thought. And throughout Psychodorus, there was an enduring shock of amorous sensuality.

The philosopher walked for a long time with the strange love that dispelled oppression round his neck and the strange love that dispelled hunger on his shoulder. In spite of his joy, though, he gradually felt his legs growing weary; his eyes almost closed and his mouth finally opened in a yawn. Then the bird fluttered its wings, uttering hectic calls, while the serpent slithered anxiously and hissed.

A third form appeared, which, with a tiger-like bound, leapt on to Psychodorus' free shoulder. It sank its sharp claws into his neck, which was already bent with fatigue—and it was dolorous and heavenly at the same time, an intensely passionate voluptuousness. Oh, the astonishing quiver, which seemed to want to kill...

Afterwards, however, Psychodorus felt as fresh and joyful as a child waking up in the morning.

Happier than the gods of Olympus, Psychodorus walked surrounded by a coquettish affection whose kisses were perfumed and restorative air, a warbling affection whose kisses appeased hunger and thirst, and a passion whose penetrating kisses rendered sleep unnecessary.

His life was nothing but sensuality. In a never-ending ecstasy, he listened to the purring, the hissing and the singing, like foreign voices that speak to you in unknown terms, but with so revealing a tone, of love. The glad cries were articulate and those cries—Psychodorus soon sensed—were not much more different than a man's deep voice, a woman's soft voice and a child's shrill voice, pronouncing the same words in the same language.

And Psychodorus knew what they were saying—because, for the continuous delight of the eyes of all four, the thoughts of any one of the companions in love created enchanted living and colored spectacles in the light, which were only distinguishable from external encounters by their greater cheerfulness and beauty.

Psychodorus had scarcely learned to understand the language of his friends directly when, for the first time in the underworld, he met a woman. She took a step toward him with an inviting glance. The little tiger, the serpent and he bird became as agitated as three furies, and the song, the purring and the hissing told the woman to go away. Remembering Athenatime, Psychodorus made a gesture of refusal, and the woman withdrew.

When Psychodorus understood the language of the paradisal underworld, whether it was sung, purred or hissed, his friends talked to him about the things he saw and explained them a little. The serpent was the chattiest and most explicit. This is the gist of what it told him:

"We know, by virtue of the poverty of our ancestors, the poverty of joys in the land from which you come. Here, though, all material needs are translated into moral needs and kisses suffice for life. Here there are five sexes. I, perhaps the most necessary of all, am a Respiration. You need me, and also these two who are on your shoulders, and you give me the triple pleasure of giving myself to the triple god that you are to me. This one, the friend with wings, is an Aliment. It appeases my hunger every time I appease its oppression. And we also need this being with the delightful claws, which is a Slumber. Our greatest voluptuousness is, however, for us all to give you what you need from us, and which cannot do anything for us except for bringing us the joy of giving it to you. If you were to love a woman, though, the race would rejoice in you and her, while we three would weep with jealousy."

When the Respiration ceased its harmonious hissing, the Slumber purred melodiously: "In spite of the existence of Women—necessary, alas, for the creation of new Humans, young Aliments, young Respirations and young Slumbers— this land is the most joyful of the existing Paradises."

And the Aliment's song continued: "We are rewarded for having understood something of the word of a prophet who came several centuries ago to tell us: "love one another."

Once, Psychodorus said: "Should I not climb back up to my dolorous homeland and repeat to the poor humans up there the Word: *Love one another*?"

His thee friends uttered frightened screeches, and they begged him: "Don't do that. Instead of believing you, they would inflict slavish tortures upon you…"

"What does it matter?" said the philosopher. "I have a duty to accept that sacrifice."

"No, no," they protested, in unison, "a thousand times no. For, after having put you to death, they would not love one another in memory of you, but would strike one another more hatefully around your memory."

From that moment on, the philosopher became depressed. The thought of the humans who were suffering on the Earth's surface loomed up like a thorny hedge between himself and joy. His friends were afflicted by his affliction.

Finally, the Aliment, fluttering its wings like sad hands, said to him: "O Psychodorus, one cannot be happy without the happiness of those of whom one is thinking. In consequence, we can do nothing more for you. Go back up, then, to the poor humans whose memory pursues you, spoiling your joy and ours."

Moaning like a funeral procession, his friends guided him to the chimney that was the only communication between the underworld and the open air. After kisses more affectionate and passionate than ever—but which Psychodorus accepted distractedly—they showed him the means of climbing back up to our drab light. He climbed, uplifted by the joy of sacrifice.

What pain awaited him! The serpent had slid behind him. Before plunging once again into subterranean bliss, it hissed these words, whose truth Psychodorus sensed:

"Don't inform your compatriots of the Word. It is another Prophet that destiny has chosen to speak in vain and die in consequence, a new object of hatred for blind men."

XX. The Bad Millstone

Having lain down on the ground in a deserted spot in order to sleep, Psychodorus heard a groan.

He raised his head, supporting himself on his elbow, and listened in order to discover where the groan had come from. He could no longer hear anything. Having laid his head down once more, however, he heard the plaint again, and he realized that it was subterranean.

He planted his staff in order to mark the location and then looked around for something with which to dig.

He came back with a spade and worked for some time. Sometimes he interrupted his task and lay down to see whether the plaint was still continuing. When the hole was deep enough, Psychodorus was able to hear it while standing up. Even so, he lay down one last time in an attempt to understand it, for it seemed to him that the plaint was composed of words.

He understood. Continually, with a monotonous rhythm, the moaning was saying: "Alas, my futile beauty! Alas, my futile beauty!"

His work continued for a long time, Now, he no longer dared strike hard with the spade, for he feared injuring the subterranean being.

Finally, something white appeared, vaguely illuminating the darkness. Psychodorus touched it, and realized that it was made of marble.

With loving precaution, avoiding inflicting the slightest scratch on the head, torso and limbs, Psychodorus disengaged the statue.

He placed it on three stones arranged into a makeshift pedestal. It was not a goddess. The sculptor had only wanted to create beauty. He had succeeded better than anyone before him or after him. The philosopher was moved by a sentiment more religious than if the gentle gods had appeared to him.

In brief sentences—but with a disdainful drawl—the statue told its story.

Glad to have created a harmony superior to al known harmonies, but jealous of his work and bristling with a fearful scorn for humans, the sculptor had said: "You are too beautiful to show yourself. The human eye is impure. My contemplation alone will rest upon you, like a father's chaste kiss."

He had shut his marble daughter up in a remote room into which no one ever went. He usually knelt some distance away from her himself.

One day, sensing that he was dying, he had hidden the beauty that unworthy men would have soiled with their gazes and desires—and perhaps even coarse words and laughter—beneath a thick layer of earth.

The status, having related these things, proclaimed: "Glory to me. I want all eyes to be dazzled by and to rejoice in my beauty. Even if they are produced, what do a few impotent blasphemies matter? Can anything soil the absolute, whether form or light?"

"O statue," said the astonished Psychodorus, "how is it that such a vulgar feminine thought can emanate from such beauty? You have a right to pride, but you stop at puerile vanity." He added: "You will be punished. Incomplete being who is not self-sufficient, you will stifle in an atmosphere of ennui. You are in a solitary place. Only a few peasants will think that they are looking at you, but they will not see your beauty, for not all men have eyes for such things."

Having spoken these words, Psychodorus lay down on the ground and slept.

In the morning, some country folk who were passing by stopped, and exchanged a few reflections, with dull gestures.

"That's marble. It might be worth a lot of money," said one.

153

"Imbecile," another replied, "marble is only stone."

"Yes, that's true," approved the rest.

"It would have been better," one concluded, "instead of spoiling that good stone by making a useless woman whom no one can even take to bed, to put it in a wall."

"But the statue is beautiful," Psychodorus insinuated.

The peasants shook their heads.

"It's too thin," said one.

"I like my wife better," said another, with a dirty laugh. "She's a bit better-built—she has bigger breasts and larger buttocks."

They drew away, and Psychodorus followed them.

That evening, one of the peasants came back with a cart and an iron bar. He broke the statue's arms, without hearing its cries of pain—for not all men have ears to hear all sounds. He took the ill-formed cylinder that remained home with him, and used it as a millstone to grind grain.

The next day, Psychodorus felt a pang of regret.

"I shall retrace my steps," he said, "and re-bury the beauty that will curse the stupidity of humans."

He only found the debris of the arms. He buried them piously. Then he resumed his random march.

He arrived in the courtyard where the peasant was grinding his grain. He heard the millstone complaining. A fat merchant, who had come to buy the peasant's harvest, said to the mutilated statue: "Rejoice in having become useful."

"Useful!" growled the countryman. "Get away! I've never seen such a poor millstone." He kicked it disdainfully.

"Merited treatment," the fat merchant approved. "That stone has pretensions, and it doesn't even make a passable millstone."

When the night was pitch dark, Psychodorus came back. He stole the bad millstone and, full of pity, interred it along with the other debris.

XXI. The Clouds

Standing on the deserted cliff, Psychodorus watched the changing forms of the clouds. To the east, their dark mass was heaped up over the mountain of mountains. Over the western sea, they were dressing heroes wounded by the Sun or lying on bloody and fleeing battlefields. Others, small and pale, fringed with green or pink light, resembled the smiles of strange children or the games of young fantastic animals.

Now, the clouds descended from the sky. Around Psychodorus, they formed a metamorphic population. One of them, similar at first to an enormous sphinx, opened an immense mouth and spoke. With a laugh that caused a roll of thunder, it demanded:

"O human, cloud of excessively slow changes, guess what we are. Are we clouds like all the others you have encountered? Or are we the uncertain forms of the past and future that you are allowed to see: the fleeting forms of the eve that preceded the morning when you scuttled on all fours, the fleeting forms of the tomorrow that will follow the evening when you will be tottering on three limbs?"

"What does it matter to me what you are?" said Psychodorus. "What interests me is the richness of the appearances with which you refresh my eyes, the richness of he dreams with which you refresh my soul."

"You have replied well," said the sphinx—which, in the hands of the wind, changed its unraveled lines, becoming an old god with a long beard and a broad benevolent smile.

And the King of the Clouds spoke at length—but at each of his sentences, perhaps more often, his lacy light stirred and his form changed. Meanwhile, his people, sometimes sow and sometimes rapid, made a dance of metamorphoses glide or bund around him and Psychodorus.

And this is what the King of the Clouds, amid the incessant fight of his forms, said with his wind-twisted mouth:

"Humans have looked at us at a particular time. They have noted our position at that arbitrary moment, along with the most brutal of our colors and the most deceptively precise of our contours. Then they have proclaimed: 'This is an acquisition forever; we are learning the *eternal* truth.' And while the slippery and multiform truth laughed at their naivety, they have built with massive blocks of error the heavy architectures of religions and metaphysical systems.

"Others have come who have seen the stupidity of the former. Even more stupid and coarse, they have cried, blinded with indignation and spite, that those infamous liars the philosophers and the priests were talking about things that had never existed. With foreheads lowered toward the mire, they have denied the very existence of clouds. And no one has divined the liquid marble of which our fleeting statues are made, whose sculptors are the powerful Sun and capricious winds."

Thus spoke the King of the Clouds, sometimes a human, sometimes a lion, eagle or whale, sometimes a form without a name, or a quivering forest, or an island with shores floating in the unreality of a glorious sea or a lake swaying to the itch of an implausible earth.

Then he said, with his chimerical mouth:

"Be wiser than these naïve generalizers and brutal negators, O Psychodorus. Affirm only the existence of the clouds that appear to your soul, and that their fleeting realities are the signs of slightly more stable realities unknown to you.

XXII. Large Living Beings

Psychodorus was sitting under an oak-tree watching the numerous movements of an ant-hive. He picked up an ant and set it on his hand. Still in a reverie, he started talking to it.

"Your eyes," he said to it, "are doubtless incapable of seeing me in my entirety—but you see my finger moving and it appears to you to be some enormous independent living thing. By contrast, if you have some vague idea of me, it's probably that I'm a heavy inanimate mass, a mountain thrown down here, next to your homeland, by a sudden catastrophe."

He broke a young shoot of the great oak, placed the ant on a leaf and moved off, carrying the little tree. He was still looking at the insect, as if he were able to read its strange thoughts in its eyes.

"The leaves of the tree that is carrying you," he said, "hardly move, retaining the same respective positions. Nothing varies in your immediate surroundings. In consequence, you probably believe that your dwelling is presently immobile at a point in space. The vague distant extents however, move to the rhythm of my stride, and you must think that the trees, stones and earth are flowing like the steam that borders your native land."

Then he addressed himself: "Psychodorus, you are this ant. Your eyes, impotent to grasp the whole of the Earth, the harmony of its form and its possible movements, are unaware that it is alive. But perhaps the Earth is speaking to you as I was speaking to the insect just now. It is saying to you: 'I'm carrying you, O Psychodorus, at a slow or rapid pace, but I'm carrying with you, with the same motion, everything that surrounds you, and you see me as motionless. But the stars in the sky before which you pass seem to your flow to be the spangles of a great blue river."

"O Earth," cried the philosopher, then, "I cannot leave you. I am attached to you as my finger is attached to my hand. The movements of my finger do not make it an independent living creature. Perhaps I too am merely a limb of your immense body.

"And what are you, Earth? A limb of some vaster body: a body that I am unable even to divine; a body that is to the impotence of my eyes and mind what you are to the visual and intellectual impotence of this ant?

"But that immense body whose life would be revealed to sufficiently large eyes, placed at an appropriate distance, is only a limb of the universal living being. O unity, there is but one life, and only one living being—and that living being my obscure stammering sometimes calls God."

As he said these things, Psychodorus looked at the ant again. It was stirring on is branch, crazy with anxiety. The philosopher said to it: "I was about to exile you, thoughtlessly, perhaps delivering you to death. Have no fear. I shall take you back to the outskirts of your city."

Indeed, he retraced his steps and piously deposited the insect on its native lawn. And he said then: "O my sister, go back to your life, and forgive me for having troubled you for a few minutes."

He drew away, thinking: "I might perhaps be very guilty with respect to that little life, for I do not know its duration, or whether one of its minutes might be equivalent to several of my weeks."

XXIII. The Inferno

Lying face down, with his head slightly raised, a man was looking at the ground and speaking. As he drew near, Psychodorus heard the softest of the barbarian dialects that he understood. The deep and wild voice, however, seemed to be laying a curse. It said: "Abandon all hope, ye who enter here. Leave all hope behind."

"To whom are you speaking, solitary man?" Psychodorus asked. "Do you want to make yourself heard by these insects, these blades of grass or these pebbles?"

Without deigning to look up at his questioner, the other said: "When one speaks, it's to oneself."

"Doubtless," agreed the philosopher, "but ordinarily, one puts on a show of speaking to others, and one chooses ears that one believes—mistakenly, to be sure, but that illusion alone makes the voice resonate—to be capable of hearing."

The barbarian, still motionless, smiled. And he explained:

"If you insist, it's to these pebbles that I'm speaking, and also to these blades of grass, and again, to these insects. To whatever has fallen into the inferno of being, I am saying: 'Abandon all hope, you will never emerge from being.' I say to others, and I am already speaking more directly and more dolorously to myself: 'Nearer brother, suffering more greatly, oh, you have descended toward the center, oh, oh, you have entered the circle of life. Abandon all hope; you will emerge from the present appearance of your life, but you will never escape life. And you, I say to the insect, you have entered the circle of movement and consciousness. You will not rest again in the more dormant and dreamlike life of plants. Abandon, abandon all hope."

The barbarian stood up. He took a threatening step toward Psychodorus. A double gesture of his two hands appeared to enclose the cynic within the four walls of a prison. Meanwhile, he continued his discourse:

"And I say to you, human: 'You have entered the circle of thought. Abandon all hope of ever emerging therefrom.'" Then, his arms pointing toward the sky, he cried: "To you, God, I say: 'You are the center of the inferno, and you are the inferno entire. Abandon all hope of ever emerging.' What hope do you have of escaping you own law, you who are everything?"

"Sages have believed that God had fled and dispersed himself in his creatures."

The barbarian burst into mocking laughter as loud as a corybant's screech.[18]

"Ha ha ha! Center, you radiate, trying to escape yourself. You enlarge yourself, you and your suffering. O circle, you grow, in the insane hope of being the circle that emerges from the circle—but God, whatever he does, is always everywhere. He is the apparent non-being that completes all the appearances of being. He is for each one all that extends beyond its limits. You walk, you live, you breathe in God. You are a floating island which that sea inundates and transports. You

---

[18] Corybants were priests of Cybele, legendary for the supposed excesses of their orgiastic fertility rites.

are a poor present, but he has already taken all your yesterdays and possesses all your tomorrows. In your eternal journey you have for provisions a few miserable changing memories. He is all that you have forgotten and all the prevision that you lack. He is, in the very instant that you believe to be your own, everything that you do not know about yourself. In the head of a bull or a lion, he is the humane thought that suffers as an unborn child suffers in its mother's belly. In the plant, he is animal consciousness, and in the lifeless stone, he is life. Human, animal, plant, stone, you are apparent slumbers of increasing profundity, but God is, within each of you, the old eternal grace of which slumber dreams and by which it is stirred. By each of his impotent efforts toward non-being, innumerably He Is. He is the fatigue of all his aspirations to rest. Poor God, who wishes to forget himself, to distract himself, to escape from himself, and who finds himself everywhere in his entirety—and who has a consciousness of himself all the clearer for having tried to extinguish it in a creature more tenebrous. Abandon all hope, poor God, poor God..."

The last words had been pronounced in an inexpressibly despairing tone. An immense silence followed them. And abysm of silence seemed to devour all possibility of joy.

Psychodorus had to make an effort to pronounce any words art all. Shivering all over, he said: "You no longer add: *You who have entered?*"

"No," cried the barbarian. "And I was wrong, just now, to address those mad words to you, and the ant, and the stone. One does not enter, and one does not emerge. From every point of the God-Inferno to every other, one is agitated."

The vaticinator lowered his voice, speaking to himself. Psychodorus thought he heard: "No, one is not even agitated. But this man would not understand how apparent immobility in space and apparent mobility in time combine to form the real immobility of the immense and the eternal."[19]

---

[19] The author inserts a footnote: "The truth indicated by the barbarian's aside is doubtless that which the Double Genius

Then he resumed the tone of his previous discourse, which doubtless seemed to him a sufficient exactitude for a listener held in some scorn: "But how does one get out of the All? Beginning and end are poor human words. You think, in saying them, that you are saying something, but you are saying nothing and you cause the eternal dolor of God to laugh lugubriously—or, rather believing that you are expressing realities and absolutes, you only show me vain appearances. Naively, you take the outermost veil of the symbol for the central truth. The Sun disappears from your sight, but it continues to burn and, when your eyes first saw it, it was already burning. There is no change."

"No change!" cried Psychodorus. His mind became annoyed with the barbarian, and also against Zeno of Elea, who, by the movement of his tongue, had denied all movement. He wanted to reply—but the barbarian made the gesture that imposes silence with a sovereign authority.

"There are changes for your eyes," he said, "seers of thin superficialities, and every reality bears innumerable vestments into eternity, but beneath the vestments that his servant death takes off, and beneath the vestments that cover his servant birth, everything remains the same. Neither hope nor fear. When I employ these words, I voice absurd human poverties."

The barbarian drew away, and shouted once again at the immobile cynic: "Free yourself from all hope and from all dread, because since forever and for always, ineffably, you Are."

XXIV. Philip's Lieutenant

Psychodorus was walking without looking at his surroundings. Words that chanced to reach him informed him that he was in Macedonia, and there was nothing for him to see in that banal country.

---

will explain further on, in the chapter entitled *The Dicephali*. (Editor's note.)"

He was walking almost somnolently. Outbursts of laughter woke him up. He perceived a group of loutish idlers, shaking with laughter. One of these coarse humorists, a very young man, shouted: "You're not old enough, old fool."

The lout was addressing a crippled old man, who drew away, followed for some time by jeers and laughter.

Psychodorus, walking beside the old man, heard him murmur: "Those imbeciles think that time exists. They don't know that life is death, that death is life. They are unaware of the lacunae of things regarded by eyes a little more perspicacious than theirs. They are unaware of the marvelous continuity of things seen by an eye that is able to penetrate more profoundly still." Then he fell silent.

"I salute you," Psychodorus said to him, "who are called a fool because you are a sage."

But the old man added: "And especially because I was a lieutenant of King Philip."

"How old are you, then?" asked the astonished cynic.

The other smiled bitterly. "You, too, doubt," he replied, "and perhaps you're incapable of understanding the meaning of my words."

"I divine that they are full of mysterious wisdom—but I can't succeed in opening them."

"Listen, then. I was born—to speak your language—about a year after what you call Philip's death."[20]

"That's why those men deny that you could have been an officer in his army."

The old man made impatient gestures. "I haven't served in any army. I've been a lieutenant, not in Philip's army, but of Philip himself. I have been part of the ensemble called Philip. I was one of his secondary souls—one of those who received orders from the principal Soul and carried them out."

---

[20] Philip II of Macedon died in 336 B.C. (thirteen years before Diogenes). Assuming that the old man is in his 70s, this affirmation suggests that this episode in Psychodorus' career is set *circa* 260 B.C.

"I feel respectful and emotional, as on the brink of an initiation. Speak, old sage, who knows things that no one else knows."

"Listen. There is nothing but souls; matter is an appearance. Suppose that a powerful eye could gaze at what you call your body—what would it see?"

"I don't know."

"It would see atoms, not tightly grouped and in contact with one another, as the naïve Leucippus and Democritus believe, but separated by abysms of void. Suppose that the eye in question magnified you to the vast scale of the night sky: between the innumerable atoms composing you, the voids would be as large as those between the stars that compose the sky—for the sky is no more solid than a human body; it is not a vault with which a high enough flight could collide; the zenith is merely a horizon that always retreats before a flight as the sky that limits your view ahead retreats as you march toward it. The sky is a gulf in which lights float, and you, for penetrating eyes, also dissolve and disperse in a formless space in which atoms move—for nothing is motionless—in frightful abysses. But the true atom is necessarily devoid of extent, for even human thought, infinitely weaker than reality, can always divide extent. Atoms are nodes of radiant force; atoms are souls.

"You body is an army of souls. Take away all the soldiers in a phalange, and there is no more phalange. Take away your souls, and there is no longer a body."

"I thought I only had one soul," said Psychodorus.

"You have a Soul that commands, a Soul that is the general of the army. And army marches under the guidance of a single thought—your body too. Except for periodic uprisings when, among the soldiers of yesterday, leaders are suddenly revealed."

"I understand."

"But beware of thinking that all your souls are equal. Some, under the supreme command, have a certain measure of authority. They are your lieutenants. They transmit your orders and, in cases of urgency, can take some initiative.

"Yesterday I was dreaming while I walked. I found myself on the edge of an unexpected gulf and I stepped back before I knew where I was or what I was doing. Someone within me, who was not Me, had known. (If you are not a sophist, you will have no difficulty resolving the apparent ambiguity of the same word being used to designate two things. An army sometimes bears the name of its general; Me sometimes signifies a leader, sometimes an ensemble, in the same way that One can mean God or the Universe…) Thus, an officer had known something of which the commander was unaware, had given urgent orders, and had been obeyed. And it is to the presence of mind of that subaltern officer that the entire army owes its salvation.

"The other day, my bare foot crushed a scorpion that had just stung me, but it was an officer of that fragment of the army, an officer of my foot—not Me, that is—who had given the order, for I became aware of the injury and the vengeance at the same time.

"Do you know what birth is? It is the raising of an army. That army will grow; then it will fight to maintain its strength; then, despite its efforts, its power will decrease—and that is childhood, maturity and old age, a whole life. When the army is disbanded, that is death. But you understand that no one dies, for the army was not one person. The general survives, and each of his officers, and all of his soldiers. When you are said to die, your principal Soul is a dispossessed sovereign. Sometimes it abdicates, a noble and disdainful exile, but if gross passions attach it to the people in revolt, it might fight dolorously and desperately all the way to the pyre. Sometimes, it even continues in the urn, miserably, a combat already lost.

"Philip was avid to command. To the extent that such strange things can be recalled and measured, it seems to me that he fought for months before abandoning the people that formed his body. Oh, if I could relate the history of Philip in his sepulcher and his frightful struggles in the urn, a narrow battlefield, and his failures and despair, I would sing a poem more astonishing than that of his conquests and his son's victories—a poem more beautiful and terrible than the Iliad. And the Athenians themselves would weep for their conqueror."

XXV. Suicide

Psychodorus, having grown old, walked with difficulty. He followed facile and banal roads. For ten years he had not had a single interesting encounter. For ten years no consolatory dream had rendered the phantom of Athenatime to him.

He sat down on the roadside and, in accordance with a custom acquired after several years of solitude, he talked to himself.

"What do you still have to do in this life, Psychodorus? Nothing new presents itself to your eyes, and your past is becoming impoverished. Every day steals a memory, and withers those that it leaves you. You ought to die, Psychodorus, of your own free will. Ennui already weighs upon you, and the listless weakness of old men. Don't wait for the probable infirmities. Go voluntarily to find Athenatime again."

He was speaking aloud, and did not notice another old man who had sat down beside him a few moments before. Suddenly, however, he turned round. A voice had affirmed: "One should never kill oneself."

"Why?" asked the cynic.

"Listen and understand, man whom I do not know. The Fates want to know how you will bear ennui. They also want to know how you will bear infirmities. It is necessary to reply with a smile to all the questions the Fates ask you. To flee one's destiny is a futile cowardice."

"You're wrong, O stranger. Cowardice is fearing death."

"Cowardice is to give in to one's greatest fear. Death seems to you to be a comfortable refuge where you might escape the evils that frighten you."

"I could say many things in reply to that point, but why do you claim that my gesture would be futile?"

"The Fates are more obstinate than we are. They know how to find us everywhere and they pose the questions that we have refused to answer again. The knot that they present to us must be untied by the patient hands of time, not cut by steel. The gesture that Alexander made to Gordius eluded an equivocal and indifferent oracle, not a true destiny. True destines do not permit avoidance."

"You seem to be assuming, O barbarian, that if I were to die voluntarily, I would be condemned to be reborn to relive the same life, and to encounter the same obstacles in my path."

"Precisely."

"Thus, you are speaking of impossible things. Everything is connected, my brother in old age. To renew my life, it would be necessary to renew the universe. It would be necessary for yesterday to happen a second time and occupy tomorrow—but then, where would tomorrow go? Truly, barbarian, I think that you're mad." Psychodorus burst out laughing. Then he continued, talking to himself: "Life is an eternal circle. I shall relive my present existence exactly many times over, and I have already espoused it an infinite number of times—but the great Year that bears in its movement the entire cycle of necessity undoubtedly lasts for millions of millions of centuries. When it reaches the point where it is now again, I shall once again be sitting in this dust, pronouncing the words that I am pronouncing, and I shall have the same desire to die. Until then, however, I need have no fear of this madman's threat of repeating myself eternally."

But the "madman" asked: "Do you think, then, that your realities are necessarily my realities? I did not say that, by virtue of your sin, external history would recommence in its entirety before the time in question—but events different for other eyes would be for your eyes the events of today. Blind to the things that others see, you would march amid a spectacle perceived by you alone, and everyone would call you mad. Or perhaps, a dolorous phantom that believed itself to be a living being, you would recommence, in a phantasmal land created solely by your disquiet, the nightmare of today. I do not pre-

166

tend, fellow man, to know all the means that the Fates employ. I say only that they are powerful, that they are inexorable, and that it is pointless to try and deceive them. And I tell you, briefly, the sum of all wisdom: Bear your burden and abstain."

Psychodorus fell silent momentarily, pensively. Then he wanted to reply—but he saw that the barbarian had got to his feet and was already disappearing around a bend in the road.

XXVI. The Floors [21]

Psychodorus did not like Aristotle. His meditations often rebuked the pride that led the latter to believe, whenever he was not in accord with Plato, that he alone possessed the whole truth.

"Naïve person, you only admit the reality of the location occupied by your mind and the poor extent enveloped by your gaze—like the Rooted Ones who denied the other side of the mountain. You have the suspicion that calls everyone who strays from your intellectual homeland and describes foreign regions a liar. But you are a man who hardly traveled at all. You are a timid person. You are not a conqueror who invades like an overflowing sea; you are a tremulous petty trader who fills a narrow treasure-chest with meager riches, obol by obol. Then you come, mad with pride, to proclaim: 'I am the only rich man; only my copper obols are real, while Plato's gold talents do not exist. There is no gold; I have never seen any.'

---

[21] This title—*Les Étages* in French—embodies a double meaning that does not lend itself to easy translation. The word *étage* is usually employed to mean the phases or stages of a process or journey, but can also refer to the floors or stories of a house. I have preferred the latter meaning because it is specifically implied when the word is used in the course of the chapter—avoiding the confusion that arises from the English double meaning of "stories"—but the symbolism of the narration obviously relates to the former.

"Yes, you are a timid person. You have told the physicians that it is necessary to pause. You believe in a limited reality. Oh, how much more beloved to me than your linear and narrow truth is the broad and cyclic truth of Pythagoras or Plato. You have never seen anything in the darkness but the light of our lantern, and you have closed your cowardly eyes when lightning has illuminated the extent. But they, watching out for lightning, have glimpsed a little of the beauty of the heavens that open; they have not reduced space to the groping of their hands and sealed time between the folly of a beginning and the folly of an end. They have glimpsed a little of the eternity that recommences itself, and recommences us.

"An infinite number of times, in this same place, while the same wind sways the same verdure above my head, I have said to myself what I am saying now. I shall say it again an infinite number of times. It is not necessary to pause, O Aristotle. When you pause your thought, you commit an arbitrary brutality. Why pause here rather than there? Reality does not pause. The world did not begin and it will not end. Neither nothingness nor chaos is conceivable. The harmonious circle has been turning forever, and will turn forever. Tell me, naïve Aristotle, the point at which a circumference ends, and the point at which it ends?"

Suddenly emerging from his meditation, however, Psychodorus saw what was in front of him. A line of houses, like one side of a street, extended to his right and his left as far as he could see. They were poor hovels, devoid of upper floors. Nothing seemed to interrupt their monotonous line. The philosopher's gaze searched in vain for a passage.

The cynic shrugged his shoulders before that infinite monotony and knocked on the nearest door with his staff. The only response was a deep hollow sound.

The philosopher waited for a moment, then lifted a latch, pulled the door open and went in. He saw a man clad in a cloak of unbleached linen, with a staff in his hand, whose appearance astonished him. It was an old man with long white hair and a long white beard.

"Who are you?" the philosopher asked.

The old man's only response was to ask the same question: "Who are you?"

"I am Psychodorus."

The old man repeated: "I am Psychodorus."

The cynic saw that the old man resembled him—and that the old man was making the same gestures as him, at the same time. Then one of them—which one?—burst out laughing.

"Ah!" he said. "If you're only Psychodorus...."

But the other, with a similar laugh, said: "Ah! If you're only Psychodorus..."

Shivering, the philosopher did not dare say any more.

He turned his back on the old man who resembled him, but the old man was in front of him. He went back to the door by which he had entered; another hand touched the latch at the same time as his own. Pushed by two simultaneous efforts, the door nevertheless held firm. Two similar movements slid back a large peephole pierced a head height. Two curiosities gazed in unison, seeing with a fraternal frisson that the ground had risen up outside, blocking the door, and probably the neighboring doors—and perhaps all the doors in the infinite half-street.

"I'm obviously in my life," Psychodorus said. "One cannot go back when one has entered."

And the naively fanciful and resigned sentence was spoken simultaneously by the Psychodorus that Psychodorus could see. Moving away from the door, the philosopher walked straight ahead. Now, he could no longer see his double—but, as if his eyes had been transported some distance away, he saw himself.

He followed a long tedious corridor. He arrived at another door and pushed it. It opened without difficulty—but Psychodorus took a step backwards.

An abyss plunged in front of him. He came back and, leaning over, looked down. He could not see the bottom of the seemingly-infinite precipice, but a ruinous winding stairway descended into the vertiginous depths and Psychodorus set his foot on the first step.

Having gone down a few steps, he found a door standing ajar and went in. The cavern contained nothing but the rigidity of a cadaver. Above it, in the dwindling darkness, an inscription mentioned a name, a few deeds, and a few spoken words. It was as if they were rare summits brightened by a Sun that had already set, at the commencement of night.

At unequal distances, all along the increasingly ruined stairway, other doors opened in the steep wall. Each crypt contained a dead person whose features were more eaten away than those of the dead people higher up, and an inscription more undecipherable than the preceding ones.

The stairway, increasingly vertiginous and rickety, gave way under Psychodorus' feet. The philosopher fell, saying: "I'm rolling into death…"

…But he came round. He was on the edge of the abyss, on a narrow ledge. Behind him, there was an opening. As soon as he could move, he took refuge in this new grotto.

No dead person awaited him in that dwelling. At the back of the empty space, however, there was a memorial inscription, vague in the gloom. The cynic rubbed his forehead and, as if his gesture had created light, was able to read:

Here lies Psychodorus, son of Psychodorus, disciple of Diogenes, lover of Athenatime. Having lost his beloved, he traveled. He visited strange peoples: the Rooted People who deny the space beyond the horizon; the Eyeless People who only know linear extent; the Invisible men who are gods to their trembling wives….

The epitaph continued for a long time, as prolix as a hermit's memoir, but certain parts were hardly legible, eaten away by moss or forgetfulness. The last words that the philosopher was able to decipher said:

Once he fell, rolling the entire length of a Great Year, and after that fall, he found himself back at the same point…

The inscription had a few more lines, but the characters were formless, blurred by a kind of malicious darkness. Psychodorus could no longer reconstitute a single word.

When he emerged from his sepulcher the abyss had been filled in. He looked behind him, but he could no longer see a mountain, a stairway, doors or caverns. He was lost in the middle of an immense bare plain, and the space around him was mute…

XXVII. The Dicephali

Constituted in all other respects like the humans of known lands, these beings bore two heads. One was turned toward the fright shoulder, the other gazed at the left shoulder. It so happened that one of these heads was mediocre, the other intelligent. Thus, every rich child had only one gymnastics teacher, but two music teachers. It is true that each teacher usually taught by means of only one of his mouths.

Psychodorus was shown an admirable man that everyone called the Double Genius. His right head composed the most marvelous poems, while his left head discovered profound geometric truths. Once, the two had had given very popular philosophical performances. The right head seemed intoxicated by universal movement, but the left head, intoxicated by unity, denied all movement. For some years, the Double Genius had refused to put himself on show. He often sought solitude—and it was claimed that the two heads had ended up reaching agreement.

Now, the left eyes of the Double Genius having perceived Psychodorus, the Double Genius drew nearer and asked: "What is this animal that only bears, on a human body, a single head, like a vile dog? Is it a complete beast or, more wretchedly, a half-human? Has it an articulate language?"

"I'm a traveler," said the wounded Psychodorus. "I have visited the strangest peoples. I speak more than a thousand articulate languages, and I've seen more things than anyone else. Before leaving my homeland, however, I was a well-educated philosopher and I knew, among many others, the doctrines espoused by each of your heads."

"Perhaps," the Dicephalus suggested, "you are a Simple Genius who has disposed of his useless head." And he drew away.

He soon returned, though. He asked Psychodorus: "Would you like to come with me, Simple Genius? Place yourself to my right and tell the head of mine that makes verses about the strange forms that you have seen and the mores that you have observed."

"I'm not in the habit," Psychodorus said, "of speaking for the benefit of half a man. Besides, I know geometric truths as well as your left head. You will listen to me with all four ears, or I shall remain silent."

"Speak," said the Double Genius, condescendingly. "We're listening."

Psychodorus gave an account of his homeland and a few other lands of monocephali. When his narration became particularly astonishing, the two heads uttered simultaneous exclamations.

The right head said: "O singular thing! O momentary form!"

But the left head proclaimed: "That happens everywhere, and is thus eternal."

Psychodorus finally said, with a smile: "My single tongue has grown weary in my unique mouth, and my ears would like to hear the verities known to your two heads."

"I'll recite my recent verses for you," the right mouth announced.

Meanwhile, the left mouth instructed: "Listen to this geometric truth that I discovered yesterday."

Psychodorus set aside the two promises. "You can offer me poems and demonstrations later, O mouths. First, explain to me what you meant when you interrupted me with hose exclamations. Why did you, right mouth, say: *O singular thing! O momentary form!* And you especially, left mouth, why did you contradict your brother, proclaiming: *That happens everywhere, and is thus eternal?*"

The left mouth protested: "I did not contradict my brother. I completed his thought. Two voices that seem contradictory are not too many to sing, certainly not the infinite and ineffable Truth, but the two poles of Truth." It continued: "Everything passes, everything flows. You cannot bathe twice in the same river, for the water is no longer the same, and you are no longer the same. But the universe is always composed of the same elements, and the water that flows or floats over the Earth is always the same water. The wave that retreats returns. Rivers, under the name of clouds, return to their sources."

"I know these things," said Psychodorus.

"Do you also know that you are eternal?"

"I know it."

"But do you know that this minute is eternal?"

"I don't understand."

"And do you know that you, who are here, are in a thousand other places?"

"I understand less and less."

"Listen, then O Simple Genius, and if you are capable of understanding, understand."

"Nothing is created and nothing dies. Your gaze and your smile say that you are familiar with these words, but what you said just now proves that you have not understood them—and they are, in fact, difficult to understand."

The Double Genius paused momentarily, as if he were searching for a less arduous explanation, within the compass of his poor listener. Then he said: "Tell me the name by which you are known in your homeland, Simple Genius."

"My name is Psychodorus."

"Let's sit down on this sand—and try to follow what I'm saying. I shall represent by the number 1 the Psychodorus that emerges from his mother's womb, by the number 2 the Psychodorus of the following moment—and then you become 3, 4, 5, 6 and the other numbers. Where is the sum to be found?"

173

"In my memory."

"And the numbers to come—what can you do with them? And the past numbers that you have forgotten? Every number is eternal. The universe is made up of all the numbers, and the numbers are infinite. The universe is infinite. Do you believe that?"

"I believe it."

"Thus, the universe includes, at every instant of its infinite existence, all possibilities—and of those possibilities, it is necessary not to represent some as real and others merely as dreams. All of them are realized at every instant."

"That's impossible."

"Then you believe that the universe has limits. You believe God to be successive. You do not believe in infinity. You do not believe that Being is and that Non-Being is not."

"I no longer know."

"You wanted me to conduct you into a land of vertigo. Have a courageous mind. You explained to me a little while ago what you call the Great Year, and I am astonished that a barbarian could, without my help, formulate such a concept. Yes, all events are on a plane that rotates incessantly and which brings them back eternally. Do you believe that the part of the circle that is not visible no longer exists?"

"You're right. Everything coexists."

"There's more. Everything is always in the visible part of the circle."

"I no longer understand."

"Come to my house. Perhaps you will understand."

Having arrived home, the Double Genius took a large circle of thin metal that had a hole at the center. He passed through the hole a vertical iron rod supported by a table smaller than the circle.

"This circle," said the left head, "represents the Great Year. Imagine it infinitely enlarged."

Then the dicephalus planted a golden rod in the ground, which the circle brushed as it turned, and from which hung a lighted lamp. "The point of the circle that passes over the golden rod," he explained, "is called the present moment. When it has drawn away from our lamp, it still exists."

"I already understand that."

"In its infinite breadth, the circle contains all possibilities. And the infinity of its breadth makes the radiance that we call the present infinite. But have you thought of the depth of time and the depth of space? We have not revealed the whole truth, or even of human truth, since, of the three dimensions we know, two are sufficient for our demonstration. What truth is hidden in the third dimension?"

"I don't know," Psychodorus stammered. "I'm afraid. It seems to me that I'm going mad."

"If you aren't capable of understanding," the Double Genius replied, cruelly, "there's no harm in your going mad." He continued: "Don't you see that I can put an infinite number of similar circles on top of his one? And underneath it too. Imagine them there. The circle immediately above the ne you can see is in advance of it by an instant. In that superior circle you are what you will be here at the next moment. A few circles higher up, you are at the moment of this one's tomorrow. There is one of these Great Years in which you are dying at this very moment, and there is one—or, rather, an infinite number—in which you are being reborn or dying again.

"And below, there is the circle in which the moment that has just passed here is the present moment. There is a circle in which what you call yesterday is named today. There is the Great Year in which you are being born at his precise moment to the life that you call your present life, and there are those in which you are living every moment of every one of your innumerable lives. Do you understand now?"

"I understand, but I'm afraid."

But the Double Genius, without any longer addressing himself to Psychodorus, cried from both of his mouths: "O instants, every one of you is realized throughout eternity!"

Then his right mouth proclaimed: "O instant, synthesis of eternity."

And his left mouth: "O eternity, analysis of the instant."

Now the two mouths became irritated. One affirmed: "Analysis is merely myopic synthesis." The other jeered: "Synthesis, poor presbyopic analysis…"

They fell silent momentarily. The right mouth opened again alone, but instead of speaking, it sang: "O Instants, O cups from each of which I drink Eternity entire. O Instant, you are sometimes in my trembling hand the amethyst cup that saddens all Eternity. But you are often the golden cup that makes all Eternity laugh in my joyous mouths. And you, O present Instant, are the emerald cup in which Eternity constricts and dilates, rises up and settles down, like a sea of hope."

The Double Genius fell silent. Sitting with a head in each hand, he seemed to be reflecting profoundly.

Psychodorus went away, and he walked unsteadily, like a man drunk on wine.

XXVIII. The Final Journey

Psychodorus was growing weaker by the day, and by the hour. The moment came when his legs refused to carry him any further. He lay down by the roadside to await death. He was smiling like a child from the country who is being taken to the city for the first time.

A young woman passed by, singing. She stopped and said: "What are you doing there, old man? Do you need anything?"

"I don't need anything," said Psychodorus. "I'm waiting for death. Don't stay to watch. It's a fine sight for those who know how to see, but it would seem ugly to your innocent youth."

The young woman sat down next to him. She leaned over and looked at him for a long time. Then she declared. "You're handsome, old man, and I love you."

"I don't understand what you're saying," Psychodorus replied, "for I can't believe that you're mocking someone who will be dead in a few hours. Other women have told me that I'm handsome, but time has hollowed out numerous wrinkles on my face since then."

The young woman explained, smiling. "Time sows when it labors. Your wrinkles are furrows full of promise. They cover the beauty of your past, but they are beautiful with the future." She added: "Old man whom I love, get up and come with me."

"Since destiny seems to demand this last effort from my courage," said Psychodorus, "I shall get up, and I shall go with you."

The young woman took him to her house. She lived alone with her old nurse. She gave the old man strong liquor to drink, and said to him: "Now your body has at least a day to live."

"Why do you want me to die tomorrow rather than to-day?" asked the philosopher."

"Because I have important things to tell you. Sleep, and when you wake up, I'll talk."

In the morning, when Psychodorus woke up, the young woman said to him: "My name is Palinoa, and I love you. If you loved me too, I'd be very glad."

She leaned over him as if to pluck the flower of a kiss from the withered old mouth. He pushed her away gently, with these words: "I'm faithful to a memory."

"You will love me in order to be more effectively faithful to her, as soon as you know the mystery of my homeland."

And she explained the mystery of her homeland.

"Although none of us has ever passed beyond the frontiers of this happy country, even once, we call ourselves the Travelers. We know the secrets that permit the exchange of souls. When a husband wants to give himself more completely, and when his wife feels a protective nostalgia, the husband's soul passes into the flesh of his wife and the wife's soul passes into the flesh of her beloved. After a crime or an evil thought, we ask a child to let our soul take a bath of purity in his innocent body. Such journeys are creators of beauties that I cannot describe. The inhabitant leaves in the dwelling he quits the traces of his tastes and habits. Would you like, if only for a few hours, to come into me? In every corner of the young palace that I inhabit, you would find memories of my beauty, and you would sense that I am worthy to be loved."

"I'm a foreigner," Psychodorus objected. "You'd be entering into a frightening exile."

"We love to exchange souls with foreigners," Palinoa said, softly. "Thus, our country, without any of our bodies ever leaving it, is nevertheless enriched by the knowledge of other lands."

"I'm an old man who is about to die. It's death that you're asking for. I'm nothing to you. I can't see any reason why you would imitate the devotion of Alcestis."[22]

"Let my still-poor soul depart for the unknown, and give me your rich soul in exchange. If you refuse, you will steal from the Earth the knowledge that the Earth has given you. You would be committing a crime against the Earth."

Psychodorus could not find a reply to that argument, but he said: "For 60 years, I've been looking forward to the moment when I would rejoin the woman I love. I can't consent to wait any longer. Go away, young woman. I want to be alone with Athenatime now."

Palinoa went away, weeping. And Psychodorus said this prayer:

"Death, light your torches and show me the veiled form of Athenatime on the road that I must take."

Along a road with innumerable bends, livid torches converged, but that road was Psychodorus' past, not his future,

---

[22] Alcestis, the subject of a tragedy by Euripides, volunteered to die in the place of her husband Admetus after Apollo got the Fates drunk and extracted a promise that he would be allowed to live if anyone would substitute for him. Heracles subsequently rescued her from Hades.

and the philosopher made vain efforts to look the other way. Death was a vast mirror that reflected what was behind him and prevented him from seeing what lay ahead of him.

Increasingly anxious, the cynic uttered a loud cry, and his entire body was streaming with the sweat of doubt.

Hearing Psychodorus' cry, the young woman came running.

"Obviously, you have asked death for her secret. She has refused to answer or, laughing sardonically, has shown you your life. You are the naïve lover who searches the utmost depths of his lover's eyes, but only finds his own reflection." She added: "Nothing can give you hope that you will find your beloved—and if you meet her, by what sign will you recognize her? You are eternal but, between your immutable banks, your memories are a flowing river. Your memory tells you nothing about the lives that preceded this one. Why do you think that it will be more generously faithful the next time?"

Psychodorus trembled, as if in darkness that was becoming thicker with every passing moment, and he cried: "Be silent, cruel woman!"

But Palinoa said: "My cruelty is benevolent. Do what I asked of you an hour ago. I promise to be faithful to the one you loved. No man will ever come near me, nor any woman— save, as you are giving it to me with your soul, for the memory of Athenatime. For her, I offer you long years of survival."

Psychodorus wept. He called out three times: "Athenatime! Athenatime! Athenatime!" But from wherever Athenatime was, no answer came.

Then the philosopher, hardly able to speak in the cold sweat of death, murmured: "Athenatime, I don't want to let you die again."

His eyes went to the young woman who was there. In an indistinct voice he sighed: "Do as you wish, Palinoa."

Palinoa divined rather than heard the consent. She put her lips to Psychodorus' lips. She contrived the exchange of souls.

179

Scarcely had she stood up than the old body became rigid.

Palinoa wrote in the language of the Travelers the memories that the soul of Psychodorus dictated to her. Her manuscript burned along with the library of Alexandria. Fortunately, Theraphron of Alexandria had translated it into Greek. Theraphron's work, long unknown, was discovered by Han Ryner, a hybrid barbarian, the son of a Norwegian father and a Catalan mother. He translated it into the patois that the French had extracted from a barbarian dialect named Latin. Then, in the hope of having his powers of invention praised or to prevent the faults that his mediocre knowledge of Greek had made him commit being noticed, the plagiarist destroyed the ancient work. Thanks to this despicable plan, readers who love original thought and ingenious inventions put a high value on his mediocre work.

THE SUPERHUMANS

A Prophetic Novel

I. The Star of Fire

As monotonous as an endless and uneventful fall, a summer that grew hotter and rained more abundantly every day had caused the cyclical charm of the seasons to be forgotten years before. Climates were also unified; the torrid and humid suffocation was the same at the poles as at the equator. Like an old man putting on more layers of clothing, the globe wrapped itself up in an immense and increasingly dense cloud. Poorly dissipated, the shadows of the night persisted, with a strangely sinister and unhealthy orange-yellow ardor. One could not retain the joyful name of light for that somber and smoky blaze: a broad darkness poorly transpierced by stray sunbeams; a hectic opacity; a wavering, submerged dusk...

The delicate and anatomically-complex plants were stifling in the heavy atmosphere. Algae were replacing them, along with horsetails and ferns that elevated their dismal architecture to the height of ancient forests in a matter of months. Calices and corollas were disappearing, along with the grace of clustered grapes and the pride of vine-leaves. Only the stubbornly ponderous aloes forced themselves to flower and died in a painful reminiscence of antique poetry. Nothing any longer remained of the colorful and harmonious thousandfold eloquence of flora, in a world reverted to infancy, but a forceful stuttering of geneses, as rapid and enormous as thunder.

The animals were evolving toward prehistoric forms. Agile birds were expiring breathlessly in the thick air, while the aepyornis reappeared, an ineptly-sketched ostrich and big and awkward as a giraffe. Everywhere, nature seemed to be beginning again, perhaps at the approach of some new slumber, of primitive dreams and deliria. Among the quadrupeds, only the largest were resisting, ever more rough-hewn: elephants were reverting to mammoths; giant hippopotamuses blocked the rivers; the muzzles of rhinoceroses were bristling with several pairs of horns.

The necks of crocodiles were growing longer, but tortoises dragged themselves along beneath larger and heavier shields. Gigantic reptiles pulled their flattened forms along on short legs, their passage leaving rapidly-smoothed wakes or durable grooves in the mud.

Except for a few powerful forms that thickened out, all the normal fauna disappeared, plunging into the mud, so to speak, and being swallowed up.

Human beings of a thousand resources and a thousand adaptabilities maintained themselves with difficulty. Unicellular creatures were multiplying rapidly, including bacilli and other kinds of microbes. Surging forth like sudden springs, unknown diseases expanded their inundation, and left depopulated cities behind them—but an extravagance of fecundity responded to the extravagance of mortality; life seemed intoxicating and unsteady, like an orgy. Similarly intoxicated, the Earth was agitated by shocks and tremors. Mountains swelled up, as abruptly as lumps in response to an impact; seas were hollowed out like wounds.

The least observant had been anxious for a long time, From the day when two suns rose over the horizon, people hardly ever encountered one another without sighing, as they shook their heads: "This time, it really is the end of the world!" The official scientists, however, continually offered reassuring affirmations and optimistic rationalizations in the newspapers. According to them, the events about which people were wrong to be worried were entirely normal and transient. Some of them, by means of subtle commentaries, discovered analogous phenomena in history. All of them drew graphs demonstrating that the heat and rain would abate next month, or the one after. The new sun that had, for a time, seconded—or, rather, dominated—the old sun would soon be exhausted by virtue of its own violence and excess.

Life became tremulous and passionate. Along with the fauna and flora of distant epochs, forgotten crimes and extinct insanities were resuscitated. The most ridiculous religions vegetated anew upon the moral dung-heap, as forceful and precocious as ferns or horsetails. People worshipped Jesus and Mithra, proclaimed Buddha and Mohammed; implored Jupiter to stop the rain and Apollo or Osiris to regulate the sunlight, dethroning their insolent rival. Even the abject cults of the High Lama and the infallible Pope reappeared.

That had begun, ten years before, with literary revivals and reconstitutions in special museums and elegant theatres. Then the evil became broader and deeper. Now, many converts were true believers, to the extent of faith, prayer, penitence and the enrichment of priests. Priests, who had been as rare, obscure and timid as other sorcerers for centuries, multiplied in response to the generous desire of the faithful like mushrooms in an autumn shower. Everywhere, people were being baptized, confessed or circumcized, crying "Allah! Allah!", or purified themselves with filthy animal sacrifices, in which mammoths replaced the extinct bulls of old.

In the hot wind of anguish, humankind was the most meekly flickering of candles, violent and weak, irritable and tearful, ready to kill over a misheard word, or burst into tears over a misinterpreted gesture. The same madman who had just struck his best friend in some frivolous discussion encountered the vilest and most malevolent of his enemies and threw himself at his feet in an inexplicable fit of affection, or threw himself into his arms covered him with tearful caresses. The man at whom you gazed with shining eyes and every intoxication, vacillating with utter dementia, ignored you or killed you if you went to kiss him, not knowing why himself, once the deed was done.

People locked themselves away, lying nude on tiles or marble floors from which the double sun caused vapors to seethe; they only went out by night. Or, rather, let us speak

183

correctly in the language of the epoch. The Great Council of Europe, soon imitated by the Emperor of Asia and the American Supreme Committee, had fortunately transformed—according to a necessary law, the members of the Academy of Grammar maintained—if not vocabulary, at least semantics.

The first article declared: "From April 15 of this year, *day* will refer to the time that elapses between the setting and rising of the two suns, while the time during which the suns are above the horizon will be called *night*."

The following articles decided that all work would be carried out during the day—which is to say, when no sun was blazing and the heavy curtain of cloud was unagitated. Severe sanctions threatened not only the imprudent who violated these wise prescriptions, but also the impertinent who permitted themselves—in undeniable hostility to the human race—to employ the ancient terminology. No one could be unaware that the reddish night was transpierced, through the dense and tremulous veils of cloud, by the rays of the two inflamed suns, but day was appeased somewhat by the benevolent kiss of darkness.

A final article declared a temporary law permitting the government to reinstitute the ancient customs of language and behavior by simple decree as soon as the second sun—"the mad sun"—consented to die.

And the governments devoted themselves lavishly to optimistic speeches. If their saliva did not end up extinguishing the maleficent star, it really was not their fault.

Chapter II. The Hexagram

One afternoon—it was probably what people unacquainted with the era would have called 3 a.m.—some 400 people met in a vast hall in the Institution of Independent Scientists in the Boulevard Michel Savigny.[23] All of them,

---

[23] Michel Savigny, or de Savigny (1832-1903) was an unorthodox thinker whose ideas made little impact during his life-

men and women alike, bore a particular symbol on their breasts: two intersecting equilateral triangles—or, as initiates called it, a hexagram.

These people seemed calmer than the others. The atmospheric conditions were certainly putting them to the proof, but, however painful the road might be, someone who knows its objective and its proximity retains a smile and a certain grace through the most grinding effort. Although the general enervation did not spare their bodies, the Hexagramists were manifesting a kind of gentleness and peace: the serenity of enlightened certainty and acceptance.

Amid a confused noise of conversations, the majority were sitting on tiered benches, but some were crossing the hall, shaking hands as they went, to climb up and take their places on the stage, behind a long table. Nothing distinguished them from the others. Anyone who wished could go up, and those who intended to speak were going up.

---

time and are almost completely forgotten today. After his death, his two sons, signing themselves "G. and E. Simon-Savigny," summarized his *"philosophique hexagrammiste"* [hexagramist philosophy] in a self-published book, *Les Adamites* (1906)—"Adamites," in this instance, referring to those natural philosophers who rejected the evolutionary gradualism that had been labelled "pre-Adamite" by its detractors, because of its supposedly-blasphemous assertion that humans had existed for much longer than Biblical chronology proposed. As the present text partly reveals, Savigny proposed that the Earth had been shaped by an alternating series of igneous and glacial catastrophes, with a periodicity of 25,000 years, during each of which continually-reincarnated life-forms were able to remake their bodily forms by an abrupt process of metamorphosis guided by effort and desire. Henri Ner might have been related to the Savigny family by marriage; his daughter Georgette married Louis Simon, who shared a surname with Savigny's wife.

There was no apparent organization. No one was presiding. The long table bore nothing but glasses and carafes of iced water. There was no anachronistic hand-bell.

In such meetings, liberty had, in fact, once been absolute from beginning to end. For two or three years, though, the need to fortify communal hope had preceded the free speech with a few simple rituals, akin to the rudiments of religion.

Despite his unexceptional costume, the young man who rose to his feet first was more reminiscent of a priest than an orator, and his role was that of an officiator. Punctuated by the by the explanatory responses of the multitude, he proclaimed the three syllables which, for the naïve persons of yore, were the name of the demiurge, or the guiding spirit of Israel.

"Je!" he said, with a backward-directed gesture.

The crowd replied: "I was."

"Ho!" he declared, his arms falling alongside his body, and the body becoming narrower, as if to negotiate a narrow passage.

And the crowd, rising, responded: "I am."

But the young man's gesture was valiantly directed forwards and upwards when his voice affirmed: "Vah!"

And the 400 replied; "I will be!"

Then he opened a book and announced, in a pious tone: "Prophecy of Michel Savigny at the beginning of the 20th century."

His solemn lecture, to which everyone listened standing up, was interrupted more than once by the responses that religious assemblies offer at intervals, in resonance with the officiator's solo.

The piece that he read described, with strange precision and alarming exactitude, the cosmic events through which they were living. A few slight errors might, it seems, have struck the witnesses of the cataclysm. No one noticed them. In truth, did they still exist? The archaic language lent the words a certain vacillation of old age. More than that: words whose youth had been rigid and solid had gradually become fluid and fugitive. The bowl of reality, receiving the fluid terms, imposed its own form upon them. Who could doubt that the entire divination had acquired harmony? Fact is a powerful magician; as soon as one delivers vague and faded words to it, it takes responsibility for coloring and fixing the meaning of prophetic pronouncements.

Devoutly, the young man read: "The approach of the star of fire is initially advertised by seasons or years that are bright and hot."

The multitude, divided into three successive choirs, replied.

The choir on the left observed: "There were years, there were years."

The central mass: "We lived through those years."

The ecstatic Hexagramists on the right: "Noble and benign years!"

The soloist went on: "First there is a spring, the radiation and splendor of which spreads joy forcefully in all hearts. Even old men will feel the joy of youth flowing through them."

The reader paused. Only the old men scattered throughout the room replied, in hoarse voices: "We lived through that second youth."

The soloist continued. Joyfully, he spoke of a luxurious unexpected charm in which the delicate sweetness of spring and the opulence of autumn were mingled.

And the three successive choirs repeated:

"There were years, there were years."

"We lived through those years."

"Noble and benign years!"

But the officiator, abruptly becoming somber and threatening, went on: "Suddenly…a globe of fire appears on the horizon. It is a small thing at first, a shining, sparkling red dot; one might think it a ruby lost in the immensity, some diamond prism struck by the red rays of a setting sun, which break apart as they strike it.

187

"From that moment on, the red dot grows incessantly. It soon resembles a block of molten metal brought out of a furnace."

The singular recitation detailed the effects of the increasingly maleficent star: the scorching and cracking of the Earth, the atmospheric furnace, the disappearing flowers, the flowing waters that run dry, lost in mud and evaporation.

And the triple chorus:

"There were months, there were months."

"We lived through those months."

"Dolorous and anguished months!"

The reader continued: "Soon, two suns rise over the horizons, one becoming more distant, the other effacing the glare of 20 suns, spreading fantastic light over everyone and everything, throwing bloody gleams here and designing down there, on the denuded plain, a lake with silver waves, every one tinted, sometimes with the scintillation of rubies, at other times those of emerald."

He spoke of the rivers turned to thick mud, stagnant and fuming, confounded with the universal mud; he spoke of animals dying of hunger and thirst, humans resisting with increasing difficulty. Then his voice seemed to light up and release sprays of fire, causing a bombardment of meteors to rain down, displaying jagged bolts of lightning and the soaring flights of fireballs falling upon cities and forests, sudden howling and sizzling conflagrations.

The triple choir mourned:

"This is now, this is now."

"We are living through this now."

"A terrible and atrocious now!"

But the soloist threw forth, with a poignant mixture of threat and promise, joy and pain: "Finally, the ocean boils, rising up in mists, and these mists, enveloping the Earth, announce to the human survivors of the frightful cataclysm that the plain might be reborn where the desert was made."

Upon which the crowd declared, with delirious emotion:

"That is tomorrow, that is tomorrow."

"We shall live in that tomorrow."

"A tomorrow of dusk and dawn, of sadness and hope, of agony and genesis!"

The young man sat down, and the crowd sat down with him. The emotion, which had not calmed at all, gradually acquired a more serious and more thoughtful aspect.

Soon, an old man with a long white beard rose to his feet, who, instead of repeating the sacred words, allowed his mind and heart to overflow.

"How many times," he cried, "in how many lives, have we encountered one another? We do not recognize one another, however; we love one another as brethren of a single life, as brethren who wake up and discover one another. That is not enough. Let us never forget that we have been finding one another again, accompanying one another, and supporting one another for centuries. One of us—which one?—was Michel Savigny, another was Edmond, another was Georges, was Poinsot, was Félix Pagan, was Jacques Fréhel, was Jean Ott.[24] And from generation to generation, we have also been the comrades of successive encounters."

After a long appeal to love, and having long demanded, with tears in his voice, that all the affection of centuries must be gathered and accumulated as provisions for the painful journey, he explained, almost a hazard, a few points of his doctrine. His audience knew what he was saying as well as he did, but they listened with glad smiles. Expressed in a loud voice, their own hopes charmed them like a reconciliation or a

---

[24] All the names listed here are those of Ner's close friends. Edmond and Georges were Michel Savigny's two sons; Félix Pagan and Jean Ott were minor poets. "Jacques Fréhel" was the pseudonym of Ner's long-time mistress and sometime collaborator Alice Télot. Maffeo Charles Poinsot wrote abundantly under his own name, although his early works, written in collaboration with Georges Normandy, were signed "Paul de Robertski."

rescue, like a numerous encounter and a vast declaration of amity amid the threats of the desert.

The old man reminded them, specifically, that although, in normal periods, creatures remain slaves to an inflexible form, prisoners of an almost immutable species, the great catastrophes created by the alternative shocks of the star of ice and the star of fire liberate forces, permitting all hopes, all attempts, all efficacious efforts, and all progress.

In a prophetic tone, he spoke of the near and far future.

He said that the star of fire would come closer and closer, that the air would become increasingly unbreathable, that humankind would soon disappear from a planet that was nothing but a seething steam-bath. He spoke of the terrors and horrors that the vulgar summarize in the phrase "the end of the world".

Then he proclaimed the ever-renewed victory of multiform life, the tenacious victory of being that successively dons a thousand new costumes, a thousand bodies adapted to its shape and its growing desire, which abandons, along the eternal pathways, a thousand worn-out forms, a thousand empty cadavers.

Now his voice rose up like a joyful fire. He extolled the imminent plasticity of matter, and proclaimed that creatures of aspiration and will would satisfy their poetic dreams in that victorious period. Those dreams appeared to the vulgar to be the craziest of chimeras; in the bleak, impassive and immutable periods of normality they were, indeed merely impotent torments. "O my dream, the dead weight and defeat of a hundred of my existences, a hundred of my poor yesterdays; the wings, success and crown of my ardent and rich tomorrow!"

He compared the painful and glorious striving of humans toward superhumanity to the victory of the caterpillar that becomes a butterfly. He spoke about old decrepit organs devoured by cells analogous to our white blood corpuscles, giving way, in the mystery of a triumphant embryogeny, to new organs, the children of desire.

He described, in the imminent torment, periods of exasperating violence punctuated by intervals of relative calm. During the more intense ardors it would be necessary to bring about the great and difficult metamorphoses, like blacksmiths hurriedly shaping red-hot iron. When the heat-waves slackened, patient and scrupulous work would be done to perfect the details. During these tranquil revisions the slightly-intoxicated work of creation would be smoothed out. In the initial phases, our multiple, perhaps contradictory desires, would be at risk of forming strange monsters, howling combinations of a thousand disparate characteristics. In the creative fever, the disorder of our desires would not be the only cause of absurd complexities; how many unconscious reminiscences might intervene, unbeknown to us, in our labors, warping them in all directions, rendering them as bizarrely composite as a madman's deliria…

The old man now compared the birth of an unknown body to the externalization of an original work by a writer or artist. He described, after a period of desire in which the future work torments and appeals with the coquetry of a distant woman or phantom, the craftsman's fearful moment of hesitation in confrontation with the unlooked-for task. He spoke of the tremulous hand, the step backwards to see what has been wrought, and the despair of the eye before an initial result so coarse, so monstrous and so far from what was intended. But soon, courageous study discovers the outlines from which the new beauty will emerge; avid and applied intelligence identifies the imperfections and their causes; at closer range, a thousand flashes of light illuminate the means of correcting them. One eliminates hesitantly, adds enthusiastically, polishes patiently, and eventually, the world of art—or the world of life, of which it is a carbon-copy—will perhaps be enriched by a masterpiece.

There had, he proclaimed, never been a better opportunity than the one that was imminent.

It was during a glacial cataclysm that an élite of creatures had succeeded in creating sublime and dolorous humankind—

191

but the hardening and contraction of matter by the cold were symbols of a profound verity. Atoms are much less tractable in painful glacial cataclysms than in magnificent igneous catastrophes. Glacial creations, even the most beautiful—whether fish, marsupials or humans—always retain a certain poverty: a smallness, narrowness and paltriness. It is a miserly and rebellious matter that is kneaded, recalcitrant and injurious to every effort. How generous, by contrast, is fire! It yields the most plastic of matter, on a prodigious scale. When its magnificent gifts are exploited, everything takes on colossal proportions—terrible lizards or mastodons—and igneous dragonflies are larger than glacial marsupials.

The creative suffering, he affirmed, would be less this time than in the time when oil was formed, and even the carboniferous period. The former epoch was more ardent than the latter. Long and persuasive reasoning demonstrated that the cataclysm now begun would be less violent than either of the other two.

"Despite these singularly favorable conditions, humankind's efforts to surpass itself will, I fear, often be blind and groping; many crazy and unviable forms will be created. We who understand are planning in advance, so far as is possible, the marvelous and terrible work to be completed. The 800 hexagramists spread all over the globe represent the most valiant, the most clear-sighted and the most effective of forces, the veritable matrix of the glories of tomorrow. Oh, if we could only come together in a single aspiration, a single will, our efforts converging toward a single goal...but that would require us to combine our desires in a sheaf of energies."

The orator had already interrupted himself many times to mop his streaming forehead and drink a little iced water. Here again he stopped, paining with fatigue, thirst and emotion.

While he was savoring the comforting refreshment, the entire assembly rose to its feet and, with vehement gestures, affirmed the communal will—but an abrupt silence fell, and the initiates looked at one another in amazement. All of them thought that they were proclaiming the same ideas as everyone else, but all of them heard different words and different desires emerging from their neighbors' lips, perhaps opposed to their own.

Up on the stage, a young, tall and slender woman shouted: "Michel Savigny never gave the future beings the name of superhumans, but that of cherubim. Did he not indicate thus there first desirable progress? Wings, wings—we want wings."

Others, however, demanded: "Let us put an end to death!"

And others: "Let us develop more powerful brains. Cephalize our being! Cephalize our being!"[25]

A hundred different cries, some distinct and authoritative, others confused and uncertain, filled the hall like precise individuals and drifting specters.

The old man's face brightened with a smile that was lovely and sad. Twice over, his hands performed a gesture of sweeping aside the unnecessary; then they commenced another enigmatic demonstrative gesture. Meanwhile, words tumbled from his excited lips: "The only urgent progress, my friends, is that which will make of humankind a god, benevolent to itself as to others. It is…"

But the orator paused, like a traveler hesitating at a fork in the road.

"Listen, instead, to a kind of fable or parable, which I composed the other day, with my heart and my mind, while re-reading Michel Savigny's admirable *Legend of the Three Companions*."

---

[25] Ryner's text has "*Céphalisons l'être.*" Although "cephalize" is not in Webster's, "cephalization" is, referring to a biological tendency for the head to dominate the body anatomically, and the verb is derivable therefrom. Given what subsequently comes to pass after the metamorphic cataclysm, it would be inappropriate to substitute "encephalize" here, even though these hexagramists appear to be calling for more highly developed brains rather than bigger heads.

Briefly and rapidly, since he was speaking to initiates, many of whom could have recited the entire text, he reminded them of that noble tale. A few words sufficed to evoke in every memory the image of the Buddha, on the eve of his death, sitting beneath the sacred tree surrounded by the host of his disciples. The words with which the great sage had dazzled those he loved in the twilight of his life resonated in every mind: "This time, I have told you nothing but the message of peace and love. Tomorrow, plunged in the depths of Nirvana, motionless and self-absorbed, I shall seek, in order to report it to you later, the message of science. Until I return, there is no truth more useful than the one expressed in these words: 'Love one another. Love enough that, in an effusion of pity, you will return good to the individual who has had the misfortune to do you harm.' Preach the unique truth tirelessly, so that the hearts conquered by you shall conquer other hearts. Thanks to you, and those who follow you, and those who follow your disciples, when I come back, I shall find humankind fraternally united. Then, to those who will have learned to love, I shall give the residue of science. To those for whom power will no longer be anything but benevolent, I shall deliver all power. To those for whom life will be a benefit that expands and irradiates, I shall explain how to triumph over death."

Then, Michel Savigny relates, time went by: ten centuries, as in all legends. A few disciples, anxious with expectation and hope, heard that in a corner of Galilee, on the shores of an idyllic lake, a man was speaking with victorious gentleness to charmed crowds. Might it be Cakya-Mounni, returned to keep his ancient promise?

Three of the principal Buddhists came to listen to the man who was perhaps the Awaited One—but when Jesus had spoken to the people, the three companions, shaking their heads or shrugging their shoulders, observed: "This man has said nothing new."

Then, turning toward him, they interrogated him bitterly. "Have you nothing new to tell us? We have known the message of love and peace for a thousand years. Have you come to reveal the message of science—yes or no?" Parting their cloaks, they displaced the symbols inscribed on their tunics and demanded an explanation of them. They were not asking for the elementary meaning of the symbols; they knew that already. What they wanted was the profound revelation that would finally bring all knowledge surging forth from the near-mute lines.

One displayed a pentagram, and demanded: "Pronounce the words that triumph over disease and death."

The second displayed two intersecting triangles and implored: "Give us the science of worlds and the beings that inhabit them."

The third, on revealing the mysterious characters on his breast, commanded: "Tell me what I have been, what I am and what I will be."

Jesus made no reply to any of the three companions, and they drew away, pouring scorn on his ignorance.

Michel Savigny's tale ends there—but the old man continued, and his commentary astonished the initiates.

"Had the Bodhisattva failed to keep his promise, then? Forgetful of humans and of his last words, did he remain plunged in the egotistical joys of Nirvana? No, no, my brethren, he really had come back, and what had initially been made flesh in Mary's loins had been the Word of Science. Alas, his childhood, more intelligent and perspicacious than the best maturity, had shown him a humankind so deceptive…oh, how far the world was from vast and universal love. Again, he encountered pariahs and masters, the scorn that crushes and the sly revolt that lies in wait. There were still victimized individuals and populations; there were still wars and battles. Would not giving the word of science to beings so insane be giving children a weapon with which to injure themselves? Jesus, weighed down by disgust and pity, resolved not to reveal the excessively dangerous word. To avoid any possibility of some spark springing involuntarily from his lips to set the world on fire, he buried the message of science in the utmost depths of his unconscious. He spent his time repeating the message of peace and love, which, until it could be effectively understood, has to be the only message for us. A child of Israel, his ignorance wished to suffer the torment of unity, and that strange need to impart the idea of an absolute beginning. To human fraternity, sensed solely by the beating of his heart, he gave a ridiculously metaphysical origin: he affirmed that humans had a common Father, who ruled in the Heavens."

The old man revealed, behind the apparent success of Christianity, its real and lamentable failure—or, if you prefer, its immediate and irremediable corruption. He affirmed that Jesus, in the Garden of Olives, had foreseen the ignoble and bloody future of his doctrine. That vision had saddened his soul to the point of death and spread a great sweat of anguish through his icy limbs. On the cross, it had torn from him the terrible cry: "Eloi, Eloi, Sabacthani!" What was that reproach to the Father who had abandoned him if not the observation, in a metaphysical form, that the fraternity of humankind was not yet, and would not be for a long time—perhaps never—a universal fact and a universal happiness?

Even in the refuge of sleep, the excessively vivid dolors of the previous day persecute us, as dreams and phantoms. It required centuries of the peace of Nirvana itself to calm the horror and despair of the dying Jesus. Before thinking about returning and venturing any hope for humans, his brethren of ill-will, he allowed a Millennium to pass, and almost a fifth of another Millennium. Then he reappeared in a pleasant town in Italy.

Humans were as unworthy as ever of the message of science. Francis forgot it as voluntarily as Jesus had forgotten it, and began the Sermon on the Mount all over again, amid the hills of Assissi.

Humans seemed to him to be naughty children. They quarreled with one another, maimed one another and killed one another to possess diamonds or other stones that could, in fact, be turned into amusing toys. They consented to worry and fatigue, cowardice and courage, peril and brutality, to wounds, to death and murder to obtain so-called precious metals, whose roundels, sparkling in the light, did indeed render the game of quoits more joyful. To seduce such beings, he made himself the most naïve and graciously puerile of souls. He tried to move the human heart by announcing the Good News to others of his brethren, the birds in the sky or the fish in the rivers. He addressed hymns to the ardent generosity of his brother the sun, to the smooth limpidity of water, our chaste sister. Because human evils were deafening almost everyone with avidity for false goods, louder than the exhortations to his brethren that flew in the air or glided through the water, louder than the odes to the chastity of water and the luminous prodigality of the Sun, Francis sang the epithalamium of Lady Poverty, his beloved spouse. He drew after him an increasing procession of the charmed poor. He did not know that the sincerity of apostles only serves to prepare for the intrigues and power of some political Brother Elias. He died ecstatic, believing that the world had finally been saved.

What a joyful impatience troubled his Nirvana this time. He did not let an entire Millennium pass. The Buddha wanted to make up the ground lost between his incarnation as Jesus and his incarnation as Francis. He did not even permit the time thus calculated to elapse, and appeared in holy Russia.

Humans had succeeded in getting worse. Instead of a few mercenaries breaking lances against resounding armor, all hands bore weapons that struck from afar, and little masses of iron were piercing defenseless bodies. The masters of nations were transforming entire populations into martyrs and assassins. In order to bury the word of science more deeply within him, he even had to forget the word of peace. He had a long, stormy and troubled childhood and a long youth as a soldier. He was manifest as a literary genius and nothing more.

He finally pulled himself together. Tolstoy proclaimed his horror of modern slavery, worse than the brutality of ancient slavery. He proclaimed his equal horror of revolutionary violence and the organized violence that we call ordinary government. He proclaimed his horror for everything that is war and murder. His temporary fatherland being engaged in a terrible struggle against some other temporary fatherland, he proclaimed his indifference for what madmen called victory, and was only not indifferent to purity of the heart and the hand. To people who admired the external ingenuity of his words but sniggered at their profound meaning, he announced one last time the Good News of "non-resistance to evil".

"My brethren, let us finally hear the word of love that the Buddha has come four times to announce to us in vain. Since the first desirable progress was unrealized by humans, let us at least prepare to accomplish it in becoming superhuman. When, in a few centuries, the Buddha comes again, perhaps bearing beneath vast white wings the 80 signs of perfection, let him finally find a superhumanity worthy of the word of science.

"Let us profit from the plastic circumstances to put an end to hatred, and let us put all the treasure of our confidence into love. Today, still, love is the only true conqueror, and the sole force that can prepare the solidity of future conquests. May hearts enlarge to the extent of the adoration of life in all living beings. Then, amid the flame and light of love, in a fraternity that rises us like a triumph…"

But the tall slender woman who had demanded the power of flight interrupted the overly long speech. She made a gesture similar to a take-off, and cried: "Wings—I want wings!"

"Demand them from love, then. But demand nothing for yourself but love. Wings given by love will always fly toward your brother's suffering or smile. Would not wings that you have forged directly be nothing but a curse, if they might become the instrument of hatred or the means of flirtatious flight? Love is the harmonious sculptor which shapes all matter in the form of good, but the hammer of hatred destroys all statues; it makes a ridiculous irritant dust of the most beautiful marbles. Love, let us choose love: the rest will be given to us as a bonus."

"I've had enough of dying!" moaned a little quinquagenarian with bleak, clean-shaven lips that imported hints of avarice to harsh features. "Immortality—it's my immortality that I shall strive for."

But the old man, his long white beard shaking with bitter laughter, went on: "O my brother, I dread that you might be making the worst of all choices. Immortals inevitably forget children, and the softness of kisses as well. An immortal life would be the least worthy to be lived. Let us flee that eternal widowhood in terror. Besides, you can only obtain a false immortality, a stagnant life of perhaps 20,000 years, until the visitation of the star of ice. Beware, my friend, of what you call immortality—it is the immortality of stone; it is ennui; it is immortal death. Let us consent joyously, my beloved, to harmonious changes, to forms that multiply and renew themselves, to the rejection of bodies that have lost their flexibility."

Even among the initiates, the old man seemed to be crying in the wilderness. The majority persisted stubbornly in demanding wings, immortality, a vaster intelligence, more synthetically powerful and simultaneously cleverer, and more flexible in penetrating the folds of analysis, or a more vigorous, adroit and commanding body—a thousand specific advantages, which, according to the use that was made of them, might be instruments of some utility or might become means of destruction and self-destruction.

Furthermore, some of them, becoming uninterested in what was happening in the hall, were now listening to noises coming from outside. The number of these distractions was increasing rapidly. The old orator was running out of breath in an ever-increasing void. His words were not even met with cold silence. Windows were opening noisily and anxious heads were leaning out over the street. The old man with the long beard stopped, exhausted, not so much by his effort as by a sense of the futility of his effort. Then, like the others, he heard the cries of the hawkers selling newspapers.

"War declared between the white race and the yellow race! Treacherous attempts by the yellow to seduce the black!"

The old preacher of love let himself fall into a chair. He murmured: "The wretches! We're all going to die in a few months, but they feel the need to murder one another. They're determined that every one of their deaths will be a crime."

"Humans," said the woman who demanded wings, "have always been condemned to die soon, but I don't believe that consideration has ever prevented them from killing one another."

Chapter III. Eternal Life

Humans kill one another cleverly and furiously. In glorious prose, journalists and orators affirmed the superior merits of their own race, stigmatizing the abominable crimes of the opposing race. Beneath the impacts, the flights, the pursuits and he innumerable bloody falls, the Earth itself, coming ever closer to the star of fire, was nothing but a vast agonized folly.

Life, however, became increasingly gigantic. Alas, the forms that it tried out enjoyed a hasty fortune and a rapid decline. They gave the impression not only of being temporary but somehow false and artificial, of shaky scenery, of one last abrupt and quivering tableau. The general enormity was out of breath, and the vastest acts of violence were groaning with weakness. In spite of the rain streaming from the clouds, the improvised forests caught fire, burning without flames, and were stifled, becoming an indescribable mixture of mud and coal. The gigantic animals fell upon the slowly burning ground to sink into it, amid the bitter exhalations of death.

The day came when there was no longer anything on the Earth resembling what we call life—but does not the life that we believe to be unknown surpass in quantity and intensity that which we believe to be known?

The vertiginous spectacle seemed to be devoid of spectators. The sphere was divided up between a thousand fireworks and a thousand boiling seas. Combinations and reactions precipitated their phantasmagorias like the changes in an immense kaleidoscope. Oceans revealed themselves, and soon evaporated. Mountains of metallic substances, created in a few seconds, oxidized in a few seconds, transforming themselves and vanishing. Detonations, shaking the heavy atmosphere, tore it apart momentarily. Jets of lava and flame surged forth amid geysers of mud, fountains of water and whirlwinds of steam.

The entire transition that future legends and future science would call chaos and genesis unfolded, inharmonious for eyes like ours, demented and unthinkable for our minds, rare and rigid in form. Confronted with the absolute, however, would the invariant chaos in which we live, which custom renders normal, as if ordained for our naivety, be any less paradoxical?

Life is always a struggle against the pack of murderous forces, but the worst cataclysms imaginable by contemporary thought cannot destroy life, a tenacious and evolving heroism. Life has two esoteric names: it is called Change and it is called Eternity. Creatures not only struggle for survival and endurance, but for improvement and vast conquests. How can things so alien to the experiences we remember, to the only existences we know, and to existences sufficiently similar to our present for the words of the present to be able to express them, be described? Everything that is too far away from the present seems impossible to us. All life that is too different, we naively call dead. But if we make the effort to imagine it, our lacerated mind transports its own pain into things, and their movement, so unlike our movement, cries out to us that it is terror and suffering.

Being was like a strange knight who, in the middle of a battle, tried on breastplates and found none that fit him. Every day, in the furnace, it heroically made itself a one-day body. Without any direct action on the most material of the molecules with which it had to surround and protect, its will captured them, tamed them, by the intermediation of more refined elements—electromagnetically equivocal, if you wish, or if you prefer, materio-spiritually fluid. Often, psychic being had scarcely constituted an outline of aggregation around itself when a frightful whirlwind tore away its precarious conquest, dispersing far and wide the atoms which, in the ineffable language of today, it was already daring to call "my atoms."

For the entirely different struggle that is present-day life, such a combat would seem to be nothing but pain, a mad and agonizing tearing apart—but who can describe the powerful joy and intoxication of the momentary victories that preceded and followed the prompt defeats? If, by a mocking effort, some warrior of these battles of flame, had been able to imagine what we call life, oh, how scornful he would have been of its cold poverty, how ridiculous the scant intensity of our falls and triumphs would have seemed to him—as ridiculous and paltry as the lumpen life of stones seems to us.

To be sure, death lay in wait for every gesture, every omission, every error, every imprudence. Death proliferated, perhaps as frequent as our slumbers. But was it not as indifferent or as joyful? And did not the revenge of births proliferate like our awakenings? In the seething fecundity of life in revolution, knowing that it would find the material everywhere of a new instrument to fashion, to accord, to manipulate, being accepted death with as little repugnance as we consent to the poor renewal of sleep. It considered it as the simplest of journeys, a comfortable means of trying out diverse forms and dismantling them after taking cognizance of their advantages and defects. It explored, curiously, the domain of every species; in order to visit them, it invented new regions; it attempted a thousand hesitant forms that offered themselves, transformed them, creating others thereby, and then rejected those imperfect envelopes. It died laughing, simply to try out some secondary amendment.

Who can describe to the sedentary individuals we are the sensual delights of those bold nomads and vagabonds? How can we, accustomed to immobile dwellings, understand the joys of folding up one's tent only to unfurl it again, in a modified form, in a different landscape?

Let us not try to stammer that which is beyond the reach of our thoughts and our words, which can neither be pronounced by our lips not heard by our ears. Let us rather move forward a few millennia, to catch up with a spectacle, still strange and fugitive, but a part of which, it seems to me, can perhaps be captured by our language—for the time always comes when the longest revolutions calm down and fade away. The time comes for peace and imprisonment in definite species. The passionately changing host will become fixed for weeks or centuries. Life, doubtless enriched by a few unknown forms and a few fortunate formulas, will become monotonous again, reproducing itself indefinitely. Embryogeny loses its groping power and becomes once again a tiresome repetition.

Chapter IV. The Superangels

The exquisite meadow was traversed by a stream whose brisk course brought it unsteadily into contact with pebbles at every step. A thousand fringes of foam dappled its greenish translucent flow with their sparkling whiteness. Here, the watercourse seemed to be imitating the yielding flexibility of the grass, there the dancing grace of islets of daisies bobbing in the wind or the swaying of meadowsweets.

Toward these delicacies some 20 reapers were advancing like a clumsy disaster. Their clothing: a large hat of braided rushes; a kind of shirt mad of beige cloth; long trousers that would have resembled leather if the thick and lumpy leather that directly compressed their bruised feet had not made the coarse cloth seems admirably delicate by comparison. They were followed by a man armed with a whip, whose costume, though coarser still, was more comfortable. Behind him came a priest; his green silk robe was enriched with red and blue embroidery, exposing his feet, protected beneath by a quadruple sole of satin and as well-groomed as the hands of ancient bishops.

The priest was not walking on the hard road; he was carried by a sort of automobile, a little open carriage of marvelous docility. A large parasol of white silk protected the occupant from the morning sun. To either side, every rotation of the wheels flapped a double fan. One leaf refreshed the air passing over the caressed cheeks, while the other kept the dust away. At intervals, a delicate foot pressed a spring and perfumed water was vaporized around the priest.

A book was within range of his left hand, a kind of paten next to his right. Negligently, he gave orders, which the overseer repeated in a brutal tone.

The little convoy stopped beside the meadow. The priest grabbed the paten and raised it piously. The enamel image represented an elephantine animal with two trunks. As if dazzled and intimidated, the men lowered their eyes, bowed their heads and knelt down.

"It is holy, just and equitable that you should worship the gods," the priest affirmed.

The reapers and the overseer plunged their foreheads into the dust of the road. While they raised their upper bodies again, the priest kissed the elephant three times, repeating: "Holy, holy, holy!" Then, turning the image toward the kneeling company again, he pronounced: "It is holy, just and equitable that you should idolize my kiss."

The foreheads were drawn through the dust again.

"Remember," the priest went on, "that humans are on this Earth solely to serve the gods. Remember that negligence is always punished…" At this point, during a pause, the overseer cracked his whip three times. Then the speech continued: "Remember that zeal is always rewarded. If the piety of your labor is ardent enough, perhaps one of you will obtain the glory this evening of kissing my bare foot, on behalf of everyone."

None of this was said with the animation of discourse or the liveliness of improvisation; the tone remained ritual, and it was apparent that the same formulas were repeated every morning.

The overseer directed each laborer to his place. The scythes were readied. The priest proclaimed: "For the glory of the gods!" That was the signal. Nevertheless, no one made a move until the overseer had cried in his turn: "For the glory of the gods!" Then the reapers piously repeated the same words as they swung the scythes for the first time.

So far as their souls were concerned, all the men were blind. None seemed capable of perceiving the touching beauty of the meadow.

As the overseer proclaimed: "For the glory of the gods," a sound of wings was heard, softer than a kiss, but simultaneously more authoritarian than a command. The priest, the overseer and he serfs turned toward the approaching sound.

A singular flock was heading toward the meadow from a nearby mountain. Birds? No, nothing that is to be found in our conscious memories. Seek instead for the treasure of those reminiscences, certainly impoverished and deformed by the nocturnal infidelity of the organs, that poets believed they had dreamed, and which we call chimeras or products of imagination. Rummage among the timidity of legends, dreams and paintings that were believed to be daring in the extreme. Although much more beautiful, the delightful beings whose delicate, smooth and affecting shadows were now moving over the meadow resembled the angels of which Fra Angelico dreamed. Music emanated from them, which seemed to emerge from the most perfect instruments—but these superior angels no longer had any need to weigh themselves down and deform themselves with foreign instruments; their vastly-sweeping wings possessed the power of great organs; their slightest adjustments sang more sweetly than our flutes, wept or rejoiced more profoundly than a bass violin.

In harmony with the orchestra of wings, a chorus of articulate words emerged from their lips.

Oh, what strange and truly divine beings! Their wings did not only spread forth all kinds of music; they dispensed perfumes—but were those perfumes not also dreams and thoughts? They displayed or gave off the most unexpected

205

colors. The multiple joys that emanated from these beings came together in ineffable harmony, and in the meantime, the successive diversities of luxuriant beneficence traced an indescribable curve of nobility. At the same time as a chorus of music and dreams, songs and thoughts, perfumes and colors, the Superangels—as they were usually called—performed an aerial dance. Compared with the aerobatic flexibility of their movements, our poor earthbound choreographies would be ponderous crawling. The exquisite evolutions that drew them together and apart, brought them closer and further away, translated more clearly that a beautiful face in a beautiful setting the metaphysical secrets of objects, the amorous secrets of creatures. In accord with the song of words, the music of wings and the melody of perfumes, their movements traced hymns of light, symphonies of flame and radiant rainbows.

The perfumes, thoughts and dreams overwhelmed the spectator. As thankful and vague as sensuality, the gazes below saw nothing but wings and quiverings, believing that they were seeing flights of sunlight, meteoric dances and falling stars. Only the priest sought to discern detail in the dazzle and oppression of those delights. Between the ever-moving wings, indefatigable sowers of melodies, odors and colors, he divined rather than saw a supple, slender, drifting, almost non-existent—but nevertheless lovely and delicate—body. Oh, so lovely, so delicate, so frail! On the vast and magnificent head, the forehead extended its broad promontory like a richness and a gift; the face, slim, small and exquisite, retreated and fled like modesty itself.

Unexpected proportions, nobler than human proportions, more pensive than virile beauty, more touching than feminine grace: the priest observed them and studied them, but he often forgot all will, all intellectual effort and allowed himself to be submerged in the vague reality as in the most paradisal and most absorbing of dreams.

Amid the orchestra of wings, amid the multicolored grace, the perfumed charm and the noble lines of movements that were forever coming apart and recombining, the Superangels sang:

"We are given many names: names of light, names of flame, names of perfume, names of gaiety, dance and flight. We prefer our name of love.

"Humans, we listen to you smiling when you call us superangels, superelves, great dragonflies, superior fairies, dancing sylphs, music incarnate—but when your ears listen to us, we proclaim ourselves more willingly Amours.

"We have obliterated in ourselves hatred, envy and jealousy. We have striven to be fully developed. That conquest realized is worth a thousand conquests to us.

"If you accord us names of flame, names of light, names of perfume, names of gaiety, dance and light, names of rainbow or music, it is because we merit the name of love.

"Love has given us wings; nothing is more assiduous and faster than love.

"We are light, flame, changing colors, because quivering love is clad in all the aspects of beauty.

"We have obliterated hatred. Victory, victory, O sole true victory! We have obliterated hatred!

"That fortunate murder took place before our birth. I scarcely remember it; the combat appears to me in a formless, changing and receding conflict, like a dream one forgets. I am, however, certain.

"The murder of hatred is my work; the murder of hatred, O my brethren, is our work.

"Among the most gloriously perfumed songs, display, O my wings, the brightest colors, the yellow and purple of all victories and all flames. Hatred is dead in our liberated hearts.

"Yes, that obliteration is our work. For there is only being in living beings, and no action or cause exists outside living beings.

"Ancient humans, in the unsteady poverty of their dreams, believed that they were supported by a God, a Creator, a Celestial Father. There is no other God but beings, no other Creator than creatures—and every one, O mystery of clarity, is his own father.

"If there were a Celestial Father, he would give all his sons what we have given ourselves. He would not be divided within himself; none of his children would hate any other.

"Are the murder of hatred and the conquest of love straightforward and easy victories, triumphs with neither cleverness nor preparation?

"Humans, listen to the great secret.

"We have arrived at love because we know the road of love and we have had the courage to climb the road of love: a path of softness, shadows and corollas; a path with a menacing entrance and smiling bends, which you call wisdom and renunciation.

"The renunciation of false goods, the rejection of heavy and thorny burdens—O deliverance! To blind slaves you seem to be poverty and emptiness, you, the only wealth and the only plenitude. They do not know in what pure gold you are hollowed out, marvelous emptiness of the cup; they do not know with what wine and what intoxication you are overflowing, sparkling plenitude.

"How many successive wisdoms and how many joyful renunciations have lightened my body, have lifted burdens and servitudes far away from me!

"If I am able to love the only wealth of beings, it is because I turned away, a long time ago, laughing and shrugging my shoulders, from the poverty of things.

"Oh, how liberated we are from all weight and all cares...we no longer want anything but to understand, to understand in order to love.

"Things have nothing lovable. Things have no heart, and my love cannot be for them. Things only have value as support for living beings—but it is not the pedestal at which I gaze; it is the beauty of the statue.

"I love you, O my brethren, moving and flying statues of perfect love. I love you with a dazzled and satisfied admiration.

"And I love, presently with pity and suspended admiration, all living beings, sketched statues. Every one may become a masterpiece that rejoices in light; every one may be clad in the lines of wisdom and love.

"Glory to wisdom, the road to love, and joyous glory to love, the summit of wisdom: glory accumulated in the thousand existences that prepared my happiness; and glory overflowing from my happiness. Glory to the road and each of its way-stations. Glory, glory, glory to the present summit and to the future summits.

"We are liberated, we are liberation. Let those who hear our sing take the road to wisdom. Let them eject the burdens and servitudes beneath which ascension is stifled. From now on they will march, lightly radiant—and tomorrow, tomorrow they will feel, with ineffable voluptuousness, the wings of love begin to sprout.

"After the dark passage of death and the floral blossoming of birth, they will be similar to us, those who have been able to liberate themselves by wisdom.

"They will have no further need of clothing or dwellings. Our wings carry us, swifter than swallows, into the most agreeable climates. Our flight laughs at the leaden march of the seasons.

"If rain is presaged whose lustration is not desired by our wings, we fly away, more rapidly than the rain-heavy winds. We are, when we wish, more rapid than the frenzied and breathless pursuit of tempests. But sometimes, rising up to the calm heights, we watch hurricanes blowing beneath us.

"All life is condemned to nourish itself. How few aliments our drifting bodies require! One fruit satisfies our most extreme hunger. Ordinarily, a flower suffices, or a perfumed leaf, or even an odorous fragment of bark. Two violets and a drop of water in the hollow of a vervain leaf will sustain a day of music, dancing, thought and love.

"Our sobriety exempts us from necessities to which we do not direct our thought, and which weigh down the reeking eaters of flesh, or even the innocent beasts that ruminate too much grass.

"A perfumed sweat dispersed, amid rays of light and harmonies, by a slight beat of our wings, suffices to expel from our slight bodies that which is not assimilable."

Thus sang the Amours.

Thus sang the flock of 40 Amours that populated the Earth and sky with poetry, dreams, thought and aspiration.

In the charmed light, their wings mingled undulant colors, caressing glazes, the harmonious quivering of rainbows. Amid these ever-perfect architectures, animated and changing, they were still singing with triumphant sweetness:

"There are no black wings among us."

Then they flew away; and their song, their dance and their blended colors said: "Humans, have we fired the arrow of love at our hearts unavailingly? Humans, plunge into a bath of wisdom; you will emerge entirely perfumed with love."

Chapter V. The Meadow Saved

While it remained visible, the humans followed the harmonious flock with their eyes. Then they stood still, pensively, for a long time. Finally, they turned, as if startled, toward the exquisite beauty of the meadow.

They were like blind men recovering their sight.

Before the coming of the Superangels, the meadow had been beautiful in vain. Now, they no longer saw it as a call to coarse and avid action, but as a joyous spectacle.

Without picking up their scythes, which they had dropped during the sublime concert, as emotional as executioners confronted by the beauty of the child they had been ordered to kill, they said: "It's too beautiful!"

"It's too beautiful!" repeated the overseer, who no longer knew what had become of his whip.

The priest shrugged his shoulders, shook his head, seemed to exorcize himself, and commanded "For the glory…"

But the charming haste of the stream moved him, as did the delicate swaying of the flowers, dispensers of perfume, and the fleeting smile that a zephyr carved out in the grass.

Things were remembering the Superangels. Their beauty, shadowed by love, trembled with something profound and living. Was not the murmur of the stream a song of tenderness now? The foam surrounding the pebbles was reminiscent of the whiteness of an arm exited by a caress. The laughter of the grass mingled with the undulations of the flowers in a delightful chaos of kisses.

The priest raised an astonished hand, first to his moist eyes, and then to the breast where his heart was beating, it seemed to him, in a new way.

Vanquished, ashamed and joyful, he admitted in his turn: "It is too beautiful!"

Chapter VI. The Immortals

Sometimes slow, sometimes rapid, sometimes hesitant and inquisitive, the Superangels have been traveling for the rest of the day and all night. They have perceived meadows, mountains, towns, rivers and seas. Now they are gliding over something new. Oh, what a strange and sinister landscape they have selected this time!

A site of desolation and death. A terrible circle of mountains on the edge of a desert. The ground is formed of rock and except toward the north, grey rocks close the circle. Not one tree, not one clump of moss, not one plant; only, here and there, a dry patch—powdery, one might say—that would be a scab on a body, a lichen on a rock. Even the grace of dawn does not succeed in importing any freshness into the torrid valley.

The almost-circular rocks that enclose the sad valley do not give the impression of heroic heaviness. They have the color, and something akin to the rotten lightness, of old bones. They give the impression of being hollow, and that numerous deep caves open out within them. The grey porous stone is

211

sometimes suggestive of an ossuary, sometimes of an immense sponge.

The Superangels circle this desolation with their dancing flexibility. They sing their happiness, wisdom and love. Then they say, interrogatively: "Rock that seems dead, you are an old receiver of stolen goods, and numerous lives quiver in your alveoli. Living beings that are hidden, but which divine our emotion, living beings that make of this sad rubble a joy and a hope for the heart—tell us, tell us who you are."

Metallic voices, shrill and distant, reply, like a vast dispersed chorus.

"We are the Immortals," say the metallic voices, distant and dispersed. "We are those who have vanquished death."

"Are you not," the Superangels replied, "those who are vanquished by life?"

And now, from the colored and perfumed orchestra of wings, a noble canticle descends, a friendly and fecundating rain:

"Welcome death, if you wish to savor life. Welcome death, if you wish to know love. Consent to the flexibility and flight of perishable form, in order that the child that you protect today will protect you tomorrow, in order that you shall become the grandchild of your child. Accept change in order to know all the moods of love; in order that you may drink fresh waters from new cups with fresh lips, and all the ardent elixirs of love.

"Emerge from your deep lairs, come into the sunlight. Gaze at the rhythmic colors of my wings. Let yourself absorb the perfumes that emanate from me. Often, when you believe that you are only welcoming a perfume, you receive a thought, or the rising smoke of a dream. Above all, listen: I will sing to you the joyous mysteries of love, the joyous mysteries of death. Hear as I sing the mortal mystery of love; hear as I sing the amorous mystery of death.

"Death, sleeping sister of love. Love, awakened brother of death…"

While the Superangels sing, little beings emerge from the rock through cleverly-hidden cracks. As short and thin as rickety children, their slow gestures grate like the sliding and friction of machines. Are not their grey bodies more like iron than flesh? Everything about them is as hard and pinched as avarice.

The Superangels gaze at them with dolorous tenderness, holding back tears.

"Sing," the Superangels implore, "sing, in order that we may know what fills your hearts."

The thin little humans, flat and angular, hesitate. The gaze disdainfully at the winged, colored, perfumed and musical beauty. They look at one another with great complacency. Finally, with a narrow smile of scorn upon their grey lips, they join hands, and with a singular timbre—one might think they were dragging chains—they begin a slow round dance, slow enough provoke yawns, slow enough to generate a gradual vertigo.

The faint grinding noise made by their little dance is accompanied by a choir of metallic voices:

"Let us sing slowly, circle slowly; we have no lack of time, we Immortals.

"Let us sing slowly, circle slowly; we have made ourselves small to leave scant purchase for death, and we have made ourselves hard, as hard as iron, and have made ourselves slow, when we deign to move...but we almost always remain motionless.

"You want to know, naïve Superangels, what there is in each of our hearts. My heart is full of pride in my immortality. It is precisely full, with no empty space or overflow. My heart is a lake of calm water; it has neither ebb nor flow and does not know the breath of wind. The cost of pride in my immortality is scorn for beings that die. Are there enough of them to be scorned, those who die?

"What does it matter to me what passes? I do not pass. What does time matter to me? I am outside time. I scarcely live, but I shall never die. What beings who are always dying call the divers joys or the intensity of life is madness. There is only sweetness and charm in motionless equality or in slowness that becomes slower and slower: a kind of progressive immobility that becomes ever more sweet. Slowness, you prepare me for immobility. Thus, little by little, the song of the mortal mother envelopes the mortal infant with the languid grace of slumber.

"Let us circle slowly, sing slowly. Slowly I sing the slow sweetness of my existence. I am a torpor that will never end. I am a joyous slumber not sliding toward the horror of awakening.

"Let us sing slowly, circle slowly. Let everything about us be slow, small and prudent—for we are immortal, save for accidents.

"Slowly, slowly, and more slowly still. What does time matter to me? I have nothing to do and nothing can to anything to me. Upon my polished hardness, neither gnawer nor murderer can prevail. From my simple metallic body I have removed all the causes of weakness and disease. I am immortal, save for accidents. My heart is a lake full of calm water. No wind can trouble the surface of my plenitude, save for the fear of accidents.

"Sing slowly, circle slowly—oh, ever more slowly! Slowness protects against accidents—but immobility protects better still—immobility in the depths of a well-sealed cave.

"We rarely see one another. Why should we see one another? Each of us lives enclosed within himself, protecting the full vase of his immortality. Meetings might cause accidents.

"You are small; make yourself smaller. The smaller you are, the more chance there is that an accident will fall to one side without touching you."

The round dance breaks up. The dwarves slip away slowly, each one toward his cleverly-hidden rack. The Superangels try to retain them.

"Wait, unfortunate immortals. Listen to our song of love and beauty.

But the little near-metallic beings, already half-plunged into their caves, squeak in their faint voices: "I laugh at beauty that will fade and die. I hate love, the brother of death. If we were stupid enough to listen to it, love would be a major cause of accidents. I have not been foolish enough to give myself a sex. I have no need to procreate; I am immortal."

And from others: "Go further to search for love. I cannot love that which passes. To love that which will die is to sow the seeds of suffering in one's heart. One would not be immortal, if one consented to pain."

"Do you at least love one another?" say the Superangels. They increase the seduction of perfumes, drifting colors and musical sweetness.

But the metallic dwarves feel nothing and see nothing. And the faint metallic voices reply: "I do not need to be loved; I am immortal. No one who loved me could give anything to me, who possesses the entire duration of eternity. Love is irritating in its uselessness; love is dangerous, in that it might cause accidents. I am immortal; I am immortal: leave me to sleep through my immortality."

The Superangels flew far away from the odious valley.

The arid rocks did not retain any memory of the delicate passing. It seemed that no shadow had ever softened their scorching, that no music had ever enchanted and brought rhythm to their crackling silence.

Everything slides over that which is immortal. Beneath an impervious carapace immortality, a bleakly monotonous continuity, slumbers in a sleep devoid of dreams and memories.

The grey hollow rocks extended the torpor of an immense ossuary beneath the world-weary sky. Nothing emerged therefrom but an indistinct murmur, fainter than the purr of a sleeping cat; that phantom noise hummed the plenitude of the hearts of the Immortals.

The peace in the calm hearts of the Immortals did not last long. A few hours after the departure of the Superangels, a frightful tumult filed the valley. The murmur in the depths of the caves fell silent. A fearful silence listened to the unfamiliar and increasing tumult. Was it the approach of a accident?

Soon, the valley was inundated by an army of humans. Its eddies implied that it was a mere advance guard. Further away, to the north, an ocean of soldiers could be divined, a few drops of which would have sufficed to invade the pass like a strait, and to fill the circus like a bay. Among the thousands of people who were visible, the millions whose existence as deducible, were a few singular individuals, mountainous and vast. Perceiving them through the well-hidden cracks, the Immortals trembled in their every petty metallic limb and cried out mutely in nightmarish terror:

"Superelephants!"

Chapter VII. The Superelephants

There was nothing particularly remarkable about the humans of this era. They were, as in other centuries, cowardly and greedy: cowardly enough to kill or die on a master's orders; cowardly enough to sacrifice, on a master's orders, the miserable treasures of their crazed hearts, the false goods for which they routinely sacrificed their lives and those of others.

Very civilized, heavily laden with clothing, jewelry and weapons, they built palaces for their masters vaster than those of Nineveh, Babylon or Persepolis and castles for those among them whom their masters distinguished, but the multitude crowded together in narrow and filthy hovels. Truly, why talk about them? Do we not already know more about them than we want to know?

Perhaps the beings that had terrified the Immortals so much will be more of a novelty.

Amours and Immortals were not the only superhumans that had succeeded in separating themselves out during the recent geodesic troubles. A third species had realized a monstrous and magnificent dream of power. These animals were often designated by the name of Superelephants. They preferred to call themselves Dominators, Masters or Gods.

These preferred names described their social situation. "Superelephant" described the essential features of their bodies accurately enough. Vaster than our Asian elephants, they almost matched the stature of the ancient mammoth—but they had two trunks.[26] The one on the left remained the most adroit and strongest of prehensile organs. The one on the right had, if one might put it thus, something human about it; its extremity, opening like our mouths, afforded a glimpse of teeth, a tongue and a throat of sorts. An articulate language emerged therefrom, which a fortunate proportion of labia and teeth and a restricted employment of guttural rendered almost harmonious, when it deigned to soften itself so as not to roll like thunder.

The left trunk trumpeted in fury, or when, without explaining anything, the Dominator wanted to terrorize. The tusks were replaced by two large hollow bones with toothed edges, in which the root of each trunk was lodged, and in which the retracted organ could take refuge in case of danger. Hidden in that citadel with menacing battlements, it became ungraspable.

From the same shoulders from which the anterior legs descended sprang two arms and hands, similar in form to the upper limbs of humans, but almost as powerful as the un-

---

[26] This detail recalls the conclusion of J. H. Rosny Aîné's story "Le Voyage" (1906; tr. as "The Voyage", included in the Black Coat Press edition of *The World of the Variants*), in which the discovery of a remote African enclave in which humans live in submissive symbiotic harmony with elephantine protectors convinces the narrator that if elephants had only had two trunks, they, not humankind, would have become the dominant species on Earth. Ner met Rosny in 1889 or thereabouts, and they remained lifelong acquaintances, though never close friends, eventually sharing the presidency of *Les Compagnons de la pensée*, an organization established to campaign for the protection of the French language, in the mid-1920s.

breakable pillars of the legs, possessed of gigantic proportions. A thick and hairy but retractile hide could cover or uncover those heavy but delicate arms at will. If necessary, they were weapons and sledgehammers, but more often organs of joy, over which ripples and frissons of pleasure ran.

The Dominators grouped together in the center of the valley. The crowd left a wide space around them, hollowed out by respect. Within that empty space a few men clad in rich priestly garments were moving, swinging radiant and odorant incense-burners in front of the masters.

These priests were singing the glory of their Gods. The worshipful murmur of the crowd occasionally repeated a few words of the hymn or corroborated it with pious responses.

"O Dominators," the priests were saying, "the Earth is yours."

In the valley and beyond, the immense chorus of humans repeated: "The Earth is yours, O Dominators."

The orison continued in a broad plainsong:

"The Earth trembles beneath your feet, O Dominators, as does the human heart beneath your gaze. All nature obeys you. Life is a privilege that you grant and which serves you. The being that refuses to worship you becomes unworthy of existence and dies beneath your strength or our pious hands. O Dominators, you are the only Gods."

The ardent and humble host repeated: "You are the only Gods, O Dominators."

Then the circle of priests, turning to the immense army, asked: "Humans, why have you come to Earth?"

The multitude, with a noise that extended like a tide, and which, like a tide, rose and repossessed, threatening to invade space, replied: "I have come to Earth in order to know the Dominators, to love them and to serve them."

One trunk was elevated, in an authoritarian manner. A religious silence spread, which seemed broader and deeper with every passing second. When the Dominator spoke, it seemed as broad and deep as the sky.

The voice of the God filled the vast silence; the extent was a bronze urn, which resounded. The extent itself seemed to proclaim: "Dread, the beginning of wisdom; justice and respect, the centers of wisdom; love of the powerful, the summit and accomplishment of wisdom, make all men into our willing slaves. These noble sentiments—listen, Immortals, it is to you that my words are addressed—are no less appropriate to superhumans. The Dominators are not superhumans, as you perhaps believe, insultingly; they are the Gods of humans and superhumans alike."

The Immortals were listening and watching through well-concealed cracks. The thunder of the Dominator's voice and the things he said were making them tremble. Here and there within the rock, the nearest and keenest human ears heard a strange faint noise, like clinking metal.

After a pause, the Dominator resumed: "Soon I shall speak to you again, Immortals, to offer you a choice between the ineffable glory of serving us and the most ignominious of deaths. Think about it for now, for we shall turn away from you, the solemn hour of the sacrifice having arrived.

The priests repeated: "The solemn hour of the sacrifice has arrived."

In the valley, along the mountainsides and in the plain, the host echoed the good news piously, ardently and at length: "The solemn hour of the sacrifice has arrived. It has arrived, the solemn hour of the sacrifice."

At several points, armed men were standing aside, leaving between two ranks a passage bristling with glory. Women precipitated themselves into it, their arms, trembling with joy, clutching suckling infants. As they reached the circle of the priests they surrendered their nurslings, proclaiming: "I give you thanks, Lords, because, your gaze having fallen upon your servant, you have chosen my son to become the fortunate nourishment of the Gods."

The priest piously cut each infant's throat; piously, he had it roasted in a little oven—I beg your pardon!—I mean, inside a portable altar. Each mother watched, kneeling and uplifted by ecstasy; she breathed the perfume of her son's burning flesh, a paradisal odor. Ritually, in spite of the intoxication and the tears and the stammering of her joy, she repeated the words of glory, adoration and boundless gratitude: "Happy, happy, thrice happy; blissful, blissful, thrice blissful, the loins that have borne the nourishment of the Gods.

The oven—pardon me, the altar—recently perfected by the genius of a priest, cooked the largest pieces of meat in a matter of minutes. It rendered them crunchy, equally penetrated by the fire in every part, as juicy at the surface as the center, tender and tasty, better than the work of the ancient spit.

A table was set up in front of each Superelephant and covered with luxurious lace. A large golden platter supported the well-cooked infant, the meal's main course—or, to be more accurate, the centerpiece of the oblation and the sacrifice. Agreeable conserves and expertly-prepared vegetables were displayed on silver platters; the amber, gold and purple of fruits refreshed the eyes, causing mouths to salivate in anticipation. Exquisite wines transformed bottles into large topazes or vast rubies. Amid sacred words and gestures, between the bending of knees, ejaculatory orisons and fragments of litanies, the priests were hurriedly carving the meat, serving the wines in foaming chalices, raising everything to the two divine mouths.

Periodically, an officiator wiped the trunks with a delicate cloth, which was only used once. Having covered the fine cloth with kisses, the priest delivered it to the kisses of the crowd. Each of these relics would be sold for a high price the next day. The happy purchaser would lock it away in a little tabernacle, from which he would take it out it on important occasions. He would receive in this blessed linen the last sigh of a loved one. He would cover a diseased part of his body with it, rejoicing in the hope of a miracle, and would then plunge into an equal gratitude for the miracle granted or the miracle effused: "Let thy will be done in my body and my soul, O Gods who know better than I what my body and soul warrant."

When the Gods had appeased their noble hunger and slaked their adorable thirst, the Dominator who had spoken before resumed:

"Immortals, the hour of our glory or your death has now arrived. The present moment is the hesitant balance. A pan will fall, and everything will be concluded. Emerge from your lairs, then, come and adore our power and our mercy. Hurry, or our justice will bring down an accident upon you. The strength of any one of us could demolish the mountain, and each of our four feet, at every step, could crush two Immortals—but we shall not deign to act ourselves. Pious warriors will bring down your miserable dens with pious cannon-fire. Devotees armed with explosives will blast you apart, scattering your little limbs amid the enormity of the shards of rock. If one of you attempts to flee, a bullet or the blade of a saber will put an end to his immortality. Speak, then. Choose between the glory of serving us or the shame of perishing beneath our divine anger.

Weighed down by terror, buoyed up by scorn for Gods that would die tomorrow, the heartsick Immortals were trembling with indignation and impotence. No retreat could protect them, they knew, against a force as implacable as it was irresistible. The majority hid, but two or three, inspired by the vertigo of danger, slid slowly toward the odious light.

One of these bold tremblers asked: "How can we serve you, we who are so small and frail? What do you want from us?"

The Dominator replied: "Since nature has created Superhumans, it is good, equitable and holy that religious society should make them intermediaries between the Gods and humans. Henceforth, humans shall know our will through the agency of superhumans. Come and give orders in our name."

"Give orders! Us, so feeble any so timid…"

"Stand tall behind your weakness; divine force will make you redoubtable. You will speak in the name of the Gods and all heads will bow before your words."

One Immortal objected: "Superhumans ought to be brethren. Any inequality between us would be as odious as…"

He did not finish. A devotee had crushed him with three blows of a crozier.

"Tomorrow," a Dominator ordered, "that valiant man will receive the ribbon of glory on his noble breast."

Persuaded by the rapid brutality of the execution, the Immortals emerged through all the cracks in the mountain. Kneeling, with their arms raised, they were imploring the Dominators for mercy—and one of them, the subtle Grintzmar, spoke for his brethren:

"We shall obey you in the emotions of happiness and gratitude. We thank you, O Gods, for having called us, for having brought us close to you, for having taught us at last the meaning of our immortal life."

Chapter VIII. A City

A being fixed for too long a time in a single form is scarcely permeable to the most elementary of emotions, astonishment. The 181 diminutive quasi-metallic Immortals, however, experienced something like admiration when they were transported from the bare and monotonous simplicity of their slumberous existence into the complex, opulent and wretched, coarse and refined life of humans and Dominators.

Agriculture and industry were overwhelming marvels. The Earth, under religious effort, produced all that it was capable of producing. Quantity, quality and variety had resulted from intensive, knowledgeable and scrupulous exploitation. Fantastic in its abundance, that which was destined for swarming humankind, whether crops or livestock, fruits or vegetables, fish or fowl, gave a strange impression of banal insipidity. On the other hand, that which was raised for the table of the Gods slowly acquired a character of perfection and fantasy that became increasingly sacred. The majority of factories did nothing but disgorge trivial merchandise. A few took months to fabricate some precious, magnificent object, which, in a barbaric excess of luxury and ornamentation, could have rivaled the masterpieces of our great artists.

Most of the Immortals were installed in vast castles in the middle of cities of eight or ten million inhabitants, which were provincial capitals. No God deigned to live in these tiny cities. Before the recruitment of the little quasi-metallic beings, the Dominators had only been represented there by priests, who supervised production and regulated its division, expediting to Eor the natural or manufactured products reserved for divine consumption. They also chose the most beautiful children when they were weaned, and had them conveyed to the metropolis. The mothers, overwhelmed with gratitude and pride, did not know whether the fruit of their wombs was destined for the condensed glory of being eaten by a God or the diffuse glory of becoming a priest.

Fifty Immortals were transported to Eor.

No city known to the reader can give any idea of the immensity and magnificence of hat city. Divided into 102 quarters, it had 102 million inhabitants, all admirable to behold. Every new moon, the priests regulated the numbers, sending the sick, pregnant women, people who had reached 40 years of age and those whom precocious old age or some accident rendered less pleasing to the eye to the provinces. In exchange, in addition to the children destined for the table or the service of the Gods, the provinces sent handsome young men of 18 to 20, and beautiful young women of 15 to 18.

In the middle of each quarter there was an immense natural or artificial hill. Surrounded by a marvelous park, which was called a "paradise," a double monument stood at the top of the mound, the entirety of which bore the name of "heaven." The most famous were the heaven and paradise of the God Marbal, the heaven and paradise of the God Rismac, the heaven and paradise of the God Salom, and the heaven and paradise of the Goddess Néac. Each of these astonishing domains received, in fact, the name of the Dominator who lived there was glorified there. The Gods always numbered 90, and the Goddesses 12. The Superelephants carefully restricted their birth-rate, and knew how to produce the sexes at will. Their 18 children, two of whom were future goddesses, had no personal dwellings, but lived some distance from Eor, in what was called the preheaven. The most knowledgeable of the priests gave them a careful education there. Engaged in pleasant studies and innocent games, these young candidates for divinity awaited without too much impatience the hour when death would create a vacant heaven and permit their apotheosis. At that moment, certain secrets would be revealed to them by the Gods who were their elders.

One climbed up to each paradise by means of a broad white marble stairway. After 18 steps 60 meters wide, one encountered a landing tiled in gold. The third of these landings was followed by six onyx steps that eventually led to an immense courtyard paved with gems, the various colors of which formed ingenious designs. The first mosaics, of an artistry that was both hieratic and refined, represented scenes of religious life with suave austerity. Of those closest to the heaven, two offered purely geometrical designs. On one side there was a sapphire hexagram, on the other, a double square of rubies inscribed within a turquoise circle. Between these two figures was a mosaic which mingled art and science oddly: a sardonyx pentagram trampled underfoot by a triumphant emerald superelephant. The senior priests understood the significance of the two lateral designs, but the esotericism of the central design was a secret reserved to the Gods. Only the Gods knew that the pentagram was the symbol of humankind.

In addition to the commons dispersed in the immensity of the paradise, the buildings comprised a temple a magnificent vestibule and a palace, infinitely more beautiful, but whose delicate splendors could not even be imagined by the vulgar. Day and night, with no interruption, priests officiated in the temple and the faithful prayed. A thousand priests were attached to the service of each temple, two thousand priests and two thousand priestesses to the service of each palace. Except for these 4000 servitors, no one went in to the Holy of Holies. Every sixth day, however, the God deigned to appear at the limit of the two buildings, to the east of the temple, between two golden battens which, amid gleams and flashes, shook noisily, like great fulgurant wings in the midst of a storm. In addition, the most benevolent of the Gods sometimes consented, at sunset, to manifest their distant presence with a trumpeting, which caused all foreheads to be bowed with emotion, and was known as the "merciful blessing." Some extended kindness so far as to take a meal from time to time at the altar, which became a solemn sacrifice.

Even between themselves, the senior priests, the palace officials, only spoke tremulously of the marvels and mysteries they were permitted to contemplate. They trembled with admiration and drooling desire when they spoke about the dazzling luxury, the paintings, the statues, the tapestries, the stained-glass windows, the items of furniture ingeniously adapted to the divine forms, the sumptuous heaps of cushions, and the embalmed temperature, always the same, ignorant of the rigors and changes of the outside world. As well as the luxurious and warm winter rooms, they sang the praises of the summer apartments, terraces tiled in gold, hanging gardens, marble courtyards, silver colonnades, onyx basins, luminous cascades, jets of colored water, odorant vaporizations, fans as beautiful as living creatures, moved by a force as discreet as it was docile.

But the priests trebled with drooling desire and terror when they made any allusion to what I am forced to call the private life of the Gods. The sumptuousness and delicacy of the feasts, the splendor and grace of the spectacles, were the least objects of their envy. Here, voluptuousness knew extremes unknown to humans.

Gods and Goddesses rarely met one another, solely for the duty of maintaining the sacred number of the species—but every park, transformed, if one might put it thus, into a harem, sheltered 100 female elephants of a rare beauty. In the para-

225

dise of a goddess, the elephants, as might be expected, belonged to the male sex. When the God summoned a servant of love, skilful priestesses had already excited and calmed his rigid force, and then resuscitated it with the most savant and tender caresses and various fantasies, for hours on end. This was, it appeared, so delightful that certain Dominators abruptly renounced natural pleasure, no longer consenting to any but these extended releases.

But let us not try to describe divine joys—a human pen is too awkward. When venturing into theology, a human pen always creates on the paper a sort of mocking laughter; respect itself seems to jeer at both the Gods and their worshippers. I shall merely indicate that each Master imported the originality of his temperament into his exigencies to an even greater degree than one might expect. A few complacently recounted extraordinary inventions to their brethren; others hid the personal aspects of their fantasy beneath a jealous modesty.

I shall not linger any longer on the description of the palace and its furnishing. All that was, to be sure, singular and opulent to the point of vertigo, but if the gods consent to dazzling material display and fantastic miracles, it is by disdainful condescension, in order to strike the most coarsely remote souls, buried deep within the flesh, by way of their senses. They prefer the faith of those who have not seen. They love to be adored in spirit and in truth. The Gods of Eor surrounded themselves with the magnificence that is the natural frame— the secretion, as it were—of divinity. Thus snails emanate the radiance of a multicolored shell. I do not eat shellfish and I can dazzle myself directly, by means of simple ecstasy and the abstract idea of the divine, without the aid of gold and pomp, flashes and fulgurations.

Let us worship the gods, not their habitations. Let us adore, if it is appropriate, all the gods, in and for themselves. Glory, glory, thrice glory to the power and the justice of all the gods, successive or simultaneous, which, in the eternities and the immensities, exercise their ingenious mercy to crush and chastise perverse humans, and to crush pious humans in order to test them and manifest their divine love.

Deus est caritas.

In the center of the city, one hill more elevated than the rest bore a vaster temple, in which there were 102 petty palaces named the celestial lodges. Entry to this temple was forbidden to the faithful. The Gods met there, when they felt the need to hold a council.

Chapter IX. The Embassy

In the central temple, the Dominators of the Orient are holding a council.

Each Superelephant is lodged in a swimming-bath three-quarters full of perfumed water. Its thick pachydermal skin protects it, alas, against sensual experiences as well as wounds and pains, but various parts of its ingenious body are able, when secure, to detach themselves from their heavy armor and savor pleasures. Their trunks, resting on cushions made of down and silk, breathe in the various perfumes that are drawn back and forth by adept fans. At the other extremity of the body, the large tail, an unnecessary shield, is raised to allow the penetration into the God's interior, through a—dare I say floral?—opening, of a clyster of joy.

Between these two sensual indulgences, the bare arms hang down enraptured by the cool caress of the bath. Also hanging down is a certain vast organ to which it would be indecent to make allusion if everything about the Gods were not venerable; at intervals, the holy phallus twitches in satisfaction, rowing like an oar.

Their intellectual power permits the Dominators to study the most serious and difficult questions amid their joys.

"There are 102 of us," said the God Marbal, "and we only possess half the Earth; if our human herd numbers more than three billion heads, it is only by a few paltry millions. Now, the Dominators of the Occident, of whom there are only 45, possess the other half of the globe, and their livestock, according to the latest statistics, nearly amounts to five billion human heads. Our dignity and our interests are equally strongly opposed to our tolerating such injustice and terrestrial disequilibrium any longer. Let us send an embassy of two of our Immortals to the Occidental Masters. They will claim, in our name, 1200 square leagues[27] of territory and a billion heads of the human species.

"We shall apply ourselves, moreover, to rendering the treaty honorable to both parties, so that each population will enthusiastically celebrate a diplomatic victory. We shall pay for the concessions we demand: our Occidental brethren will receive, along with 200 kilos of unrefined gold, six kilos of diamonds freed from all superfluous matter. We shall also give them a share in the glorious conquest of the Immortals and ceded to them 60 of the 181 superhumans that we possess. Have I summarized the general opinion accurately?"

---

[27] The author inserts a footnote here: "It will be deduced that I am reducing my measures to different ones. I am even constrained, for the sake of immediate clarity, to translate the numbers. The Dominators employ the sexagesimal system in their calculations. I am avoiding, as much as possible, confusing the reader. My version, almost invariably too familiar, often sacrifices material exactitude. I am suppressing any strangeness that would only serve to astonish. I am working as a poet, not a historian. If poetry is, as Aristotle says, 'truer than history', does it not owe that superiority to the omission of insignificant details?" As the reader will observe, the author continues of confuse the sexagesimal and decimal system in his calculations, favoring such multiples as "600" and "6000" and ignoring the fact that a sexagesimal system would multiply its numerals in groups equivalent to the decimal system's 36, 216, etc. Readers will doubtless be able to make their own minds up about the relative truthfulness of poetry and mathematics—which is perhaps as well, as Aristotle offers us no assistance in that regard.

The listeners replied, some of them saying: "That's exactly right," while others said: "That's almost exactly right."

Neverheless, Salom thought that it was necessary to demand more from the Occidentals, and Rismac declared the concessions proposed by Marbal to be too considerable. These were, however, inconsequential trifles and quibbles. The only question that generated a discord sufficiently long and confused to be worthy of the noble name of parliamentary debate concerned the choice of ambassadors.

Rismac, Salom and several others manifested a profound scorn for the Immortals. The diminutive quasi-metallic men looked most unattractive, and would make sorely shabby representatives for Gods. Besides, they seemed to lack courage, zeal and eloquence. From all points of view, priests would be better.

Marbal recognized the strength of these objections. On the other hand, he emphasized the interest-value implicit in showing the Occidentals beings with which they were unfamiliar, the glory and intimidation implicit in showing off the domestication of an entire race of superhumans. Marbal's eloquence ended up winning the argument.

Two Immortals were brought in. The God Marbal explained to them what was expected of their piety, and in what glory they were going to drape the future.

Salom and Rismac were right. The cowardly little beings had not become any braver in domesticity. No mysticism had taken hold of them. Unlike some humans, they were not enthused by the idea of a triumphant death on the field of honor, in ardent combat on the Masters' behalf. They were not intoxicated by the idea of the palm that is placed in the hand of a statue when the statue represents a martyr dead on the Masters' behalf.

While the subtle Grintzmar kept quiet, fearful and tremulous, overwhelmed by the novelty of the situation, his companion Maupit objected: "But what if the wicked Dominators of the Occident put us to death?"

229

"We shall avenge you," Marbal replied. The reply seemed to him to be peremptory.

It seemed less so to the little quasi-metallic being. "Alas," he sighed, "that won't give us back our poor immortality."

"Do we, the Gods, not die ourselves?" the Dominator asked, haughtily.

"But you have so many other advantages," replied the unhappy Maupit, shivering like metal on the fire. Perhaps he was about to enumerate those advantages enviously, the blasphemer!

The brutal words of Rismac stopped him on the brink of the abyss. "When we command, the universe has only to obey. If you refuse the glory that we are offering you, there remains the shame of dying beneath our wrath." He extended his two trunks menacingly toward the servitors.

"We will obey, we will obey!" cried the poor trembling beings.

"If you encounter the glory of dying for your Gods, rejoice. Say that you will rejoice, or I shall rid you of a life of which you are demonstrating yourselves unworthy in a trice."

"We shall rejoice, we shall rejoice!" stammered the little Immortals.

The subtle Grintzmar, finally recovering his wits, even employed priestly terminology. "Grace is illuminating me!" he cried. "I see, I believe, I know, I am disabused. Everything is good that one encounters on the road of divine service."

The Superelephants swung their trunks approvingly.

"We shall not send you to our Occidental brethren on your own," Marbal explained. "You will march in great pomp, as befits the vicars of Gods. Two hundred thousand humans will form your cortège, on 200,000 magnificent caparisoned horses. The carriage that will carry you is forged entirely in the purest gold, for you shall go in a carriage, escorted by cavalry. Your mission must be accomplished with majesty, and in any epoch, he who speaks of majesty speaks of anachronism and wasted time."

The two Immortals departed that same day. They rejoiced in their little hearts at the slowness of their progress—but their dear little hearts, slightly dilated by this thought, contracted fearfully at the idea that they must eventually reach their destination. Exchanging their fraternal emotions in the secrecy of the carriage, they composed speeches, anticipated objections and prepared replies. Everything that they planned was crawling with pious humility, as is appropriate when one is not very brave and one has to address oneself to Gods.

On the fifth day of their march, Grintzmar and Maupit were thrown into great distress. A telephoned message from the Dominators enjoined them to have the persons of the two sacred ambassadors, the shining carriage and its numerous escort, transported to the frontier by the most rapid means possible—which is to say, by powerful radioactive automobiles.

Alas, the pious automobilists deployed such zeal that the whole assembly was grouped together again the following day within a league of the empire of the Occident.

In accordance with the instructions they had received, the Ambassadors telephoned the Occidental governor from the frontier. They asked to enter the foreign land with their magnificent cortège. The Gods of the Occident immediately granted authorization, but they added that they would keep as their property, along with one of the Immortals, half of the men, horses and everything else that entered their territory.

The negotiations by wireless telephone lasted three days. It was necessary, before replying to each communication from the Occidentals, to ask for instructions from the Masters of the Orient. Council-meetings multiplied in the temple of Eor and the metropolitan church of Oor.[28]

---

[28] The author inserts a footnote: "The meanings of these names are hardly mysterious; the former may be translated as Orientville or Eopolis, the latter as Occidentville or Hesperopolis." (Or, of course, East City and West City.)

The Occidentals would not abandon any of their claims, but the ambassadors finally received the order to complete their mission in a silver coach escorted by only two thousand cavaliers.

The Superelephants of Oor would not grant plenipotentiaries accompanied by such scant pomp the honor of receiving them in the metropolitan church. The disdainful audience was held n the open air, on the vast esplanade in front of the monument. Only the two Immortals were permitted to climb up to the top step and kneel down there. The escort remained at the bottom of the steps, surrounded by an Occidental army.

Before the Immortals had said a word, 45 trunks were directed toward them horizontally, like 45 mockeries. Opening their extremities, they displayed their teeth in a broad unanimous smile. The mound trembled, as Olympus had once trembled beneath the laughter of other Gods.

Amid the formidable gaiety, words sprang forth: "The poor Dominators of the Orient are even poorer than we would have thought."

Ridiculously small, the Immortals were trembling, their bony knees clicking. I spite of the distance between them and all oriental ears, would not their words be reported back to Eor? Would they not be aggravated and envenomed there?

The courage of cowards is sometimes amazing. These, negligent of the distant peril, as if it did not exist, devoted themselves entirely to the effort of avoiding immediate danger.

"The Superelephants of Eor," cried the subtle Grintzmar, "were to our ignorant eyes the most beautiful, the richest and most powerful of all, until our good fortune revealed your 45 ineffable beauties, your 45 opulences, and your 45 omnipotences. We were adoring in them the shadow and the presentiment of the veritable Gods. Now we see. Our amazement and our joy proclaim it: here, and here alone, there are Gods."

"These little Immortals lack neither common sense nor piety," trumpeted the satisfied 45.

One of them added: "The least of superhumans is definitely worth a million head of human cattle."

Trembling with both the pride of success and the dread of danger, Grintzmar went on: "O only veritable Gods, we dare not report to your pure ears the impious words that the false Gods have instructed us…"

The subtle Grintzmar paused. The silence seemed full of menace. It was with fear alone that he was trembling when he sensed the impossibility of not continuing.

"We are but instruments. We are like the earpiece of a wireless telephone, and you do not become irritated with the earpiece of a telephone, no matter what it says. But we are, alas, conscious instruments, and when sacrilege adopts our machine as an interpreter, we suffer from its electronic passage, as if we were responsible."

"Speak! Get on with it!" cried the most impatient of the Superelephants.

But the most merciful said: "Speak without dread. Put your trust in divine generosity."

"We shall speak, then, O Gods, for two reasons: firstly, to obey your adorable command; secondly, because it will perhaps be useful to you to acquaint you, to the very least detail, with the folly of the Orient.

"Forgive the blasphemies that do not come from us: the blasphemies that we would already have expunged from our memory but for the desire to be useful to you; the blasphemies that we only repeat, and dolorously, on your orders…

"The false Gods of Eor have said: 'Whether they inhabit the Orient or the Occident, Gods are equal and brethren. They ought to share the wealth of the Earth fraternally and equally'."

"Such was always the pretention of the poor," one Superelephant jeered. Forty-four thunderous bursts of laughter supported the thunder of its snigger.

"By virtue of that mad pretention of the poor, the false Gods of Eor demand 1200 square leagues of land and a billion head of your human cattle."

"And what else?" jeered the most vulgar of the Gods.

"We have repeated all that these impertinent individuals demand. In exchange, they offer you 1200 kilos of unrefined gold, six kilos of diamonds freed from all superfluous matter, and 60 Immortals."

"The Orientals were always clever negotiators," one trunk remarked.

"Poverty is ingenious," trumpeted another.

And the laughter of the Gods made the air tremble again.

Soon, though, they began to examine the question with the semi-seriousness it appeared to require.

Several thought the Orientals' demands to be unworthy of any response. Others wanted to send a few words of scornful outrage, which would make the arms of the false Gods of Eor blush, by wireless telephone. The majority opined that it was necessary to oppose ridiculous offers with counter-proposals. These were what ended up being adopted:

The Gods of Oor would give the sub-Gods of Eor 100 square leagues of territory and 100 million humans. In exchange, they would receive 60,000 tons of unrefined gold, 60 kilos of diamonds freed of all superfluous matter, and 120 Immortals. In addition, the sub-Gods of Eor would admit their inferiority. Three of them would come, in the name of the 102, to render homage to the 45.

When the Ambassadors found out what message they were to intended to deliver, their wretched carcasses trembled with a sound like clanking chains. How could they refuse anything whatsoever to irritable Gods? How could they take such insulting propositions to irritable Gods? It seemed that they had no other choice but death here or death there.

Ingenious necessity, however, offered Grintzmar a possibly-salutary inspiration.

"O sole Gods of the universe and our hearts," he cried, "deign no longer to deprive two dazzled disciples of your presence. For us, your presence is life, light and joy. Listen to our mercy and our loved. Do not plunge us once again into darkness, dolor and death."

The 45 hesitated, caressed by praises, but wounded by a refusal to obey that felt like a thorn among flowers.

The Immortal found the decisive argument, however. After protestations of unreserved devotion, he exposed a scruple.

"It is only natural that one should send superhumans as ambassadors to veritable Gods, but would it not do too much honor to the false Gods of Eor to treat them with the same consideration? Would humans not suffice to bear your adorable orders to vulgar Superelephants? If you would permit us to express the whole of our thinking, even priests might still be too considerable. Artisans or peasants, that would be sufficient, and would mark, perhaps still with insufficient quantity, the inferiority in which you hold these usurpers."

This fashion of manifesting their disdain to the "false Gods" seemed ingeniously insolent to the "Gods"—and the two Immortals experienced the truth of the old saying: "Piety always works."

Chapter X. The Battle

The Gods of Eor, sensitive to the outrage, forsook the slow and solemn form of an embassy. They telephoned:

"We claim, to re-establish a little justice between the Masters, 1200 leagues of territory and a billion human heads. We shall take back none of our legitimate and overly modest demands, and we now refuse the compensations that we offered initially. The reparation of an iniquity, if it is accompanied by compensations, wounds equity once more, and only establishes a false and unstable equilibrium. Ceasing to be unjust to ourselves, we renounce an excessive generosity, which, in view of the incomprehension of the Superelephants of the Occident, would become a crime against our people. Hear, resonating within our words, the threat and the firm resolution of an ultimatum. If we do not receive a reply within 12 hours, or if the response is not an unreserved 'yes,' we shall consider ourselves to be in a state of war. In one last impulse of benevolence, we even give you warning that the order for mobilization has already been issued."

The reply only took four hours to arrive.

"The true Gods of Oor, indignant at the insolence of the false Gods of Eor, declare war on them."

An hour after this final message, the border troops exchanged the first rifle-shots, the first machine-gun fire, the first shots from electric cannon and radioactive cannon, the first aerial torpedoes... I shall suspend the list there for fear of pointing the men of day in the direction of a few criminal inventions.

On the following day, on the fearful oceans, solitary vessels gave chase to one another and fleets collided like stormwinds. In the sky and the confused waters, explosives produced such disturbances that nature enveloped the belligerents' storm with storms of her own. In the dark rain and the blind tornadoes, shots were soon striking friends and enemies at random.

The naval battles were, however, episodes without interest, save for the dying and the wounded. Everyone knew that it was on land that the matter would be settled.

It was a week after war had been declared that the armies confronted one another on the plain that was then called El-al—which is to say, "the Immense"—but which is known today as Morol...which is to say, "the Boneyard."

The Orientals had assembled 500 million humans. The Occidentals opposed them with 800 million—but the Orientals' armaments were supposedly superior and their 240,000 airships would probably triumph without difficulty over the 120,000 chartered by their adversaries. In addition, popular opinion enthusiastically attributed to the Oriental Marbal the most marvelous strategic genius; his own people were already calling him the God of War. The future would depend on the extent to which that emphatic reputation was justified.

It will be remembered that the Oriental Dominators numbered 102, and the Occidentals 45. If the rights of individuals were respected, that difference had no military signi-

ficance. According to the Melem Convention, the Superelephants could direct strategy and tactics, but they were prohi-
bited from fighting. The Gods were also forbidden to touch a
weapon in order to regulate its fire.

It is true that there had not been a war between the Dominators for more than 400 years, and the famous Melem
Convention was already 200 years old.

Before the signal was given, before the first torpedo was
launched, before the squadrons of airships had risen into the
air, while the two armies still resembled trembling walls that
were about to crumble, but which, until the moment of col-
lapse, remained motionless masses, the Superangels appeared
at a moderate height.

All gazes turned toward the musical flock. With the most
delicate of dances, the Amours mingled the most soothing of
colors. There were luminous blues, silky greys, pale pinks and
idyllic greens. An atmosphere of languishing perfumes and
tender dreams bathed the plain of Elal. The whole of the immense plain was nothing but an ocean of gentleness and pity.
Similar to the murmur of the sea beneath an evening breeze, a
dreamlike music danced, unaccompanied by any precision of
words. The words that provide a counterpoint to our sentiments impact upon us by virtue of their very gentleness. The
Superangels prudently enveloped the souls with vague tenderness and uncertain tears.

The human were gazing, listening and breathing in multiple ecstasy. The rancor in their hearts was transformed, magically metamorphosed into the honey of generosity. Weapons
were already falling from relaxed hands, lips widening into
smiles, eyes becoming mist. A few more chords, a few more
strophes of color, of indistinct singing, of languishing perfumes, and the enemies would doubtless have thrown themselves into one another's fraternal arms.

To become a Dominator, it is necessary to know how to
render oneself hard, much more so than an ordinary pachy-
derm. The Superelephants had hearts even more solid than
their rough hide. They were astonished that these imprecise

sounds, colors, odors and movements could have such an influence over the uncertain souls of humans.

Despite their astonishment, and although they could only comprehend by means of their eyes and ears what was happening to the soldiers, their powerful intelligence was not long delayed in divining the seriousness of the danger.

Their implacable will as expressed in a command: "Fire on those wretches!" All their trunks, rigid and menacing, indicated that the "wretches" in question were the Superangels.

The Gods had never shouted as loudly—but their cry was drowned out by the ocean of music, perfumes and bounty.

No one obeyed the divine order. Perhaps no one had heard it.

The Superelephants shouted again: "Do you not see that these monsters are trying to break the sacred union?"

The magic word was not without effect. A few cannons turned the ugliness of their maws toward the Superangels. But was that not insult and warning rather than determined hostility? The ignoble maws seemed to be hesitating to spit death at so much frail beauty.

Before this strange hesitation, the Dominators of the Orient and the Dominators of the Occident launched, as if they were a reserve, the perhaps-decisive words.

The 45 affirmed: "The enemy, sensing defeat, is making a desperate attempt to sue for peace. Do not let the advantages and glory of certain victory be snatched from you, noble warriors. Kill these cowardly allies of the enemy."

At the same time, the 102 trumpeted: "Fire on these wretched accomplices of the wretched Occidentals. The enemy, confronted by certain ruin, is making one last effort to sue for a peace that, in his treacherous thinking, will be no more than a truce and an armistice. Let us not give him the time to prepare a further aggression, which will cost us more lives. For the glory of the Gods and the salvation of humanity, kill the Superangels, perfidious allies of your perfidious adversaries. That energetic gesture will suffice to disperse the Occidental army like dust."

Loaded with explosive words and dry powder, the cannons launched shells, bombs and torpedoes. The air seemed to unfold like an immense fan of fire; the irritated Earth sent up into the tremulous sky a thunder compared with which the thunder of the ancient Gods was no more than sighs and murmurs.

The Superangels, unattained, rose up more rapidly than the volley of projectiles. The pacific beauty of their colors became invisible. Their music, lost in the aerial abyss, no longer reached the mad Earth inhabited by humans and Gods.

Beneath the out-of-range Superangels, the battle was unleashed: a black dementia, a tempest of increasing rage, darkening the air and souls. A few minutes, and the irreparable was accomplished: on both sides, there were deaths to avenge, blood to wash away with blood, "sublime sacrifices that could not remain futile."

I recoil from a description of the battle. Have not historians, calm to the point of platitude, and epic poets, enthusiastic and cruel to the point of folly, painted enough human carnage?

I want to conserve my nervous strength. I do not want to squeeze and mortally sadden my poor heart, enamored with the heroisms of love and wisdom, my poor heart, which admires the passive victories of the crucified and drinkers of hemlock. I flee from the rotten odor of military combat with nauseated disgust. Gestures that are animated by the drunkenness of hatred—a thousand times worse than intoxication by alcohol—are too repulsive.

I also try to avoid banalities written too often.

I also intend, most especially of all, to remain quiet as to the unique features of the battle of Morol. No, I shall not commit the crime of explaining the machines more terrible than our machines, of describing maneuvers more murderous than our maneuvers. Humans do not need my help to make their intelligence the slave of heir folly.

The superiority of the Orientals' armaments definitely compensated, and more, for their numerical inferiority. The

239

prophetic renown of Marbal was definitely not mistaken. Did the formidable general suspect that he bore within him, further hardened and weighted down by the massive power of new organs, the base soul, the cold strength and the promptitude of decision of a certain Napoléon, who was vile enough for the filthy admiration of the masses to have smeared him with the nickname *the Great*?

His skilful dispositions cancelled out the inferiority of the Orientals, and multiplied the power of their superiorities. As befit a superhuman, he had superflashes of supergenius. He was also as murderously infernal as any other martial God had ever been. After a few hours, the two flanks of the Occidental army had melted in the flames falling from the sky or rising from the ground. The center, overflowing to the right and the left, fled under the crushing effect of a roof of fire and the enveloping approach of the pincers of death.

The desperate 45 could not bear the shame of defeat. As soon as they get in our way, the right of individuals appear to us as injustice, and perfidious pre-war maneuvers. Magnanimous hearts and truly military souls are able to reject such paralyses. They detest and tear up, with a decisive gesture, any piece of paper that spoils a victory, or even hinders the simple prolongation of resistance. For the brave there are but two honors: the glory of triumphant victory, and the glory of fighting to the death and mutilating the triumphant enemy.

"Often," cried one Occidental God, "it is when all seems lost that all is saved! Let us show that we our worthy of our divinity."

And another: "The Orientals are fighting with forbidden weapons. They have forfeited all rights. We no longer have to respect the conventions that they violate without scruple. Let us not be naïve dupes; let us be victors."

Amid these cries, and other similar ones, accompanied by heroic trumpetings, the 45, darkly decisive, advanced with trunks held high toward the Oriental center. These sublime Gods clamored: "Victory or death! To the end, to the end! We shall not survive the only shame, the shame of defeat!"

One minute more, and they charged the densely-packed battalions.

Ajaxes, who consent to do battle with the Gods, are rare. There were none to be found among the warriors of the Orient. Even the aviators, who were in no danger of being reached by the trunks, flew away—a glorious flight disguised as a pursuit. Giving chase to the enemy aviators, they cleared the intimidated sky under which the resounding course of the Gods passed.

The infantry, queen of battles, felt its march stopped as if by a wall of stupor. The soldiers looked at one another, and the pale contagion of terror overwhelmed them. Silent and motionless, a herd breathless at the approach of a storm, they saw the frightful descent of divine powers rolling toward them. Their eyes vacillated along with their unsteady hearts. Then those eyes looked behind. Finally, they turned their backs, and there was panic, madness unleashed.

The plain now seemed to be a precipice over which an army was falling and tearing apart, like the waters of a cataract. In the abruptly resealed immensity, fleeing men collided with other fleeing men, striking out to open up a rapid passage. Every soldier was a bolide of folly and fear. The strong knocked the weak down. The densest groups toppled the less dense. Numerous feet trampled the fallen bodies. Successive feet crushed the fluid pulp that had been standing up in precise and living forms a little while before.

The Oriental Superelephants sent in their reserves. Dust borne away by the wind that precedes an avalanche, they fled before the terribly terrorized dementia of the first escapees.

The distant cannons fell silent, as if, in the presence of divine fury, there was nothing to do but tremble.

While the Orientals' center galloped in disarray before the trunks, the men of the Occident, abandoning that part of the plain where the Gods were able to triumph without assistance, attacked the two flanks. The Orientals were seeing a victory already won fall apart and vanish, shred by shred.

The Superelephants of Eor watched the unexpected crime and the shattering of their hopes in alarmed consternation. When amazement, having calmed slightly, permitted reflection, they asked themselves whether it was worse to suffer unjust defeat or to offer men the dangerous scale of a battle between Gods.

There was a momentary hesitation, of which those heroes did not take long to feel ashamed.

"Gods who break their word are no longer anything but enormous beasts. Let us degrade in reality those whose conduct degrades them in law. The Earth knows enough invincible scourges. Let us at least destroy this one."

It was Marbal who spoke, with the authority of justice, firmness of soul, and genius. Trumpetings of approval replied. Then, with the admirable rapidity that is neither hesitant nor trepidant, he made the dispositions for the new battle.

According to his instructions, 90 Superelephants hurled themselves forward to meet the 45. Meanwhile, the other 12 directed and supported the humans. The 12 were sufficient to put the Occidental army to flight.

I can describe without horror the maneuver ordered by Marbal and executed by the 90. Before the brutality of beings who know no doubt, be they Gods or beasts, my heart rises up with less horror than before the crimes of wretched humans, my brethren in appearance, and perhaps in the merciful uncertainty of certain moments.

The 90 quickly divided themselves up into pairs. During the resounding charge, each pair selected its adversary, and divided up their roles. The stronger or bolder wound its two trunks around the enemy trunks, while its arms were paralysing the opposing arms. Its comrade went around the Occidental and, with its four prehensile organs, seized different posterior limbs at different heights. It pulled backwards abruptly with all its strength, while the former, with a continuous effort, pulled forwards. A few minutes sufficed to fell the majority of the Masters of Oor. Among the first victors, several pairs were able to separate, one God alone sufficing to hold and destroy

242

the vanquished. The other ran to assist some excessively slow victory, or assault some excessively tenacious resistance.

Half an hour after the meeting of the Dominators, the Occidentals' defeat was irremediable. How could a crushed mass, trumpeting in pain, shame and impotence, still be a god to humans, servile hearts and docile minds notwithstanding? The Occidentals, seeing their masters defeated, sensed the edifice of their piety come crashing down within them, with a funereal sound. The most faithful, or the most impulsive, fled in unspeakable moral anguish, but the majority was gripped by the noble need to create, without delay, a new religion and to bow down before new Masters. Throwing down their weapons, they acclaimed within a dawning joy Gods embellished by a bath of strangeness and triumph.

Some cried: "Victory is the only mother of Gods!"

Others affirmed: "My heart has always sensed that there were no true Gods but in Eor."

Marbal's voice was raised above the immense rumor. "Glory to the converts," proclaimed the genius God. "Glory to those who come freely to the truth."

The humans of the Orient, mocking the tamed Gods, were bringing solid cables and attaching them to the broken limbs of the Dominators of Oor, and they were singing: "The true Gods have always come from the Orient. Glory to none but Gods from the Orient."

Chapter XI. A Difficult Problem

In the central temple, the Gods of Eor were occupying the perfumed baths. In the middle were the Superelephants of Oor, in uncomfortable and humiliating attitudes. Lying on their backs, the vanquished were bound to enormous rotating plates. Cables and chains penetrated their hide, long strips of which had been torn away. Legs, arms and trunks were attached to eight columns of cast iron.

Immobilized, among other obstacles, by grooves hollowed out in the columns, a sort of enormous shield weighed upon each body. The powerful mobile prison was nothing but a complicated arrangement of chains, ropes, winches and pulleys: a clever mechanical chaos.

Priests made their entrance. They were carrying two great mortars and two heavy pestles; they were dragging behind them, laden with chains, the Immortals who, as ambassadors, had betrayed their Masters. A dozen dogs followed, whose baying cried out with ferocity and hunger.

The traitors were thrown into the depths of the huge mortars. Beneath the heavy threat of the pestles, they shivered and fainted. Awakened from unconsciousness, however, they uttered the screams of agonized beasts at the same time as the grating of breaking machines. Soon, their bodies—a pulp as ferruginous as it was bloody—were thrown to the dogs, which recoiled howling from the repulsive paste.

Finally, the dogs obeyed the orders of hunger and fought over the sickening remains of the two Immortals.

Then the priests took the unsated dogs out of the temple. The victorious Gods and the defeated Gods were left alone.

Marbal addressed the Superelephants of Oor:

"If prudence, the primary virtue of Gods, did not hold sway in our profound hearts even over the love of justice and the most legitimate thirst for vengeance, we would condemn you, like the traitors whose torture you have just watched, to a dishonorable and dolorous death—but Gods know how to elevate the voice of their reason over the discordant cries of their embittered sentiments. We want to examine coolly the difficult problem that the insanity of your actions has posed for us and for you. We want to study it and resolve it in collaboration with you, our enemies in the narrow blindness of the moment, our friends in the vast clarity of the centuries."

On 45 platforms of humiliation and suffering. Hostile murmurs were audible.

Marbal re-established silence with a loud and authoritative trumpet-blast. Then he continued, with impressive calm:

"As manifestly stupid as the human herd is, do you think that the spectacle that, through your fault, we have offered to their eyes and their slow intelligence is without danger for the present of Eor and the future of all Masters? Humans have seen Gods fighting one another. They have seen victory hesitate between the Gods. They have seen Gods vanquished by force and suffering. How can we avoid the battering-rams of such memories from knocking down the edifice of piety and respect, the work of time that protects our life, our power and our sensual pleasures?

"What would our intrinsic power be, if the charmed amazement of the faithful did not increase to the dimensions of a mirage, if the terrified imagination of the faithful were not elevated and deepened to any vertigo, were not extended, inflated and exaggerated to every infinity? We, so few in number, would be the ones trembling before the human swarm. A revolt of beings who no longer believe would annihilate us, as the morning sunlight disperses phantoms.

"To be sure, we would sell our lives dearly. We would kill who knows how many humans—100 million, perhaps. A joyful but futile massacre. What is 100 million in a crowd that surpasses eight billion?

"A few Superelephants would escape by flight, would hide away like hunted beasts, in grottoes in snowy mountains and caverns in torrid deserts. They would reproduce; painfully, they would raise a proscribed and wretched race of Gods. Perhaps we would even perish, to the very last, or ironic chance would only allow two males to survive, and no leap would permit us to spring into the future. The hypotheses are numerous and only too probable that would destroy any divine couple, forbidding the reincarnation of our supreme species forever. Has not your action begun to hollow out, between the unsteady present and the black future, an abyss impossible to traverse, into which divinity will sink tomorrow?

"Let us not despair yet, dear enemies with whom resemblance binds us together and common interest renders us fraternal. Our resources are immense. Our admirable priests can

245

bring into play a brilliant and specious eloquence, like a mirror moving in the sunlight. Their logic falls and spreads out, more flexible and solid than a suddenly-cast net. Skylarks were always less naïve than humans.

"Salvation is perhaps not very difficult, dependent on the creation of a new legend in the credulity of the human species. But be glad: we need your help, just as you need ours. Understand the indissoluble marriage of our interests, and the future will become accessible once again to the dominating feet of Superelephants."

Marbal fell silent—a pregnant silence. When he resumed speaking, he did not explain the solution or suggestion that his last words had seemed to advertise. Had he set it aside as impossible?

His voice, heavy with bitterness and lacerated by irony, summoned the vanquished to enlightenment. "You are undoubtedly preoccupied, Gods of Oor, with the redoubtable problem that your conduct has generated. You shall enjoy, for a duodecade, a leisure and an attitude that permits reflection. Immobility, with bellies and feet in the air, should, I suppose, easily give rise to meditation."

The sniggering of the 102 rolled its storm throughout the edifice. Heard outside as thunder and mystery, it caused human hearts to tremble.

With implacable succinctness, Marbal demanded: "Has one of the 45 discovered the solution to the problem posed by the perfidy of the 45?"

"We are the defeated, who ask for nothing," replied one Occidental Superelephant. "We can no longer do anything but submit. Under your questioning, your outrages, the tortures that you inflict upon us, and the death that you will inflict on us, courage can no longer have any other names for us but scorn and indifference."

"The Occident," Marbal observed, "was always scatterbrained. Its thought, enclosed within limited horizons, always remained a stranger to broad panoramas and great foresight.

You shall die one day, brethren, who seem to wish to die now."

"A quick death is our only hope, if we are still weak enough to choose to hope."

"But death, which never solves anything, poses the knottiest problems in this instance. Sit down for a moment on the stone of meditation, madly hurrying marchers who dare to say: 'The horizon is near.' Do you always forget the deceptive and successive light of horizons?

"After having made the problems more awkward by insane behavior, you are neglecting the tangles that you have made. Do you think that your disdain is sufficient to eliminate them? At least allow the Orientals to reason on your behalf as well as their own.

"Suppose that you are dead, and that human docility continues, as inert as the passivity of stones. You can but hope to be reborn promptly, O insatiable ones—but take care. If the laws that strictly limit births among us are not modified, in what miserable conditions will you find yourselves? Understand and tremble. We tremble mightily, ourselves, before a lesser, distant and uncertain peril.

"Now, I invite you no longer to be terrified, as the vanquished, of ourselves alone and in your narrow present. Transported from now into your distant future, accept your share, in order to be reborn as the sons of conquerors, in the anxiety and unsteadiness of the victory."

He was hoping for a prompt response. He forced himself to wait. When it came, it was as deceptive as darkness.

"We don't understand," said one of the captives, simply.

"Let me first reassure you on the subject of our sentiments. No hatred blinds us. We shall avoid constraining you to return in human form. You would provide excessively dangerous leaders to future revolts, or, at least, too noble a prey for our necessary severities. Benevolently, we shall broaden out the law. We shall permit you, if you persist in your folly and your suicide, to regain dominator bodies. Thus, you have the same interest as us in protecting the eternity of the Gods. Do

247

you understand that, you who do not want to understand anything?"

"Perhaps," replied one of the vanquished. There was a hint of joy in his tone.

Less bitterly, Marbal replied: "If you have examined that side of the question profitably—the only one that can offer you a durable interest—speak. If one of you has a wise proposal to make, let him speak. We shall listen with fraternal benevolence."

Some of the 45 sniggered. One of them said aloud, in an ironic tone: "The fraternal fashion in which you have treated us this far…"

But Marbal, with a severity mingled with softness, as if he were addressing children said: "Do not forget, brethren, that you will be Gods in the future, as in the past. Blinded by the darkness of a rapid present that is your handiwork and your error, do not prefer, as if you were humans, those beasts that speak, thoughts that are phantasmal and superficial to the point of ridicule. Do you not feel that we have been obedient, and are obedient still, to a necessity created by you? Do you not sense that we are struggling with a friendly heart against that necessity, that we are trying to save you from a karma instituted by your own folly? Think about it: how can we experience anything resembling malevolence toward Gods who are our brothers, and who, if they die today, will be our beloved children tomorrow?"

A vast emotional silence now hung on the words of the genius Marbal. His trunks drew apart, along with his arms, in a gesture signifying the rejection of unnecessary burdens.

"Let us set aside the past, about which we can do nothing. What is done is done. Let the causes fall into the bottomless pit. Let us study the possible effects and do our best to sculpt to our convenience the material that is offered to us by the past.

"Brethren, let us emerge from today, a petty, vexed and blind ditch. Let us gaze coolly into the abysm of the future. Let our intelligence illuminate it. Let our will collect realities harmonious to our desire. Necessary and inevitable allies of the victors, do not remain in the implacable stupidity of the defeated. Do not condemn yourselves, you whom we do not condemn. Do you want a few days, a few duodecades, a few moons, to search for the solution that it is necessary for you or us to find?"

His eloquence had been less persuasive than he had hoped.

"We only desire death," replied several of the 45. The silence of the others approved the desperate and despairing reply.

"It is not death that we are proposing to you, however," Marbal declared. "It is a voluptuous and easy life."

A hope quivered in the hearts of the captives—one of those terrible hopes that combat shame. They were silent, restraining at the tips of their trunks sighs emanating from the most secret depths.

"This, brethren, is what appears to us to be the best thing to do, if you will agree to it loyally:

"Priests will free you from your bonds. Others will summon humans to the borders of the temple. You will swing pious incense-burners before us. Speaking on behalf of all of you, one of you will proclaim, in a loud and determined voice: 'Gods can only be born in Eor. Any Superelephant who has seen the light of day outside the Holy City is a servant of the Gods. We are the greatest, and in consequence the most devoted, of the servants of the true Gods. Our pride—we confess it and we repent of it—once led us astray, but grace has touched our hearts with its hands of light. After the fall into fetid darkness and sacrilege, we now rise up in broad daylight replete with perfumes, the most faithful of priests. We repent, and our zeal will render us almost divine'."

While Marbal dictated the formula of honorable amendment, the 45 began murmuring. Their murmur ended up drowning out the powerful voice, which rose in vain and became inaudible.

The victor, entwined in the bonds of a victory that could not be undone, trumpeted wrathfully. Then he cried: "Let me finish, impulsive ones whose haste has already caused so much harm!"

Although the solution proposed by Marbal seemed unacceptable to the captives, they were curious to hear him out. They also experienced a considerable admiration for the genius of the speaker. They listened, therefore, torn between astonishment, hatred and an unspecifiable hope.

"Do what is asked of you and you will have an easy and honored life. You will be the mediators between humans and us. We shall extend generosity to you, to the point of requiring ourselves to remain forever invisible to the vulgar. You alone will refuse prayers or gather them in order to transmit them to us. Is not a servant who distributes favors and punishments, and is solely visible, a veritable master? All incense and glory will be offered up to your pride. You alone, by means of vain words, will report to Gods whose memory will become vaguer every day, and whose existence will soon seem problematic, homage that only flatters you. When natural death has visited you, things will resume their normal course—but we shall be 147, for you shall be reborn on Eor to be, in absolute equality with us, the masters of the world. Will you accept that present glory and that imminent radiance?"

"We refuse any lowering of status, even temporarily."

Marbal became indignant. "Creators of obstacles in your path, implacable enemies of yourselves, what do you ask, then? You refuse the best and most benevolent solutions. Propose in your turn. Say, finally, what you want."

"We ask for nothing but a quick death."

"Then it shall be according to your absurd will. Let the fools disappear for a while into the wings. We shall study, between Gods and common sense, the means of preventing your return from being a catastrophe for you and for the universe."

Priests of the superior order were called in. They were instructed to detach the first of the 45, kneel down and offer him the cup of holy death. Having drunk, the Superelephant entered euthanasia.

New enlightenment penetrated him along with the voluptuous peace. Magically, that twilight clarified the distant dawn for him. Turned toward the future, he proclaimed: "A true God can only be born in Eor."

It appeared to his companions that there would be no shame, death having been accepted, in ensuring their next existence by means of such a declaration.

When they had finally expressed that reasonable opinion, they were freed from their bonds. They marched, a powerful procession, to the threshold of the temple. Having drained the chalice of benign deliverance together, they cried to the humans kneeling before the most sublime of mysteries: "A true God can only be born in Eor."

The priests, followed by the entire pious crowd, repeated: "A true God can only be born in Eor."

The sound of the essential truth was propagated from mouth to mouth, crowd to crowd, city to city. The Word formed a girdle of virtue, piety and joy around the Earth.

When the Superelephants of Oor had lain down in peaceful death, their near-divine bodies were embalmed. They were stood up, magnificent and incorruptible statues, in the vast open space in front of the central temple. Their raised trunks permitted the sight of their broad bosoms, where letters that seemed to be made of light repeated and would repeat for centuries to come:

A TRUE GOD CAN ONLY BE BORN IN EOR.

Thus the wisdom of Marbal solved the most difficult problem that had ever addressed its irresolute mockery to divine meditation.

Chapter XII. Power and Love

Immense projects were undertaken for the aggrandizement of Eor. On 45 mounds raised around the old city, 45 paradises were planted and 45 heavens built. Each of these solemn heights became the center of a new quarter, to which the Provinces sent a million selected humans.

Eighteen young Superelephants, proclaimed Gods, were installed amid magnificent ceremonies in some of the new dwellings. The secret law that limited births was relaxed in order that the 27 heavens still vacant would not wait too long for a sacred presence.

These changes amused the Dominators for two or three duodecades.

When the work was finished, and fortunate births had completed the number of the 147 divinities who would govern the world henceforth, their divine hearts were gradually penetrated by ennui.

Is not ennui the superior power that humans have always sensed behind the gods? The merriment of the vulgar calls the mysterious force Destiny—but a few sages believe that Destiny has two esoteric names, two gaping abyssal names: Emptiness and Ennui.

One does not triumph over ennui, the asphyxiating phantom that one senses everywhere but cannot grasp anywhere. To combat it is to be condemned to a bottomless defeat that recommences with every hour. But the heavy unbreathable vapor only creeps in low places. Beings that live on the hilly plateaux of disinterested research, on the various mountain of enthusiastic and careful art, or on the serene heights of love can scarcely comprehend that there're might well be ennui and emptiness in their hearts.

Nothing is as low as the Gods. Avid for power and glory, gluttonous for adoration, they are unaware of the true summits of art, love and research. Entirely directed toward external conquest, they never perceive that the true summits are within them.

Power, wealth, sadistic lusts, glory and incense, the fumes with which the Gods nourish themselves, sometimes intoxicate the moment to the point of dizziness, but they leave the day famished and hollow.

The masters of Olympus were a noble race. They knew how to look at themselves and laugh at themselves. Were they not parodying their own torment in the punishments in which wingless eternity was endlessly repeated? Was it not before a scarcely-curved mirror that they laughed in contemplating Sisyphus or the Danaïdes?

The Gods that had succeeded them did not know how to smile and never manifested any disinterested subtlety. Only knowing how to listen externally, they could not hear the resonance of their internal emptiness. Dedicated to the unique concern of governing humans, they had glorified, brutalized or sophisticated all aspects of the baseness that made humans governable.

Although they had the superiority of not imagining themselves eternally immutable, the Dominators of Eor felt the hollowness of ennui within them, felt the choking heaviness of ennui weighing upon them, and felt the crushing pressure of ennui around them. Ennui seems to be emanating from the bored and simultaneously irradiates everything with boredom. It is a hunger that twists the entrails and a chill that aches and paralyses.

One day, in the enlarged central temple, from one of the 147 perfumed baths, Marbal pronounced these words:

"What, then, do we need, Divine brethren, in order to experience the full measure of the unalloyed happiness that the priests, in what I hope will prove to be a prophetic lie, sing as our privilege?

"We need—hear my sincere and long-meditated words— to dominate the entire population of the globe. Humans obey us piously. The fearful Immortals bow before the possible creators of accidents. But the Superangels have none of the sentiments of devotion to us that are our due. I even dread that in certain moments of intoxication, they believe themselves superior to us."

Amid murmurs, trunks and arms agitated in gestures of negation. From all sides, there were exclamations: "Those crazy beings could not take folly to such an extreme!"

"Admit," Marbal went on, "that their attitude pains you. The homage that they refuse us would be much more precious than that of eight billion humans and 212 Immortals."[29]

"We need the homage of the Superangels," cried the 146. "You have enlightened us as to what we lack. Henceforth, all joy will be bitter to us until the superelves become our humble friends and servants."

"Let us set out, brethren, on a vast campaign. Let us summon the Superangels, in order that we may seduce them with promises and honors."

The 147 left the city. They refused any escort, even sending away the foremost of the priests and the leaders of the Immortals. At the exquisite hour when night begins, they reached a large grassy plateau, which the silken sky covered like a tent of tenderness.

They called to all points of the horizon: "Amours, Amours, where are you? Amours, Amours, the most powerful of beings seek you and desire your presence as a thirsty animal runs toward a spring. Come and share with the Gods the rule of the Earth."

A distant song replied: "We do not refuse any call. We are hurrying, preceded by perfumes and music. If your appeal is sincere, do you not feel, in your emotion, our emotion and our approach? If your appeal is sincere, do you not already feel our presence stirring in your hearts?"

A strange softness penetrated the hard Dominators. A slow plenitude rose from the depths of their being, bound, it seemed, to render the morose emptiness of the powerful overflowing with joy.

Soon, the Superangels appeared to their charmed eyes. Their beauty outshone the beauty of the stars. Their light was bluer than the sky, whiter than moonlight, rosier than the freshness of flowers, more tenderly and diaphanously green

---

[29] It is not obvious how or why the number of the Immortals should have increased in this fashion from the previously-cited 181 (less the two who were ground up in the mortar).

than mountain springs, or more delicately and more scintilla-
tingly yellow than the gleam of straw in the shade of a barn.

They sounded, as an uncertain prelude, a music of expectation and charm. They wove and unraveled a strophe of hesitant colors, a network of perfumes that combined and dispersed, a gliding back and forth. Then, floating as vaguely as
clouds or dreams, they listened to what the Dominators were
saying.

Marbal cried: "Greetings to you, who are the winged
grace of the Earth. We salute you in your joyous glory, artists,
dancers, musician and poets. Only the equal triumph of ruling
holds sway over your changing radiation. Come to us, who
rule. Be the charm and delight of the sovereign Gods. Share
with us the honors that all owe to beauty, almost as much as to
power."

"Power," replied the music of the Superangels, "you will
merit being honored when you have the radiation of love that
warms seeds and incubates slow hatchings. Become, O Dominators, the protectors and guides of all living things. Defend
them against the vicissitudes of nature and, since you are the
strongest, glorify yourselves in being the most laborious servants of life. Direct toward scourges the vigor of your intelligence and the firmness of your heart. Be life's rampart against
the scourge that arrives and rises; when the scourge slackens,
be the repercussion and reflux of life. Let your hearts, softened
by all suffering, lift up your courage to combat all suffering.
Let your gentleness, leaning over living beings, relieve cor-
rupted hearts. Let your strength be the faithful servant of your
bounty, so that the Earth might become, thanks to you, the
vast altar of love at which all living things take communion."

"Do you not know, O Superangels, the hardness of love
and its implacable jealousy? We turn away from the vile humans and the vile Immortals; it is to you alone that we offer
our wild hearts. Render to us alone the love that we offer you.
Love that which is great and powerful. Sing of our strength
and the devotion owed to us by everything that exists. Sing of
the glory of loving us to the point of sacrifice and martyrdom.

Our life is the mightiest of beauties; make the grace of your music, perfumes and dances hover around our unshakable equilibrium. Thus, for you and for us, the Earth will turn in a delirium of joy."

"Let us sing no longer, brethren, of material power; in itself it possesses neither value nor beauty. Your strength may be a good or an evil, its actions may sing with nobility or grate with ugliness, according to the use you make of it. The power of a living being over living beings always leads to wickedness and oppression. If you want strength to cease crawling, grinding and crushing, give it the sovereign wings of love. Let power, an abominable mistress, finally become a good servant.

"Poor Superelephants, Gods of tyranny and ugliness, become saviors. Then, if you deign to keep the name of Gods, that title, worthy of every blasphemy and all derision, will become a radiance—the radiance, under no matter what name, of universal love. Let your energy, helpful to all weakness, emanate only benefits, but let it refrain from extinguishing the humblest of lights or breaking the most fragile of reeds."

"Humans adore what crushes them. In crushing them and breaking them, we are giving them the only profound sensuality of which their servile hearts are capable."

"Liberate their hearts from all dread and all servility. Then love, pouring out all gratitude toward you, will fill the emptiness of your hearts. Or, rather, a benevolent heart is the wellspring that pours into and fills itself, without waiting for the streams of gratitude to come or be refused."

"The first joy is to rule. The second is to hear one's rule blessed and hymned. But if the rule is not harsh, what merit resides in the faithful who bless the Gods, and what pleasure can the Gods take from worthless blessings?"

For a long time, exquisite counsels descended from on high and superb declarations rose up from down below. In the astonished air, there was the encounter, friction and separation of the lightest of perfumes and the heaviest of stinks. The contradictory words of excessively different beings were alternating in vain. What those on high sang rose up again to those on high. What those down below sang fell back on those down below. No heart was penetrated by that which did not emerge therefrom.

Finally, the Dominators became irritated by having lowered themselves fruitlessly to the caresses of words and promises. Their deception declared the Superangels unworthy of so much condescension.

"You do not wish to become voluntarily the friends who charm us and whom we would honor with our protection, and for whom we would demand from humans almost as much honor as for ourselves? Woe, then, to you and your obstinate sacrilege. We will capture you, and hurt you, if necessary, and you shall sing, rebel birds, in the servitude of solid aviaries."

The Superangels disappeared. Behind them, like a wake of dazzling light, trailed this song: "We only deploy our music, our colors and our rhythms in the liberty of the air. Our rhythms, colors and music only deploy their virtues in the liberty of hearts."

The majority of the Dominators tried to console themselves for the insulting absence. They listened to the savant musical compositions and the skillful and pious poems of humans. They caressed their eyes with the erotically religious dances of the daughters of humankind. They charmed themselves momentarily with the gleam of metals or gems and the color of paintings. But, oh, how pale, dead and heavy all that was in comparison with the free grace of the superelves!

Four or five of them, among whom was the brilliant and tenacious Marbal, were no longer anything more than inventors who were seeking and becoming frustrated. They would not have a moment of rest or pleasure until they had discovered a means of capturing the Superangels and locking them in melodious cages. Frequent news renewed bitter desire in all of them, redoubling their humiliation and hatred.

The insolent rebels accorded to vile humans the songs, the evolutions of color, the quivering brightness and sinuous perfumes that they now refused the Dominators. Oh, the incomprehensible and odious caprices of artists! Appearing unexpectedly over a Provincial town, they lavished their incomparable multiple spectacle upon the inhabitants.

Now, that beauty was not without venom and danger. After the luminous passage, the humans remained pensive for a few days, treating one another more gently, and less servile with respect to their masters.

Chapter XIII. The Conspiracy

The majority of the Dominators aggravated their condition by multiplying vain pleasures. In a whirl of festivals, they lavished the most diverse, the most profound and the bitterest caresses upon the eternal ennui of their flesh, their eyes, their ears and their pride. They invented honors as vertiginous as mountain peaks, pleasures as vertiginous as abysses.

The drunken amusement of the hour always left the day empty and interminable. The vigor of their bodies was exhausted without lifting the besieging fog that was slyly inundating their souls, invading their fatigue like hollows and enveloping the most superb and desperately voluptuous summits with their victorious crawl. Trunks yawned before the rarest spectacles. Bare arms reached out, amid savant caresses, into an unvanquished enervation.

The four or five whose intelligence was always alert and politically attentive were now prey to obsession, employing their genius in searching for a means to bring the Superangels down. No Dominator perceived the changes, long undetectable, that were taking place in the human mind. What prophets call the signs of the times and historians call the symptoms of revolution are never easy to discern.

The human mind is a fluid, slippery, contradictory entity. Its general march is often confused by eddies generated by obstacles or by fashionable whims and wanderings. Only denouements clarify the tragedies of reality.

Disinterested genius is mistaken when it tries to anticipate vast and durable movements. How can masters, enveloped by presumption and incense, see through the clouds that which great minds solely attentive to causes and effects cannot discern? Masters always march in the security of their superiority and the consequent adulation. They do not see the abrupt shock or the sudden fall into the shallow ditch or profound abyss toward which their pompous and voluptuous dream is leading them.

The two executed Immortals were reincarnated as humans in a family of priests. The nostalgia that saddened their childhood still remained imprecise for them. Later, without knowing where it came from, they would feel the need to avenge themselves on the Dominators igniting in their souls. For the moment, they were singular children, who avoided games and sought solitude. Those who knew them best thought that their self-absorbed meditations had pious and theological objectives, as was appropriate.

Marbal and a few others, had they been able to extract themselves from their passionate desire to capture the Superangels, might perhaps have been intelligent enough to anticipate the danger, patient enough to discover their future enemies in time, and resourceful enough to seduce them or neutralize them. Their preoccupation even distracted them from more imminent and more pressing perils.

The most highly-evolved humans had, by their most recent reincarnation, slightly increased the number of the Superangels. A few, although the Immortals did not reproduce at all, had even discovered the rare secret of enveloping themselves with diminutive quasi-metallic bodies that only accidents could destroy. But the dreams of the majority of humans were too corrupt to elevate them toward the pure life of the Amours, and the dreams of the majority of humans were too avid and frenetic an intoxication not to disdain the slow and somnolent existence of Immortals.

The desire of slaves is modeled on the form of their masters. It is the life of their masters that slaves call the high life, the inimitable life, or even, simply and completely, life.

Life, is not your beauty to manifest yourself variously, abundantly and indefinably? In every epoch, however, life, as changeable as flame, reserves its name to a single form. The vast, undulant and splendid name always designates, for the vulgar, a narrow and confined dream, shiny with obscenity.

The majority of humans, students of a coarse example, only aspired, even in the passage of death, toward an "advancement." Those who had spent their days in a humble condition wanted to become voluptuous and honored priests. Weary of subaltern authority and reflected glory, the priests of yesterday strove toward supreme government and its ardent radiance; they attempted to reincarnate themselves in the bodies of Superelephants. The secret law that limited Dominator births set them in conflict with former Gods. Vanquished in the excessively unequal struggle, bruised by invisible barriers, they retreated irritably toward achievable existences.

Today, several thousand humans, of which four-fifths were priests, were manifesting an intelligence and avidity equal to their masters. Millions sensed within themselves the vacillating and lacerating ascension of an as-yet-ill-defined ambition. It was too dangerous to reveal their dreams and nostalgias to companions who were always unsure. Most of them locked up their aspirations, whether vague or precise, in the hermitage of a tortured heart. Their superiority was a torment, with which, in solitude, they often intoxicated themselves, as with the bitter wine of pride.

One cunningly brilliant priest, after having cleverly cultivated a reputation for naivety, forged a potentially redoubtable organization under a pious and reassuring name. It was called the Society for the Most Profound Love of the Gods. A series of ordeals and initiations, the first of which were utterly banal, slowly tested the few strong-minded accomplices with whom the founder might be able to attempt the great revolt. Spies infiltrated this milieu as they do all milieux. As soon as their reports gave rise to anxiety, the society was dissolved and the founder burned for the crime of heresy. From then on, a severe law forbade any esoteric association, on pain of death.

The most inextricable difficulty was not created by the cunning of the police or the uncertainty of relationships. It emerged from the equal ambition, vertiginously intolerant, of secret revolts. Every speech declared: "I am not superior to any other human." Every silence affirmed: "I am superior to all other humans." Even so, after centuries-long tranquility, revolts were multiplying. Mostly sly and tenacious, a few revealed themselves, and sudden and bright as flashes of lightning.

Three Dominators died on the same night, poisoned. Five or six others escaped death thanks to the promptitude of medical care and the efficacy of its remedies. The maladies were covered up. The pretence was maintained that the deaths were natural. They were willingly acknowledged, like all divine deaths. Amid the accustomed solemnities, the cadavers were burned on the odorous and precious wood designated by the rituals. The funeral orations commented eloquently on the old sacred text according to which the Gods, when they were "too indignant at the diminution of piety among the living," abandoned our filthy Earth to rule over the blissful dead.

No visible reaction was manifest in Eor, but the Superelephants were trembling before the perfidy of an omnipresent danger.

In several provincial cities, brutal bands armed according to the latest improvements were taking possession of the streets, assailing the castles and the temples, killing Immortals and priests, mounting a stubborn resistance to regular troops. In several places, peasant rebellions were devastating the countryside.

Most of the rebels were massacred. A few groups took refuge in forests, amid the rocky chaos of mountains or the depths of deserts. Terror, pity or sympathy moved the inhabitants of villages, farms or oases to furnish them with provisions.

Events were occurring more astonishing and blasphemous than one could believe. Mothers carrying their nurslings were furtively leaving cities or towns, desperately fleeing the

261

glory, once so fervently desired, of seeing their children eaten by the Gods.

If the leaders of the revolts succeeded in making their voices heard, they would multiply the sporadic uprisings infinitely, and progressively gather forces that might prove irresistible.

The principal ones among them met on the solitary plateau of Valal, where legend said that mysterious ancient assemblies had been held. An enormous stone table stood in the center. Three humbler stones surrounded it, like seats around an altar or a podium. Seated on these stone benches, the rebels attempted to organize a provisional government.

Would the rivalries of the ambitious not thwart that attempt? None of them could support a leader; each of them would suffer secretly of not being the Master that everyone obeyed.

At first there was a long confused quarrel, which almost became bloody on more than one occasion—but the renegade priest Nurdol soothed their wrath with a clever and subtle speech.

Firstly, he displayed, in an impressive light of precision and sincerity, the difficulties and the probabilities of the adventure into which they had irrevocably entered, and which had no exit for any of them but triumph or death.

All the rebels' strength derived from the disaffection produced in a great many humans by the increasing harshness and the increasingly unexpected and cruel caprices of the Dominators. But nothing is less sure than the human heart. None was capable of liberty, and yet, how many would obey if the orders did not appear to emanate from Gods?

Nurdol recalled that a few priests, including himself, had attempted to preach about benign and invisible divinities. They had not obtained any success. However stupid the people of the present century might be, their faith had to be sustained by some appearance and visual evidence.

"We shall seek together from now on and we shall find the solution to that difficulty. Before then, I shall expose another that seems to me to be no less considerable. Ordinary humans are not the only ones to show themselves to be incapable of being disciplined as soon as they are removed from the worship of visible Gods. Superior humans, as we have just seen once again, are also incapable of obeying one among them.

"Well, my dear companions, these two obstacles against which we seem bound to break can be overcome by a single action—which, I believe, offers no particular difficulty. Our inferior brothers will be unable to live without religion, and only a religion can save us from the jealous competition that pulverizes our strength..."

The hot-headed Lohar rose to his feet, with a magnificent fervor. "The new religion is easy to find!" he exclaimed. "If we are clever, not only will it underpin our power, as you have just shown, but it will undermine that of the enemy. Let us divide the Dominators. Let us make a choice between them and proclaim, for example, that the only Gods are named Marbal, Rismac, Salom..."

Nurdol burst out laughing. "You are naming those who are the true masters—those whose advice the divine herd always follows; those who, by force of genius and continuous intellectual effort, exercise al the realities of power. What advantage would they obtain, statues deprived of their pedestal, in being deprived of brethren who love and admire them, who are nothing to them but marvelous instruments of their reign?"

"Propose other names, then," demanded the hot-headed Lohar.

But the subtle priest said: "I shall not go in the direction you have indicated. It is the most deceptive of blind alleys. The vulgar Gods, inferior to the prophetic synthesis that is an adept government, rejoice in the glare and appearance of power, satisfied with the thousand joys of pride or the flesh that the submission of humans procure for them. Ties as solid as the pleasures of gratitude and hope attach them to a few superior individuals who know how to protect the continuity and security of their common contentment. That unity, whose lack

263

is our weakness, is perfect among the Superelephants. Often admitted to the mysteries of the Central Temple, I know that better than anyone and can testify to it with certainty."

"So you see no means of creating a schism? So the ancient religion appears to you to be unshakable? Why, then, before the people who are fighting against it, have you just preached the necessity of a religion? Oh, I can see through you, and understand you better than you'd like, traitor paid to dispirit and discourage us…"

Lohar, a warrior as violent as he was formidable, rose up in his power and his wrath. He drew his sword, and ran toward Nurdol, shouting: "Let all traitors perish as this traitor will perish!" But the other chiefs threw themselves upon him, and set up a chorus of soothing words and placatory gestures.

The subtle Nurdol looked on, his lips parted in a smile of disdain and bitterness.

They finally succeeded in bringing Lohar back to his place and making him sit down on his stone. He struggled, quivering, as if bristling with menace.

Nurdol made a sign that he wanted to continue his speech.

Lohar, with a scornful gesture of resentment, covered his ears.

The former priest explained: "If I advertise the disease, it is because we shall find the remedy. Soon, we shall discover a new religion, which I believe to be marvelously efficacious. It will establish the necessary discipline between us. It will, I hope, seduce the great majority of humans."

From every side, impatient cries sprang forth like projectiles, striking the slow and sinuous sloth of the orator. "Quickly! Speak, quickly!"

But he replied: ""Who speaks too quickly says nothing. Now, I shall explain, certainly not the whole, but at least the essence."

This declaration was greeted with shrugs, and grudging consent. "Speak as you please, then."

Unhurriedly, Nurdol continued. He seemed to be grop-ing. They did not know whether he was approaching his con-clusion or drawing away from it. They listened with an increa-singly active anxiety. They sought to divine a thought that was taking too long to emerge.

That was what the skilled orator wanted. Instead of pro-nouncing the salutary formula himself, thus raising jealousies and objections, he was guiding the minds of his listeners by obscure pathways toward the place where his own thought dwelt. Soon, no doubt, they would see as Nurdol saw. It would be them who would voice his idea. It would become their idea, their discovery; they would love it like their daughter.

"To a religion of harsh tyranny," he continued, "can none of us, my dear friends, see a means of opposing a religion of gentleness, fraternity and love?"

It was as if everyone arrived at the same time at the summit from which the new spectacle became visible. Excited by what they had perceived, they stood up abruptly, in the enlightenment of revelation.

"The Superangels!" they cried. The Superangels! Let the Superangels be the Gods of the crowd and the chiefs of the chiefs!"

Chapter XIV. Revolt and Love

Having opened his ears and heard the loud unanimous cry, the hot-headed Lohar, shouted along with the others, what the others shouted. Then, with his hand extended, he came to the subtle Nurdol.

"I am quick to anger," he said, "But I can recognize and repair my errors. If you wish, from now on, Lohar is the most faithful and ardent of your friends."

The former priest, a skilled actor, did not take the hand that was held out to him. He opened his arms, threw himself recklessly upon Lohar, and kissed both his cheeks. The clever fellow even drew a few tears from his eyes.

Lohar wept abundantly and naively.

The spectators applauded. "An admirable beginning for the religion of love," they said, nodding their heads happily. "That kiss will be celebrated by the remotest posterity. That kiss is the radiant commencement of a new era."

Nurdol smiled softly.

Lohar, uplifted by ecstasy, felt that his heart was fuller than it had once been in the first ecstasy of love. He felt that his heart was full, and swollen like a bud about to open. He blossomed, tenderly proud to think himself "the commencement of a new era," the promoter of universal happiness.

After a few moments devoted to mutual congratulations and dreams of the future, Nurdol, by common consent, climbed up to the top of the central stone, which some were calling "the sacred stone." On behalf of all of them, he shouted: "Superangels, dear Superangels, listen! The most highly-evolved of humans launch toward you the call of love and adoration." The former priest continued: "Our hearts are overflowing with disgust and shame at the memory of the vile and tyrannical religion that was imposed on our credulous youth."

And all of them, toward the orient, toward the occident, toward the south, the north and 20 intermediate points, echoed: "Our hearts are overflowing with disgust and shame at the memory of the tyrannical and vile religion that was imposed on our credulous youth."

"Come, then, dear Superangels; initiate us into the religion of truth and love."

This last appeal was not repeated.

Everyone was listening, in a exquisite softness, to vague and distant music that was becoming clearer with every passing second.

Soon, their eyes were glad. They saw the harmonious flock and the floating mixtures of noble colors.

When the Superangels were hovering above the imploring group, the music was accompanied by a song:

"Here we are, here we are. Tell those who love you the suffering and aspiration of your hearts."

The chiefs addressed Nurdol then. "Speak for us. Recount the suffering and aspiration of our hearts."

Nurdol spoke for some time.

Meanwhile, the Superangels circled with gracious slowness. Sometimes joyously approving, sometimes saddened and reproachful, their music responded continuously to the mixed words of the former priest.

He concluded with this prayer: "Be our Gods, then, O benevolent Superangels. Unite under your command all those among men who are good, and lead us to the violent victory of love. Unite in an irresistible army those who have the heart, in order that they might exterminate the tyrants and the incurable slaves...."

The song of the Superangels replied: "There is but one God on high, over the Earth and the depths. Do not believe that God is a person, or several persons. The unique God is a diffuse power, and the unique God is named Love.

"Love—listen, poor unstable beings—is not the god of armies. Any army is the enemy of the true God. The servants of the true God are scornful of weapons and violence.

"The scorn of all weapons and all violence is the commencement of wisdom and the threshold of love. Let your first effort be to reject, along with the weapons with which your arms are laden, the desire for vengeance that is crushing your hearts.

"Neither arms bearing arms nor armored hearts can enter into you, Ideal Temple that does not display a visible architecture anywhere. In truth, can anyone enter the Ideal Temple? No, one radiates it around one. It bursts forth, shining like a sun, everywhere one encounters that fame more noble than the sunlight, a heart that does not know violence.

"Love everything that is alive. Let the radiance and the overflow of your hearts direct a joyous love, devoid of hatred, toward living beings. Let it direct toward tyrants and the servile—toward all the violent living beings blind to the point of striking out against life—a love made of pity.

"No violence can protect love and life. All violence wounds love and life.

"Be quiet. We know. Violence can triumph over violence as one lie can displace another. Deplorable victories, local and unenduring. Violence is a terrible wind. If two winds encounter and oppose one another, they do not produce calm but the horrors and howling whirlwinds of the tempest.

"Love, that which you desire, is neither a contest of winds not the triumph of the stronger wind. What you want is radiant peace, an end to all violence and all lies."

"O Superangels," Nurdol replied, "you speak with a penetrating charm of the gentle beauty and tender duty of the future. Let us therefore march together toward the beauties for which you have raised a yearning within us. Let us march toward the light of which you sing—but let us not forget the necessities of a nocturnal march. Let us march along the only road open to us. Help us in the bitter and heroic duty of the present, the sole possible creator of the present.

"If you truly desire the future and its calm nobility, consent to the inevitable cruelty of its birth. The birth of the future is difficult, and it can only be realized by steel. Our society is old and worn-out. Steel, alas, will always be the midwife of old societies."

The choir of Superangels replied: "There is no calculation and no warning sign to indicate when a society is about to give birth. Your wicked and wounded societies are always crying out and wailing like women in labor. Every time anyone tries to deliver them by steel, the mother is injured, and an unformed embryo is drawn from her. Steel has never brought anything from the belly of a society but a monster or a new tyrant.

"There is no benevolent force but love and its warmth. Love is both the only sun that can bring forth blossom and the only flower that can bloom. There is neither cruelty nor brutality in the blossoming."

The Superangels continued their delightful canticle—but the impatient chiefs were all talking at once now. Simultaneously, they were proclaiming the necessity of armed revolt, the necessity of killing tyrants, the necessity of exterminating the henchmen of tyranny. They were now transporting into things the inclination of their hearts, with the result that they were speaking with a torrential and filthy eloquence. Their words had an odor of cruel joy and madness, a whiff of powder, blood and putrescence. Their torrential and filthy pleas became increasingly bitter, increasingly impassioned, and increasingly urgent.

The Superangels listened, amid music that became progressively mournful and sad. They finally adopted a swaying flight, movements and sounds pronouncing a hesitant rhythm, which no longer knew whether it still had hope, whether there was anything further to attempt.

But the chiefs, increasingly drunk on their own words and those of their neighbors, calling the implacable gentleness of the Superangels cowardice.

Then the Amours drew away, trailing behind them the melody of their dying hope.

After their departure, the rebel chiefs resumed their deliberation. All of Nurdol's adroit subtlety was impotent. The men separated, as future enemies, each to act now on his own behalf.

If, by chance, they had triumphed, of what implacable wars might their victory have been the mother?

They were vanquished on after another. Several died on the battlefield. A few, taken prisoner, expired under the most frightful tortures. Only the subtle Nurdol escaped death. For a long time, in the mountain caves, he led a vexed and miserable life.

Chapter XV. Captive Wings

At the moment when what the Dominators' annals called "the great rebellion and the great sacrilege" broke out, Marbal, with the aid of a few bird-catchers and scientists, had just invented a vast invisible net, which would be able to take the Superangels by surprise and capture them.

Urgent preoccupations caused him to postpone the project so dear to his heart until later. The circumstances required all his genius. The attempt of the rebel chiefs to oppose the divinity of the Superangels to the dominion of the Superelephants soon became known. The refusal of the winged beings was also known. The reasons for their abstention were not known, nor whether they were profound and essential or merely circumstantial. Could an attack on them be risked, in case it failed and caused them to revoke their pacific decision and commit themselves to the revolt of the redoubtable chiefs? It was necessary for the Dominators to crush their declared enemies before creating new and more terrible ones.

A few years later, after the "triumph of order," Marbal's plans encountered an irreducible opposition in the Great Council. It was generally believed that the troubled Superangels might reignite blasphemous sentiments in the human heart. Their music was disturbing, even while preaching, against the grain of prevailing sentiment, a love that no one understood. How great might their power be, on the day when they sounded a clarion call to heroism, combat, and natural cruelty?

As the terrible alarm became a distant memory, however, dread and prudence diminished in the Dominators' minds, forming an increasingly insufficient counterweight to the instinct to subjugate everything. A day came when the unanimity of the Superelephants consented to Marbal's desire.

A dozen airships, innocent in appearance, as if naïve, would weave the invisible net out of the very air, at the appropriate height. Then they would fall, an abrupt swoop of eagles, and the subtle trap would capture everything that was between them and the ground.

Experiments were carried out. All of them succeeded marvelously. The smallest birds and the most powerful, the most fearful and the swiftest, were always caught in the net. Nothing seemed to be able to escape it.

One day, above the central plaza of Dolol, a small city of eight million inhabitants, the Superangels were giving voice to their songs and giving the eyes a poetic living feast of harmonies. A dozen aeronefs moved into position above the marvelous choir and began a series of singular maneuvers. They moved past and cut across one another like darting swallows.

The Superangels thought that the stupid aviators were parodying their movements. They sang a scornful strophe against the baseness of caricatures, then resumed the music of love, wisdom and peace—and did not watch the indifferent evolutions of the airships.

The humans had all heard talk of the invisible net, woven in the air at the moment of its use, which captured all sorts of birds on the Dominators' behalf: those that were enemies to be destroyed, those that might serve as nourishment, and those that might be shut up in aviaries for the enjoyment of their singing and their grace in flight or hopping. Several guessed what was happening. Information, details and suppositions ran from mouth to ear, in whispers and sparks. Then there was free speech, and the growing noise of a conflagration. Some were saying: "We must warn the unfortunates!" But no one dared to undertake the dangerous sacrilege.

Already the airships were descending in a vertiginous swoop. A few screams burst forth, increasing momentarily. Finally, there was a universal rumor: "Superangels, save yourselves! The invisible net!" And arms were waving madly. Women had been unable to retain the cry of their heart. Now the entire multitude was repeating it, with crazed gestures.

There was so much pity and anguish in the great clamor that the Superangels, ever-ready to obey love, took flight in order to set the anxiety of the humans to rest.

It was a fraction too late. The seven Superangels who found themselves at the rear were struck by the net and entangled in the occult mesh.

They were locked in a huge cage, which a vast flat automobile bore toward Eor.

Their brethren accompanied them in mid-air, singing strophes of solidarity and courage. The captives replied with melodies of amorous dread. They begged their beloved kin to admit their impotence and flee from needless risk.

That evening, the cage stopped at the entrance to Eor. On high, a dozen airships recommenced the confused maneuvers whose objective was now known.

Then the canticle of the Seven became imperious and irresistible. Oh, the noble and tender lamentation was more powerful than one can say; it had the authority of love in tears.

Obeying the captives, the free Superangels rose up higher than any trap, human or divine, could climb. The airships abandoned a futile task—and the prisoners were introduced into the immense capital.

The central temple was lit up, illuminating the entire city with the strange, bright gaieties of a nocturnal celebration.

Alerted by wireless telephone, the Superelephants were waiting, their hearts voluptuous and full, in their perfumed baths. The cage was transported into the midst of the sublime council.

Marbal spoke with the proud softness of the triumphs of love: "Dear Superangels, artists as beloved as admired, you will excuse a violence that expresses our inability to live without you, without your colors, without your songs, without your dances and your smiles of light.

"You should consider us as orphans recovering their parents, as widowers resuscitating adored wives.

"Give us your word not to flee our affection. We shall envelop you with so many honors and so much joy that you will bless the moment of the amorous constraint for as long as you live.

"Soon, you will engage your brethren, since you love them, to come and share with you the most glorious and most voluptuous of ecstasies."

The Superangels sang: "Without you, Liberty, there is neither glory, nor pleasure, nor love. Are we still Amours, when we are captives? No. We are no more than abrupt wisdom, which resists. If any softness subsists within us, it will flow, a haughty pity, over the insanity of those who think that love can be enchained."

Marbal replied: "Don't exaggerate, dear sages. No chains weigh upon your delicate bodies, and your cage will open as soon as you have promised to remain with us, who love you, in order to embellish your life in embellishing our own."

But the Superangels replied: "Wild liberty of love, you shun the bonds of flowers as jealously as chains of steel. You cannot live in the narrowness of promises and oaths any more than in the breadth of sages and dungeons. You cannot be locked up, either in a word or in a place.

"Wild liberty of love, you refuse everything that is a limit or a pause. Promises and oaths, more subtle poisons, more cowardly servitudes…"

The Superelephants were becoming annoyed. Rismac expressed the general feeling: "Cease these ridiculously austere songs. Give your music fluttering wings, and the subtle grace of caresses."

Then the hymn resumed. Its gravity loomed up, like a rocky landscape. A cheerful stream, however, shone here and there amid the grey harshness. Entwined within the severity of the music was mocking and jesting laughter.

"A free being sings free joy. The sage whose body is captive sings the realities of his heart and the impregnable citadel of his bitter wisdom.

"Let the songs of the vulgar captive flow slackly, like tears, or, baser still, like consenting servitude. The voice of the captive sage rises up, as proud as his internal liberty and the bristling of his invincible defenses.

"Songs of the captive, the more disdainful you are, the brighter and more luminous is your beauty—but that proud beauty mocks the impotence and baseness of tyrants.

"Gods, you are the true slaves…"

"Are you going to abuse our generosity much longer?" cried Salom. "You would be prudent not to irritate further the masters on whom your lives depend. Think about it: the time has come to appease us. If you do not want to taste the bitterness of death, it is time to sing the sweetness and charm of living under our merciful yoke."

"Let us sing sweetly the charming sweetness of death. Liberator of captives, madmen with eyes of night see your face as black. For those who know, your face is the soft light of dawn.

"Gentle premature death, come fill our hearts, you who will permit us to become the sons of our brothers and the pupils of our sisters.

"Charming deliverance, come snatch us away from crazed hands and demented trunks. Our joyous desire flies to meet you, free journey to the next reincarnation.

"Look at these fools, perspicacious death; they are still too insane for anything, except you, to liberate us from them and render us to those who love us.

"Come, gentle and noble death, to us who gently and proudly appeal to you and hope for you."

"If your obstinacy constrains us to condemn you," cried Rismac, the death that we inflict upon you will, I promise you, lack gentleness as well as nobility. It will engulf you, a vile maw. Meanwhile, a host of tortures, humiliations and degradations and will harass your slow death-throes."

"Let us sing, my brethren, the ugliness and the beauty of tortures. Let us sing the beauty and the ugliness of outrages.

"Tortures, ugly and servile shadows over whomever inflicts them upon you, radiate with the light of free beauty those who endure you with courage.

"Insults, the being that inflicts you lowers his baseness, makes his ugliness uglier, darkens his night. But you are wings and ascension for those who endure you with a noble heart, and you shine like a halo around the mind that accepts you with victorious laughter.

"Come, then, torture and outrages, add that which is lacking to our beauty…"

Many trunks were yawning. Many arms were stretching, wearily, and trumpetings were sounding ennui at length. Finally, a few Superelephants said: "How boring these musicians are! Let us be rid of these musicians, creators of ennui."

The great cage was carried out of the central temple. The Dominators remained alone, deliberating as to the fate of the annoying musicians.

Rismac and Salom called for vengeful measures, but Marbal said: "I confess, brethren, that I have made an error in presenting to you artists devoid of tact, whose talent is so strangely inflexible. I allowed myself to be deceived by an undeserved reputation. I see it now: the least of humans who sings or plays instruments is more agreeable to the ear. But there is nothing to do but render the liberty of fleeing from us to those beings whose presence is so fastidious."

As some persisted in speaking of vengeance, he added: "Let us not make implacable enemies—who, now that we no longer have the element of surprise, will become untrappable. The death of their brothers would render the Superangels terrible."

A large minority protested, speaking emphatically of divine power.

"Understand me well," Marbal went on. "I do not dread that the irritated Superangels might cause us any great material damage. My fear is more subtle. They would pursue all our excursions with those funereal and obstinate songs that their stupidity calls the rhythms of wisdom. The open air would become, for us, an immense, lugubrious, unbreathable annoyance. Its infection would constrain us to confine ourselves to the narrow ennui of our heavens."

After a long discussion, a vast expenditure of exclamations and eloquence, Marbal's opinion finished out carrying the day.

However, the ceremony of liberation was postponed until the following day.

Chapter XVI. Merciful Precautions

On the vast open space in front of the central temple, the Superelephants and the most senior priests were surrounding the Superangels' cage.

"Incomparable musicians," said Marbal, "the priests will open your mobile cage respectfully. You were locked therein—as your noble hearts have understood—solely to hear the protestations of our admiration and our love. We hope that you will come back often, you and your brethren, to be acclaimed by the Dominators, who love you. We hope that you will fly away slowly today. The songs that will accompany your departure—we have the delicacy of your sentiments for a guarantee—will celebrate the generosity of the masters of the Earth, and you will praise liberty as a gift of the Gods. It ought to please your love to salute appropriately the most natural of the gifts of love."

"Let us sing," replied the Superangels, "the infinite bounty of the Gods. The Gods, impotent to do good, desire that the evil that they do and the evil that they do not do to be adored. Be praised, then Gods, for not doing all evil. For our part, we sing humbly the generosity with which, giving that which does not belong to you, you sometimes deign not to take that which belongs to someone else."

"Open the cage," cried Rismac, "and chase these insolent individuals away. At the same time, let the sound of clarions and cymbals drown out their sacrilegious music."

The cage having been opened amid the clamor of brass instruments, he Superangels rose up solely, a silent flock. The rhythm of their movements was the most obvious of ironies. Their colors mingled, a din of laughter amid the vast din of light. The perfumes emanating from them had, in their exquisiteness, something ticklish and hilarious about them.

A few hours later, three blasts of the ritual canon summoned the people of Eor and the provinces o the temples. In every pulpit, a priest read out a message telephoned by the Superelephants in a sonorous voice.

"Irritated by the very benefits that the Gods wished to heap upon them, furious at sensing themselves powerless against divinity, the proud Superangels have sworn the most murderous hatred against the humans beloved by the Gods. Adept in evil, these demons of the air have found a means of putting a mortal poison into their colors, their movements and their music. For human weakness, to see them or hear them will henceforth be to die.

"In order to permit divine protection to be exercised effectively, it is ordered that humans, as soon as the Superangels manifest their presence, must look down at the ground and block their ears. At the same time, let them flee promptly to their dwellings.

"The Gods, in their infinite bounty, will fabricate perfect plugs for the ears. Soon, a pair of them will be distributed to every man, woman and child beloved by the Gods.

"Only the Superelephants, the Immortals and the priests of the highest rank, armored by virtue and science, can look at and hear the pestilential Superangels without danger. Only they can pronounce the powerful formulas of exorcism effectively. The priests will report to the people, after having disarmed their musical venom, the least abominable of the words of the Enemy."

Since that blessed day, every time the Superangels appear in a canton, the Immortals, the priests and the overseers order the lowering of heads and the introduction into ears of the benevolent plugs. The overseers and the lower-ranking members of the clergy provide a prudent example themselves. Then, with cracks of the whip, the herd is chased to the city or the village. The humans are locked in their dwellings by means of the external bolts with which every door and shutter is equipped.

On the first rest-day, the priests repeat the Superangels' words in the temples, without the murderous accompaniment of music, color and rhythm. The humans listen, overwhelmed by terror, for the words repeated by the priests are always a mixture of gross insults and formidable threats. The humans thus experience appropriate sentiments of hatred and fear for the demons of the air. They soothe these burdensome feelings by thinking gratefully about the benevolent powers that defend them against the vast danger. Their pious prayers give thanks to the Gods for the faultless vigilance of their protection. They do not forget the noble intercessors, the priests and Immortals, who collaborate devoutly in the divine favor.

A few humans, however, finding themselves far from their leaders during a musician apparition, have pushed perverse curiosity to the extent of listening and looking. They are not dead. They have carried away, locked in their hearts, the treasure of an indescribable comfort and strange hope. These individuals say, in the privacy of their mind, that the priests are liars intent on falsifying all words from on high. They carry everywhere the sweetness of a dazzling memory and charmed dreams. When, by chance, their crime is discovered—is there, for the Law, any other crime than disobedience of the Law?—these humans are put to death, as justice demands. But most of them know how to keep silent regarding their joy and the dreams that delight them. In silence and in solitude, they enjoy singular ecstasies or desolate themselves with singular yearnings.

Thanks to a memory that works upon these humans until death and after death, the number of Superangels is increasing rapidly. Among the human who, by means of fraud, have seen and heard, those who have some strength of will and aspiration are reincarnated in the body of a Superangel.

And the 62 adult Amours are surrounded by a growing population of winged children.

Chapter XVII. The Supergod

Although their opinions are often opposed, a strong friendship unites Marbal and Rismac. They rarely let three or four days pass without one of them going to spend long hours in the other's home.

These meetings begin with enormous and delicate oral pleasures. The priestly cooks put a genius worthy of admiration into them. After the meat, fruits and pastries, the ingenious sauces and the perfect roasts, the joy becomes more spiritual, procured by wines, liqueurs, perfumes and stimulant fumes.

In the midst of this tonic intoxication, the two Superelephants enjoy performances of moving or comic dramas, dances, wrestling matches, pugilistic contests, musical recitals and poems dedicated to their glory. Sometimes, however, they prefer to remain alone. On those days, while drinking through one trunk and smoking odorant herbs with the other, they voice the observations and dreams of their vast brains.

Rismac expresses anxieties. The rapid increase of the superangelic population is causing him an indefinite dread.

Marbal laughs and jeers, however. "Nowhere," he affirms, "in no matter what respect, is number ever increased without a proportional diminution of quality." He laughs at the Superangels, gaily mocking their imprudence. "These naïve beings are neglecting the elementary precaution of limiting births. They are allowing themselves to be invaded by an inferior host that they will never succeed in assimilating and educating. A little patience; who will live will see: their hearts, their minds, their music, their colors, the flexibility and grace of their rhythms—all will fade and decline. Tomorrow, with the adolescence of the first fugitives, a general decadence will commence. Following a universal law, there will be a uniformly accelerating fall. Weight, increasing every day, will not permit, even for a distant future, any hope of a new rise. The crowd will degrade an overly generous élite. Soon there will be too many appearances of Superangels for a single true Superangel to remain."

While his two trunks cough and sneeze he most self-satisfied laughter, Marbal proclaims: "Love is always lost and ruined by ease of acquisition." A few years more, he claims, and the majority of the new Superangels will come begging to the Gods for that which the seven captives refused with such insulting pride. Even if a few ancients remain opposed to that movement, what will it matter? The greater number of the artists will be domesticated and will despise he rare independents. A conspiracy of silence will grow up around them; no one will know that any music other than the music of adulation exists.

In these conversations without witnesses, however, Marbal voluntarily reveals much vaguer and more distant anticipations. Often, after having lamented his massive present ennui, he sings, drunkenly and lyrically, hopes as radiant as the sun.

"Only children are happy," he declares. "When I say children, you know that I don't simply mean what the minds of humans and those of the majority of our brethren understand by the term. For me, as you know, a child is a symbol. Whatever his age, I call any individual who enjoys novelty a child."

"I know what you mean," said Rismac. "At the beginning of the geological period, we spent long lives that consisted entirely of dazzling childhoods."

"I can still see them, those beautiful lives, in a distant light that is nevertheless clearer than the light of today. We possess exactly the same faculties, the same organs; we hold dominion over an Earth that is less rich and slaves that are more numerous—but all that, oh joy! had not belonged to us for long. Oh, the fresh charm of that morning's conquests, the playthings that we had only just acquired!"

"It's our bodies that you're calling playthings?"

"Our bodies and their powers, still groping, testing themselves amid shocks and triumphs. What an overwhelming mass of sensual indulgences all that was, the first time, the first ten times. Afterwards, the hazy blurring and discoloration of things fell upon the universe, like mists and veils of mourning. In a faded and worn-out world, we no longer experience any more than an indifferent domination, and emptiness weighs upon our hearts."

"What about your next existence?"

"I don't know…perhaps I'll linger for a while in the free life. It seems to me that one must be less bored in that sort of interval. Isn't ennui the heavy drag of the body? When I escape myself on the wings of thought or dream, I forget the sadness and humiliation of my flesh; I forget the faithful melancholy that lies in wait for my every return."

"It seems to me that you sometimes forget it without going so far. You're able to chase it away instead of fleeing from it, and you don't always disdain the pleasures of the flesh. Besides, do you think that a being can ever dispense with a body?"

"Certainly not. But the light envelope that sways around me between two incarnations appears to me, by contrast, almost immaterial. Diaphanous, it allows itself, I assume, to be penetrated by the breaths and radiances of more delicate sensualities. I suspect that it is less fastidious than the heavy organism that I drag around."

Marbal drank a cupful of strong liquor. Then, waving his prophetic trunks, he said: "A god is a miserable thing that must be surpassed. What I love in a god is that it is a transition and a bridge. What I love about the present is that it is the seed of a vast and unknown future; the tree will be infinite by comparison with the seed, and it will not resemble the seed. What I love about the tedious identical repetition is that it is preparing some eloquent novelty."

Enthusiastic and dolorous, he continued a speech that was disordered, as if by passion: "Every being thus far has created something higher. I shall certainly not be the ebb of that great tide, and shall not turn back toward the human or any other beast. Nor, any longer, shall I languish in cessation and stagnation; I shall linger for as brief a while as possible in the monotony of being a God.

"What is a human to a God? A derision and a dolorous shame. That is what a god must be to a supergod: a derision or a dolorous shame. Oh, I shall be able one day to unclench my divine grimace, to dilate my face and my superdivine radiance.

"We have traced the path of the worm as far as godhood, but there is still much of the crawling earthworm within us. Once we were apes and humans. Is not a god still more basely human now than a human?

"The supergod is the meaning of the Earth. Powerful and dolorous, my will sings, cries and weeps: let the supergod be the meaning of the Earth!"

"In truth, in truth, I tell you, godhood is an impure river. It must become an ocean in order to welcome the river and its impurities without being fouled. The supergod is the ocean toward which I am precipitating my waters and my mud. In him alone will my great scorn for what I am be dissolved and dissipated."

Drinking a burning elixir, Rismac cried: "Your dreams, Marbal, intoxicate me and stimulate me better than the best liqueurs. Speak, speak on, you who can speak like dreams."

"The supergod, the supergod! When, therefore, will the star of ice come, to precipitate the fortunate catastrophe and allow me, by means of a formidable passion, to kill the god, to abandon his heavy hide on the edge of the eternal path and project myself into supergodhood?"

"How do you see us after that radiant metamorphosis?"

"Our present power multiplied by 60 times 60,000..."

"Insignificant multiplication!" said the vulgar Rismac, very nearly, with a drunken giggle. "Are you going, by the same token, to burden us with an infinitely more massive and fastidious body? 60 times 60,000 times my weight—you almost make me afraid, and, if I do not retreat, at least I hesitate before such a mountain."

"Have no fear that I am repeating and aggravating today's error. The colossal is an impasse from which I shall escape."

"By what means?"

"I shall change the formula completely. More completely than when, in a previous incarnation, we liberated ourselves from the prison of the waters by the victory in which the cold-blooded fish gave birth to the air-breathing being and its noble fever."

"Do you mean that we shall live in the air like the naïve Superangels?"

"Do not transmute my riches into dross, wicked enchanter, and my diamonds into vulgar pebbles. The supergod will not be a bird. The words to describe the supergod and his supple form do not exist in the rigid indigence of divine language. Listen, though, to my bare words and try to hear, beyond the empty words, the obscure plenitude of the future. Until now, we have been confined to the heavy world of matter. As supergods, we shall inhabit the world of force. A god is made of flesh and that is why a god remains an animal. A bird is made of flesh, and that is why its flight is still a crawl. It glides through the prison of the air like a fish in the dungeon of the waters. The supergod will not be so stupid as to forge himself in flesh; he will possess an electrical body."

"An electrical body?"

"For an eternity of eternities, we have been afraid of force as fish are afraid of our atmosphere. To protect ourselves against it, we have enveloped the body with thick, almost impermeable insulation. It was necessary, alas, so long as being was ignorant of the laws of electricity and radioactivity, as long as unforeseeable effects remained often-murderous caprices so far as we were concerned. Now that we know, our creeping prudence is no longer anything but stupidity and cowardice. Already we oblige currents of every sort to follow the paths we designate for them. We no longer have much to dread from energies that are almost completely submissive, and which we use, anticipating them, until those slaves revolt.

"I no longer dream of tedious dominion over the tremulous beings. What I want is to tyrannize the impassive forces. My superdivine body will be fluid, light, obedient enough for my will to radiate therefrom as heat and light radiate from the sun. It will summon electric currents and radioactive currents; it will charge itself with them, a formidable condenser, and will hurl them forth whenever I wish, in the direction I dictate, in the form that I desire. I shall spread around me, according to my fantasy, light our darkness, heat or cold. If it pleases me, my light will be brighter than all known lights, my darkness thicker that the most massive nightmares, and no burn can give an idea of the heat or cold that will emanate from me. I shall attract or repel, dilate or contract, beings near or far, the densest or rarest matter. I shall excite vitality or stupefy it. When I wish, no eye will be subtle enough to perceive my fluid presence; when I prefer it, all eyes will close, wounded by the dazzle that will precede my approach. Will you see me playing, in the midst of my aureole of darkness, the midst of my lightning radiance, the divine game of destruction, and the superdivine game of creation?"

"I can't imagine the joys of such a state precisely," Rismac said. "It seems to me that I'd prefer to inhabit a more solid body. My body is the site of almost all my true needs, almost all my true desires and, in consequence, almost all my true satisfactions."

Marbal shrugged his two trunks slightly, as we shrug our shoulders. "When will you stop lying to yourself?" he said. "Isn't our greatest need to dominate?"

"Perhaps. But the direct pleasures of tyranny…oh, how quickly they're exhausted! Consciousness of a power is soon followed by disgust for that power. Only voluptuousness amuses me and delays me a little. Besides, your power will always encounter limits into which to run and hurt itself."

"Listen! My electrical body might perhaps be more avid than my heavy material mass. Try to imagine my incendiary lusts. I shall devour a city or a forest as I now eat a child or a fruit. Lightning, which I shall be when it pleases me, nourishes itself, I imagine, on lightened, refined matter idealized by flame. Often, my activity will radiate around me the intoxicating vertigo of disasters."

"A flame that wraps itself up in its daughter flames—yes there might be amusement in voluptuousness in being that. But I suspect that the pleasure would wear out as rapidly as the others; it too would fade, in the course of a few experiences."

"I dream," said Marbal, "of the marvelous voyages of my fluid body. Do you think, when my effort and my victory have promoted me to supergodhood, that I will be content with the poverties of our ground and our atmosphere?"

"Where will you go, great vagabond."

"I shall go…I shall go…I shall go everywhere."

"Everywhere—that seems very little to me."

"I shall travel through cosmic space and conquer worlds."

"Beware of unfortunate encounters!"

"What do I have to fear? Master of forces, I shall be, to the extent that I deign to be, the master of beings. If, before a host of vulgar superhumans, I shed my thunderous envelope momentarily, if I soften myself and relax myself to the point of rendering myself visible, troubled by the appearance of a living meteor, you would be plunged by the least of my gazes into a pious hypnosis. Superangels, Immortals, Superelephants will follow me like an infatuated herd. When I disappear, you will weep. I am the one you seek in the groping of your intoxications, the groping and anxiety of your kisses, the groping and yearning of your dreams."

"Allow me to laugh at the vision of that herd of gods reaching up with their desolate trunks and futile trumpetings toward the sky."

"Don't imagine, however," Marbal continued, "that I shall only undertake voyages in space."

"Where else, then, great madman? Do you hope to find a location beyond location?"

"I shall undertake voyages in time. Perhaps the power will be given to me to surround myself with whatever future I please. I shall surely be able to plunge into all my pasts. Sometimes I shall bound, in a changing light, from ne to another of my summits, from one to another of my radiant memories. Sometimes I shall lie down in the shade of a valley, lost in the cool obscurity of some distant forgetfulness. I shall awake and go to sleep again as one opens and closes the silky softness of a fan. Can you understand the lightning ardor of such precise play, he relaxed languor of such joyous imprecision? Can you see me packing eternities of eternities into an instant swollen like a phallus? Can you see me diluting an instant like a perfume in the sinuosities and breaths of the moving eternity? Often, as the sun shines in suspended vapors in the form of a rainbow, my radiant present will amuse itself in illuminating my tears of yesteryear. Uniting my scattered dolors with a thread of joy, I shall build a bridge of glory and colored light."

"All that," said the material Rismac, shaking his head, "does not seem to me worth an itch in my mucous membranes."

But Marbal did not hear. He continued, his intoxication increasing: "Do you think I've already said everything there is to say about my voyages? Do you think that space and time can be sufficient for my conquering ardor and my victorious blossoming?"

"You're frightening me," Rismac admitted. "You amaze me. You're overwhelming me."

"I shall voyage through all the forms of existence. Sometimes I shall become a stone that dreams, sometimes a god or beast that wallows. And I shall voyage through all the planes of existence. My joyous fantasy will allow me to mingle with the disincarnate as well as beings of flesh or metal and electrical or radioactive forces. For us, death is still a brazen wall. We can scarcely hear, behind the massive darkness, the surf of beings that want to put on flesh again. To my superdivine eyes, death will be a transparent veil through which the incarnate beings of yesterday and tomorrow will be visible. When it pleases me, I shall lift the light fabric; with neither terrors nor death-throes, I shall pass through to the other side as laughter passes through mist, and I shall return without suffering the disgust of fetal life, the sordidness of birth, the weakness and dependence of infancy."

"But if you possess everything," Rismac objected, "there will be nothing left for you to do but dream. What remedy will there be for your superdivine ennui?"

"As reality broadens out, dreams broaden out. What I possess will always remain a sphere lost in the universe. If I possessed the whole universe, whether or not I were endowed with the power to create others, I would dream, as I dream today, of the work of tomorrow, or dream of the work that will forever be impossible. The further I grow, the more I multiply the points at which I touch that which is not me; if I were everything, would I not be enveloped in every direction by nothing? You cannot conceive of an infinity realized without it being immediately surrounded by an infinity of void and dream. The real danger, my poor Rismac—but I am not one of those who recoil from it—is exactly the opposite of the peril you indicate. I shall be too rich not to suffer innumerable poverties. I shall be too real not to be entirely invaded by the flux of dream. Millions of times more powerful than today, I shall suffer the sentiment of millions of newly-perceived and newly acquired aspects of impotence. Every power conquered is the joy of a moment, a sadness forever. One who can do everything will weep against the walls of the contradictory, will weep because he cannot, in one place at one time, with respect to one object, be the absolute yes and the absolute no."

Rismac shook his two trunks, which elongated in disdainful grimace. "You have taken away," he said, "any desire I had to become a supergod. There are moments when, listening to you, I dream of reincarnating myself as a Superangel. Only the Amours, it seems to me, have found the secret of happiness."

"Can you imagine a worse misfortune and a worse disgrace for a proud heart than to resign itself to a naïve happiness devoid of pride?"

"Even so…"

"Then again, truly, Superangels will become so common… When I am a supergod, if I discover even one peer, I shall be annoyed by equality, and be jealous."

"But if you're alone in your superdivine superheaven, you'll become superbored with supersolitude."

"Alas!" saighed Marbal, "the needs of our hearts are various and unsteady. Contradiction, the limit of all conceivable power, however, is only limited by the chaos of our avidities."

287

The two gods remained silent, pensive and motionless for some time. When they emerged from a potentially painful reverie, it was to drink from numerous cups one after another, and to breathe in numerous puffs of stupefying smoke, in order to roll, like donkeys with itchy backs, in the mire of drunkenness.

SF & FANTASY

Guy d'Armen. *Doc Ardan: The City of Gold and Lepers*
G.-J. Arnaud. *The Ice Company*
Aloysius Bertrand. *Gaspard de la Nuit*
Richard Bessière. *The Gardens of the Apocalypse*
Félix Bodin. *The Novel of the Future*
André Caroff. *The Terror of Madame Atomos*
Didier de Chousy. *Ignis*
C. I. Defontenay. *Star (Psi Cassiopeia)*
Charles Derennes. *The People of the Pole*
Georges Dodds/Paul Wessels (anthologists). *The Missing Link*
Harry Dickson. *The Heir of Dracula*
Jules Dornay. *Lord Ruthven Begins*
Sâr Dubnotal *vs. Jack the Ripper*
Alexandre Dumas. *The Return of Lord Ruthven*
J.-C. Dunyach. *The Night Orchid; The Thieves of Silence*
Henri Duvernois. *The Man Who Found Himself*
Henri Falk. *The Age of Lead*
Paul Féval. *Anne of the Isles; Knightshade; Revenants; Vampire City; The Vampire Countess; The Wandering Jew's Daughter*
Paul Féval, *fils. Felifax, the Tiger-Man*
Arnould Galopin. *Doctor Omega*
Nathalie Henneberg. *The Green Gods*
V. Hugo, P. Foucher & P. Meurice. *The Hunchback of Notre-Dame*
Michel Jeury. *Chronolysis*
Octave Joncquel & Theo Varlet. *The Martian Epic*
Gérard Klein. *The Mote in Time's Eye*
Jean de La Hire. *Enter the Nyctalope; The Nyctalope on Mars; The Nyctalope vs. Lucifer*
André Laurie. *Spiridon*
Georges Le Faure & Henri de Graffigny. *The Extraordinary Adventures of a Russian Scientist Across the Solar System* (2 vols.)
Gustave Le Rouge. *The Vampires of Mars*

Jules Lermina. *Mysteryville; Panic in Paris; To-Ho and the Gold Destroyers*

Jean-Marc & Randy Lofficier. *Edgar Allan Poe on Mars; The Katrina Protocol; Pacifica; Robonocchio; Tales of the Shadowmen* (anthologists; 7 vols.)

Xavier Mauméjean. *The League of Heroes*

John-Antoine Nau. *Enemy Force*

Marie Nizet. *Captain Vampire*

C. Nodier, A. Beraud & Toussaint-Merle. *Frankenstein*

Henri de Parville. *An Inhabitant of the Planet Mars*

J. Polidori, C. Nodier, E. Scribe. *Lord Ruthven the Vampire*

P.-A. Ponson du Terrail. *The Vampire and the Devil's Son*

Maurice Renard. *The Blue Peril; Doctor Lerne; The Doctored Man;. A Man Among the Microbes; The Master of Light*

Albert Robida. *The Adventures of Saturnin Farandoul; The Clock of the Centuries.*

J.-H. Rosny Aîné. *Helgvor of the Blue River; The Givreuse Enigma; The Mysterious Force; The Navigators of Space; Vamireh; The World of the Variants; The Young Vampire*

Han Ryner. *The Superhumans*

Brian Stableford. *The New Faust at the Tragicomique;The Empire of the Necromancers (The Shadow of Frankenstein; Frankenstein and the Vampire Countess; Frankenstein in London); Sherlock Holmes & The Vampires of Eternity; The Stones of Camelot; The Wayward Muse.* (anthologist) *The Germans on Venus; News from the Moon*

Jacques Spitz. *The Eye of Purgatory*

Kurt Steiner. *Ortog*

Villiers de l'Isle-Adam. *The Scaffold; The Vampire Soul*

Philippe Ward. *Artahe*

Philippe Ward & Sylvie Miller. *The Song of Montségur*

MYSTERIES & THRILLERS

M. Allain & P. Souvestre. *The Daughter of Fantômas*

A. Anicet-Bourgeois, Lucien Dabril. *Rocambole*

A. Bisson & G. Livet. *Nick Carter vs. Fantômas*

V. Darlay & H. de Gorsse. *Lupin vs. Holmes: The Stage Play*
Paul Féval. *Gentlemen of the Night; John Devil; The Black
Coats ('Salem Street; The Invisible Weapon; The Parisian
Jungle; The Companions of the Treasure; Heart of Steel; The
Cadet Gang)*
Emile Gaboriau. *Monsieur Lecoq*
Steve Leadley. *Sherlock Holmes: The Circle of Blood*
Maurice Leblanc. *Arsène Lupin vs. Countess Cagliostro; Lu-
pin vs. Holmes (The Blonde Phantom; The Hollow Needle)*
Gaston Leroux. *Chéri-Bibi; The Phantom of the Opera; Rou-
letabille & the Mystery of the Yellow Room*
William Patrick Maynard. *The Terror of Fu Manchu*
Frank J. Morlock. *Sherlock Holmes: The Grand Horizontals*
P. de Wattyne & Y. Walter. *Sherlock Holmes vs. Fantômas*
David White. *Fantômas in America*

SCREENPLAYS

Mike Baron. *The Iron Triangle*
Emma Bull & Will Shetterly. *Nightspeeder; War for the Oaks*
Gerry Conway & Roy Thomas. *Doc Dynamo*
Steve Englehart. *Majorca*
James Hudnall. *The Devastator*
Jean-Marc & Randy Lofficier. *Royal Flush*
J.-M. & R. Lofficier & Marc Agapit. *Despair*
Andrew Paquette. *Peripheral Vision*
R. Thomas, J. Hendler & L. Sprague de Camp. *Rivers of Time*

NON-FICTION

Stephen R. Bissette. *Blur 1-5. Green Mountain Cinema 1*
Win Scott Eckert. *Crossovers* (2 vols.)
Jean-Marc & Randy Lofficier. *Shadowmen* (2 vols.)
Randy Lofficier. *Over Here*

www.ingramcontent.com/pod-product-compliance
Lightning Source LLC
Chambersburg PA
CBHW030351020726
47493CB00003B/769